TWO
ROADS

Dear Reader

Two Roads is dedicated to finding the best and most compelling stories and *Water for Elephants* is one of the best. Ever since I first published this book in 2006, I have been an enormous fan of Sara Gruen and her ability to evoke a magical world.

As the story starts, Jacob Jankowski, now an old man forgotten and alone in a nursing home, wants to get a secret off his chest: when he was a young man, homeless and desperate, he jumped a train. Not just any train, but that of The Benzini Brothers Most Spectacular Show on Earth – a second rate circus going from one second rate town to another in Depression era America.

There's murder and mayhem, fabulous escapist entertainment, a cast of heroes and villains, grifters and freaks. There is a beautiful heroine with whom Jacob falls in love, another heroine who weighs 2500 pounds, a wicked villain and all the thrill of the big top. As Jacob tells the story of the secret he's kept for seventy years, the world of the circus and its unforgettable characters, both human and animal, comes alive right to the last affecting twist in the tale.

There's a reason why this book has sold millions of copies, been made into a huge film and delighted so many people. I think it's the power of great storytelling.

Lisa Highton
PUBLISHER

PRAISE FOR *WATER FOR ELEPHANTS*

'There is a tender story of first love, murder, mayhem and
animal and human brutality, of hucksters, whores and the
general hoopla created when the circus rolls into town . . . This
book is every bit the fabulous escapist entertainment that the
big top once was.'
—*Sunday Express*

'You are so immersed in circus life that you are completely
blinded by the thrilling, fatal dazzle of sequins and sawdust.'
—*Daily Telegraph*

'An imaginative modern fairystory teeming with eccentric
characters.'
—*The Times*

'Similar in tone to *Carter Beats the Devil*, filled with eccentric
characters, unlikely love matches and errant animals . . .'
—*The London Paper*

'[This] sprightly tale has a ringmaster's crowd-pleasing pace.'
—*Entertainment Weekly*

'I loved Water for Elephants . . . Great story, loads of fun;
hard to put down. So what if the heroine weighs
2500 pounds?'
— Stephen King

'Great!'
— Giffords Circus

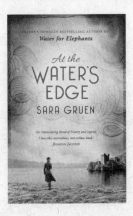

Coming in May 2015.

A gripping and poignant love story set in a remote village in the Scottish Highlands at the end of the Second World War – perfect for all the fans of *Water For Elephants*.

After embarrassing themselves at the social event of the year in high society Philadelphia on New Year's Eve of 1944, Maddie and Ellis Hyde are cut off financially by Ellis's father, a former army Colonel who is already ashamed of his colour-blind son's inability to serve in WWII.

To Maddie's horror, Ellis decides that the only way to regain his father's favour (and generosity) is to succeed in a venture his father attempted and very publicly failed at: he will hunt the famous Loch Ness monster and when he finds it he will restore his father's name and return to his father's good graces.

In January 1945 they hitch a ride on a ship across the Atlantic while the war is still raging all around them. And Maddie, now alone and virtually abandoned in a foreign country, must begin to work out who she is and what she wants - the vacuous life she left behind or something more real? What she discovers – about the larger world and about herself – opens her eyes not only to the dark forces that exist around her but to the beauty and surprising possibilities of life.

Water for Elephants

SARA GRUEN

TWO
ROADS

This edition specially produced
for
World Book Night UK
2015

www.tworoadsbooks.com

First published in Great Britain in 2006 by
Hodder & Stoughton
An Hachette UK company

This edition published in 2011 by Two Roads
An imprint of Hodder & Stoughton
21

A CIP catalogue record for this title is available from the British Library.

Paperback ISBN (B format) 978 0 340 962725
Paperback ISBN (film tie-in) 978 1 444 71600 9
Paperback ISBN (A format) 978 1 444 71598 9
eBook ISBN 978 1 444 71629 0

Printed and bound in the UK by
Clays Ltd, St Ives plc

Text printed on Bulky FSC 50gsm manufactured by Stora Enso Anjala Mill in Finland
Paper supplied by Paper Management Services and Stora Enso

Hodder & Stoughton policy is to use papers that are natural, renewable
and recyclable products and made from wood grown in sustainable
forests. The logging and manufacturing processes are expected to
conform to the environmental regulations of the country of origin.

Two Roads
Hodder & Stoughton Ltd
338 Euston Road
London NW1 3BH

For Bob,
Still my secret weapon

Acknowledgments

I am indebted to the following people for their contributions to this book:

To my husband, Bob – my love and greatest champion.

To my editor, Chuck Adams, who provided me with the kind of criticism, attention to detail, and support that took this story to a different level.

To my critique partner, Kristy Kiernan, and my first readers, Karen Abbott, Maureen Ogle, Kathryn Puffett (who happens to be my mother), and Terence Bailey (who happens to be my father), for their love and support and for talking me off the ledge at regular intervals.

To Gary C. Payne, for answering my questions on all things circus, offering anecdotes, and checking my manuscript for accuracy.

To Fred D. Pfening III, Ken Harck, and Timothy Tegge, for graciously allowing me to use photographs from their collections. Special thanks to Fred for reading and helping me fine-tune the text.

To Heidi Taylor, assistant registrar at the Ringling Museum of Art, for helping me track down and secure the rights to various photographs, and to Barbara Fox McKellar, for allowing me to use her father's photograph.

To Mark and Carrie Kabak, both for their hospitality and for introducing me to Mark's former charges at the Kansas City Zoo.

To Andrew Walaszek, for providing and checking Polish translations.

To Keith Cronin, both for valuable criticisms and for coming up with a title.

To Emma Sweeney, for continuing to be all I could ask for in an agent.

And finally, to the members of my writing group. I don't know what I'd do without you.

I meant what I said, and I said what I meant . . .
An elephant's faithful – one hundred per cent!

— Theodore Seuss Geisel, *Horton Hatches the Egg*, 1940

PROLOGUE

Only three people were left under the red and white awning of the grease joint: Grady, me, and the fry cook. Grady and I sat at a battered wooden table, each facing a burger on a dented tin plate. The cook was behind the counter, scraping his griddle with the edge of a spatula. He had turned off the fryer some time ago, but the odor of grease lingered.

The rest of the midway – so recently writhing with people – was empty but for a handful of employees and a small group of men waiting to be led to the cooch tent. They glanced nervously from side to side, with hats pulled low and hands thrust deep in their pockets. They wouldn't be disappointed: somewhere in the back Barbara and her ample charms awaited.

The other townsfolk – rubes, as Uncle Al called them – had already made their way through the menagerie tent and into the big top, which pulsed with frenetic music. The band was whipping through its repertoire at the usual earsplitting volume. I knew the routine by heart – at this very moment, the tail end of the Grand Spectacle was exiting and Lottie, the aerialist, was ascending her rigging in the center ring.

I stared at Grady, trying to process what he was saying. He glanced around and leaned in closer.

'Besides,' he said, locking eyes with me, 'it seems to me you've got a lot to lose right now.' He raised his eyebrows for emphasis. My heart skipped a beat.

Thunderous applause exploded from the big top, and the band slid seamlessly into the Gounod waltz. I turned instinctively toward the menagerie because this was the cue for the elephant act. Marlena was either preparing to mount or was already sitting on Rosie's head.

'I've got to go,' I said.

'Sit,' said Grady. 'Eat. If you're thinking of clearing out, it may be a while before you see food again.'

That moment, the music screeched to a halt. There was an ungodly collision of brass, reed, and percussion – trombones and piccolos skidded into cacophony, a tuba farted, and the hollow clang of a cymbal wavered out of the big top, over our heads and into oblivion.

Grady froze, crouched over his burger with his pinkies extended and lips spread wide.

I looked from side to side. No one moved a muscle – all eyes were directed at the big top. A few wisps of hay swirled lazily across the hard dirt.

'What is it? What's going on?' I said.

'*Shh*,' Grady hissed.

The band started up again, playing 'Stars and Stripes Forever.'

'Oh Christ. Oh shit!' Grady tossed his food onto the table and leapt up, knocking over the bench.

'What? What is it?' I yelled, because he was already running away from me.

'The Disaster March!' he screamed over his shoulder.

I jerked around to the fry cook, who was ripping off his apron. 'What the hell's he talking about?'

'The Disaster March,' he said, wrestling the apron over his head. 'Means something's gone bad – real bad.'

'Like what?'

'Could be anything – fire in the big top, stampede, whatever. Aw sweet Jesus. The poor rubes probably don't even know it yet.' He ducked under the hinged door and took off.

Chaos – candy butchers vaulting over counters, workmen staggering out from under tent flaps, roustabouts racing headlong across the lot. Anyone and everyone associated with the Benzini Brothers Most Spectacular Show on Earth barreled toward the big top.

Diamond Joe passed me at the human equivalent of a full gallop. 'Jacob – it's the menagerie,' he screamed. 'The animals are loose. Go, go, *go!*'

He didn't need to tell me twice. Marlena was in that tent.

A rumble coursed through me as I approached, and it scared the hell out of me because it was on a register lower than noise. The ground was vibrating.

I staggered inside and met a wall of yak – a great expanse of curly-haired chest and churning hooves, of flared red nostrils and spinning eyes. It galloped past so close I leapt backward on tiptoe, flush with the canvas to avoid being impaled on one of its crooked horns. A terrified hyena clung to its shoulders.

The concession stand in the center of the tent had been flattened, and in its place was a roiling mass of spots and stripes – of haunches, heels, tails, and claws, all of it roaring, screeching, bellowing, or whinnying. A polar bear towered above it all, slashing blindly with skillet-sized paws. It made contact with a llama and knocked it flat – BOOM. The llama hit the ground, its neck and legs splayed like the five points of a star. Chimps screamed and chattered, swinging on ropes to stay above the cats. A wild-eyed zebra zigzagged too close to a crouching lion, who swiped, missed, and darted away, his belly close to the ground.

My eyes swept the tent, desperate to find Marlena. Instead I saw a cat slide through the connection leading to the big top – it was a panther, and as its lithe black body disappeared into the canvas tunnel I braced myself. If the rubes didn't know, they were about to find out. It took several seconds to come, but come it did – one prolonged shriek followed by another, and then another, and then the whole place exploded with the thunderous sound of bodies trying to shove past other bodies and off the stands. The band screeched to a halt for a second time, and this time stayed silent. I shut my eyes: *Please God let them leave by the back end. Please God don't let them try to come through here.*

I opened my eyes again and scanned the menagerie, frantic to find her. How hard can it be to find a girl and an elephant, for Christ's sake?

When I caught sight of her pink sequins, I nearly cried out in relief – maybe I did. I don't remember.

She was on the opposite side, standing against the side-wall, calm as a summer day. Her sequins flashed like liquid diamonds, a shimmering beacon between the multi-colored hides. She saw me, too, and held my gaze for what seemed like forever. She was cool, languid. Smiling even. I started pushing my way toward her, but some-thing about her expression stopped me cold.

That son of a bitch was standing with his back to her, red-faced and bellowing, flapping his arms and swinging his silver-tipped cane. His high-topped silk hat lay on the straw beside him.

She reached for something. A giraffe passed between us – its long neck bobbing gracefully even in panic – and when it was gone I saw that she'd picked up an iron stake. She held it loosely, resting its end on the hard dirt. She looked at me again, bemused. Then her gaze shifted to the back of his bare head.

'Oh Jesus,' I said, suddenly understanding. I stumbled forward, screaming even though there was no hope of my voice reaching her. 'Don't do it! *Don't do it!*'

She lifted the stake high in the air and brought it down, splitting his head like a watermelon. His pate opened, his eyes grew wide, and his mouth froze into an *O*. He fell to his knees and then toppled forward into the straw.

I was too stunned to move, even as a young orangutan flung its elastic arms around my legs.

So long ago. So long. But still it haunts me.

* * *

5

I don't talk much about those days. Never did. I don't know why – I worked on circuses for nearly seven years, and if that isn't fodder for conversation, I don't know what is.

Actually I do know why: I never trusted myself. I was afraid I'd let it slip. I knew how important it was to keep her secret, and keep it I did – for the rest of her life, and then beyond.

In seventy years, I've never told a blessed soul.

ONE

I am ninety. Or ninety-three. One or the other. When you're five, you know your age down to the month. Even in your twenties you know how old you are. I'm twenty-three, you say, or maybe twenty-seven. But then in your thirties something strange starts to happen. It's a mere hiccup at first, an instant of hesitation. How old are you? Oh, I'm – you start confidently, but then you stop. You were going to say thirty-three, but you're not. You're thirty-five. And then you're bothered, because you wonder if this is the beginning of the end. It is, of course, but it's decades before you admit it.

You start to forget words: they're on the tip of your tongue, but instead of eventually dislodging, they stay there. You go upstairs to fetch something, and by the time you get there you can't remember what it was you were after. You call your child by the names of all your other children and finally the dog before you get to his. Sometimes you forget what day it is. And finally you forget the year.

Actually, it's not so much that I've forgotten. It's more like I've stopped keeping track. We're past the millennium, that much I know – such a fuss and bother over nothing, all those young folks clucking with worry and buying canned food because somebody was too lazy to leave space for four digits instead of two – but that could have been last month or three years ago. And besides, what does it really matter? What's the difference between three weeks or three years or even three decades of mushy peas, tapioca, and Depends undergarments?

I am ninety. Or ninety-three. One or the other.

Either there's been an accident or there's roadwork, because a gaggle of old ladies is glued to the window at the end of the hall like children or jailbirds. They're spidery and frail, their hair as fine as mist. Most of them are a good decade younger than me, and this astounds me. Even as your body betrays you, your mind denies it.

I'm parked in the hallway with my walker. I've come a long way since my hip fracture, and thank the Lord for that. For a while it looked like I wouldn't walk again – that's how I got talked into coming here in the first place – but every couple of hours I get up and walk a few steps, and with every day I get a little bit farther before feeling the need to turn around. There may be life in the old dog yet.

There are five of them now, white-headed old things

huddled together and pointing crooked fingers at the glass. I wait a while to see if they wander off. They don't.

I glance down, check that my brakes are on, and rise carefully, steadying myself on the wheelchair's arm while making the perilous transfer to the walker. Once I'm squared away, I clutch the gray rubber pads on the arms and shove it forward until my elbows are extended, which turns out to be exactly one floor tile. I drag my left foot forward, make sure it's steady, and then pull the other up beside it. Shove, drag, wait, drag. Shove, drag, wait, drag.

The hallway is long and my feet don't respond the way they used to. It's not Camel's kind of lameness, thank God, but it slows me down nonetheless. Poor old Camel – it's been years since I thought of him. His feet flopped loosely at the end of his legs so he had to lift his knees high and throw them forward. My feet drag, as though they're weighted, and because my back is stooped I end up looking down at my slippers framed by the walker.

It takes a while to get to the end of the hall, but I do – and on my own pins, too. I'm pleased as punch, although once there I realize I still have to find my way back.

They part for me, these old ladies. These are the vital ones, the ones who can either move on their own steam or have friends to wheel them around. These old girls still have their marbles, and they're good to me. I'm a rarity here – an old man among a sea of widows whose hearts still ache for their lost men.

'Oh, here,' clucks Hazel. 'Let's give Jacob a look.'

She pulls Dolly's wheelchair a few feet back and shuffles up beside me, clasping her hands, her milky eyes

9

flashing. 'Oh, it's so exciting! They've been at it all morning!'

I edge up to the glass and raise my face, squinting against the sunlight. It's so bright it takes a moment for me to make out what's happening. Then the forms take shape.

In the park at the end of the block is an enormous canvas tent, thickly striped in white and magenta with an unmistakable peaked top—

My ticker lurches so hard I clutch a fist to my chest.

'Jacob! Oh, Jacob!' cries Hazel. 'Oh dear! Oh dear!' Her hands flutter in confusion, and she turns toward the hall. 'Nurse! Nurse! Hurry! It's Mr Jankowski!'

'I'm fine,' I say, coughing and pounding my chest. That's the problem with these old ladies. They're always afraid you're about to keel over. 'Hazel! I'm fine!'

But it's too late. I hear the squeak-squeak-squeak of rubber soles, and moments later I'm engulfed by nurses. I guess I won't have to worry about getting back to my chair after all.

'So what's on the menu tonight?' I grumble as I'm steered into the dining room. 'Porridge? Mushy peas? Pablum? Oh, let me guess, it's tapioca isn't it? Is it tapioca? Or are we calling it rice pudding tonight?'

'Oh, Mr Jankowski, you are a card,' the nurse says flatly. She doesn't need to answer, and she knows it. This being Friday, we're having the usual nutritious but uninteresting combination of meat loaf, creamed corn, reconstituted mashed potatoes, and gravy that may have been waved over a piece of beef at some point in its life. And they wonder why I lose weight.

I know some of us don't have teeth, but I do, and I want pot roast. My wife's, complete with leathery bay leaves. I want carrots. I want potatoes boiled in their skins. And I want a deep, rich cabernet sauvignon to wash it all down, not apple juice from a tin. But above all, I want corn on the cob.

Sometimes I think that if I had to choose between an ear of corn or making love to a woman, I'd choose the corn. Not that I wouldn't love to have a final roll in the hay – I am a man yet, and some things never die – but the thought of those sweet kernels bursting between my teeth sure sets my mouth to watering. It's fantasy, I know that. Neither will happen. I just like to weigh the options, as though I were standing in front of Solomon: a final roll in the hay or an ear of corn. What a wonderful dilemma. Sometimes I substitute an apple for the corn.

Everyone at every table is talking about the circus – those who can talk, that is. The silent ones, the ones with frozen faces and withered limbs or whose heads and hands shake too violently to hold utensils, sit around the edges of the room accompanied by aides who spoon little bits of food into their mouths and then coax them into masticating. They remind me of baby birds, except they're lacking all enthusiasm. With the exception of a slight grinding of the jaw, their faces remain still and horrifyingly vacant. Horrifying because I'm well aware of the road I'm on. I'm not there yet, but it's coming. There's only one way to avoid it, and I can't say I much care for that option either.

The nurse parks me in front of my meal. The gravy

on the meat loaf has already formed a skin. I poke experimentally with my fork. Its meniscus jiggles, mocking me. Disgusted, I look up and lock eyes with Joseph McGuinty.

He's sitting opposite, a newcomer, an interloper – a retired barrister with a square jaw, pitted nose, and great floppy ears. The ears remind me of Rosie, although nothing else does. She was a fine soul, and he's – well, he's a retired lawyer. I can't imagine what the nurses thought a lawyer and a veterinarian would have in common, but they wheeled him on over to sit opposite me that first night, and here he's been ever since.

He glares at me, his jaw moving back and forth like a cow chewing cud. Incredible. He's actually eating the stuff.

The old ladies chatter like schoolgirls, blissfully unaware.

'They're here until Sunday,' says Doris. 'Billy stopped to find out.'

'Yes, two shows on Saturday and one on Sunday. Randall and his girls are taking me tomorrow,' says Norma. She turns to me. 'Jacob, will you be going?'

I open my mouth to answer, but before I can Doris blurts out, 'And did you see those horses? My word, they're pretty. We had horses when I was a girl. Oh, how I loved to ride.' She looks into the distance, and for a split second I can see how lovely she was as a young woman.

'Do you remember when the circus traveled by train?' says Hazel. 'The posters would appear a few days ahead – they'd cover every surface in town! You couldn't see a brick in between!'

'Golly, yes. I certainly do,' Norma says. 'They put posters on the side of our barn one year. The men told

Father they used a special glue that would dissolve two days after the show, but darned if our barn wasn't still plastered with them months later!' She chuckles, shaking her head. 'Father was fit to be tied!'

'And then a few days later the train would pull in. Always at the crack of dawn.'

'My father used to take us down to the tracks to watch them unload. Gosh, that was something to see. And then the parade! And the smell of peanuts roasting—'

'And Cracker Jack!'

'And candy apples, and ice cream, and lemonade!'

'And the sawdust! It would get in your nose!'

'I used to carry water for the elephants,' says McGuinty.

I drop my fork and look up. He is positively dripping with self-satisfaction, just waiting for the girls to fawn over him.

'You did not,' I say.

There is a beat of silence.

'I beg your pardon?' he says.

'You did not carry water for the elephants.'

'Yes, I most certainly did.'

'No you didn't.'

'Are you calling me a liar?' he says slowly.

'If you say you carried water for elephants, I am.'

The girls stare at me with open mouths. My heart's pounding. I know I shouldn't do this, but somehow I can't help myself.

'How dare you!' McGuinty braces his knobby hands on the edge of the table. Stringy tendons appear in his forearms.

'Listen pal,' I say. 'For decades I've heard old coots like

you talk about carrying water for elephants and I'm telling you now, it never happened.'

'Old coot? *Old coot?*' McGuinty pushes himself upright, sending his wheelchair flying backward. He points a gnarled finger at me and then drops as though felled by dynamite. He vanishes beneath the edge of the table, his eyes perplexed, his mouth still open.

'Nurse! Oh, Nurse!' cry the old ladies.

There's the familiar patter of crepe-soled shoes and moments later two nurses haul McGuinty up by the arms. He grumbles, making feeble attempts to shake them off.

A third nurse, a pneumatic black girl in pale pink, stands at the end of the table with her hands on her hips. 'What on earth is going on?' she asks.

'That old S-O-B called me a liar, that's what,' says McGuinty, safely restored to his chair. He straightens his shirt, lifts his grizzled chin, and crosses his arms in front of him. '*And* an old coot.'

'Oh, I'm sure that's not what Mr Jankowski meant,' the girl in pink says.

'It most certainly is,' I say. 'And he is, too. *Pffffft.* Carried water for the elephants indeed. Do you have any idea how much an elephant drinks?'

'Well, I never,' says Norma, pursing her lips and shaking her head. 'I'm sure I don't know what's gotten into you, Mr Jankowski.'

Oh, I see, I see. So that's how it is.

'It's an outrage!' says McGuinty, leaning slightly toward Norma now that he sees he's got the popular vote. 'I don't see why I should have to put up with being called a liar!'

'And an old coot,' I remind him.

'Mr Jankowski!' says the black girl, her voice raised. She comes behind me and releases the brakes on my wheelchair. 'I think maybe you should spend some time in your room. Until you calm down.'

'Now wait just a minute!' I shout as she swings me away from the table and toward the door. 'I don't need to calm down. And besides, I haven't eaten!'

'I'll bring your dinner in,' she says from behind.

'I don't want it in my room! Take me back! You can't do this to me!'

But it appears she can. She wheels me down the hall at lightning speed and turns sharply into my room. She jams the brakes on so hard the whole chair jars.

'I'll just go back,' I say as she raises my footrests.

'You'll do no such thing,' she says, setting my feet on the floor.

'This isn't fair!' I say, my voice rising in a whine. 'I've been sitting at that table forever. He's been there two weeks. Why is everyone siding with him?'

'Nobody's siding with anyone.' She leans forward, slinging her shoulder under mine. As she lifts me, my head rests next to hers. Her hair is chemically straightened and smells of flowers. When she sets me on the edge of the bed, I am at eye level with her pale pink bosom. And her name tag.

'Rosemary,' I say.

'Yes, Mr Jankowski?' she says.

'He *is* lying, you know.'

'I know no such thing. And neither do you.'

'I do, though. I was on a show.'

She blinks, irritated. 'How do you mean?'

15

I hesitate and then change my mind. 'Never mind,' I say.

'Did you work on a circus?'

'I said never mind.'

There's a heartbeat of uncomfortable silence.

'Mr McGuinty could have been seriously hurt, you know,' she says, arranging my legs. She works quickly, efficiently, but stops just short of being summary.

'No he couldn't. Lawyers are indestructible.'

She stares at me for a long time, actually looking at me as a person. For a moment I think I sense a chink. Then she snaps back into action. 'Is your family taking you to the circus this weekend?'

'Oh yes,' I say with some pride. 'Someone comes every Sunday. Like clockwork.'

She shakes out a blanket and spreads it over my legs. 'Would you like me to get your dinner?'

'No,' I say.

There's an awkward silence. I realize I should have added 'thank you,' but it's too late now.

'All right then,' she says. 'I'll be back in a while to see if you need anything else.'

Yup. Sure she will. That's what they always say.

But Dagnammit, here she is.

'Now don't tell anyone,' she says, bustling in and sliding my dinner-table-cum-vanity over my lap. She sets down a paper napkin, plastic fork, and a bowl of fruit that actually looks appetizing, with strawberries, melon, and apple. 'I packed it for my break. I'm on a diet. Do you like fruit, Mr Jankowski?'

I would answer except that my hand is over my mouth and it's trembling. Apple, for God's sake.

She pats my other hand and leaves the room, discreetly ignoring my tears.

I slip a piece of apple into my mouth, savoring its juices. The buzzing fluorescent fixture above me casts its harsh light on my crooked fingers as they pluck pieces of fruit from the bowl. They look foreign to me. Surely they can't be mine.

Age is a terrible thief. Just when you're getting the hang of life, it knocks your legs out from under you and stoops your back. It makes you ache and muddies your head and silently spreads cancer throughout your spouse.

Metastatic, the doctor said. A matter of weeks or months. But my darling was as frail as a bird. She died nine days later. After sixty-one years together, she simply clutched my hand and exhaled.

Although there are times I'd give anything to have her back, I'm glad she went first. Losing her was like being cleft down the middle. It was the moment it all ended for me, and I wouldn't have wanted her to go through that. Being the survivor stinks.

I used to think I preferred getting old to the alternative, but now I'm not sure. Sometimes the monotony of bingo and sing-alongs and ancient dusty people parked in the hallway in wheelchairs makes me long for death. Particularly when I remember that I'm one of the ancient dusty people, filed away like some worthless tchotchke.

But there's nothing to be done about it. All I can do is put in time waiting for the inevitable, observing as the ghosts of my past rattle around my vacuous present. They crash and bang and make themselves at home, mostly because there's no competition. I've stopped fighting them.

They're crashing and banging around in there now.

Make yourselves at home, boys. Stay awhile. Oh, sorry – I see you already have.

Damn ghosts.

TWO

I'm twenty-three and sitting beside Catherine Hale; or rather, she's sitting beside me, because she came into the lecture hall after I did, sliding nonchalantly across the bench until our thighs were touching and then shrinking away with a blush as though the contact were accidental.

Catherine is one of only four women in the class of '31 and her cruelty knows no bounds. I've lost track of all the times I've thought *Oh God, oh God, she's finally going to let me,* only to be hit in the face with *Dear God, she wants me to stop NOW?*

I am, as far as I can tell, the oldest male virgin on the face of the earth. Certainly no one else my age is willing to admit it. Even my roommate Edward has claimed victory, although I'm inclined to believe the closest he's ever come to a naked woman was between the covers of one of his eight-pagers. Not too long ago some of the guys on my football team paid a woman a quarter apiece to let them do it, one after the other, in the cattle barn. As much as I had hoped to leave my virginity behind at Cornell, I couldn't bring myself to take part. I simply couldn't do it.

And so in ten days, after six long years of dissections, castrations, foalings, and shoving my arm up a cow's rear end more times than I care to remember, I, and my faithful shadow, Virginity, will leave Ithaca and join my father's veterinary practice in Norwich.

'And here you can see evidence of thickening of the distal small intestine,' says Professor Willard McGovern, his voice devoid of inflection. Using a pointer, he pokes languidly at the twisted intestines of a dead salt-and-pepper milk goat. 'This, along with enlarged mesenteric lymph nodes indicates a clear pattern of—'

The door squeaks open and McGovern turns, his pointer still buried in the doe's belly. Dean Wilkins walks briskly into the room and mounts the stairs to the podium. The two men confer, standing so close their foreheads nearly touch. McGovern listens to Wilkins' urgent whispers and then turns to scan the rows of students with worried eyes.

All around me, students fidget. Catherine sees me looking and slides one knee over the other, smoothing her skirt with languorous fingers. I swallow hard and look away.

'Jacob Jankowski?'

In my shock, I drop my pencil. It rolls under Catherine's feet. I clear my throat and rise quickly. Fifty-some pairs of eyes turn to look at me. 'Yes, sir?'

'Can we have a word, please?'

I close my notebook and set it on the bench. Catherine retrieves my pencil and lets her fingers linger on mine as she hands it to me. I make my way to the aisle, bumping knees and stepping on toes. Whispers follow me to the front of the room.

Dean Wilkins stares at me. 'Come with us,' he says.

I've done something, that much is clear.

I follow him into the hallway. McGovern walks out behind me and closes the door. For a moment the two of them stand silently, arms crossed, faces stern.

My mind races, dissecting my every recent move. Did they go through the dorm? Did they find Edward's liquor – or maybe even the eight-pagers? Dear Lord – if I get expelled now, my father will kill me. No question about it. Never mind what it will do to my mother. Okay, so maybe I drank a little whiskey, but it's not like I had anything to do with the fiasco in the cattle—

Dean Wilkins takes a deep breath, raises his eyes to mine, and claps a hand on my shoulder. 'Son, there's been an accident.' A slight pause. 'An automobile accident.' Another pause, longer this time. 'Your parents were involved.'

I stare at him, willing him to continue.

'Are they . . . ? Will they . . . ?'

'I'm sorry, son. It was instant. There was nothing anyone could do.'

I stare at his face, trying to maintain eye contact, but it's difficult because he's zooming away from me, receding to the end of a long black tunnel. Stars explode in my peripheral vision.

'You okay, son?'

'What?'

'Are you okay?'

Suddenly he's right in front of me again. I blink, wondering what he means. How the hell can I be okay? Then I realize he's asking whether I'm going to cry.

He clears his throat and continues. 'You'll have to go back today. To make a positive identification. I'll drive you to the station.'

The police superintendent – a member of our congregation – is waiting on the platform in street clothes. He greets me with an awkward nod and stiff handshake. Almost as an afterthought, he pulls me into a violent embrace. He pats my back loudly and expels me with a shove and a sniff. Then he drives me to the hospital in his own car, a two-year-old Phaeton that must have cost the earth. So many things people would have done differently had they known what would happen that fateful October.

The coroner leads us to the basement and slips through a door, leaving us in the hall. After a few minutes a nurse appears, holding the door open in wordless invitation.

There are no windows. There is a clock on one wall, but the room is otherwise bare. The floor is linoleum, olive green and white, and in the middle are two gurneys. Each has a sheet-covered body on it. I can't process this. I can't even tell which end is which.

'Are you ready?' the coroner asks, moving between them.

I swallow and nod. A hand appears on my shoulder. It belongs to the superintendent.

The coroner exposes first my father and then my mother.

They don't look like my parents, and yet they can't be anyone else. Death is all over them – in the mottled patterns of their battered torsos, the eggplant purple on bloodless white; in the sinking, hollowed eye sockets. My mother – so pretty and meticulous in life – wears a stiff grimace in death. Her hair is matted and bloodied, pressed into the hollow of her crushed skull. Her mouth is open, her chin receding as though she were snoring.

I turn as vomit explodes from my mouth. Someone is there with a kidney dish, but I overshoot and hear liquid splash across the floor, splattering against the wall. Hear it, because my eyes are squeezed shut. I vomit again and again, until there's nothing left. Despite this, I remain doubled over and heaving until I wonder if it's possible to turn inside out.

They take me somewhere and plant me in a chair. A kindly nurse in a starched white uniform brings coffee, which sits on the table next to me until it grows cold.

Later, the chaplain comes and sits beside me. He asks if there is anyone he can call. I mumble that all my relatives are in Poland. He asks about neighbors and members of our church, but for the life of me I can't come up with a single name. Not one. I'm not sure I could come up with my own if asked.

When he leaves I slip out. It's a little over two miles to our house, and I arrive just as the last sliver of sun slips beneath the horizon.

The driveway is empty. Of course.

I stop in the backyard, holding my valise and staring at the long flat building behind the house. There's a new sign above the entrance, the lettering glossy and black:

E. JANKOWSKI AND SON
Doctors of Veterinary Medicine

After a while I turn to the house, climb the stoop, and push open the back door.

My father's prized possession – a Philco radio – sits on the kitchen counter. My mother's blue sweater hangs on the back of a chair. There are ironed linens on the kitchen table, a vase of wilting violets. An overturned mixing bowl, two plates, and a handful of cutlery set to dry on a checked dish towel spread out by the sink.

This morning, I had parents. This morning, they ate breakfast.

I fall to my knees, right there on the back stoop, howling into splayed hands.

The ladies of the church auxiliary, alerted to my return by the superintendent's wife, swoop down on me within the hour.

I'm still on the stoop, my face pressed into my knees. I hear gravel crunching under tires, car doors slamming, and next thing I know I'm surrounded by doughy flesh, flowered prints, and gloved hands. I am pressed against soft bosoms, poked by veiled hats, and engulfed by jasmine, lavender, and rose water. Death is a formal affair, and they're dressed in their Sunday best. They pat and they fuss, and above all, they cluck.

Such a shame, such a shame. And such good people, too. It's hard to make sense of such a tragedy, surely it is, but the good Lord works in mysterious ways. They will take care of everything. The guest room at Jim and Mabel Neurater's house is already made up. I am not to worry about a thing.

They take my valise and herd me toward the running car. A grim-faced Jim Neurater is behind the wheel, gripping it with both hands.

Two days after I bury my parents, I am summoned to the offices of Edmund Hyde, Esquire, to hear the details of their estate. I sit in a hard leather chair across from the man himself as it gradually sinks in that there is nothing to discuss. At first I think he's mocking me. Apparently my father has been taking payment in the form of beans and eggs for nearly two years.

'Beans and eggs?' My voice cracks in disbelief. *'Beans and eggs?'*

'And chickens. And other goods.'

'I don't understand.'

'It's what people have, son. The community's been hit right hard, and your father was trying to help out. Couldn't stand by and watch animals suffer.'

'But . . . I don't understand. Even if he took payment in, uh, whatever, how does that make everything belong to the bank?'

'They fell behind on their mortgage.'

'My parents didn't have a mortgage.'

He looks uncomfortable. Holds his steepled fingers in front of him. 'Well, yes, actually, they did.'

'No, they didn't,' I argue. 'They've lived here for nearly thirty years. My father put away every cent he ever made.'

'The bank failed.'

I narrow my eyes. 'I thought you just said it all goes to the bank.'

He sighs deeply. 'It's a different bank. The one that gave them the mortgage when the other one closed,' he says. I can't tell if he's trying to give the appearance of patience and failing miserably or is blatantly trying to make me leave.

I pause, weighing my options.

'What about the things in the house? In the practice?' I say finally.

'It all goes to the bank.'

'What if I want to fight it?'

'How?'

'What if I come back and take over the practice and try to make the payments?'

'It doesn't work like that. It's not yours to take over.'

I stare at Edmund Hyde, in his expensive suit, behind his expensive desk, in front of his leather-bound books. Behind him, the sun streaks through lead-paned windows. I am filled with sudden loathing – I'll bet he's never taken payment in the form of beans and eggs in his life.

I lean forward and make eye contact. I want this to be his problem, too. 'What am I supposed to do?' I ask slowly.

'I don't know, son. I wish I did. The country's fallen on hard times, and that's a fact.' He leans back in his chair, his fingers still steepled. He cocks his head, as though an idea has just occurred to him. 'I suppose you could go west,' he muses.

It dawns on me that if I don't get out of this office right now, I'm going to slug him. I rise, replace my hat, and leave.

When I reach the sidewalk something else dawns on me. I can think of only one reason my parents would need a mortgage: to pay my Ivy League tuition.

The pain from this sudden realization is so intense I double over, clutching my stomach.

Because no other options occur to me, I return to school – a temporary solution at best. My room and board is paid up until the end of the year, but that is only six days away.

I've missed the entire week of review lectures. Everyone is eager to help. Catherine hands me her notes and then hugs me in a way that suggests I might get different results if I were to attempt the usual quest. I pull away. For the first time in living memory, I have no interest in sex.

I can't eat. I can't sleep. And I certainly can't study. I stare at a single paragraph for a quarter of an hour but can't absorb it. How can I, when behind the words, on the white background of the paper, I'm watching an endless loop of my parents' deaths? Watching as their cream-colored Buick flies through the guardrail and over the side of the bridge to avoid old Mr McPherson's red truck? Old Mr McPherson, who confessed as he was led from the scene that he wasn't entirely sure what side of the road he should have been on and thinks that maybe he hit the gas instead of the brake? Old Mr McPherson, who showed up at church one legendary Easter without trousers?

*   *   *

The proctor shuts the door and takes his seat. He glances at the wall clock and waits until the minute hand wobbles forward.

'You may begin.'

Fifty-two exam booklets flip over. Some people riffle through it. Others start writing immediately. I do neither.

Forty minutes later, I have yet to touch pencil to paper. I stare at the booklet in desperation. There are diagrams, numbers, lines and charts – strings of words with terminal punctuation at the end – some are periods, some question marks, and none of it makes sense. I wonder briefly if it is even English. I try it in Polish, but that doesn't work either. It might as well be hieroglyphics.

A woman coughs and I jump. A bead of sweat falls from my forehead onto my booklet. I wipe it off with my sleeve, then pick the booklet up.

Maybe if I bring it closer. Or hold it farther away – I can see now that it is in English; or rather, that the individual words are English, but I cannot read from one to another with any sense of continuity.

A second drop of sweat falls.

I scan the room. Catherine is writing quickly, her light brown hair falling over her face. She is left-handed, and because she writes in pencil her left arm is silver from wrist to elbow. Beside her, Edward yanks himself upright, glances at the clock in panic, and slumps back over his booklet. I turn away, toward a window.

Snatches of sky peek through leaves, a mosaic in blue and green that shifts gently with the wind. I stare into it, allowing my focus to soften, looking beyond the leaves and branches. A squirrel bounds fatly across my sight line, its full tail cocked.

I shove my chair back with a violent screech and stand up. My brow is beaded, my fingers shaking. Fifty-two faces turn to look.

I should know these people, and up until a week ago I did. I knew where their families lived. I knew what their fathers did. I knew whether they had siblings and whether they liked them. Hell, I even remember the ones who had to drop out after the Crash: Henry Winchester, whose father stepped off the ledge of the Board of Trade Building in Chicago. Alistair Barnes, whose father shot himself in the head. Reginald Monty, who tried unsuccessfully to live in a car when his family could no longer pay for his room and board. Bucky Hayes, whose unemployed father simply wandered off. But these ones, the ones who remain? Nothing.

I stare at these faces without features – these blank ovals with hair – looking from one to the next with increasing desperation. I'm aware of a heavy, wet noise, and realize it's me. I'm gasping for breath.

'Jacob?'

The face nearest me has a mouth and it's moving. The voice is timid, unsure. 'Are you okay?'

I blink, unable to focus. A second later I cross the room and toss the exam booklet on the proctor's desk.

'Finished already?' he says, reaching for it. I hear paper rustling as I head for the door. 'Wait!' he calls after me. 'You haven't even started! You can't leave. If you leave I can't let you—'

The door cuts off his final words. As I march across

the quad, I look up at Dean Wilkins' office. He's standing at the window, watching.

I walk until the edge of town and then veer off to follow the train tracks. I walk until after dark and the moon is high, and then for several hours after. I walk until my legs hurt and my feet blister. And then I stop because I am tired and hungry and have no idea where I am. It's as though I've been sleepwalking and suddenly woken to find myself here.

The only sign of civilization is the track, which rests on a raised bed of gravel. There is forest on one side and a small clearing on the other. From somewhere nearby I hear water trickling, and I pick my way toward it, guided by the moonlight.

The stream is a couple of feet wide at most. It runs along the tree line at the far side of the clearing and then cuts off into the woods. I peel off my shoes and socks and sit at its edge.

When I first submerge my feet in the frigid water, they hurt so badly I yank them out again. I persist, dunking them for longer and longer periods, until the cold finally numbs my blisters. I rest my soles against the rocky bottom and let the water wriggle between my toes. Eventually the cold causes its own ache, and I lie back on the bank, resting my head on a flat stone while my feet dry.

A coyote howls in the distance, a sound both lonely and familiar, and I sigh, allowing my eyes to close. When it is answered by a yipping only a few dozen yards to my left, I sit forward abruptly.

The faraway coyote howls again and this time is

answered by a train whistle. I pull on my socks and shoes and rise, staring at the edge of the clearing.

The train is closer now, rattling and thumping toward me: *CHUNK-a-chunk-a-chunk-a-chunk-a, CHUNK-a-chunk-a-chunk-a-chunk-a, CHUNK-a-chunk-a-chunk-a-chunk-a* . . .

I wipe my hands on my thighs and walk toward the track, stopping a few yards short. The acrid stink of oil fills my nose. The whistle shrieks again—

TWE-E-E-E-E-E-E-E-E-E—

A massive engine explodes around the bend and barrels past, so huge and so close I'm hit by a wall of wind. It churns out rolling clouds of billowing smoke, a fat black rope that coils over the cars behind it. The sight, the sound, the stink are too much. I watch, stunned, as half a dozen flat cars whoosh by, loaded with what look like wagons, although I can't quite make them out because the moon has gone behind a cloud.

I snap out of my stupor. There are people on that train. It matters not a whit where it's going because wherever it is, it's away from coyotes and toward civilization, food, possible employment – maybe even a ticket back to Ithaca, although I haven't a cent to my name and no reason to think they'd take me back. And what if they will? There is no home to return to, no practice to join.

More flat cars pass, loaded with what look like telephone poles. I look behind them, straining to see what follows. The moon slips out for a second, shining its bluish light on what might be freight cars.

I start running, moving the same direction as the train. My feet slip in the sloping gravel – it's like running in sand, and I overcompensate by pitching forward. I stumble, flailing and trying to regain my balance before any part of me comes between the huge steel wheels and the track.

I recover and pick up speed, scanning each car for something to grab on to. Three flash by, locked up tight. They're followed by stock cars. Their doors are open but filled by the exposed tail ends of horses. This is so odd I take note, even though I'm running beside a moving train in the middle of nowhere.

I slow to a jog and finally stop. Winded and very nearly hopeless, I turn my head. There's an open door three cars behind me.

I lunge forward again, counting as they pass.

One, two, three—

I reach for the iron grab bar and fling myself upward. My left foot and elbow hit first, and then my chin, which smashes onto the metal edging. I cling tightly with all three. The noise is deafening, and my jawbone bangs rhythmically on the iron edging. I smell either blood or rust and wonder briefly if I've destroyed my teeth before realizing the point is in serious danger of becoming moot – I'm balanced perilously on the edge of the doorway with my right leg pointed at the undercarriage. With my right hand I cling to the grab bar. With my left I claw the floorboards so desperately the wood peels off, under my nails. I'm losing purchase – I have almost no tread on my shoes and my left foot slides in short jerks toward the door. My right leg now dangles so far under the train I'm sure I'm going to lose it. I brace for it even, squeezing my eyes shut and clenching my teeth.

After a couple of seconds, I realize I'm still intact. I

open my eyes and weigh my options. There are only two choices here, and since there's no dismounting without going under the train, I count to three and buck upward with everything I've got. I manage to get my left knee up over the edge. Using foot, knee, chin, elbow, and finger-nails, I scrape my way inside and collapse on the floor. I lie panting, utterly spent.

Then I realize I'm facing a dim light. I jerk upright on my elbow.

Four men are sitting on rough burlap feed sacks, playing cards by the light of a kerosene lantern. One of them, a shrunken old man with stubble and a hollow face, has an earthenware jug tipped up to his lips. In his surprise, he seems to have forgotten to put it back down. He does so now and wipes his mouth with the back of his sleeve.

'Well, well, well,' he says slowly. 'What have we here?'

Two of the men sit perfectly still, staring at me over the top of fanned cards. The fourth climbs to his feet and steps forward.

He is a hulking brute with a thick black beard. His clothes are filthy, and the brim of his hat looks like someone has taken a bite out of it. I scramble to my feet and stumble backward, only to find that there's nowhere to go. I twist my head around and discover that I'm up against one of a great many bundles of canvas.

When I turn back, the man is in my face, his breath rank with alcohol. 'We don't got room for no bums on this train, brother. You can git right back off.'

'Now hold on, Blackie,' says the old man with the jug. 'Don't go doin' nothing rash now, you hear?'

'Rash nothin',' says Blackie, reaching for my collar. I

swat his arm away. He reaches with his other hand and I swing up to stop him. The bones in our forearms meet with a crack.

'*Woohoo*,' cackles the old man. 'Watch yourself, pal. Don't you go messin' with Blackie.'

'It seems to me maybe Blackie's messing with me,' I shout, blocking another blow.

Blackie lunges. I fall onto a roll of canvas, and before my head even hits I'm yanked forward again. A moment later, my right arm is twisted behind my back, my feet hang over the edge of the open door, and I'm facing a line of trees that passes altogether too quickly.

'Blackie,' barks the old guy. 'Blackie! Let 'im go. Let 'im go, I tell ya, and on the inside of the train, too!'

Blackie yanks my arm up toward the nape of my neck and shakes me.

'Blackie, I'm tellin' ya!' shouts the old man. 'We don't need no trouble. Let 'im go!'

Blackie dangles me a little further out the door, then pivots and tosses me across the rolls of canvas. He returns to the other men, snatches the earthenware jug, and then passes right by me, climbing over the canvas and retreating to the far corner of the car. I watch him closely, rubbing my wrenched arm.

'Don't be sore, kid,' says the old man. 'Throwing people off trains is one of the perks of Blackie's job, and he ain't got to do it in a while. Here,' he says, patting the floor with the flat of his hand. 'Come on over here.'

I shoot another glance at Blackie.

'Come on now,' says the old man. 'Don't be shy. Blackie's gonna behave now, ain't you, Blackie?'

Blackie grunts and takes a swig.

I rise and move cautiously toward the others.

The old man sticks his right hand up at me. I hesitate and then take it.

'I'm Camel,' he says. 'And this here's Grady. That's Bill. I believe you've already made Blackie's acquaintance.' He smiles, revealing a scant handful of teeth.

'How do you do,' I say.

'Grady, git that jug back, will ya?' says Camel.

Grady trains his gaze on me, and I meet it. After a while he gets up and moves silently toward Blackie.

Camel struggles to his feet, so stiff that at one point I reach out and steady his elbow. Once he's upright he holds the kerosene lamp out and squints into my face. He peers at my clothes, surveying me from top to bottom.

'Now what did I tell you, Blackie?' he calls out crossly. 'This here ain't no bum. Blackie, git on over here and take a look. Learn yourself the difference.'

Blackie grunts, takes one last swallow, and relinquishes the jug to Grady.

Camel squints up at me. 'What did you say your name was?'

'Jacob Jankowski.'

'You got red hair.'

'So I've heard.'

'Where you from?'

I pause. Am I from Norwich or Ithaca? Is where you're from the place you're leaving or where you have roots?

'Nowhere,' I say.

Camel's face hardens. He weaves slightly on bowed

legs, casting an uneven light from the swinging lantern. 'You done something, boy? You on the lam?'

'No,' I say. 'Nothing like that.'

He squints at me a while longer and then nods. 'All right then. None of my business no-how. Where you headed?'

'Not sure.'

'You outta work?'

'Yes sir. I reckon I am.'

'Ain't no shame in it,' he says. 'What can you do?'

'About anything,' I say.

Grady appears with the jug and hands it to Camel. He wipes its neck with his sleeve and passes it to me. 'Here, have a belt.'

Now, I'm no virgin to liquor, but moonshine is another beast entirely. It burns hellfire through my chest and head. I catch my breath and fight back tears, staring Camel straight in the eyes even as my lungs threaten to combust.

Camel observes and nods slowly. 'We land in Utica in the morning. I'll take you to see Uncle Al.'

'Who? What?'

'You know. Alan Bunkel, Ringmaster Extraordinaire. Lord and Master of the Known and Unknown Universes.'

I must look baffled, because Camel lets loose with a toothless cackle. 'Kid, don't tell me you didn't notice.'

'Notice what?' I ask.

'Shit, boys,' he hoots, looking around at the others. 'He really don't know!'

Grady and Bill smirk. Only Blackie is unamused. He scowls, pulling his hat farther down over his face.

Camel turns toward me, clears his throat, and speaks

slowly, savoring each word. 'You didn't just jump a train, boy. You done jumped the Flying Squadron of the Benzini Brothers Most Spectacular Show on Earth.'

'The *what?*' I say.

Camel laughs so hard he doubles over.

'Ah, that's precious. Precious indeed,' he says, sniffing and wiping his eyes with the back of his hand. 'Ah, me. You done landed yer ass on a circus, boy.'

I blink at him.

'That there's the big top,' he says, lifting the kerosene lamp and waving a crooked finger at the great rolls of canvas. 'One of the canvas wagons caught the runs wrong and busted up real good, so here it is. Might as well find a place to sleep. It's gonna be a few hours before we land. Just don't lie too close to the door, that's all. Sometimes we take them corners awful sharp.'

THREE

I awake to the prolonged screeching of brakes. I'm wedged a good deal farther between the rolls of canvas than I was when I fell asleep, and I'm disoriented. It takes me a second to figure out where I am.

The train shudders to a stop and exhales. Blackie, Bill, and Grady roll to their feet and drop wordlessly out the door. After they're gone, Camel hobbles over. He leans down and pokes me.

'Come on, kid,' he says. 'You gotta get out of here before the canvas men arrive. I'm gonna try to set you up with Crazy Joe this morning.'

'Crazy Joe?' I say, sitting up. My shins are itchy and my neck hurts like a son of a bitch.

'Head horse honcho,' says Camel. 'Of baggage stock, that is. August don't let him nowhere near the ring stock.

Actually, it's probably Marlena that don't let him near, but it don't make no difference. She won't let you nowhere near, neither. With Crazy Joe at least you got a shot. We had a run of bad weather and muddy lots, and a bunch of his men got tired of working Chinese and moped off. Left him a bit short.'

'Why's he called Crazy Joe?'

'Don't rightly know,' says Camel. He digs inside his ear and inspects his findings. 'Think he was in the Big House for a while but I don't know why. Wouldn't suggest you ask, neither.' He wipes his finger on his pants and ambles to the doorway.

'Well, come on then!' he says, looking back at me. 'We don't got all day!' He eases himself onto the edge and slides carefully to the gravel.

I give my shins one last desperate scratch, tie my shoes, and follow.

We are adjacent to a huge grassy lot. Beyond it are scattered brick buildings, backlit by the predawn glow. Hundreds of dirty, unshaven men pour from the train and surround it, like ants on candy, cursing and stretching and lighting cigarettes. Ramps and chutes clatter to the ground, and six- and eight-horse hitches materialize from nowhere, spread out on the dirt. Horse after horse appears, heavy bob-tailed Percherons that clomp down the ramps, snorting and blowing and already in harness. Men on either side hold the swinging doors close to the sides of the ramps, keeping the animals from getting too close to the edge.

A group of men marches toward us, heads down.

'Mornin', Camel,' says the leader as he passes us and

climbs into the car. The others clamber up behind him. They surround a bundle of canvas and heave it toward the entrance, grunting with effort. It moves about a foot and a half and lands in a cloud of dust.

'Morning, Will,' says Camel. 'Say, got a smoke for an old man?'

'Sure.' The man straightens up and pats his shirt pockets. He digs into one and retrieves a bent cigarette. 'It's Bull Durham,' he says, leaning forward and holding it out. 'Sorry.'

'Roll-your-own suits me fine,' says Camel. 'Thanks, Will. Much obliged.'

Will jerks his thumb at me. 'Who's that?'

'A First of May. Name's Jacob Jankowski.'

Will looks at me, and then turns and spits out the door. 'How new?' he says, continuing to address Camel.

'Real new.'

'You got him on yet?'

'Nope.'

'Well, good luck to ya.' He tips his hat at me. 'Don't sleep too sound, kid, if you know what I mean.' He disappears into the interior.

'What does that mean?' I say, but Camel is walking away. I jog a little to catch up.

There are now hundreds of horses among the dirty men. At first glance the scene looks chaotic, but by the time Camel has lit his cigarette, several dozen teams are hitched and moving alongside the flat cars, pulling wagons toward the runs. As soon as a wagon's front wheels hit the sloped wooden tracks, the man guiding its pole leaps out of the way. And it's a good thing, too. The heavily loaded wagons come barreling down the runs and don't stop until they're a dozen feet away.

In the morning light I see what I couldn't last night – the wagons are painted scarlet, with gold trim and sunburst wheels, each emblazoned with the name BENZINI BROS MOST SPECTACULAR SHOW ON EARTH. As soon as the wagons are hitched to teams, the Percherons lean into their harnesses and drag their heavy loads across the field.

'Watch out,' says Camel, grabbing my arm and pulling me toward him. He braces his hat with his other hand, the lumpy cigarette clenched in his teeth.

Three men on horseback gallop past. They swerve and cross the length of the field, tour its perimeter, and then swing back around. The one in the lead turns his head from side to side, shrewdly assessing the ground. He holds both reins in one hand and with the other retrieves flagged darts from a leather pouch, flinging them into the earth.

'What's he doing?' I ask.

'Laying out the lot,' says Camel. He comes to a stop in front of a stock car. 'Joe! Hey, Joe!'

A head appears in the doorway.

'I got a First of May here. Fresh from the crate. Think you can use him?'

The figure steps forward onto the ramp. He pushes up the brim of a battered hat with a hand missing three of its fingers. He scrutinizes me, shoots an oyster of dark brown tobacco juice out the side of his mouth, and goes back inside.

Camel pats my arm in a congratulatory fashion. 'You're in, kid.'

'I am?'

'Yep. Now go shovel some shit. I'll catch up with you later.'

The stock car is an ungodly mess. I work with a kid named Charlie whose face is smooth as a girl's. His voice hasn't even broken yet. After we shovel what seems like a cubic ton of manure out the door, I pause, surveying the remaining mess. 'How many horses do they load in here, anyway?'

'Twenty-seven.'

'Jesus. They must be packed in so tight they can't move.'

'That's the idea,' Charlie says. 'Once the wedge horse loads, none of 'em can go down.'

The exposed tails from last night suddenly make sense.

Joe appears in the doorway. 'Flag's up,' he growls.

Charlie drops his shovel and heads for the door.

'What's going on? Where are you going?' I say.

'The cookhouse flag's up.'

I shake my head. 'I'm sorry, I still don't understand.'

'Chow,' he says.

Now *that* I understand. I, too, drop my shovel.

Canvas tents have popped up like mushrooms, although the largest one – obviously the big top – still lies flat on the ground. Men stand over its seams, bending at the waist and lacing its pieces together. Towering wooden poles stick up through its center line, already flying Old Glory. With the rigging on the poles, it looks like the deck and mast of a sailboat.

All around its perimeter, eight-man sledge teams pound in stakes at breakneck speed. By the time one sledge hits the stake, five others are in motion. The resulting noise is as regular as machine-gun fire, cutting through the rest of the din.

Teams of men are also raising enormous poles. Charlie and I pass a group of ten throwing their combined weight against a single rope as a man off to the side chants, 'Pull it, shake it, break it! Again – pull it, shake it, break it! Now downstake it!'

The cookhouse couldn't be more obvious – never mind the orange and blue flag, the boiler belching in the background, or the stream of people heading for it. The smell of food hits me like a cannonball in the gut. I haven't eaten since the day before yesterday, and my stomach twists with hunger.

The sidewalls of the cookhouse have been raised to allow for a draft, but it is divided down the center by a curtain. The tables on this side are graced with red and white checked tablecloths, silverware, and vases of flowers. This seems wildly out of sync with the line of filthy men snaking behind the steam tables.

'My God,' I say to Charlie as we take our place in line. 'Look at this spread.'

There are hash browns, sausages, and heaping baskets of thickly sliced bread. Spiral cut ham, eggs cooked every which way, jam in pots, bowls of oranges.

'This ain't nothin',' he says. 'Big Bertha's got all this, and waiters, too. You just sit at your table and they bring it right to you.'

'Big Bertha?'

'Ringling,' he says.

'You worked for them?'

'Uh . . . no,' he says sheepishly. 'But I know people who have!'

I grab a plate and scoop up a mountain of potatoes, eggs, and sausages, trying to keep from looking desperate. The scent is overwhelming. I open my mouth, inhaling deeply – it's like manna from heaven. It *is* manna from heaven.

Camel appears from nowhere. 'Here. Give this here to that fella there, at the end of the line,' he says, pressing a ticket into my free hand.

The man at the end of the line sits in a folding chair, looking out from under the brim of a bent fedora. I hold out the ticket. He looks up at me, arms crossed firmly in front of him.

'Department?' he says.

'I beg your pardon?' I say.

'What's your department?'

'Uh . . . I'm not sure,' I say. 'I've been mucking out stock cars all morning.'

'That don't tell me nothin',' he says, continuing to ignore my ticket. 'That could be ring stock, baggage stock, or menagerie. So which is it?'

I don't answer. I'm pretty sure Camel mentioned at least a couple of those, but I don't remember the specifics.

'If you don't know your department, you ain't on the show,' the man says. 'So, who the hell are you?'

'Everything okay, Ezra?' says Camel, coming up behind me.

'No it ain't. I got me some smart-ass rube trying to filch breakfast from the show,' says Ezra, spitting on the ground.

'He ain't no rube,' says Camel. 'He's a First of May and he's with me.'

'Yeah?'

'Yeah.'

The man flicks the brim of his hat up and checks me out, head to toe. He pauses a few beats longer and then says, 'All right, Camel. If you're vouching for him, I reckon that's good enough for me.' The hand comes out, snatches my ticket. 'Somethin' else. Teach him how to talk before he gets the shit kicked out of him, will ya?'

'So, what's my department?' I ask, heading for a table.

'Oh no you don't,' says Camel, grabbing my elbow. 'Them tables ain't for the likes of us. You stick close to me till you learn your way around.'

I follow him around the curtain. The tables in the other half are set end to end, their bare wood graced only with salt and pepper shakers. No flowers here.

'Who sits on the other side? Performers?'

Camel shoots me a look. 'Good God, kid. Just keep your trap shut till you learn the vernacular, would ya?'

He sits down and immediately shoves half a piece of bread into his mouth. He chews on it for a minute and then looks across at me. 'Oh go on, don't be sore. I'm just looking out for ya. You saw how Ezra was, and Ezra's a pussycat. Sit yourself down.'

I look at him for a moment longer and then step over the bench. I set my plate down, glance at my manure-stained hands, wipe them on my pants, and, finding them no cleaner, dig into my food anyway.

'So, what's the vernacular then?' I say finally.

'They're called kinkers,' says Camel, talking around a mouthful of chewed food. 'And your department is baggage stock. For now.'

'So where are these kinkers?'

'They'll be pulling in any time. There's two more sections of train still to come. They stay up late, sleep late, and arrive just in time for breakfast. And while we're on the subject, don't you go calling them "kinkers" to their faces, neither.'

'What do I call them?'

'Performers.'

'So why can't I just call them performers all the time?' I say with a note of irritation creeping into my voice.

'There's them and there's us, and you're us,' says Camel. 'Never mind. You'll learn.' A train whistles in the distance. 'Speak of the devil.'

'Is Uncle Al with them?'

'Yep, but don't you go getting any ideas. We ain't going near him till later. He's cranky as a bear with toothache when we're still setting up. Say, how you making out with Joe? Had enough of horse shit yet?'

'I don't mind.'

'Yeah, well I figure you for better'n that. I been talking to a friend of mine,' Camel says, crushing another piece of bread between his fingers and using it to wipe grease from his plate. 'You stick with him the rest of the day, and he'll put in a word for you.'

'What'll I be doing?'

'Whatever he says. And I mean that, too.' He cocks an eyebrow for emphasis.

Camel's friend is a small man with a large paunch and booming voice. He's the sideshow talker, and his name is Cecil. He examines me and declares me suitable for the job at hand. I – along with Jimmy and Wade, two other men deemed presentable enough to mix with the towns-folk – are supposed to position ourselves around the edges of the crowd and then, when we get the signal, step forward and jostle them toward the entrance.

The sideshow is on the midway, which teems with activity. On one side, a group of black men struggles to put up the sideshow banners. On the other, there's clinking and shouting as white-jacketed white men set up glass after glass of lemonade, forming pyramids of full glasses on the counters of their red and white striped concession stands. The air is filled with the scents of corn popping, peanuts roasting, and the tangy under-tone of animal.

At the end of the midway, beyond the ticket gate, is a huge tent into which all manner of creatures is being carted – llamas, camels, zebras, monkeys, at least one polar bear, and cage after cage of cats.

Cecil and one of the black men fuss with a banner featuring an enormously fat woman. After a couple of seconds Cecil slaps the other man's head. 'Get with it, boy! We're going to be crawling with suckers in a minute. How are we gonna bring them in if they can't see Lucinda's splendors?'

A whistle blows and everyone freezes.

'Doors!' booms a male voice.

All hell breaks loose. The men at the concession stands scurry behind their counters, making final adjustments to their wares and straightening their jackets and caps. With the exception of the poor soul still working on Lucinda's banner, all the black men slip through the canvas and out of sight.

'Get that goddamned banner up and get out of here!' Cecil screams. The man makes one final adjustment and disappears.

I turn. A wall of humans swells toward us with squealing children leading the way, yanking their parents forward by the hand.

Wade jabs an elbow in my side. '*Pssst* . . . You wanna see the menagerie?'

'The what?'

He cocks his head at the tent between us and the big top. 'You been craning your neck since you got here. Wanna take a peek?'

'What about him?' I say, jerking my eyes toward Cecil.

'We'll be back before he misses us. Besides, we can't do nothin' till he gets a crowd going.'

Wade leads me to the ticket gate. Old men guard it, sitting behind four red podiums. Three ignore us. The fourth glances at Wade and nods.

'Go on. Have a peek,' says Wade. 'I'll keep an eye on Cecil.'

I peer inside. The tent is enormous, as tall as the sky and supported by long, straight poles jutting at various angles. The canvas is taut and nearly translucent – sunlight filters through the material and seams, illuminating the largest candy stand of all. It's smack in the center of the menagerie, under rays of glorious light, surrounded by banners advertising sarsaparilla, Cracker Jack, and frozen custard.

Brilliantly painted red and gold animal dens line two of the four walls, their sides propped open to reveal lions, tigers, panthers, jaguars, bears, chimps, and spider monkeys – even an orangutan. Camels, llamas, zebras, and horses stand behind low ropes slung between iron stakes, their heads buried in mounds of hay. Two giraffes stand within an area enclosed by chain-link fence.

I'm searching in vain for an elephant when my eyes come to an abrupt stop on a woman. She looks so much like Catherine I catch my breath – the plane of her face, the cut of her hair, the slim thighs I've always imagined were under Catherine's staid skirts. She's standing in front of a row of black and white horses, wearing pink sequins, tights, and satin slippers, talking to a man in top hat and tails. She cups the muzzle of one of the white horses, a striking Arabian with a silver mane and tail. She lifts a hand to push back a piece of her light brown hair and adjust her headdress. Then she reaches up and smoothes the horse's forelock against his face. She grasps his ear in her fist, letting it slide through her fingers.

There's an enormous crash, and I spin to find that the side of the closest animal den has slammed shut. When I turn back, the woman is looking at me. Her brow furrows, as though in recognition. After a few seconds I realize I should smile or drop my eyes or do something, but I can't. Eventually the man in the top hat puts his hand on her shoulder and she turns, but slowly, reluctantly. After a few seconds she steals another glance.

Wade is back. 'Come on,' he says, slapping me between the shoulder blades. 'It's showtime.'

'Ladies-s-s-s-s-s and gentlemen-n-n-n-n-n-n! Twen-n-n-n-ty-five minutes till the big show! Twen-n-n-n-ty-five minutes! More than enough time to avail yourselves of the amazing, the unbelievable, the m-a-a-a-a-a-rvelous wonders we have gathered from all four corners of the earth, and still find a good seat in the big top! Plenty of time to see the oddities, the freaks of nature, the spectacles! Ours is the most dazzling collection in the world, ladies and gentlemen! In the world, I tell you!'

Cecil stands on a platform beside the sideshow's entrance. He struts back and forth, gesturing grandly. A crowd of about fifty hovers loosely. They are uncommitted, more paused than stopped.

'Step right this way, to see the gorgeous, the *enormous*, the Lovely Lucinda – the world's most beautiful fat lady! Eight hundred and eighty-five pounds of pudgy perfection, ladies and gentlemen! Come see the human ostrich – he can swallow and return anything you hand him. Give it a try! Wallets, watches, even lightbulbs! You name it, he'll regurgitate it! And don't miss Frank Otto, the world's most tattooed man! Held hostage in the darkest jungles of Borneo and tried for a crime he didn't commit, and his punishment? Well, folks, his punishment is written all over his body in permanent ink!'

The crowd is denser, their interest piqued. Jimmy, Wade, and I mingle near the back.

'And now,' says Cecil, swinging around. He puts his finger to his lips and winks grotesquely – an exaggerated gesture that pulls the side of his mouth up toward his eye. He raises a hand in the air, asking for quiet. 'And now – my apologies, ladies, but this is for the gentlemen only – the gentlemen only! Because we're in mixed company, for delicacy's sake, I can only say this once. Gentlemen, if you're a red-blooded American, if you've got manly blood flowing through your veins, then this is something you don't want to miss. If you'll follow that there fella – right there, just right over there – you'll see something so amazing, so shocking, it's guaranteed to—'

He stops, closes his eyes, and lifts a hand. He shakes his head with remorse. 'But no,' he continues. 'In the interest of decency and on account of being in mixed company, I can't say any more than that. Can't say any more, gentlemen. Except this – *you don't want to miss it!* Just hand your quarter to this fella here, and he'll take you right on in. You'll never remember the quarter you spent here today, and you'll never forget what you see. You'll be talking about this for the rest of your lives, fellas. The rest of your lives.'

Cecil straightens up and adjusts his checked waistcoat, tugging the hem with both hands. His face assumes a deferential expression and he gestures broadly toward an entrance on the opposite side. 'And ladies, if you'll kindly come this way – we have wonders and curiosities suitable for your delicate sensibilities, too. A gentleman would never forget the ladies. Especially such lovely ladies as yourselves.' With this he smiles and closes his eyes. The women in the crowd glance nervously at the disappearing men.

A tug-of-war has broken out. A woman holds fast to her husband's sleeve with one hand and bats him with the other. He grimaces and frowns, ducking to avoid her blows. When he finally breaks free, he straightens his lapels and glowers at his now-sulking wife. As he struts off to hand over his quarter, someone clucks like a hen. Laughter ripples through the crowd.

The rest of the women, perhaps because they don't want to make a spectacle, watch reluctantly as their men drift off and get in line. Cecil sees this and comes down from his platform. He is all concern, all gallant attention, gently drawing them toward more savory matters.

He touches his left earlobe. I push imperceptibly forward. The women move closer to Cecil and I feel like a sheepdog.

'If you'll step this way,' Cecil continues, 'I'll show you ladies something you've never seen before. Something so unusual, so extraordinary, you never dreamed it existed, and yet it's something you can talk about at church this Sunday, or with Grandma and Grandpa at the dinner table. Go ahead and bring the little fellas, this here is strictly family fun. See a horse with his head where his tail should be! Not a word of a lie, ladies. A living creature with his tail where his head should be. See it with your own eyes. And when you tell your menfolk about it, maybe they'll wish they'd stayed with their lovely ladies instead. Oh yes, my dears. They will indeed.'

By now I'm surrounded. The men have all but disappeared, and I let myself drift along in the current of churchgoers and ladies, of young fellas and the rest of the non-red-blooded Americans.

The horse with his tail where his head should be is exactly that – a horse backed into a standing stall so that his tail hangs into his feed bucket.

'Oh, for crying out loud,' says one woman.

'Well, I never!' says another, but mostly there is relieved laughter, because if this is the horse with the tail where his head should be, then how bad can the men's show be?

There's a scuffling outside the tent.

'You goddamned sons of bitches! You're damned right I want my money back – you think I'm gonna pay a quarter to see a goddamned pair of suspenders? You talk about red-blooded Americans, well, this one's red-blooded all right! I want my goddamned money back!'

'Excuse me, ma'am,' I say, wedging my shoulder between the two women ahead of me.

'Hey, mister! What's your hurry?'

'Excuse me. Beg your pardon,' I say, pushing my way out.

Cecil and a red-faced man are squaring off. The man advances, places both hands on Cecil's chest, and shoves him backward. The crowd parts, and Cecil crashes against the striped skirt of his platform. The patrons close in behind, standing on tiptoe, gawking.

I launch myself through them, reaching Cecil just as the other man hauls off and swings – his fist is but an inch or two from Cecil's chin when I snatch it from the air and twist it behind his back. I lock an arm around his neck and drag him backward. He sputters, reaching up and clawing my forearm. I tighten my grip until my tendons dig into his windpipe and half-drag, half-march him to beyond the end of the midway. Then I chuck him into the dirt. He lies in a cloud of dust, wheezing and grasping his throat.

Within seconds, two suited men breeze past me, lift him by the arms and haul him, still coughing, toward town. They lean into him, pat his back, and mutter encouragement. They straighten his hat, which has miraculously stayed in place.

'Nice work,' says Wade, clapping a hand on my shoulder. 'You done good. Come on back. They'll take care of it from here.'

'Who are they?' I say, examining the row of long scratches, beaded with blood, on my forearm.

'Patches. They'll calm him down and make him happy. That way we won't catch any heat.' He turns to address the crowd, clapping once – loudly – and then rubbing his hands in front of him. 'Okay, folks. Everything's fine. Nothing more to see here.'

The crowd is reluctant to leave. When the man and his escorts finally disappear behind a redbrick building they start to dribble away, but continue to glance hopefully over their shoulders, afraid they'll miss something.

Jimmy pushes his way through the stragglers.

'Hey,' he says. 'Cecil wants to see you.'

He leads me through to the back end. Cecil sits on the very edge of a folding chair. His legs and spat-clad feet stick straight out. His face is red and moist, and he fans himself with a program. His free hand pats various pockets and then reaches into his vest. He pulls out a flat, square bottle, curls his lips back, and pulls the cork out with his teeth. He spits it off to the side and tips the bottle up. Then he catches sight of me.

He stares for a moment, the bottle poised at his lips. He lowers it again, resting it on his rounded belly. He drums his fingers against it, surveying me.

'You handled yourself pretty well out there,' he says finally.

'Thank you, sir.'

'Where'd you learn that?'

'Dunno. Football. School. Wrangling the odd bull who objected to losing his testicles.'

He watches me a moment longer, fingers still drumming, lips pursed. 'Camel got you on the show yet?'

'Not officially. No sir.'

There's another long silence. His eyes narrow to slits. 'Know how to keep your mouth shut?'

'Yes sir.'

He takes a long slug from his bottle and relaxes his eyes. 'Well, okay then,' he says, nodding slowly.

It's evening, and while the kinkers are delighting the crowd in the big top I'm standing near the back of a much smaller tent on the far edge of the lot, behind a row of baggage wagons and accessible only through word of mouth and a fifty-cent admission fee. The interior is dim, illuminated by a string of red bulbs that casts a warm glow on the woman methodically removing her clothes.

My job is to maintain order and periodically smack the sides of the tent with a metal pipe, the better to discourage peeping toms; or rather, to encourage peeping toms to come around front and pay their fifty cents. I am also supposed to keep a lid on the kind of behavior I witnessed at the sideshow earlier, although I can't help thinking that the fellow who was so upset this afternoon would find little to complain about here.

There are twelve rows of folding chairs, every one of them occupied. Moonshine is passed from man to man, each blindly groping for the bottle because no one wants to take his eyes off the stage.

The woman is a statuesque redhead with eyelashes too long to be real and a beauty spot painted next to her full lips. Her legs are long, her hips full, her chest a stupefaction. She is down to a G-string, a glimmering translucent shawl, and a gloriously overflowing brassiere. She shakes her shoulders, keeping gelatinous time with the small band of musicians to her right.

She takes a few strides, sliding across the stage in feathered mules. The snare drum rolls, and she stops, her mouth open in mock surprise. She throws her head back, exposing her throat and sliding her hands down around the cups of her brassiere. She leans forward, squeezing until the flesh swells between her fingers.

I scan the sidewalls. A pair of shoe tips peeks under the edge of the canvas. I approach, keeping close to the wall. Just in front of the shoes, I swing the pipe and smack the canvas. There's a grunt, and the shoes disappear. I pause with my ear to the seam, and then return to my post.

The redhead sways with the music, caressing her shawl with lacquered nails. It has gold or silver woven through it and sparkles as she slides it back and forth across her shoulders. She drops forward suddenly at the waist, throws her head back, and shimmies.

The men holler. Two or three stand, shaking their fists in encouragement. I glance at Cecil, whose steely gaze tells me to watch them.

The woman stands up, turns her back, and strides to the center of the stage. She passes the shawl between her legs, slowly grinding against it. Groans rise from the audience. She spins so she's facing us and continues sliding the shawl back and forth, pulling it so tight the cleft of her vulva shows.

'Take it off, baby! Take it all off!'

The men are getting rowdier; more than half are on their feet. Cecil beckons me forward with one hand. I step closer to the rows of folding chairs.

The shawl drops to the floor and the woman turns her back once again. She shakes her hair so it ripples over her shoulder blades and raises her hands so that they meet at the clasp of her brassiere. A cheer rises from the crowd. She pauses to look over her shoulder and winks, running the straps coquettishly down her arms. Then she drops the bra to the floor and spins around, clutching her breasts in her hands. A howl of protest rises from the men.

'Aw, come on, sugar, show us what you got!'

She shakes her head, pouting coyly.

'Aw, come on! I spent fifty cents!'

She shakes her head, blinking demurely at the floor.

Suddenly her eyes and mouth spring open and she pulls her hands away.

Those majestic globes drop. They come to an abrupt stop before swinging gently, even though she's standing perfectly still.

There's a collective intake of breath, a moment of awed silence before the men whoop in delight.

'Atta girl!'

'Lord have mercy!'

'Hot *damn!*'

She caresses herself, lifting and kneading, rolling her nipples between her fingers. She stares lasciviously down at the men, running her tongue across her upper lip.

A drum roll begins. She grasps each hardened point firmly between thumb and forefinger and pulls one breast so that its nipple points at the ceiling. Its shape changes utterly as the weight redistributes. Then she drops it – it falls suddenly, almost violently. She hangs onto the nipple and lifts the other in the same upward arc. She alternates, picking up speed. Lifting, dropping, lifting, dropping – by the time the drum cuts out and the trombone kicks in, her arms move so fast they're a blur, her flesh an undulating, pumping mass.

The men holler, screaming their approval.

'Oh *yeah!*'

'Gorgeous, baby! Gorgeous!'

'Praise the sweet Lord!'

Another drum roll begins. She leans forward at the waist and those glorious tits swing, so heavy, so low – a foot long, at least, wider and rounded at the ends, as though each contains a grapefruit.

She rolls her shoulders; first one, and then the other, so her breasts move in opposite directions. As the speed increases, they swing in ever-widening circles, lengthening as they gain momentum. Before long, they're meeting in the center with an audible slap.

Jesus. There could be a riot in the tent and I wouldn't know it. There's not a drop of blood left in my head.

The woman straightens up and then drops into a curtsy. When she stands, she scoops a breast up to her face and slides her tongue around its nipple. Then she slurps it into her mouth. She stands there shamelessly sucking her own tit as the men wave their hats, pump their fists, and scream like animals. She drops it, gives the slick nipple a final tweak, and then blows the men a kiss. She leans down long enough to retrieve her diaphanous shawl and disappears, her arm raised so that the shawl trails behind her, a shimmering banner.

'All right then, boys,' says Cecil, clapping his hands and climbing the stairs to the stage. 'Let's have a big hand for our Barbara!'

The men cheer and whistle, clapping with hands held high.

'Yup, ain't she something? What a lady. And it's your lucky day, boys, because for tonight only, she'll be accepting a limited number of gentleman callers after the show. This is a real honor, fellas. She's a gem, our Barbara. A real gem.'

The men crowd toward the exit, slapping each other on the back, already exchanging memories.

'Did you see those titties?'

'Man, what a rack. What I wouldn't give to play with those for a while.'

I'm glad nothing requires my intervention, because I'm trying hard to maintain my composure. This is the first time I've ever seen a woman naked and I don't think I'll ever be the same.

FOUR

I spend the next forty-five minutes standing guard outside Barbara's dressing tent as she entertains gentleman callers. Only five are prepared to part with the requisite two dollars, and they form a surly line. The first goes in and after seven minutes of huffing and grunting emerges again, struggling with his fly. He staggers off and the next enters.

After the last of them leaves, Barbara appears in the doorway. She is nude except for an Oriental silk dressing gown she hasn't bothered to tie. Her hair is mussed, her mouth smudged with lipstick. She holds a burning cigarette in one hand.

'That's it, honey,' she says, waving me away. There's whiskey on her breath and in her eyes. 'No freebies tonight.'

I return to the cooch tent to stack chairs and help

dismantle the stage while Cecil counts the money. At the end of it, I'm a dollar richer and stiff all over.

The big top still stands, glowing like a ghostly coliseum and pulsing with the sound of the band. I stare at it, entranced by the sound of the audience's reactions. They laugh, clap, and whistle. Sometimes there's a collective intake of breath or patter of nervous shrieks. I check my pocket watch; it's quarter to ten.

I consider trying to catch part of the show, but am afraid that if I cross the lot I'll get shanghaied into some other task. The roustabouts, having spent much of the day sleeping in whatever corner they could find, are dismantling the great canvas city as efficiently as they put it up. Tents drop to the ground, and poles topple. Horses, wagons, and men trek across the lot, hauling everything back to the side rail.

I sink to the ground and rest my head on raised knees.

'Jacob? Is that you?'

I look up. Camel limps over, squinting. 'By gum, I thought it was,' he says. 'The old peepers ain't workin' so good no more.'

He eases himself down next to me and pulls out a small green bottle. He picks the cork out and takes a drink.

'I'm gettin' too old for this, Jacob. I ache all over at the end of every day. Hell, I ache all over now, and we ain't even at the end of the day yet. The Flying Squadron won't pull out for probably two more hours, and we start the whole danged thing over again five hours after that. It's no life for an old man.'

He passes me the bottle.

'What the hell is this?' I say, staring at the brackish liquid.

'It's jake,' he says, snatching it back.

'You're drinking extract?'

'Yeah, so?'

We sit in silence for a minute.

'Damn Prohibition,' Camel finally says. 'This stuff used to taste just fine till the government decided it shouldn't. Still gets the job done, but tastes like hell. And it's a damn shame because it's all that keeps these old bones going anymore. I'm about used up. Ain't good for nothin' but ticket seller, and I reckon I'm too ugly for that.'

I glance over and decide he's right. 'Is there something else you can do instead? Maybe behind the scenes?'

'Ticket seller's the last stop.'

'What'll you do when you can't manage anymore?'

'I reckon I'll have an appointment with Blackie. Hey,' he says, turning to me hopefully. 'Got any cigarettes?'

'No. Sorry.'

'I didn't suppose,' he sighs.

We sit in silence, watching team after team haul equipment, animals, and canvas back to the train. Performers leaving the back end of the big top disappear into dressing tents and emerge in street clothes. They stand in groups, laughing and talking, some still wiping their faces. Even out of costume they are glamorous. The drab workmen scuttle all around, occupying the same universe but seemingly on a different dimension. There is no interaction.

Camel interrupts my reverie. 'You a college boy?'

'Yes sir.'

'I figured you for one.'

He offers the bottle again, but I shake my head.

'Did you finish?'

'No,' I say.

'Why not?'

I don't answer.

'How old are you, Jacob?'

'Twenty-three.'

'I got a boy your age.'

The music has ended, and townspeople start to trickle from the big top. They stop, perplexed, wondering what happened to the menagerie through which they entered. As they leave by the front, an army of men enter by the back and return carting bleachers, seats, and ring curbs, which they fling noisily into lumber wagons. The big top is being gutted before the audience has even left it.

Camel coughs wetly, the effort wracking his body. I look to see if he needs a thump on the back, but he's holding up a hand to stop me. He snorts, hawks, and then spits. Then he drains the bottle. He wipes his mouth with the back of his hand and looks over at me, eyeing me from head to toe.

'Listen,' he says. 'I ain't trying to know your business, but I do know you ain't been on the road long. You're too clean, your clothes are too good, and you don't got a possession in the world. You collect things on the road – maybe not nice things, but you collect them all the same. I know I ain't got no talking room, but a boy like you shouldn't be on the bum. I been on the bum and it ain't no life.' His forearms rest on his raised knees, his face turned to mine. 'If you got a life to go back to, I reckon that's what you should do.'

It's a moment before I can answer. When I do, my voice cracks. 'I don't.'

He watches me for a while longer and then nods. 'I'm right sorry to hear that.'

The crowd disperses, moving from the big top to the parking lot and beyond, to the edges of the town. From behind the big top, the silhouette of a balloon rises into the sky, followed by a child's prolonged wail. There is laughter, the sound of car engines, voices raised in excitement.

'Can you believe she bent like that?'

'I thought I was going to *die* when that clown dropped his drawers.'

'Where's Jimmy – Hank, have you got Jimmy?'

Camel scrambles suddenly to his feet. 'Ho! There he is. There's that old S-O-B now.'

'Who?'

'Uncle Al! Come on! We gotta get you on the show.'

He limps off faster than I would have thought possible. I get up and follow.

There is no mistaking Uncle Al. He has ringmaster written all over him, from the scarlet coat and white jodhpurs to the top hat and waxed curled moustache. He strides across the lot like the leader of a marching band, ample belly thrust forward and issuing orders in a booming voice. He pauses to let a lion's den cross in front of him and then continues past a group of men struggling with a rolled canvas. Without breaking stride, he smacks one of them on the side of the head. The man yelps and turns, rubbing his ear, but Uncle Al is gone, trailed by followers.

'That reminds me,' Camel says over his shoulder, 'whatever you do, don't mention Ringling in front of Uncle Al.'

'Why not?'

'Just don't.'

Camel scurries up to Uncle Al and steps into his path. 'Er, there you are,' he says, his voice artificial and mewling. 'I was wondering if I could have a word, sir?'

'Not now, boy. Not now,' booms Al, goose-stepping past like the Brownshirts you see in the grainy news trailers at the movies. Camel limps weakly behind, popping his head around one side, and then falling back and running along the other like a disgraced puppy.

'It won't take but a moment, sir. It's just I was wondering if any of the departments was short of men.'

'Thinking of changing careers, are we?'

Camel's voice rises like a siren. 'Oh no, sir. Not me. I'm happy right where I am. Yes sir. Happy as a clam, that's me.' He giggles maniacally.

The distance between them widens. Camel stumbles and then comes to a stop. 'Sir?' he calls across the growing distance. He comes to a stop. 'Sir?'

Uncle Al is gone, swallowed whole by people, horses, and wagons.

'Goddammit. God*dammit!*' says Camel, tearing his hat from his head and throwing it to the ground.

'It's okay, Camel,' I say. 'I appreciate you trying.'

'No, it ain't okay,' he shouts.

'Camel, I—'

'Just shut it. I don't want to hear it. You're a good kid, and I ain't about to stand by and watch you mope off

66

'cuz that fat old grouch don't got time. I just ain't. So have a little respect for your elders and don't give me no trouble.'

His eyes are burning.

I lean over, retrieve his hat, and brush the dirt off. Then I hold it out to him.

After a moment, he takes it. 'All right then,' he says gruffly. 'I guess that's all right.'

Camel takes me to a wagon and tells me to wait outside. I lean against one of the large spoked wheels and pass the time alternately picking slivers from beneath my nails and chewing long pieces of grass. At one point my head bobs forward, on the cusp of sleep.

Camel emerges an hour later, staggering, holding a flask in one hand and a roll-your-own in the other. His eyelids flutter at half-mast.

'This here's Earl,' he slurs, sweeping an arm behind him. 'He's gonna take care of ya.'

A bald man steps down from the wagon. He is enormous, his neck thicker than his head. Blurred green tattoos run across his knuckles and up his hairy arms. He holds out his hand.

'How do you do,' he says.

'How do you do,' I say, perplexed. I swing around to Camel, who's zigzagging through the crispy grass in the general direction of the Flying Squadron. He's also singing. Badly.

Earl cups his hands around his mouth. 'Shut it, Camel! Get yourself on that train before it leaves without you!'

Camel drops to his knees.

'Ah Jesus,' says Earl. 'Hang on. I'll be back in a minute.'

He walks over and scoops the older man off the ground as easily as if he were a child. Camel lets his arms, legs, and head dangle over Earl's arms. He giggles and sighs.

Earl sets Camel on the edge of a car's doorway, consults with someone inside, and then returns.

'Stuff's gonna kill the old fellow,' he mutters, marching straight past me. 'If he don't rot out his guts, he'll roll off the goddamned train. Don't touch the stuff myself,' he says, looking over his shoulder at me.

I'm rooted to the spot where he left me.

He looks surprised. 'You coming, or what?'

When the final section of the train pulls out, I'm crouched under a bunk in a sleeping car wedged against another man. He is the rightful owner of the space but was persuaded to let me hang out for an hour or two for a price of my one dollar. He grumbles anyway, and I hug my knees to make myself as compact as possible.

The odor of unwashed bodies and clothes is over-whelming. The bunks, stacked three high, hold at least one and sometimes two men, as do the spaces beneath them. The fellow wedged in the floor space across from me punches a thin gray blanket, trying in vain to form a pillow.

A voice carries across the jumble of noise: '*Ojcze nasz któryś jest w niebie, swięć sie imie Twoje, przyjdź królestwo Twoje—*'

'Jesus Christ,' my host says. He pokes his head into the aisle. 'Speak in English, you fucking Polack!' Then he retreats back under the bunk, shaking his head. 'Some of these guys. Right off the fucking boat.'

'*—i nie wódz nasź na pokuszenie ale nas zbaw ode złego. Amen.*'

I nestle against the wall and close my eyes. 'Amen,' I whisper.

The train lurches. The lights flicker for a moment and go out. From somewhere ahead of us a whistle screeches. We begin rolling forward and the lights come back on. I'm tired beyond words, and my head bumps unbuffered against the wall.

I wake some time later and find myself facing a pair of huge work boots.

'You ready then?'

I shake my head, trying to get my bearings.

I hear tendons creaking and snapping. Then I see a knee. Then Earl's face. 'You still down there?' he says, peering under the bunk.

'Yeah. Sorry.'

I shimmy out and struggle to my feet.

'Hallelujah,' says my host, stretching out.

'*Pierdol się,*' I say.

A snort of laughter comes from a bunk a few feet away.

'Come on,' says Earl. 'Al's had enough to loosen him up but not enough to get mean. I figure this is your opportunity.'

He leads me through two more sleeping cars. When we reach the platform at the end, we're facing the back of a different kind of car. Through its window I can see burnished wood and intricate light fixtures.

Earl turns to me. 'You ready?'

'Sure,' I say.

I am not. He grabs me by the scruff and smashes my face into the doorframe. With his other hand, he yanks open the sliding door and chucks me inside. I fall forward, my hands outstretched. I come to a stop against a brass rail and straighten up, looking back at Earl in shock. Then I see the rest of them.

'What is this?' says Uncle Al from the depths of a winged chair. He is seated at a table with three other men, twaddling a fat cigar between the finger and thumb of one hand and holding five fanned cards in the other. A snifter of brandy rests on the table in front of him. Just beyond it is a large pile of poker chips.

'Jumped the train, sir. Found him sneaking through a sleeper.'

'Is that a fact?' says Uncle Al. He takes a leisurely drag from his cigar and sets it on the edge of a standing ashtray. He sits back, studying his cards and letting smoke waft from the corners of his mouth. 'I'll see your three and raise you five,' he says, leaning forward and flinging a stack of chips into the kitty.

'You want I should show him the door?' says Earl. He advances and lifts me from the floor by the lapels. I tense and close my fists around his wrists, intending to hang on if he tries to throw me again. I look from Uncle Al to the lower half of Earl's face – which is all I can see – and then back again.

Uncle Al folds his cards and sets them carefully on the table. 'Not yet, Earl,' he says. He reaches for the cigar and takes another drag. 'Set him down.'

Earl lowers me to the floor with my back to Uncle Al. He makes a halfhearted attempt to smooth my jacket.

'Step forward,' says Uncle Al.

I oblige, happy enough to be out of Earl's reach.

'I don't believe I've had the pleasure,' he says, blowing a smoke ring. 'What's your name?'

'Jacob Jankowski, sir.'

'And what, pray tell, does Jacob Jankowski think he is doing on my train?'

'I'm looking for work,' I say.

Uncle Al continues to stare at me, blowing lazy smoke rings. He rests his hands on his belly, drumming a slow beat on his waistcoat.

'Ever worked on a show, Jacob?'

'No sir.'

'Ever been to a show, Jacob?'

'Yes, sir. Of course.'

'Which one?'

'Ringling Brothers,' I say. A sharp intake of breath causes me to turn my head. Earl's eyes are wide in warning.

'But it was terrible. Just terrible,' I add hastily, turning back to Uncle Al.

'Is that a fact,' says Uncle Al.

'Yes, sir.'

'And have you seen our show, Jacob?'

'Yes, sir,' I say, feeling a blush spread across my cheeks.

'And what did you think of it?' he asks.

'It was . . . spectacular.'

'What was your favorite act?'

I grasp wildly, pulling details out of the air. 'The one

71

with the black and white horses. And the girl in pink,' I say. 'With the sequins.'

'You hear that, August? The boy likes your Marlena.'

The man opposite Uncle Al rises and turns – he's the man from the menagerie tent, only now he's minus the top hat. His chiseled face is impassive, his dark hair shiny with pomade. He also has a moustache, but unlike Uncle Al's, his lasts only the length of his lip.

'So what exactly is it that you envision yourself doing?' asks Uncle Al. He leans forward and lifts a snifter from the table. He swirls its contents, and drains it in a single gulp. A waiter emerges from nowhere and refills it.

'I'll do just about anything. But if possible I'd like to work with animals.'

'Animals,' he says. 'Did you hear that, August? The lad wants to work with animals. You want to carry water for elephants, I suppose?'

Earl's brow creases. 'But sir, we don't have any—'

'Shut up!' shrieks Uncle Al, leaping to his feet. His sleeve catches the snifter and knocks it to the carpet. He stares at it, his fists clenched and face growing darker and darker. Then he bares his teeth and screams a long, inhuman howl, bringing his foot down on the glass again and again and again.

There's a moment of stillness, broken only by the rhythmic clacking of ties passing beneath us. Then the waiter drops to the floor and starts scooping up glass.

Uncle Al takes a deep breath and turns to the window with his hands clasped behind him. When he eventually turns back to us, his face is once again pink. A smirk plays around the edges of his lips.

'I'm going to tell you how it is, *Jacob Jankowski*.' He spits my name out like something distasteful. 'I've seen your sort a thousand times. You think I can't read you like a book? So what's the deal – did you and Mommy have a fight? Or maybe you're just looking for a little adventure between semesters?'

'No, sir, it's nothing like that.'

'I don't give a damn what it is – even if I gave you a job on the show, you wouldn't survive. Not for a week. Not for a day. The show is a well-oiled machine, and only the toughest make it. But then you wouldn't know anything about tough, would you, Mr College Boy?'

He glares at me as though challenging me to speak. 'Now piss off,' he says, waving me away. 'Earl, show him the door. Wait until you actually see a red light before chucking him off – I don't want to catch any heat for hurting *Mommy's widdle baby*.'

'Hang on a moment, Al,' says August. He's smirking, clearly amused. 'Is he right? Are you a college boy?'

I feel like a mouse being bounced between cats. 'I was.'

'And what did you study? Something in the fine arts, perhaps?' His eyes gleam in mockery. 'Romanian folk dancing? Aristotelian literary criticism? Or perhaps – Mr *Jankowski* – you completed a performance degree on the accordion?'

'I studied veterinary sciences.'

His mien changes instantly, utterly. 'Vet school? You're a vet?'

'Not exactly.'

'What do you mean, "not exactly"'

'I never wrote my final exams.'

'Why not?'

'I just didn't.'

'And those final exams, those were in your final year?'

'Yes.'

'What college?'

'Cornell.'

August and Uncle Al exchange glances.

'Marlena said Silver Star was off,' says August. 'Wanted me to get the advance man to arrange for a vet. Didn't seem to understand that the advance man was gone out *in advance*, hence the name.'

'What are you suggesting?' says Uncle Al.

'Let the kid have a look in the morning.'

'And where do you propose we put him for tonight? We're already past capacity.' He snatches his cigar from the ashtray and taps it on the edge. 'I suppose we could just send him out on the flats.'

'I was thinking more along the lines of the ring stock car,' says August.

Uncle Al frowns. 'What? With Marlena's horses?'

'Yes.'

'You mean in the area where the goats used to be? Isn't that where that little shit sleeps – oh, what's his name?' he says, snapping his fingers. 'Stinko? Kinko? That clown with the dog?'

'Precisely,' smiles August.

August leads me back through the men's bunk cars until we're standing on a small platform facing the back of a stock car.

'Are you sure-footed, Jacob?' he inquires graciously.

'I believe so,' I answer.

'Good,' he says. Without further ado, he leans forward, catches hold of something around the side of the stock car, and climbs nimbly to the roof.

'Jesus Christ!' I yell, looking in alarm first at the point where August disappeared, and then down at the bare coupling and ties that race beneath the cars. The train jerks around a curve. I throw my hands out to keep my balance, breathing hard.

'Come on then,' yells a voice from the roof.

'How the hell did you do that? What did you grab?'

'There's a ladder. Just around the side. Lean forward and reach for it. You'll find it.'

'What if I don't?'

'Then I guess we'll take our leave, won't we?'

I advance gingerly to the edge. I can see just the edge of a thin iron ladder.

I train my eyes on it and wipe my hands on my thighs. Then I tip forward.

My right hand meets ladder. I grasp wildly with my left until I ensnare the other side. I jam my feet in the rungs and cling tightly, trying to catch my breath.

'Well, come on then!'

I look up. August peers down at me, grinning, his hair blowing in the wind.

I climb to the roof. He moves over, and when I sit down next to him he claps a hand on my shoulder. 'Turn around. I want you to see something.'

He points down the length of the train. It stretches behind us like a giant snake, the linked cars jiggling and bending as it rounds a curve.

'It's a beautiful sight, isn't it, Jacob?' says August. I look back at him. He's staring right at me, his eyes glowing. 'Not quite as beautiful as my Marlena, though – hey hey?' He clicks his tongue and winks.

Before I can protest, he stands and tap-dances across the roof.

I crane my neck and count stock cars. There are at least six.

'August?'

'What?' he says, stopping midtwirl.

'Which car is Kinko in?'

He crouches suddenly. 'This one. Aren't you a lucky boy?' He pries off a roof vent and disappears.

I scuttle over on hands and knees.

'August?'

'What?' returns a voice from the darkness.

'Is there a ladder?'

'No, just drop down.'

I lower myself inside until I'm hanging by my fingertips. Then I crash to the floor. A surprised nicker greets me.

Thin strips of moonlight filter through the slatted sides of the stock car. On one side of me is a line of horses. The other side is blocked by a wall that is clearly homemade.

August steps forward and shoves the door inward. It crashes against the wall behind it, revealing a makeshift room lit by kerosene lamp. The lamp is on an upturned crate next to a cot. A dwarf is lying on his stomach with a thick book open in front of him. He's about my age and, like me, has red hair. Unlike me, his stands straight up from his head, an unruly thatch. His face, neck, arms, and hands are heavily freckled.

'Kinko,' says August in disgust.

'August,' says the dwarf, equally disgusted.

'This is Jacob,' August says, taking a tour of the tiny room. He leans over and fingers things as he passes. 'He's going to bunk with you for a while.'

I step forward, holding out my hand. 'How do you do,' I say.

Kinko regards my hand coolly and then looks back at August. 'What is he?'

'His name is Jacob.'

'I said what, not who.'

'He's going to help out in the menagerie.'

Kinko leaps to his feet. 'A menagerie man? Forget it. I'm a performer. There's no way I'm bunking with a working man.'

There's a growl from behind him, and for the first time I see the Jack Russell terrier. She's standing on the end of the cot with her hackles raised.

'I am the equestrian director and superintendent of animals,' August says slowly, 'and it is by the grace of my generosity you are allowed to sleep here at all. It is also by the grace of my generosity that it's not filled with roustabouts. Of course, I can always change that. Besides, this gentleman is the show's new veterinarian – from Cornell no less – which puts him a good deal higher than you in my estimation. Perhaps you'd like to consider offering him the cot.' The lamp's flame flickers in August's eyes. His lip quivers in its shadowy glow.

After a moment he turns to me and bows low, clicking

his heels. 'Good night, Jacob. I'm sure Kinko will make you comfortable. Won't you, Kinko?'

Kinko glowers at him.

August smoothes both sides of his hair with his hands. Then he leaves, pulling the door shut behind him. I stare at the rough-hewn wood until I hear his footsteps clatter over top of us. Then I turn around.

Kinko and the dog are staring at me. The dog lifts her lip and snarls.

I spend the night on a crumpled horse blanket against the wall, as far from the cot as I can. The blanket is damp. Whoever covered the slats when they turned this into a room did a lousy job, so the blanket's been rained on and reeks of mildew.

I wake with a start. I've scratched my arms and neck raw. I don't know if it's from sleeping on horsehair or vermin and don't want to know. The sky that shows between the patched slats is black, and the train is still moving.

I awoke because of a dream, but I can't recall specifics. I close my eyes, reaching tentatively for the corners of my mind.

It's my mother. She's standing in the yard in a corn-flower blue dress hanging laundry on the line. She has wooden clothes pegs in her mouth and more in an apron tied around her waist. Her fingers are busy with a sheet. She's singing quietly in Polish.

Flash.

I'm lying on the floor, looking up at the stripper's dangling breasts. Her nipples, brown and the size of silver dollar pancakes, swing in circles – out and around, SLAP. Out and around, SLAP. I feel a pang of excitement, then remorse, and then nausea.

And then I'm . . .

I'm . . .

FIVE

I'm blubbering like the ancient fool I am, that's what.

I guess I was asleep. I could have sworn that just a few seconds ago I was twenty-three, and now here I am in this wretched, desiccated body.

I sniff and wipe my stupid tears, trying to pull myself together because that girl is back, the plump one in pink. She either worked all night or I lost track of a day. I hate not knowing which.

I also wish I could remember her name, but I can't. That's how it is when you're ninety. Or ninety-three.

'Good morning, Mr Jankowski,' the nurse says, flipping on the light. She walks to the window and adjusts the horizontal blinds to let in sunlight. 'Time to rise and shine.'

'What for?' I grumble.

'Because the good Lord has seen fit to bless you with another day,' she says, coming to my side. She presses a button on my bedrail. My bed starts to hum. A few seconds later I'm sitting upright. 'Besides, you're going to the circus tomorrow.'

The circus! So I haven't lost a day.

She pops a disposable cone on a thermometer and sticks it in my ear. I get poked and prodded like this every morning. I'm like a piece of meat unearthed from the back of the fridge, suspect until proven otherwise.

After the thermometer beeps, the nurse flicks the cone into the wastebasket and writes something on my chart. Then she pulls the blood pressure cuff from the wall.

'So, do you want to have breakfast in the dining room this morning, or would you like me to bring you something here?' she asks, wrapping the cuff around my arm and inflating it.

'I don't want breakfast.'

'Come now, Mr Jankowski,' she says, pressing a stethoscope to the inside of my elbow and watching the gauge. 'You've got to keep your strength up.'

I try to catch sight of her name tag. 'What for? So I can run a marathon?'

'So you don't catch something and miss the circus,' she says. After the cuff deflates, she removes the apparatus from my arm and hangs it back on the wall.

Finally! I can see her name.

'I'll have it in here then, Rosemary,' I say, thereby proving that I remembered her name. Keeping up the appearance of having all your marbles is hard work but important. Anyway, I'm not really addled. I just have more facts to keep track of than other people.

'I do declare you're as strong as a horse,' she says, writing one last thing down before flipping my chart shut. 'If you keep your weight up, I'll bet you could go on another ten years.'

'Swell,' I say.

When Rosemary comes to park me in the hallway, I ask her to take me to the window so I can watch the goings-on at the park.

It's a beautiful day, with the sun streaming down between puffy clouds. Just as well – I remember all too well what it's like to work on a circus lot when the weather is foul. Not that the work is anything like what it used to be. I wonder if they're even called roustabouts any more. And sleeping quarters sure have improved – just look at those RVs. Some of them even have portable satellite dishes attached to them.

Shortly after lunch, I spot the first nursing home resident being wheeled up the street by relatives. Ten minutes later there's a veritable wagon train. There's Ruthie – oh, and Nellie Compton, too, but what's the point? She's a turnip, she won't remember a thing. And there's Doris – that must be her Randall she's always talking about. And there's that bastard McGuinty. Oh yes, cock-of-the-walk, with his family surrounding him and a plaid blanket spread over his knees. Spouting elephant stories, no doubt.

There's a line of glorious Percherons behind the big top, every one of them gleaming white. Maybe they're for vaulting? Horses in vaulting acts are always white so that the powdered rosin that makes the performer's feet stick to their backs won't show.

Even if it is a liberty act, there's no reason to think it could hold a candle to Marlena's. There's nothing and no one who could compare to Marlena.

I look for an elephant, with equal parts dread and disappointment.

The wagon train returns later in the afternoon with balloons tied to their chairs and silly hats on their heads. Some even hold bags of cotton candy in their laps – bags! For all they know, the floss could be a week old. In my day it was fresh, spun from a drum onto a paper cone.

At five o'clock, a slim nurse with a horse face comes to the end of the hall. 'Are you ready for your dinner, Mr Jankowski?' she says, kicking off my brakes and spinning me around.

'*Hrrmph,*' I say, cranky that she didn't wait for an answer.

When we get to the dining room, she steers me toward my usual table.

'No, wait!' I say. 'I don't want to sit there tonight.'

'Don't worry, Mr Jankowski,' she says. 'I'm sure Mr McGuinty has forgiven you for last night.'

'Yeah, well, I haven't forgiven him. I want to sit over there,' I say, pointing at another table.

'But there's nobody at that table,' she says.

'Exactly.'

'Oh, Mr Jankowski. Why don't you just let me—'

'Just put me where I asked you to, damn it.'

My chair stops and there is dead silence from behind it. After a few seconds we start moving again. The nurse parks me at my chosen table and leaves. When she returns to plunk a plate down in front of me, her lips are pursed primly.

The main difficulty with sitting at a table by yourself is that there's nothing to distract you from hearing other people's conversations. I'm not eavesdropping; I just can't help hearing it. Most of them are talking about the circus, and that's okay. What's *not* okay is Old Fart McGuinty sitting at *my* regular table, with *my* lady friends, and holding court like King Arthur. And that's not all – apparently he told someone who worked for the circus that he used to carry water for the elephants, and they *upgraded his ticket to a ringside seat!* Incredible! And there he sits, yammering on and on about the special treatment he received while Hazel, Doris, and Norma stare adoringly.

I can stand it no longer. I look down at my plate. Stewed something under pale gravy with a side of pockmarked Jell-O.

'Nurse!' I bark. 'Nurse!'

One of them looks up and catches my eye. Since it's clear I'm not dying, she takes her sweet time getting to me.

'What can I do for you, Mr Jankowski?'

'How about getting me some real food?'

'I beg your pardon?'

'Real food. You know – that stuff people on the outside get to eat.'

'Oh, Mr Jankowski—'

'Don't you "Oh, Mr Jankowski" me, young lady. This

is nursery food, and last I looked I wasn't five years old. I'm ninety. Or ninety-three.'

'It's not nursery food.'

'Yes it is. There's no substance. Look—' I say, dragging my fork through the gravy-covered heap. It falls off in glops, leaving me holding a coated fork. 'You call that food? I want something I can sink my teeth into. Something that crunches. And what, exactly, is this supposed to be?' I say, poking the lump of red Jell-O. It jiggles outrageously, like a breast I once knew.

'It's salad.'

'*Salad?* Do you see any vegetables? I don't see any vegetables.'

'It's fruit salad,' she says, her voice steady but forced.

'Do you see any fruit?'

'Yes. As a matter of fact I do,' she says, pointing at a pock. 'There. And there. That's a piece of banana, and that's a grape. Why don't you try it?'

'Why don't *you* try it?'

She folds her arms across her chest. The schoolmarm has run out of patience. 'This food is for the residents. It's designed specifically by a nutritionist who specializes in geriatric—'

'I don't want it. I want real food.'

There's dead silence in the room. I look around. All eyes are trained on me. 'What?' I say loudly. 'Is that so much to ask? Doesn't anyone else here miss real food? Surely you can't all be happy with this . . . this . . . *pap?*' I put my hand on the edge of my plate and give it a shove.

Just a little one.

Really.

My plate shoots across the table and crashes to the floor.

Dr Rashid is summoned. She sits at my bedside and asks questions that I try to answer courteously, but I'm so tired of being treated as though I'm unreasonable that I'm afraid I may come off as a bit crotchety.

After a half hour she asks the nurse to come into the hallway with her. I strain to hear, but my old ears, for all their obscene hugeness, pick up nothing but snippets: 'serious, serious depression' and 'manifesting as aggression, not uncommon in geriatric patients.'

'I'm not deaf, you know!' I shout from my bed. 'Just old!'

Dr Rashid peers in at me and takes the nurse's elbow. They move down the hall and out of earshot.

That night, a new pill appears in my paper cup. The pills are already in my palm before I notice it.

'What's this?' I ask, pushing it around. I flip it over and inspect the other side.

'What?' says the nurse.

'This,' I say, poking the offending pill. 'This one right here. It's new.'

'It's called Elavil.'

'What's it for?'

'It's going to help you feel better.'

'What's it for?' I repeat.

She doesn't answer. I look up. Our eyes meet.

'Depression,' she says finally.

'I won't take it.'

'Mr Jankowski—'

'I'm not depressed.'

'Dr Rashid prescribed it. It's going to—'

'You want to drug me. You want to turn me into a Jell-O-eating sheep. I won't take it, I tell you.'

'Mr Jankowski. I have twelve other patients to take care of. Now please take your pills.'

'I thought we were residents.'

Every one of her pinched features hardens.

'I'll take the others but not this,' I say, flicking the pill from my hand. It flies through the air and lands on the floor. I toss the others into my mouth. 'Where's my water?' I say, my words garbled because I'm trying to keep the pills on the center of my tongue.

She hands me a plastic cup, retrieves the pill from the floor, and goes into my bathroom. I hear a flush. Then she comes back.

'Mr Jankowski. I am going to go get another Elavil and if you won't take it, I will call Dr Rashid, and she will prescribe an injectable instead. Either way, you are taking the Elavil. How you do so is up to you.'

When she brings the pill, I swallow it. A quarter of an hour later, I also get an injection – not of Elavil, of something else, but still it doesn't seem fair because I took their damned pill.

Within minutes, I am a Jell-O-eating sheep. Well, a sheep at any rate. But because I keep reminding myself of the incident that brought this misfortune upon me, I realize that if someone brought pockmarked Jell-O right now and told me to eat it, I would.

What have they done to me?

I cling to my anger with every ounce of humanity left in my ruined body, but it's no use. It slips away, like a wave from shore. I am pondering this sad fact when I realize the blackness of sleep is circling my head. It's been there awhile, biding its time and growing closer with each revolution. I give up on rage, which at this point has become a formality, and make a mental note to get angry again in the morning. Then I let myself drift, because there's really no fighting it.

SIX

The train groans, straining against the increasing resistance of air brakes. After several minutes and a final, prolonged shriek, the great iron beast shudders to a stop and exhales.

Kinko throws back his blanket and stands up. He's no more than four feet tall, if that. He stretches, yawns, and smacks his lips, then scratches his head, armpits, and testicles. The dog dances around his feet, her stump of a tail wagging furiously.

'Come on, Queenie,' he says, scooping her up. 'You want to go outside? Queenie go outside?' He plants a kiss in the middle of her brown and white head and crosses the little room.

I watch from my crumpled horse blanket in the corner.

'Kinko?' I say.

If it weren't for the vehemence with which he slams the door, I might think he didn't hear me.

We are on a side rail behind the Flying Squadron, which has obviously been here a few hours. The tent city has already risen, to the delight of the crowd of townspeople hanging around watching. Rows of children sit on top of the Flying Squadron surveying the lot with shining eyes. Their parents congregate beneath, holding the hands of younger siblings and pointing to various marvels appearing in front of them.

The workmen from the main train climb down from the sleeper cars, light cigarettes, and trek across the lot toward the cookhouse. Its blue and orange flag is already flying and the boiler beside it belches steam, bearing cheerful witness to the breakfast within.

Performers emerge from sleepers closer to the back of the train and of obviously better quality. There's a clear hierarchy: the closer to the back, the more impressive the quarters. Uncle Al himself climbs from a car right in front of the caboose. I can't help but notice that Kinko and I are the human occupants closest to the engine.

'Jacob!'

I turn. August strides toward me, his shirt crisp, his chin scraped smooth. His slick hair bears the recent impression of a comb.

'How are we this morning, my boy?' he asks.

'All right,' I say. 'A little tired.'

'Did that little troll give you any trouble?'

'No,' I say. 'He was fine.'

'Good, good.' He claps his hands together. 'Shall we

have a look at that horse then? I doubt it's anything serious. Marlena coddles them terribly. Oh, here's the little lady now. Come here, darling,' he calls brightly. 'I want you to meet Jacob. He's a fan of yours.'

I feel a blush creep across my face.

She comes to a stop beside him, smiling up at me as August turns toward the stock car. 'It's a pleasure to meet you,' she says, extending her hand. Up close she still looks remarkably like Catherine – delicate features, pale as porcelain, with a smattering of freckles across the bridge of her nose. Shimmering blue eyes, and hair just dark enough to disqualify as blonde.

'The pleasure is mine,' I say, painfully aware that I haven't shaved in two days, my clothes are stiff with manure, and that manure is not the only unpleasant scent rising from my body.

She cocks her head slightly. 'Say, you're the one I saw yesterday, aren't you? In the menagerie?'

'I don't think so,' I say, lying instinctively.

'Sure you are. Right before the show. When the chimp den slammed shut.'

I glance at August, but he's still facing the other way. She follows my gaze and seems to understand.

'You're not from Boston, are you?' she says, her voice lowered.

'No. I've never been.'

'Huh,' she says. 'It's just you look familiar somehow. Oh well,' she continues brightly. 'Auggie says you're a vet.' At the sound of his name, August spins around.

'No,' I say. 'I mean, not exactly.'

'He's being modest,' says August. 'Pete! Hey, Pete!'

A group of men stand in front of the stock car's door, attaching a ramp with built-in sides. A tall one with dark hair turns. 'Yeah, boss?' he says.

'Get the others unloaded and bring out Silver Star, will you?'

'Sure.'

Eleven horses later – five white and six black – Pete goes inside the stock car once again. A moment later he's back. 'Silver Star don't want to move, boss.'

'Make him,' says August.

'Oh no you don't,' says Marlena, shooting August a dirty look. She marches up the ramp and disappears.

August and I wait outside, listening to passionate entreaties and tongue clicks. After several minutes she reappears in the doorway with the silver-maned Arabian.

Marlena steps out in front of him, clicking and murmuring. He raises his head and pulls back. Eventually he follows her down the ramp, his head bobbing deeply with each step. At the bottom he pulls back so hard he almost sits on his haunches.

'Jesus, Marlena – I thought you said he was a bit off,' says August.

Marlena is ashen. 'He was. He wasn't anything like this bad yesterday. He's been a bit lame for a few days, but *nothing* like this.'

She clicks and tugs until the horse finally steps onto the gravel. He stands with his back hunched, his hind legs bearing as much weight as they can. My heart sinks. It's the classic walking-on-eggshells stance.

'What do you think it is?' says August.

'Give me a minute,' I say, although I'm already ninety-nine percent sure. 'Do you have hoof testers?'

'No. But the smithy does. Do you want me to send Pete?'

'Not yet. I might not need them.'

I crouch beside the horse's left shoulder and run my hands down his leg, from shoulder to fetlock. He doesn't flinch. Then I lay my hand across the front of his hoof. It's radiating heat. I place my thumb and forefinger on the back of his fetlock. His arterial pulse is pounding.

'Damn,' I say.

'What is it?' says Marlena.

I straighten up and reach for Silver Star's foot. He leaves it firmly on the ground.

'Come on, boy,' I say, pulling on his hoof.

Eventually he lifts it. The sole is bulging and dark, with a red line running around the edge. I set it down immediately.

'This horse is foundering,' I say.

'Oh dear God!' says Marlena, clapping a hand to her mouth.

'What?' says August. 'He's what?'

'Foundering,' I say. 'It's when the connective tissues between the hoof and the coffin bone are compromised and the coffin bone rotates toward the sole of the hoof.'

'In English, please. Is it bad?'

I glance at Marlena, who is still covering her mouth. 'Yes,' I say.

'Can you fix it?'

'We can bed him up real thick, and try to keep him off his feet. Grass hay only and no grain. And no work.'

'But can you fix it?'

I hesitate, glancing quickly at Marlena. 'Probably not.'

August stares at Silver Star and exhales through puffed cheeks.

'Well, well, well!' booms an unmistakable voice from behind us. 'If it isn't our very own animal doctor!'

Uncle Al floats toward us in black and white checked pants and a crimson vest. He carries a silver-topped cane, which he swings extravagantly with each step. A handful of people straggle behind him.

'So what says the croaker? Did you sort out the horse?' he asks jovially, coming to a stop in front of me.

'Not exactly,' I say.

'Why not?'

'Apparently he's foundering,' says August.

'He's what?' says Uncle Al.

'It's his feet.'

Uncle Al bends over, peering at Silver Star's feet. 'They look fine to me.'

'They're not,' I say.

He turns to me. 'So what do you propose to do about it?'

'Put him on stall rest and cut his grain. Other than that, there's not much we can do.'

'Stall rest is out of the question. He's the lead horse in the liberty act.'

'If this horse keeps working, his coffin bone will rotate until it punctures his sole, and then you'll lose him,' I say unequivocally.

Uncle Al's eyelids flicker. He looks over at Marlena.

'How long will he be out?'

I pause, choosing my next words carefully. 'Possibly for good.'

'*Goddammit!*' he shouts, stabbing his cane into the earth. 'Where the hell am I supposed to get another liberty horse midseason?' He looks around at his followers.

They shrug, mumble, and avert their gazes.

'Useless sons of bitches. Why do I even keep you? Okay, you—' He points his cane at me. 'You're on. Fix this horse. Nine bucks a week. You answer to August. Lose this horse and you're out of here. In fact, first hint of trouble and you're out of here.' He steps forward to Marlena and pats her shoulder. 'There, there, my dear,' he says kindly. 'Don't fret. Jacob here will take good care of him. August, go get this little girl some breakfast, will you? We have to hit the road.'

August's head jerks around. 'What do you mean, "hit the road"?'

'We're tearing down,' says Uncle Al, gesturing vaguely. 'Moving along.'

'What the hell are you talking about? We just got here. We're still setting up!'

'Change of plans, August. Change of plans.'

Uncle Al and his followers walk away. August stares after them, his mouth open wide.

Rumors abound in the cookhouse.

In front of the hash browns:

'Carson Brothers got caught short-changing a few weeks ago. Burned the territory.'

'Ha,' snorts someone else. 'That's usually our job.'

In front of the scrambled eggs:

'They heard we was carrying booze. There's gonna be a raid.'

'There's gonna be a raid, all right,' comes the reply. 'But it's on account of the cooch tent, not the booze.'

In front of the oatmeal:

'Uncle Al stiffed the sheriff on the lot fee last year. Cops say we got two hours before they run us out.'

Ezra is slouched in the same position as yesterday, his arms crossed and his chin pressed into his chest. He pays me no attention whatever.

'Whoa there, big fella,' says August as I head for the canvas divider. 'Where do you think you're going?'

'To the other side.'

'Nonsense,' he says. 'You're the show's vet. Come with me. Although I must say, I'm tempted to send you over there just to find out what they're saying.'

I follow August and Marlena to one of the nicely dressed tables. Kinko sits a few tables over, with three other dwarves and Queenie at his feet. She looks up hopefully, her tongue lolling off to the side. Kinko ignores her and everyone else at his table. He stares straight at me, his jaw moving grimly from side to side.

'Eat, darling,' says August, pushing a bowl of sugar toward Marlena's porridge. 'There's no point fretting. We've got a bona fide veterinarian here.'

I open my mouth to protest, then shut it again.

A petite blonde approaches. 'Marlena! Sweetie! You'll never guess what I heard!'

'Hi, Lottie,' says Marlena. 'I have no idea. What's up?'

Lottie slides in beside Marlena and talks nonstop, almost without pausing for breath. She's an aerialist and she got the straight scoop from a good authority – her spotter heard Uncle Al and the advance man exchanging heated words outside the big top. Before long a crowd surrounds our table, and between Lottie and the tidbits tossed out by her audience, I hear what amounts to a crash course on the history of Alan J. Bunkel and the Benzini Brothers Most Spectacular Show on Earth.

Uncle Al is a buzzard, a vulture, an eater of carrion. Fifteen years ago he was the manager of a mud show: a ragtag group of pellagra-riddled performers dragged from town to town by miserable thrush-hoofed horses.

In August of 1928, through no fault of Wall Street, the Benzini Brothers Most Spectacular Show on Earth collapsed. They simply ran out of money and couldn't make the jump to the next town, never mind back to winter quarters. The general manager caught a train out of town and left everything behind – people, equipment, and animals.

Uncle Al had the good fortune to be in the vicinity and was able to score a sleeping car and two flats for a song from railroad officials desperate to free up their siding. Those two flats easily held his few decrepit wagons, and because the train cars were already emblazoned with BENZINI BROS MOST SPECTACULAR SHOW ON EARTH, Alan Bunkel retained the name and officially joined the ranks of train circuses.

When the Crash came, larger circuses started going down and Uncle Al could hardly believe his luck. It started with the Gentry Brothers and Buck Jones in 1929. The next year saw the end of the Cole Brothers, the Christy Brothers, and the mighty John Robinson. And every time a show closed, there was Uncle Al, sopping up the remains: a few train cars, a handful of stranded performers, a tiger, or a camel. He had scouts everywhere – the moment a larger circus showed signs of trouble, Uncle Al would get a telegram and race to the scene.

He grew fat off their carcasses. In Minneapolis, he picked up six parade wagons and a toothless lion. In Ohio, a sword swallower and a flat car. In Des Moines, a dressing tent, a hippopotamus and matching wagon, and the Lovely Lucinda. In Portland, eighteen draft horses, two zebras, and a smithy. In Seattle, two bunk cars and a bona fide freak – a bearded lady – and this made him happy, for what Uncle Al craves above all else, what Uncle Al dreams of at night, are freaks. Not made freaks: not men covered head to toe in tattoos, not women who regurgitate wallets and lightbulbs on command, not moss-haired girls or men who pound stakes into their sinus cavities. Uncle Al craves real freaks. Born freaks. And that is the reason for our detour to Joliet.

The Fox Brothers Circus has just collapsed, and Uncle Al is ecstatic because they employed the world-famous Charles Mansfield-Livingston, a handsome, dapper man with a parasitic twin growing out of his chest. He calls it Chaz. It looks like an infant with its head buried in his ribcage. He dresses it in miniature suits, with black patent shoes on its feet, and when Charles walks, he holds its little hands in his. Rumor has it that Chaz's tiny penis even gets erections.

Uncle Al is desperate to get there before someone else snaps him up. And so, despite the fact that our posters are all over Saratoga Springs; despite the fact that it was supposed to be a two-day stop and we've just had 2,200 loaves of bread, 116 pounds of butter, 360 dozen eggs, 1,570 pounds of meat, 11 cases of sauerkraut, 105 pounds of sugar, 24 crates of oranges, 52 pounds of lard, 1,200 pounds of vegetables, and 212 cans of coffee delivered to the lot; despite the tons of hay and turnips and beets and other food for the animals that is piled out back of the menagerie tent; despite the hundreds of townspeople gathered at the edge of the lot right now, first in excitement, and then in bewilderment, and now in fast-growing anger; despite all this, we are tearing down and moving out.

The cook is apoplectic. The advance man is threatening to quit. The boss hostler is furious, whacking the beleaguered men of the Flying Squadron with flagrant abandon.

Everyone here has been down this route before. Mostly they're worried they won't be fed enough during the three-day journey to Joliet. The cookhouse crew are doing their best, scrabbling to haul as much food as they can back to the main train and promising to hand out dukeys – apparently some kind of boxed meal – at the first opportunity.

When August learns we have a three-day jump in front of us, he lets loose a string of curses, then strides back and forth, damning Uncle Al to hell and barking orders at the rest of us. While we haul food for the animals back to the train, August goes off to try to persuade – and if necessary, to bribe – the cookhouse steward into parting with some of the food meant for humans.

Diamond Joe and I carry buckets of offal from behind the menagerie to the main train. It's from the local stockyards, and is repulsive – smelly, bloody, and charred. We put the buckets just inside the entrance of the stock cars. The inhabitants – camels, zebras, and other hay burners – kick and fuss and make all manner of protest, but they are going to have to travel with the meat because there is no other place to put it. The big cats travel on top of the flat cars in parade dens.

When we're finished, I go looking for August. He's behind the cookhouse loading a wheelbarrow with the odds and ends he's managed to beg off the cookhouse crew.

'We're pretty much loaded,' I say. 'Should we do anything about water?'

'Dump and refill the buckets. They've loaded the water wagon, but it won't last three days. We'll have to stop along the way. Uncle Al may be a tough old crow, but he's no fool. He won't risk the animals. No animals, no circus. Is all the meat on board?'

'As much as will fit.'

'Priority goes to the meat. If you have to toss off hay to make room, do it. Cats are worth more than hay burners.'

'We're packed to the gills. Unless Kinko and I sleep somewhere else, there's no room for anything else.'

August pauses, tapping his pursed lips. 'No,' he says finally. 'Marlena would never tolerate meat on board with her horses.'

At least I know where I stand. Even if it is somewhere below the cats.

* * *

The water at the bottom of the horses' buckets is murky and has oats floating in it. But it's water all the same, so I carry the buckets outside, remove my shirt and dump what's left over my arms, head, and chest.

'Feeling a little less than fresh, Doc?' says August.

I'm leaning over with water dripping from my hair. I wipe both eyes clear and stand up. 'Sorry. I didn't see any other water to use, and I was just going to dump it, anyway.'

'No, quite right, quite right. We can hardly expect our vet to live like a working man, can we? I'll tell you what, Jacob. It's a little late now, but when we get to Joliet I'll arrange for you to start getting your own water. Performers and bosses get two buckets apiece; more, if you're willing to grease the water man's palm,' he says, rubbing his fingers and thumb. 'I'll also set you up with the Monday Man and see about getting you another set of clothes.'

'The Monday Man?'

'What day did your mother do the washing, Jacob?'

I stare at him. 'Surely you don't mean—'

'All that wash hanging up on lines. It would be a shame to let it go to waste.'

'But—'

'Never you mind, Jacob. If you don't want to know the answer to a question, don't ask. And don't use that slime to clean up. Follow me.'

He leads me back across the lot to one of only three tents left standing. Inside are hundreds of buckets, lined up two deep in front of trunks and clothes racks, with names or initials painted on the sides. Men in various states of undress are using them to bathe and shave.

'Here,' he says, pointing at a pair of buckets. 'Use these.'

'But what about Walter?' I ask, reading the name from the side of one of them.

'Oh, I know Walter. He'll understand. Got a razor?'

'No.'

'I have some back there,' he says, pointing across the tent. 'At the far end. They're labeled with my name. Hurry up though – I'm guessing we'll be out of here in another half an hour.'

'Thanks,' I say.

'Don't mention it,' he says. 'I'll leave a shirt for you in the stock car.'

When I return to the stock car, Silver Star is against the far wall in knee-deep straw. His eyes are glassy, his heart rate high.

The other horses are still outside, so I get my first good look at the place. It has sixteen standing stalls, which are formed by dividers that swing across after each horse is led in. If the car hadn't been adulterated for the mysterious and missing goats, it would hold thirty-two horses.

I find a clean white shirt laid across the end of Kinko's cot. I strip out of my old one and toss it onto the horse blanket in the corner. Before I put the new shirt on, I bring it to my nose, grateful for the scent of laundry soap.

As I'm buttoning it, Kinko's books catch my eye. They're sitting on the crate beside the kerosene lamp. I tuck in my shirt, sit on the cot, and reach for the top one.

It's the complete works of Shakespeare. Underneath is

a collection of Wordsworth poems, a Bible, and a book of plays by Oscar Wilde. A few small comic books are hidden inside the front cover of the Shakespeare. I recognize them immediately. They're eight-pagers.

I flip one open. A crudely drawn Olive Oyl lies on a bed with her legs open, naked but for her shoes. She spreads herself with her fingers. Popeye appears in a thought bubble above her head, with a bulging erection that reaches to his chin. Wimpy, with an equally enormous erection, peers through the window.

'What the hell do you think you're doing?'

I drop the comic, then bend quickly to retrieve it.

'Just leave it the hell alone!' says Kinko, storming over and snatching it from my hands. 'And get the hell off my bed!'

I leap up.

'Look here, pal,' he says, reaching up to jab his finger into my chest. 'I'm not exactly thrilled about having to bunk with you, but apparently I don't have a choice in the matter. But you better believe I have a choice about whether you mess with my stuff.'

He is unshaven, his blue eyes burning in a face that is the color of beets.

'You're right,' I stammer. 'I'm sorry. I shouldn't have touched your things.'

'Listen, pisshead. I had a nice gig going here until you came along. Plus I'm in a bad mood anyway. Some asshole used my water today, so you'd best stay out of my way. I may be short, but don't think I can't take you.'

My eyes widen. I recover but not soon enough.

His eyes narrow to slits. He scans the shirt, my clean-shaven face. He chucks the eight-pager onto his cot. 'Aw hell. Haven't you done enough already?'

'I'm sorry. Honest to God, I didn't know it was yours. August said I could use it.'

'Did he also say you could go through my stuff?'

I pause, embarrassed. 'No.'

He gathers his books and stuffs them into the crate.

'Kinko – Walter – I'm sorry.'

'That's Kinko to you, pal. Only my friends call me Walter.'

I walk to the corner and sink down on my horse blanket. Kinko helps Queenie onto the bed and lies down beside her, staring so pointedly at the ceiling I half-expect it to start smoldering.

Before long, the train pulls out. A few dozen angry men chase us for a while, swinging pitchforks and baseball bats, although it's mostly for the benefit of the tale they'll get to tell at dinner tonight. If they had really wanted a fight there was plenty of time before we pulled out.

It's not that I can't see their point – their wives and children had been looking forward to the circus for days, and they themselves had probably been looking forward to some of the other entertainments rumored to be available in the back of our lot. And now, instead of sampling the charms of the magnificent Barbara, they'll have to content themselves with their eight-pagers. I can see why a guy might get steamed.

Kinko and I clatter along in hostile silence as the train gets up to speed. He lies on his cot, reading. Queenie rests her head on his socks. Mostly she sleeps, but whenever she's awake, she watches me. I sit on the horse blanket, bone-weary but not yet tired enough to lie down and suffer the indignities of vermin and mildew.

At what should be dinnertime, I get up and stretch. Kinko's eyes dart over from behind his book, and then back to the text.

I walk out to the horses and stand looking over their alternating black and white backs. When we reloaded them, we moved everyone up to give Silver Star all four empty stalls' worth of space. Even though the rest of the horses are now in unfamiliar slots, they seem largely unperturbed, probably because we loaded them in the same order. The names scratched into the posts no longer match the occupants, but I can extrapolate who's who. The fourth horse in is Blackie. I wonder if his personality is anything like his human namesake's.

I can't see Silver Star, which means he must be lying down. That's both good and bad: good, because it keeps the weight off his feet, and bad because it means he's in enough pain he doesn't want to stand. Because of the way the stalls are constructed, I can't check on him until we stop and unload the other horses.

I sit across from the open door and watch the landscape pass until it gets dark. Eventually I slide down and fall asleep.

It seems like only minutes later when the brakes begin screeching. Almost immediately, the door to the goat room opens and Kinko and Queenie come out into the rough foyer. Kinko leans one shoulder against the wall, hands pushed deep in his pockets and ignoring me studiously. When we finally come to a stop, he jumps to the ground, turns, and claps twice. Queenie leaps into his arms and they disappear.

I climb to my feet and peer out the open door.

We're on a siding in the middle of nowhere. The other two sections of train are also stopped, stretched out before us on the track, a half mile between each.

People climb down from the train in the early morning light. The performers stretch grumpily and gather in groups to talk and smoke as the workmen drop ramps and unload stock.

August and his men arrive within minutes.

'Joe, you deal with the monkeys,' says August. 'Pete, Otis, unload the hay burners and get them watered, will you? Use the stream instead of troughs. We're conserving water.'

'But don't unload Silver Star,' I say.

There's a long silence. The men look first at me and then at August, whose gaze is steely.

'Yes,' August finally says. 'That's right. Don't unload Silver Star.'

He turns and walks away. The other men regard me with wide eyes.

I jog a little to catch up with August. 'I'm sorry,' I say, falling into stride beside him. 'I didn't mean to give orders.'

He stops in front of the camel car and slides the door open. We're greeted by the grunts and complaints of distressed dromedaries.

'That's all right, my boy,' August says cheerily, slinging a bucket of meat at me. 'You can help me feed the cats.'

I catch the bucket's thin metal handle. A cloud of angry flies rises from it.

'Oh my God,' I say. I set the bucket down and turn

away, retching. I wipe tears from my eyes, still gagging. 'August, we can't feed them this.'

'Why not?'

'It's gone off.'

There's no answer. I turn and find that August has set a second bucket beside me and left. He's marching up the tracks carting another two buckets. I grab mine and catch up.

'It's putrid. Surely the cats won't eat this,' I continue.

'Let's hope they do. Otherwise, we'll have to make some hard decisions.'

'Huh?'

'We're still a long way from Joliet, and, alas, we're out of goats.'

I am too stunned to answer.

When we reach the second section of the train, August hops up onto a flat car and props open the sides of two cat dens. He opens the padlocks, leaves them hanging on the doors, and jumps down to the gravel.

'Go on then,' he says, thumping me on the back.

'What?'

'They get a bucket each. Go on,' he urges.

I climb reluctantly onto the bed of the flat car. The odor of cat urine is overwhelming. August hands me the buckets of meat, one at a time. I set them on the weathered wooden boards, trying not to breathe.

The cat dens have two compartments each: to my left is a pair of lions. To my right, a tiger and a panther. All four are massive. They lift their heads, sniffing, their whiskers twitching.

'Well, go on then,' says August.

'What do I do, just open the door and toss it in?'

'Unless you can think of a better way.'

The tiger rises, six hundred glorious pounds of black, orange, and white. His head is huge, his whiskers long. He comes to the door, swings around, and walks away. When he returns, he growls and swipes at the latch. The padlock rattles against the bars.

'You can start with Rex,' says August, pointing at the lions, which are also pacing. 'That's him on the left.'

Rex is considerably smaller than the tiger, with mats in his mane and ribs showing under his dull coat. I steel myself and reach for a bucket.

'Wait,' says August, pointing at a different bucket. 'Not that one. This one.'

I can't see the difference, but since I've already ascertained that it's a bad idea to argue with August, I oblige.

When the cat sees me coming, he lunges at the door. I freeze.

'What's the matter, Jacob?'

I turn around. August's face is glowing.

'You're not afraid of Rex, are you?' he continues. 'He's just a *widdle kitty cat.*'

Rex pauses to rub his mangy coat against the bars at the front of the cage.

With fumbling fingers, I remove the padlock and lay it by my feet. Then I lift the bucket and wait. The next time Rex turns away from the door, I swing it open.

Before I can tip the meat out, his huge jaws chomp down on my arm. I scream. The bucket crashes to the floor, splattering chopped entrails everywhere. The cat drops off my arm and pounces on the meat.

I slam the door and hold it shut with my knee while I check whether I still have an arm. I do. It is slick with saliva and as red as if I had dunked it in boiling water, but the skin isn't broken. A moment later, I realize August is laughing uproariously behind me.

I turn to him. 'What the hell is wrong with you? You think that's funny?'

'I do, yes,' says August, making no effort to contain his mirth.

'You're seriously fucked, you know that?' I jump down from the flat car, check my intact arm once more, and stalk off.

'Jacob, wait,' laughs August, coming up behind me. 'Don't be sore. I was just having a little fun with you.'

'What fun? I could have lost my arm!'

'He hasn't got any teeth.'

I halt, staring at the gravel beneath my feet as this fact sinks in. Then I continue walking. This time, August doesn't follow.

Furious, I head for the stream and kneel beside a couple of men watering zebras. One of the zebras spooks, barking and throwing his striped muzzle high in the air. The man holding the lead rope shoots a succession of glances at me as he struggles to maintain control. 'Goddammit!' he shouts. 'What is that? Is that blood?'

I look down. I am spattered with blood from the entrails. 'Yes,' I say. 'I was feeding the cats.'

'What the hell is wrong with you? You trying to get me killed?'

I walk downstream, looking back until the zebra calms

down. Then I crouch by the water to rinse the blood and cat saliva from my arms.

Eventually I head back to the second section of the train. Diamond Joe is up on a flat, next to a chimp den. The sleeves of his gray shirt are rolled up, exposing hairy, muscled arms. The chimp sits on his haunches, eating fistfuls of cereal mixed with fruit and watching us with shiny black eyes.

'Need help?' I ask.

'Naw. About done, I think. I hear August got you with old Rex.'

I look up, prepared to be angry. But Joe's not smiling.

'Watch yourself,' he says. 'Rex might not take your arm, but Leo will. You can bet on that. Don't know why August asked you to do it anyway. Clive is the cat man. Unless he wanted to make a point.' He pauses, reaches into the den, and touches fingers with the chimp before shutting the door. Then he jumps down from the flat. 'Look, I'm only going to say this once. August's a funny one, and I don't mean funny ha-ha. You be careful. He don't like no one questioning his authority. And he has his moments, if you know what I mean.'

'I believe I do.'

'No, I don't think you do. But you will. Say, you eaten yet?'

'No.'

He points up the track to the Flying Squadron. There are tables set up alongside the track. 'Cookhouse crew got up a breakfast of sorts. Also put up some dukey boxes. Make sure you grab one, 'cuz that probably means we're not stopping again until tonight. Get it while the getting's good, I always say.'

'Thanks, Joe.'

'Don't mention it.'

I return to the stock car with my dukey box, which contains a ham sandwich, apple, and two bottles of sarsaparilla. When I see Marlena sitting in the straw beside Silver Star, I set my dukey box down and walk slowly toward her.

Silver Star lies on his side, his flanks heaving, his respiration shallow and fast. Marlena sits at his head with her legs curled beneath her.

'He's not any better, is he?' she says, looking up at me. I shake my head.

'I don't understand how this could happen so fast.' Her voice is tiny and hollow, and it occurs to me that she's probably going to cry.

I crouch beside her. 'Sometimes it just does. It's not because of anything you did, though.'

She strokes his face, running her fingers around his dished cheek and down under his chin. His eyes flicker.

'Is there anything else we can do for him?' she asks.

'Short of getting him off the train, no. Even under the best of circumstances, there's not a lot you can do but take them off their feed and pray.'

She glances at me and does a double take when she sees my arm. 'Oh my God. What happened to you?'

I look down. 'Oh, that. It's nothing.'

'No it's not,' she says, climbing to her knees. She takes my forearm in her hands and moves it to catch the sunlight coming in through the slats. 'It looks new. It's going to be a heck of a bruise. Does this hurt?' She takes the back of my arm in one hand and runs the other over the blue patch that's spreading beneath my skin. Her palm is cool and smooth, and leaves my hair standing on end.

I close my eyes and swallow hard. 'No, really, I'm—'

A whistle blows, and she looks toward the door. I take the opportunity to extricate my arm and rise.

'Twen-n-n-n-n-n-nty minutes!' bellows a deep voice from somewhere near the front of the train. 'Twen-n-n-n-n-n-n-nty minutes to push-off!'

Joe pokes his head through the open doorway. 'Come on! We gotta load these animals! Oh, sorry ma'am,' he says, tipping his hat to Marlena. 'I didn't see you there.'

'That's okay, Joe.'

Joe stands awkwardly in the doorway, waiting. 'It's just that we've got to do it now,' he says in desperation.

'Go ahead,' says Marlena. 'I'm going to ride this leg with Silver Star.'

'You can't do that,' I say quickly.

She looks up at me, her throat elongated and pale. 'Why ever not?'

'Because once we get the other horses loaded you'll be trapped back here.'

'That's all right.'

'What if something happens?'

'Nothing's going to happen. And if it does, I'll climb over them.' She settles into the straw, curling her legs back under her.

'I don't know,' I say doubtfully. But Marlena is gazing at Silver Star with an expression that makes it perfectly clear she's not budging.

I look back at Joe, who raises his hands in a gesture of exasperation and surrender.

After a final glance at Marlena, I swing the stall divider into place and help load the rest of the horses.

Diamond Joe is right about the long haul. It's early evening before we stop again.

Kinko and I haven't exchanged a word since we left Saratoga Springs. He clearly hates me. Not that I blame him – August set it up that way, although I don't suppose there's any point in trying to explain that to him.

I stay up front with the horses to let him have some privacy. That, and I'm still nervous at the thought of Marlena trapped at the end of a row of thousand-pound animals.

When the train stops she climbs nimbly over their backs and drops to the floor. When Kinko emerges from the goat room, his eyes crinkle in momentary alarm. Then they shift from Marlena to the open door with studied indifference.

Pete, Otis, and I unload and water the ring stock, camels, and llamas. Diamond Joe, Clive, and a handful of cage hands head up to the second section of the train to deal with the animals in dens. August is nowhere to be seen.

After we get the animals back on board, I climb into the stock car and poke my head into the room.

Kinko sits cross-legged on the bed. Queenie sniffs a bedroll that has replaced the infested horse blanket. Sitting on top is a neatly folded red plaid blanket and a pillow in a smooth white case. A square sheet of cardboard lies in the center of the pillow. When I lean over to pick it up, Queenie leaps as though I've kicked her.

Mr and Mrs August Rosenbluth request the pleasure of your immediate presence in stateroom 3, car 48, for cocktails, followed by a late dinner.

I look up in surprise. Kinko is staring daggers at me. 'You wasted no time ingratiating yourself, did you?' he says.

SEVEN

The cars are not sequentially numbered, and it takes me a while to find car 48. It is painted a deep burgundy and trimmed with foot-tall gold lettering trumpeting BENZINI BROS MOST SPECTACULAR SHOW ON EARTH. Just beneath that, visible only in relief under the shiny fresh paint, is another name: CHRISTY BROS CIRCUS.

'Jacob!' Marlena's voice floats from a window. A few seconds later she appears on the platform at the end, swinging out from the handrail so that her skirt swirls around her. 'Jacob! Oh, I'm so glad you could make it. Please come in!'

'Thanks,' I say, glancing around. I climb up and follow her down the interior passageway and through the second door.

Stateroom 3 is glorious as well as a misnomer – it

constitutes half the car, and contains at least one additional room, which is cordoned off with a thick velvet curtain. The main room is paneled in walnut and outfitted with damask furniture, a dinette, and a Pullman kitchen.

'Please make yourself comfortable,' says Marlena, waving me toward one of the chairs. 'August will be along in a minute.'

'Thank you,' I say.

She sits opposite me.

'Oh,' she says leaping up again. 'Where are my manners? Would you like a beer?'

'Thank you,' I say. 'That would be swell.'

She flutters past me to an icebox.

'Mrs Rosenbluth, can I ask you something?'

'Oh, please, call me Marlena,' she says, popping the bottle cap. She tips a tall glass and pours beer slowly down its side, avoiding a foam head. 'And yes, by all means. Ask away.' She hands me the glass, and then returns to get another.

'How is it that everyone on this train has so much alcohol?'

'We always head to Canada at the beginning of the season,' she says, taking her seat again. 'Their laws are much more civilized. Cheers,' she says, holding out her glass.

I touch mine to hers and take a sip. It's a cold, clean lager. Magnificent. 'Don't the border guards check?'

'We put the booze in with the camels,' she says.

'I'm sorry, I don't understand,' I say.

'Camels spit.'

I nearly spurt beer through my nose. She giggles too, and brings a hand demurely to her mouth. Then she sighs and puts her beer down. 'Jacob?'

'Yes?'

'August told me about what happened this morning.'

I glance at my bruised arm.

'He feels terrible. He likes you. He really does. It's just . . . Well, it's complicated.' She looks into her lap, blushing.

'Hey, it's nothing,' I say. 'It's fine.'

'Jacob!' shouts August from behind me. 'My dear fellow! So glad you could join our little soirée. I see Marlena has set you up with a drinky-poo; has she shown you the dressing room yet?'

'The dressing room?'

'Marlena,' he says, turning and shaking his head sadly. He waggles a finger in reprimand. '*Tsk tsk,* darling.'

'Oh!' she says, leaping to her feet. 'I completely forgot!'

August walks to the velvet curtain and whisks it aside. 'Ta-dah!'

There are three outfits lying side by side on the bed. Two tuxedos, complete with shoes, and a beautiful rose silk dress with beading on its neck and hemline.

Marlena squeals, clapping her hands in delight. She rushes to the bed and grabs the dress, pressing it to her body and twirling.

I turn to August. 'These aren't from the Monday Man—'

'A tux on a wash line? No, Jacob. Being equestrian director has the odd perk. You can clean up in there,' he says, pointing to a polished wooden door. 'Marlena and I will change out here. Nothing we haven't seen before, eh darling?' he says.

She grabs a rose silk shoe by the heel and chucks it at him.

The last thing I see as I shut the bathroom door is a tangle of feet toppling forward onto the bed.

When I come back out, Marlena and August are the picture of dignity, hovering in the background as three white-gloved waiters fuss with a small wheeled table and silver-domed platters.

The neckline of Marlena's dress barely covers her shoulders, exposing her collarbone and a slim bra strap. She follows my gaze and tucks the strap back under the material, blushing once again.

The dinner is sublime: We start with oyster bisque and follow with prime rib, boiled potatoes, and asparagus in cream. Then comes lobster salad. By the time dessert appears – English plum pudding with brandy sauce – I don't think I can take another bite. And yet a few minutes later I find myself scraping my plate with my spoon.

'Apparently Jacob doesn't find dinner up to snuff,' August says in a slow drawl.

I freeze midscrape.

Then he and Marlena dissolve into fits of giggles. I set my spoon down, mortified.

'No, no, my boy, I'm joking – obviously,' he chortles, leaning over to pat my hand. 'Eat. Enjoy yourself. Here, have some more,' he says.

'No, I couldn't possibly.'

'Well, have some more wine then,' he says, refilling my glass without waiting for a response.

August is gracious, charming, and mischievous – so much so that as the evening wears on I begin to think the incident with Rex was just a joke gone awry. His face glows with wine and sentiment as he regales me with the tale of how he wooed Marlena. Of how he recognized her powerful way with horses the very moment she entered his menagerie tent three years before – sensed it from the horses themselves. And how, to the great distress of Uncle Al, he refused to budge until he had swept her off her feet and married her.

'It took some doing,' says August, emptying the remains of one champagne bottle into my glass and then reaching for another. 'Marlena's no pushover, plus she was practically engaged at the time. But this beats being the wife of a stuffy banker, doesn't it, darling? At any rate, it's what she was born to do. Not everyone can work with liberty horses. It's a God-given talent, a sixth sense, if you will. This girl speaks horse, and believe me, they listen.'

Four hours and six bottles into the evening, August and Marlena dance to 'Maybe It's the Moon,' while I lounge in an upholstered chair with my right leg draped over its arm. August twirls Marlena around and then stops with her extended from the end of his straightened arm. He's weaving, his dark hair tousled. His bow tie trails from either side of his collar and the first few buttons of his shirt are undone. He stares at Marlena with such intensity he looks like a different man.

'What's the matter?' says Marlena. 'Auggie? Are you all right?'

He continues to stare into her face, cocking his head as though evaluating her. The edge of his lip curls. He starts to nod, slowly, barely moving his head.

Marlena's eyes grow wide. She tries to step backward, but he catches her chin with his hand.

I sit forward, suddenly on full alert.

August stares for a moment longer, his eyes shiny and hard. Then his face transforms again, becoming so sloppy that for a moment I think he's going to burst into tears. He pulls her to him by the chin and kisses her full on the lips. Then he steers himself into the bedroom and collapses face first onto the bed.

'Excuse me a moment,' Marlena says.

She goes into the bedroom and rolls him over so he's sprawled across the center of the bed. She removes his shoes and drops them to the floor. When she comes out, she pulls the velvet curtain shut and immediately changes her mind. She pulls it open again, turns off the radio, and sits opposite me.

A snore of kingly proportions rumbles from the bedroom.

My head is buzzing. I am entirely drunk.

'What the hell was that?' I ask.

'What?' Marlena kicks off her shoes, crosses her legs, and leans forward to rub the arch of her foot. August's fingers have left red marks on her chin.

'That,' I sputter. 'Just now. When you were dancing.'

She looks up sharply. Her face contorts, and for a moment I'm afraid she's going to cry. Then she turns to the window and holds a finger to her lips. She is silent for almost half a minute.

'You have to understand something about Auggie,' she says, 'and I don't quite know how to explain it.'

I lean forward. 'Try.'

'He's . . . mercurial. He's capable of being the most charming man on earth. Like tonight.'

I wait for her to continue. 'And . . . ?'

She leans back in her chair. 'And, well, he has . . . moments. Like today.'

'What about today?'

'He nearly fed you to a cat.'

'Oh. That. I can't say I was thrilled, but I was hardly in danger. Rex has no teeth.'

'No, but he's four hundred pounds and he has claws,' she says quietly.

I set my wineglass on the table as the enormity of this sinks in. Marlena pauses, then lifts her eyes to meet mine. 'Jankowski is a Polish name, isn't it?'

'Yes. Of course.'

'Poles do not, in general, like Jews.'

'I didn't realize August was Jewish.'

'With a name like Rosenbluth?' she says. She looks at her fingers, twisting them in her lap. 'My family is Catholic. They disowned me when they found out.'

'I'm sorry to hear that. Although I'm not surprised.'

She looks up sharply.

'I didn't mean it like that,' I say. 'I'm not . . . like that.'

An uncomfortable silence stretches between us.

'So why am I here?' I finally ask. My drunken brain is unable to process all this.

'I wanted to smooth things over.'

'You did? He didn't want me here?'

'No, of course he did. He wanted to make it up to you, too, but it's harder for him. He can't help his little moments. They embarrass him. The best thing to do is pretend they didn't happen.' She sniffs and turns to me with a tight smile. 'And we had a lovely time, didn't we?'

'Yes. Dinner was lovely. Thank you.'

As yet another silence engulfs us, it dawns on me that unless I want to try leaping across train cars drunk and in the dead of night, I'll be sleeping right where I am.

'Please, Jacob,' says Marlena. 'I do so want things to be all right between us. August is simply delighted you've joined us. And so is Uncle Al.'

'And why is that, exactly?'

'Uncle Al was touchy about not having a vet, and then out of blue, here you are, from an Ivy League school no less.'

I stare, still trying to comprehend.

'Ringling has a vet,' Marlena continues, 'and being like Ringling makes Uncle Al happy.'

'I thought he hated Ringling.'

'Darling, he wants to *be* Ringling.'

I lean my head back and shut my eyes, but this results in disastrous spinning, so I open them again and try to focus on the feet dangling from the end of the bed.

When I wake up, the train has stopped – can I really have slept through the screeching brakes? The sun is shining on me through the window, and my brain pounds against my skull. My eyes ache and my mouth tastes like a sewer.

I stagger to my feet and glance into the bedroom. August is curled around Marlena, his arm lying across her. They are on top of the bedspread, still fully dressed.

I get a few odd looks when I emerge from car 48 dressed in a tux with my other clothes tucked under my arm. At this end of the train, where most of the onlookers are performers, I am regarded with frosty amusement. As I pass the working men's sleepers, the glances become harder, more suspicious.

I climb gingerly into the stock car and push open the door of the little room.

Kinko is sitting on the edge of his cot, an eight-pager in one hand and his penis in the other. He stops midstroke, its slick purple head extending beyond his fist. There's a heartbeat of silence followed by the whoosh of an empty Coke bottle flying at my head. I duck.

'Get out!' Kinko screams as the bottle explodes against the doorframe behind me. He leaps up, causing his erection to bounce wildly. 'Get the hell out!' He lobs another bottle at me.

I turn to the door, shielding my head and dropping my clothes. I hear a zipper running up, and a moment later the complete works of Shakespeare smash into the wall beside me. 'Okay, okay!' I shout. 'I'm leaving!'

I pull the door shut behind me and lean against the wall. The curses continue unabated.

Otis appears outside the stock car. He looks in alarm at the closed door and then shrugs. 'Hey, fancy boy,' he says. 'You gonna help us with these animals or what?'

'Sure. Of course.' I jump to the ground.

He stares at me.

'What?' I say.

'Ain't you gonna change out of the monkey suit first?'

I glance back at the closed door. Something heavy slams against the interior wall. 'Uh, no. I think I'll stay like I am for the time being.'

'Your call. Clive's cleaned out the cats. He wants us to bring the meat.'

There's even more noise coming from the camel car this morning.

'Them hay burners sure don't like traveling with meat,' says Otis. 'Wish they'd stop kicking up such a fuss, though. We got a fair bit farther to go.'

I slide the door open. Flies explode outward. I see the maggots just as the smell hits. I manage to stagger a few feet away before vomiting. Otis joins me, doubled over, clasping his hands to his gut.

After he finishes throwing up, he takes a few deep breaths and pulls a filthy handkerchief from his pocket. He clasps it over his mouth and nose, and returns to the car. He grabs a bucket, runs to the tree line and dumps it. He holds his breath until he's halfway back. Then he stops, bent over with his hands on his knees, gasping for air.

I try to help, but every time I get near, my diaphragm erupts in fresh spasms.

'I'm sorry,' I say when Otis returns. I'm still gagging. 'I can't do it. I just can't.'

He shoots me a dirty look.

'My stomach's off,' I say, feeling the need to explain. 'I drank too much last night.'

'Yeah, I'll bet you did,' he says. 'Have a seat, monkey boy. I'll take care of it.'

Otis dumps the rest of the meat at the tree line, leaving it in a heap that buzzes with flies.

We leave the door to the camel car wide open, but it's clear a simple airing out won't be sufficient.

We lead the camels and llamas down the tracks and tie them to the side of the train. Then we slosh buckets of water across the floorboards, using push brooms to sluice the resulting muck from the car. The stench is still overwhelming, but it's the best we can do.

After we tend to the rest of the animals, I return to the ring stock car. Silver Star is lying on his side, and Marlena is kneeling next to him, still wearing the rose dress from the night before. I walk past the long line of open stall dividers and stand beside her.

Silver Star's eyes are barely open. He flinches and grunts in reaction to some unseen stimulus.

'He's worse,' Marlena says without looking at me.

After a moment I say, 'Yes.'

'Is there any chance he'll recover? Any chance at all?'

I hesitate, because what's on the tip of my tongue is a lie and I find I can't utter it.

'You can tell me the truth,' she says. 'I need to know.'

'No. I'm afraid there's no chance at all.'

She lays a hand on his neck, holding it there. 'In that case, promise me it will be quick. I don't want him to suffer.'

I understand what she's asking me, and shut my eyes. 'I promise.'

She rises and stands staring down at him. I'm marveling

and not just a little unnerved at her stoic reaction when a strange noise rises from her throat. It's followed by a moan, and next thing I know she's bawling. She doesn't even try to wipe the tears that slide down her cheeks, just stands hugging her arms with shoulders heaving, gasping for breath. She looks like she's going to collapse in on herself.

I stare in horror. I have no sisters and my limited experience with comforting women has always been over something a hell of a lot less devastating than this. After a few moments of indecision, I lay a hand on her shoulder.

She turns and falls against me, pressing her wet cheek into my – August's – tuxedo shirt. I rub her back, making shushing noises until her tears finally subside into jerky hiccups. Then she pulls away.

Her eyes and nose are swollen and pink, her face slick with mucus. She sniffs and wipes her lower lashes with the back of each hand, as though that will do any good. Then she straightens her shoulders and leaves without looking back, her high heels tapping down the length of the car.

'August,' I say, standing beside the bed and shaking his shoulder. He flops limply, as responsive as a corpse.

I lean and shout in his ear. 'August!'

He grunts, irritated.

'August! Wake up!'

Finally he shifts, rolling and placing a hand over his eyes. 'Oh God,' he says. 'Oh God, I think my head is going to explode. Close the curtain, will you?'

'Do you have a gun?'

The hand drops from the eyes. He sits up.

'What?'

'I have to put Silver Star down.'

'You can't.'

'I have to.'

'You heard Uncle Al. If anything happens to that horse, you'll be redlighted.'

'Which means what, exactly?'

'Chucked from the train. When it's moving. If you're lucky, within sight of a train yard's red lights so you can find your way to town. If you're not, well, you'd just better hope they don't open the door while the train's crossing a trestle.'

Camel's remark about having an appointment with Blackie suddenly makes sense – as do various comments from my first meeting with Uncle Al. 'In that case I'll take my chances and stay right here when the train pulls out. But either way, that horse needs putting down.'

August stares at me with black-ringed eyes.

'Shit,' he says finally. He swings his legs around so that he's sitting at the edge of the bed. He rubs his stubbled cheeks. 'Does Marlena know?' he asks, leaning over to scratch his black-socked toes.

'Yes.'

'Fuck,' he says, getting to his feet. He holds one hand to his head. 'Al's going to have a fit. Okay, meet me at the stock car in a few minutes. I'll bring the gun.'

I turn to leave.

'Oh, Jacob?'

'Yes?' I say.

'Change out of my tux first, will you?'

When I get back to the stock car, the interior door is open. I poke my head in with more than a little trepidation, but Kinko is gone. I go inside and change into my regular clothes. A few minutes later, August shows up with a rifle.

'Here,' he says, climbing the ramp. He hands me the gun and drops two shells into my other palm.

I slip one into my pocket and hold the other one out. 'I only need one.'

'What if you miss?'

'For crying out loud, August, I'm going to be standing right next to him.'

He stares at me, and then takes the extra shell. 'Okay, fine. Take him a good ways from the train to do it.'

'You've got to be kidding. He can't walk.'

'You can't do it here,' he says. 'The other horses are right outside.'

I just look at him.

'Shit,' he says finally. He turns and leans against the wall, his fingers beating a tattoo against the slats. 'Okay. Fine.'

He walks to the door. 'Otis! Joe! Get the other horses out of here. Take them at least as far up as the second section.'

Someone outside mumbles.

'Yeah, I know,' says August. 'But they're just going to have to wait. Yeah, I know that. I'll talk to Al and tell him we have a little . . . complication.'

He turns back to me. 'I'm going to find Al.'

'You better find Marlena, too.'

'I thought you said she knew?'

'She does. But I don't want her to be alone when she hears that shot. Do you?'

August stares at me long and hard. Then he clomps down the ramp, planting his feet with such force the boards bounce beneath him.

I wait a full fifteen minutes, both to give August time to find Uncle Al and Marlena and also to let the other men move the rest of the animals far enough away.

Finally I pick up the rifle, slide the shell into the chamber, and throw the bolt. Silver Star's muzzle is pressed up against the end of his stall, his ears twitching. I lean over and run my fingers down his neck. Then I place the muzzle of the gun under his left ear and pull the trigger.

There's an explosion of sound and the butt of the rifle bucks into my shoulder. Silver Star's body seizes, his muscles responding to one last synaptical spasm before finally falling still. From far away, I hear a single desperate whinny.

My ears are ringing as I climb down from the stock car, but even so it seems to me that the scene is eerily silent. A small crowd of people has gathered. They stand motionless, their faces long. One man pulls his hat from his head and presses it to his chest.

I walk a few dozen yards from the train, climb the grassy bank, and sit rubbing my shoulder.

Otis, Pete, and Earl enter the stock car and then

reappear, hauling Silver Star's lifeless body down the ramp by a rope tied to his hind feet. Upside down his belly looks huge and vulnerable, a smooth expanse of snowy white dotted by black-skinned genitals. His lifeless head nods in agreement with each yank of the rope.

I sit for close to an hour, staring at the grass between my feet. I pluck a few blades and roll them in my fingers, wondering why the hell it's taking them so long to pull out.

After a while August approaches. He stares at me, and then leans over to pick up the rifle. I hadn't been aware of bringing it with me.

'Come on, pal,' he says. 'Don't want to get left behind.'

'I think I do.'

'Don't worry about what I said earlier – I talked to Al, and no one's getting redlighted. You're fine.'

I stare sullenly at the ground. After a while, August sits beside me.

'Or are you?' he says.

'How's Marlena?' I respond.

August watches me for a moment and then digs a package of Camels from his shirt pocket. He shakes one loose and offers it to me.

'No thanks,' I say.

'Is that the first time you've shot a horse?' he says, plucking the cigarette from the package with his teeth.

'No. But it doesn't mean I like it.'

'Part of being a vet, my boy.'

'Which, technically, I'm not.'

'So you missed the exams. Big deal.'

'It is a big deal.'

'No it isn't. It's just a piece of paper, and nobody here gives a damn about that. You're on a show now. The rules are different.'

'How so?'

He waves toward the train. 'Tell me, do you honestly think this is the most spectacular show on earth?'

I don't answer.

'Eh?' he says, leaning into me with his shoulder.

'I don't know.'

'No. It's nowhere near. It's probably not even the fiftieth most spectacular show on earth. We hold maybe a third of the capacity Ringling does. You already know that Marlena's not Romanian royalty. And Lucinda? Nowhere near eight hundred and eighty-five pounds. Four hundred, tops. And do you really think Frank Otto got tattooed by angry headhunters in Borneo? Hell no. He used to be a stake driver on the Flying Squadron. He worked on that ink for nine years. And you want to know what Uncle Al did when the hippo died? He swapped out her water for formaldehyde and kept on showing her. For two weeks we traveled with a pickled hippo. The whole thing's illusion, Jacob, and there's nothing wrong with that. It's what people want from us. It's what they expect.'

He stands up and holds out a hand. After a moment, I take it and let him pull me to my feet.

We walk toward the train.

'Damn, August,' I say. 'I almost forgot. The cats haven't eaten. We had to dump their meat.'

'It's all right, my boy,' he says. 'It's already been taken care of.'

'What do you mean, taken care of?'

I stop in my tracks.

'August? What do you mean it's been taken care of?'

August continues walking, the gun slung casually over his shoulder.

EIGHT

Wake up, Mr Jankowski. You're having a bad dream.'

My eyes snap open. Where am I? Oh, hell and damnation.

'I wasn't dreaming,' I protest.

'Well, you were talking in your sleep, sure enough,' says the nurse. It's the nice black girl again. Why do I have such trouble remembering her name? 'Something about feeding stars to cats. Now don't you go fretting about those cats – I'm sure they got fed, even if it was after you woke up. Now why did they go and put these on you?' she muses, ripping open my Velcro wrist restraints. 'You didn't try to run off now, did you?'

'No. I had the audacity to complain about that pablum they feed us.' I glance sideways at her. 'And then my plate sort of slid off the table.'

She stops and looks at me. Then she bursts out laughing. 'Oh, you're a live one, all right,' she says, rubbing my wrists between her warm hands. 'Oh my.'

It comes to me in a flash: Rosemary! Ha. So I'm not senile after all.

Rosemary. Rosemary. Rosemary.

I must think of a way to commit it to memory, a rhyme or something. I may have remembered this morning, but that's no guarantee I'll remember it tomorrow or even later today.

She goes to the window and opens the blinds.

'Do you mind?' I say.

'Do I mind what?' she replies.

'Correct me if I'm wrong, but isn't this my room? What if I don't want the blinds open? I tell you, I'm getting mighty sick of everyone thinking they know better than I do about what I want.'

Rosemary gazes at me. Then she drops the blinds and marches from the room, letting the door shut behind her. My mouth opens in surprise.

A moment later there are three taps on the door. It opens a crack.

'Good morning, Mr Jankowski, may I come in?'

What the hell game is she playing?

'I said, may I come in?' she repeats.

'Of course,' I sputter.

'Thank you kindly,' she says coming in and standing at the foot of my bed. 'Now, would you like me to open the blinds and let the good Lord's sun shine in on you, or would you rather sit here in pitch darkness all day long?'

'Oh, go ahead and open them. And stop it with that nonsense.'

'It's not nonsense, Mr Jankowski,' she says, going to the window and opening the blinds. 'Not a bit of it. I'd never thought of it that way before, and I thank you for opening my eyes.'

Is she making fun of me? I narrow my eyes, examining her face for clues.

'Now, am I correct in thinking you'd like breakfast in your room?'

I don't answer, as I'm still undecided as to whether I smell a rat. You'd think they'd have that preference written on my chart by now, but they ask me the same damned question every morning. Of course I would rather take my breakfast in the dining room. Taking it in my bed makes me feel like an invalid. But breakfast follows the early-morning diaper change, and the smell of feces fills the hallway and makes me retch. It's not until an hour or two after each and every one of the incapacitated folks has been cleaned, fed, and parked outside their doors that it's safe to poke your head out.

'Now, Mr Jankowski – if you expect people to try to do things your way, you're going to have to give some hints as to what that way is.'

'Yes. Please. I'll have it in here,' I say.

'All right, then. Would you like your shower before or after breakfast?'

'What makes you think I need a shower?' I say, thoroughly offended, even though I'm not at all sure I don't need a shower.

'Because this is the day your people visit,' she says,

flashing that big smile again. 'And because I thought you'd like to be nice and fresh for your outing this afternoon.'

My outing? Ah, yes! The circus. I must say, waking up two days in a row and having the prospect of a visit to the circus ahead of me has been nice.

'I think I'll take it before breakfast if you don't mind,' I say pleasantly.

One of the greatest indignities about being old is that people insist on helping you with things like bathing and going to the washroom.

I don't in fact require help with either, but they're all so afraid I'm going to slip and break my hip again that I get a chaperone whether I like it or not. I always insist on walking into the washroom myself, but there's always someone there, just in case, and for some reason it's always a woman. I make whoever it is turn around while I drop my drawers and sit, and then I send her outside until I'm finished.

Bathing is even more embarrassing, because I have to strip down to my birthday suit in front of a nurse. Now, there are some things that never die, so even though I'm in my nineties my sap sometimes rises. I can't help it. They always pretend not to notice. They're trained that way, I suppose, although pretending not to notice is almost worse than noticing. It means they consider me nothing more than a harmless old man sporting a harmless old penis that still gets uppity once in a while. Although if one of them took it seriously and tried to do something about it, the shock would probably kill me.

Rosemary helps me into the shower stall. 'There, now you just hold on to that bar over there—'

'I know, I know. I've had showers before,' I say, grabbing the bar and easing myself onto the bath chair. Rosemary runs the shower head down the pole so I can reach it.

'How's that for temperature, Mr Jankowski?' she asks, waving her hand in and out of the stream and keeping her gaze discreetly averted.

'Fine. Just give me some shampoo and go outside, will you?'

'Why, Mr Jankowski, you *are* in a mood today, aren't you?' She opens the shampoo and squeezes a few drops onto my palm. It's all I need. I've only got about a dozen hairs left.

'You give me a shout if you need anything,' she says, pulling the curtain across. 'I'll be right out here.'

'*Hrrrmph,*' I say.

Once she's gone I quite enjoy my shower. I take the shower head from its mount and spray my body from up close, aiming it over my shoulders and down my back and then over each of my skinny limbs. I even hold my head back with my eyes shut and let the spray hit my face full on. I pretend it's a tropical shower, shaking my head and reveling in it. I even enjoy the feel of it down there, on that shriveled pink snake that fathered five children so long ago.

Sometimes, when I'm in bed, I close my eyes and remember the look – and especially the feel – of a woman's naked body. Usually it's my wife's, but not always. I was completely faithful to her. Not once in more than sixty years did I stray, except in my imagination, and I have a feeling she wouldn't have minded that. She was a woman of extraordinary understanding.

Dear Lord, I miss that woman. And not just because if she were still alive, I wouldn't be here, although that's the God's truth. No matter how decrepit we became, we would have looked after each other, like we always did. But after she was gone, I didn't stand a chance against the kids. The first time I took a fall, they had it sewn up as quick as you can say Cracker Jack.

But Dad, they said, you broke your hip, as though maybe I hadn't noticed. I dug in my heels. I threatened to cut them off without a cent until I remembered they already controlled my money. They didn't remind me – they just let me rail on like an old fool until I remembered of my own accord, and that made me even angrier because if they had any respect for me at all they would have at least made sure I had the facts straight. I felt like a toddler whose tantrum was being allowed to run its course.

As the enormity of my helplessness dawned on me, my position began to slip.

You're right, I conceded. I guess I could use *some* help. I suppose having someone come in during the day wouldn't be so bad, just to help out with the cooking and cleaning. No? Well, how about a live-in? I know I've let things slip *a little* since your mother died . . . But I thought you said . . . Okay, then one of you can move in with me . . . But I don't understand . . . Well, Simon, your house is large. Surely I could . . . ?

It was not to be.

I remember leaving my house for the last time, bundled

up like a cat on the way to the vet. As the car pulled away, my eyes were so clouded by tears I couldn't look back.

It's not a nursing home, they said. It's assisted living – progressive, you see. You'll only have help for the things you need, and then when you get older . . .

They always trailed off there, as though that would prevent me from following the thought to its logical conclusion.

For a long time, I felt betrayed that not one of my five children offered to take me in. No longer. Now that I've had time to mull it over, I see they've got enough problems without adding me into the mix.

Simon is around seventy and has had at least one heart attack. Ruth has diabetes, and Peter has prostate trouble. Joseph's wife ran off with a cabana boy when they were in Greece, and while Dinah's breast cancer seems to have gone into remission – thank God – now she's got her granddaughter living with her, trying to get the girl back on track after two illegitimate children and an arrest for shoplifting.

And those are just the things I know about. There are a host of others they don't mention because they don't want to upset me. I've caught wind of several, but when I ask questions they clam right up. Mustn't upset Grandpa, you know.

Why? That's what I want to know. I hate this bizarre policy of protective exclusion, because it effectively writes me off the page. If I don't know what's going on in their lives, how am I supposed to insert myself in the conversation?

I've decided it's not about me at all. It's a protective mechanism for *them*, a way of buffering themselves against my future death, like when teenagers distance themselves from their parents in preparation for leaving home. When Simon turned sixteen and got belligerent, I thought it was just him. By the time Dinah got there, I knew it wasn't her fault – it was programmed into her.

But despite bowdlerizing content, my family has been entirely faithful about visiting. Someone comes every single Sunday, come hell or high water. They talk and they talk and they talk, about how fine/foul/fair the weather is, and what they did on vacation, and what they ate for lunch, and then at five on the nose they look gratefully at the clock and leave.

Sometimes they try to get me to go to the bingo game down the hall on their way out, like the batch from two weeks ago. Wouldn't you like to join in? they said. We could take you there on our way out. Doesn't it sound like fun?

Sure, I said. Maybe if you're a rutabaga. And they laughed, which pleased me even though I wasn't joking. At my age, you take credit for whatever you can. At least it proved they were listening.

My platitudes don't hold their interest and I can hardly blame them for that. My real stories are all out of date. So what if I can speak firsthand about the Spanish flu, the advent of the automobile, world wars, cold wars, guerrilla wars, and Sputnik – that's all ancient history now. But what else do I have to offer? Nothing happens to me anymore. That's the reality of getting old, and I guess that's really the crux of the matter. I'm not ready to be old yet.

But I shouldn't complain, this being circus day and all.

Rosemary returns with a breakfast tray, and when she pulls off the brown plastic lid I see that she's put cream and brown sugar on my porridge.

'Now don't you go telling Dr Rashid about the cream,' she says.

'Why not? I'm not supposed to have cream?'

'Not you specifically. It's part of the specialized diet. Some of our residents can't digest rich things the way they used to.'

'What about butter?' I'm outraged. My mind skips back over the last weeks, months, and years, trying to remember the last appearance of cream or butter in my life. Dang it, she's right. Why didn't I notice? Or maybe I did, and that's why I dislike the food so much. Well, it's no wonder. I suppose we're on reduced salt as well.

'It's supposed to keep you healthier for longer,' she says, shaking her head. 'But why you folks shouldn't enjoy a bit of butter in your golden years, I don't know.' She looks up sharply. 'You still have your gall-bladder, don't you?'

'Yes.'

Her face softens again. 'Well, in that case you enjoy that cream, Mr Jankowski. Do you want your TV on while you eat?'

'No. There's nothing but garbage on these days, anyway,' I say.

'I couldn't agree more,' she says, refolding the blanket

at the foot of my bed. 'You give me a buzz if you need anything else.'

After she leaves, I resolve to be nicer. I'll have to think of a way of reminding myself. I suppose I could wrap a bit of napkin around my finger since I don't have any string. People were always doing that in movies when I was younger. Wrapping strings around their fingers to remember things, that is.

I reach for the napkin, and as I do I catch sight of my hands. They are knobby and crooked, thin-skinned, and – like my ruined face – covered with liver spots.

My face. I push the porridge aside and open my vanity mirror. I should know better by now, but somehow I still expect to see myself. Instead, I find an Appalachian apple doll, withered and spotty, with dewlaps and bags and long floppy ears. A few strands of white hair spring absurdly from its spotted skull.

I try to brush the hairs flat with my hand and freeze at the sight of my old hand on my old head. I lean close and open my eyes very wide, trying to see beyond the sagging flesh.

It's no good. Even when I look straight into the milky blue eyes, I can't find myself anymore. When did I stop being me?

I'm too sickened to eat. I put the brown lid back on the porridge and then, with considerable difficulty, locate the pad that controls my bed. I press the button that flattens its head, leaving the table hovering over me like a vulture. Oh wait, there's a control here that lowers the bed, too. Good. Now I can roll onto my side without hitting the damned table and spilling the porridge. Don't want to do that again – they may call it a display of temper and summon Dr Rashid.

Once my bed is flat and as low as it will go, I roll onto my side and stare out the venetian blinds at the blue sky beyond. After a few minutes I'm lulled into a sort of peace.

The sky, the sky – same as it always was.

NINE

I'm daydreaming, staring out the open door at the sky when the brakes start their piercing shriek and everything lurches forward. I brace myself against the rough floor and then, after I regain my balance, run my hands through my hair and tie my shoes. We must have finally reached Joliet.

The rough-hewn door beside me squeaks open and Kinko comes out. He leans against the frame of the main door with Queenie at his feet, staring intently at the passing landscape. He hasn't looked at me since yesterday's incident, and to be frank, I find it difficult to look at him, vacillating as I do from feeling the deepest empathy for his mortification to being barely able not to laugh. When the train finally chugs to a stop and sighs, Kinko and Queenie disembark with the usual clap-clap and flying leap.

The scene outside is eerily quiet. Although the Flying Squadron pulled in a good half hour ahead of us, its men stand around silently. There is no ordered chaos. There is no clatter of runs or chutes, no cursing, no flying coils of rope, no hitching of teams. There are simply hundreds of disheveled men staring in bafflement at the pitched tents of another circus.

It's like a ghost town. There is a big top, but no crowd. A cookhouse, but no flag. Wagons and dressing tents fill the back end, but the people who are left mill about aimlessly or sit idly in the shade.

I jump down from the stock car just as a black and beige Plymouth roadster pulls into the parking lot. Two men in suits climb out, carrying briefcases and scanning the scene from under homburgs.

Uncle Al strides toward them, *sans entourage*, wearing his top hat and swinging his silver-tipped cane. He shakes hands with both men, his face jovial, cordial. As he talks, he turns to gesture broadly across the lot. The businessmen nod, crossing their arms in front of them, figuring, considering.

I hear gravel crunching behind me, and then August appears at my shoulder. 'That's our Al,' he says. 'He can smell a city official a mile off. You watch – he'll have the mayor eating out of his hand by noon.' He claps me on the shoulder. 'Come on.'

'Where to?' I ask.

'Into town, for breakfast,' he says. 'Doubt there's any food here. Probably won't be until tomorrow.'

'Jesus – really?'

'Well, we'll try, but we hardly gave the advance man time to get here, did we?'

'What about them?'

'Who?'

I point at the defunct circus.

'Them? When they get hungry enough they'll mope off. Best thing for everyone, really.'

'And our guys?'

'Oh, them. They'll survive until something shows up. Don't you worry. Al won't let them die.'

We stop at a diner not far down the main strip. It has booths along one wall and a laminate counter with red-topped stools along the other. A handful of men sit at the counter, smoking and chatting with the girl who stands behind it.

I hold the door for Marlena, who goes immediately to a booth and slides in against the wall. August drops onto the opposite bench, so I end up sitting next to her. She crosses her arms and stares at the wall.

'Mornin'. What can I get you folks?' says the girl, still behind the counter.

'The works,' says August. 'I'm famished.'

'How do you like your eggs?'

'Sunny side up.'

'Ma'am?'

'Just coffee,' Marlena says, sliding one leg over the other and jiggling her foot. The motion is frenetic, almost aggressive. She does not look at the waitress. Or August. Or me, come to think of it.

'Sir?' says the girl.

'Uh, same as him,' I say. 'Thanks.'

August leans back and pulls out a pack of Camels. He

flicks the bottom. A cigarette arcs through the air. He catches it in his lips and leans back, eyes bright, hands spread in triumph.

Marlena turns to look at him. She claps slowly, deliberately, her face stony.

'Come now, darling. Don't be a wet noodle,' says August. 'You know we were out of meat.'

'Excuse me,' she says, sliding toward me. I leap out of her way. She marches out the door, shoes tap-tapping and hips swaying under her flared red dress.

'Women,' says August, lighting his cigarette from behind a cupped hand. He snaps his lighter shut. 'Oh, sorry. Want one?'

'No thanks. I don't smoke.'

'No?' he muses, sucking in a lungful. 'You should take it up. It's good for your health.' He puts the pack back in his pocket and snaps his fingers at the girl behind the counter. She's standing at the griddle, holding a spatula.

'Make it snappy, would you? We don't have all day.'

She freezes, spatula in the air. Two of the men at the counter turn slowly to look at us, eyes wide.

'Um, August,' I say.

'What?' He looks genuinely puzzled.

'It's coming just as fast as I can make it,' the waitress says coldly.

'Fine. That's all I was asking,' says August. He leans toward me and continues in a lowered voice. 'What did I tell you? Women. Must be a full moon, or something.'

When I return to the lot, a selected few of the Benzini Brothers tents are up: the menagerie, the stable tent, and the cookhouse. The flag is flying, and the smell of sour grease permeates the air.

'Don't even bother,' says a man coming out. 'Fried dough and nothing but chicory to wash it down.'

'Thanks,' I say. 'I appreciate the warning.'

He spits and stalks off.

The Fox Brothers employees who remain are lined up in front of the privilege car. A desperate hopefulness surrounds them. A few smile and joke, but their laughter is high-pitched. Some stare straight ahead, their arms crossed. Others fidget and pace with bowed heads. One by one, they are summoned inside for an audience with Uncle Al.

The majority climb out defeated. Some wipe their eyes and confer quietly with others near the front of the line. Others stare stoically ahead before walking toward town.

Two dwarves enter together. They leave a few minutes later, grim-faced, pausing to talk to a small group of men. Then they trudge down the tracks, side by side, heads high, stuffed pillowcases slung over their shoulders.

I scan the crowd for the famous freak. There are certainly oddities: dwarves and midgets and giants, a bearded lady (Al's already got one, so she's probably out of luck), an enormously fat man (could get lucky if Al wants a matching set), and an assortment of generally sad-looking people and dogs. But no man with an infant sticking out of his chest.

After Uncle Al has made his selections, our workmen tear down all of the other circus's tents except for the stable and menagerie. The remaining Fox Brothers men, no longer on anyone's payroll, sit and watch, smoking and spitting wads of tobacco juice into tall patches of Queen Anne's lace and thistles.

When Uncle Al discovers that city officials have yet to itemize the Fox Brothers baggage stock, a handful of nondescript horses get spirited from one stable tent to another. Absorption, so to speak. And Uncle Al's not the only one with that idea – a handful of farmers hang around the edges of the lot, trailing lead ropes.

'They're just going to walk out of here with them?' I ask Pete.

'Probably,' he says. 'Don't bother me none so long as they don't touch ours. Keep your eyes open, though. It's gonna be a day or two before anybody knows what's what, and I don't want none of ours going missing.'

Our baggage stock has done double duty, and the big horses are foaming and blowing hard. I persuade a city official to open a hydrant so we can water them, but they're still without hay or oats.

August returns as we're filling the last trough.

'What the hell are you doing? Those horses have been on a train for three days – get out there on the pavement and hard-ass them so they don't go soft.'

'Hard-ass, my ass,' replies Pete. 'Look around you. Just what the hell do you think they've been doing for the last four hours?'

'You used our stock?'

'What the hell did you want me to use?'

'You should've used their baggage stock!'

'I don't know their fucking baggage stock!' shouts Pete. 'And what's the point of using their baggage stock if we're just going to have to hard-ass ours to keep 'em in shape, anyway!'

August's mouth opens. Then it shuts and he disappears.

Before long, trucks converge on the lot. One after another backs up to the cookhouse, and unbelievable amounts of food disappear behind it. The cookhouse crew gets right to work, and in no time at all, the boiler is running and the scent of good food – real food – wafts across the lot.

The food and bedding for the animals arrives shortly thereafter, in wagons rather than trucks. When we cart the hay into the stable tent, the horses nicker and rumble and stretch out their necks, snatching mouthfuls before it even hits the ground.

The animals in the menagerie are no less happy to see us – the chimps scream and swing from the bars of their dens, flashing toothy grins. The meat eaters pace. The hay burners toss their heads, snorting, squealing, and even barking in agitation.

I open the orangutan's door and set a pan of fruits, vegetables, and nuts on the floor. As I close it, her long arm reaches through the bars. She points at an orange in another pan.

'That? You want that?'

She continues to point, blinking at me with close-set eyes. Her features are concave, her face a wide platter fringed with red hair. She's the most outrageous and beautiful thing I've ever seen.

'Here,' I say, handing her the orange. 'You can have it.'

She takes it and sets it on the floor. Then she reaches out again. After several seconds of serious misgivings, I hold out my hand. She wraps her long fingers around it, then lets go. She sits on her haunches and peels her orange.

I stare in amazement. She was thanking me.

'So that's that,' says August as we emerge from the menagerie. He claps a hand on my shoulder. 'Join me for a drink, my boy. There's lemonade in Marlena's dressing tent, and not that sock juice from the juice joint either. We'll put a drop of whiskey in, hey hey?'

'I'll be along in a minute,' I say. 'I need to check the other menagerie.' Because of the peculiar status of the Fox Brothers baggage stock – whose numbers have been depleting all afternoon – I've seen for myself that they were fed and watered. But I have yet to lay eyes on their exotics or ring stock.

'No,' August says firmly. 'You'll join me now.'

I look over, surprised by his tone. 'All right. Sure,' I say. 'Do you know if they got fed and watered?'

'They'll get fed and watered. Eventually.'

'What?' I say.

'They'll get fed and watered. Eventually.'

'August, it's damned near ninety degrees. We can't leave them without at least water.'

'We can, and we will. It's how Uncle Al does business. He and the mayor will play chicken for a while, the mayor will figure out he doesn't have a fucking clue what to do with giraffes and zebras and lions, he'll drop his prices, and then – and only then – we'll move in.'

'I'm sorry, but I can't do that,' I say, turning to walk away.

His hand locks around my arm. He comes in front of

me and leans in so close his face is inches from mine. He lays a finger alongside my cheek. 'Yes, you can. They will get cared for. Just not yet. That's how it works.'

'That's bullshit.'

'Uncle Al has made an art form out of building this circus. We are what we are because of it. Who the hell knows what's in that tent? If there's nothing he wants, then fine. Who cares? But if there's something he wants and you mess with his business and he ends up paying more because of it, you better believe that Al is going to mess with you. Do you understand?' He speaks through clenched teeth. 'Do . . . you . . . understand?' he repeats, coming to a full stop after each word.

I stare straight into his unblinking eyes. 'Entirely,' I say.

'Good,' he says. He takes his finger out of my face and steps backward. 'Good,' he says again, nodding and allowing his face to relax. He forces a laugh. 'I'll tell you what, that whiskey will go down well.'

'I think I'll pass.'

He watches me for a moment and then shrugs. 'Suit yourself,' he says.

I take a seat some distance from the tent housing the abandoned animals, watching it with increasing desperation. The sidewall billows inward from a sudden gust of wind. There isn't even a cross draft. I have never been more aware of the heat beating down on my own head and the dryness of my own throat. I remove my hat and wipe a gritty arm across my forehead.

When the orange and blue flag goes up over the cookhouse for dinner, a handful of new Benzini Brothers employees join the lineup, identifiable by the red dinner tickets they clutch in their hands. The fat man was lucky, as was the bearded lady and a handful of dwarves. Uncle Al took on only performers, although one unfortunate fellow found himself unemployed again within a matter of minutes when August caught him looking a little too appreciatively at Marlena as he exited the privilege car.

A few others try to join the lineup, and not a one of them gets by Ezra. His only job is to know everyone on the show, and by God, he's good at it. When he jerks his thumb at some unfortunate, Blackie steps forward to take care of it. One or two of the rejects manage to scarf a fistful of food before flying headfirst out of the cook-house.

Drab, silent men hang all around the perimeter with hungry eyes. As Marlena steps away from the steam tables, one of them addresses her. He's a tall man, gaunt, with deeply creased cheeks. Under different circumstances, he would probably be handsome.

'Lady – hey, lady. Can you spare a little? Just a piece of bread?'

Marlena stops and looks at him. His face is hollow, his eyes desperate. She looks at her plate.

'Aw, come on, lady. Have a heart. I ain't ate in two days.' He runs his tongue across cracked lips.

'Keep moving,' says August, taking Marlena's elbow and steering her firmly toward a table in the center of the tent. It's not our usual table, but I've noticed that people tend not to argue with August. Marlena sits silently, looking occasionally at the men outside the tent.

'Oh, it's no good,' she says, flinging her cutlery to the

table. 'I can't eat with those poor souls out there.' She stands and picks up her plate.

'Where are you going?' August says sharply.

Marlena stares down at him. 'How am I supposed to sit here and eat when they've had nothing for two days?'

'You are not giving that to him,' says August. 'Now *sit down.*'

People from several other tables turn to look. August smiles nervously at them and leans toward Marlena. 'Darling,' he says urgently, 'I know this is hard on you. But if you give that man food, it will encourage him to hang around, and then what? Uncle Al's already made his picks. He wasn't one of them. He's got to move on, that's all – and the sooner the better. It's for his own good. It's a kindness, really.'

Marlena's eyes narrow. She sets her plate down, stabs a pork chop with her fork, and slaps it on a piece of bread. She swipes August's bread, slaps it on the other side of the pork chop, and storms off.

'What do you think you're doing?' shouts August.

She walks straight to the gaunt man, picks up his hand, and plants the sandwich in it. Then she marches off to scattered applause and whistles from the working men's side of the tent.

August vibrates with anger, a vein pulsing at his temple. After a moment he rises, taking his plate. He tilts its contents into the trash and leaves.

I stare at my plate. It's piled high with pork chops, collard greens, mashed potatoes, and baked apples. I worked like a dog all day, but I can't eat a thing.

* * *

Although it's nearly seven, the sun is still high and the air heavy. The terrain is very different from what we left behind in the northeast. It's flat here, and dry as a bone. The lot is covered in long grass, but it's brown and trampled, crispy as hay. At the edges, near the tracks, tall weeds have taken over – tough plants with stringy stalks, small leaves, and compact flowers. Designed to waste energy on nothing but getting their blooms up toward the sun.

As I pass the stable tent, I see Kinko standing in its scant shade. Queenie squats in front of him, defecating loosely, scootching a few inches forward after each fresh burst of liquid.

'What's up?' I say, coming to a stop beside him.

Kinko glares at me. 'What the hell does it look like? She's got the trots.'

'What did she eat?'

'Who the fuck knows?'

I step forward and peer closely at one of the small puddles, checking for signs of parasites. She seems clear. 'See if the cookhouse has any honey.'

'Huh?' Kinko says, straightening up and squinting at me.

'Honey. If you can get hold of any slippery elm powder, add a bit of that as well. But a spoonful of honey should help on its own,' I say.

He frowns at me for a moment, arms akimbo. 'Okay,' he says doubtfully. Then turns back to his dog.

I walk on, eventually settling on a patch of grass some distance from the Fox Brothers menagerie. It stands in ominous desertion, as though there's a minefield around it. No one comes within twenty yards. The conditions inside must be deadly, but short of tying up Uncle Al and August and hijacking the water wagon, I can't think of a damned thing to do. I grow more and more desperate, until I can sit still no longer. I climb to my feet and go instead to our menagerie.

Even with the benefit of full water troughs and a cross-breeze, the animals are in a heat-induced stupor. The zebras, giraffes, and other hay burners remain on their feet but with their necks extended and eyes half-closed. Even the yak is motionless, despite the flies that buzz mercilessly around his ears and eyes. I swat a few away, but they land again immediately. It's hopeless.

The polar bear lies on his stomach, head and snout stretched in front of him. In repose he looks harmless – cuddly even, with most of his bulk concentrated in the lower third of his body. He takes a deep, halting breath and then exhales a long, rumbling groan. Poor thing. I doubt the temperature in the Arctic ever climbs anywhere close to this.

The orangutan lies flat on her back, arms and legs spread out. She turns her head to look at me, blinking mournfully as though apologizing for not making more of an effort.

It's okay, I say with my eyes. *I understand.*

She blinks once more and then turns her face so she's looking at the ceiling again.

When I get to Marlena's horses, they snort in recognition and flap their lips against my hands, which still smell like baked apples. When they find I have nothing for them, they lose interest and drift back into their semi-conscious state.

The cats lie on their sides, perfectly still, their eyes not quite closed. If it weren't for the steady rise and fall of their rib cages, I might think they were dead. I press my forehead up against the bars and watch them for a long time. Finally I turn to leave. I'm about three yards away when I suddenly turn back. It's just dawned on me that the floors of their dens are conspicuously clean.

Marlena and August are arguing so loudly I can hear them twenty yards off. I pause outside her dressing tent, not at all sure I want to interrupt. But neither do I want to listen – I finally steel myself and press my mouth to the flap.

'August! Hey, August!'

The voices drop. There's a shuffling, and someone shushing someone.

'What is it?' calls August.

'Did Clive feed the cats?'

His face appears in the crack of the flap. 'Ah. Yes. Well, that presented a bit of difficulty, but I've worked something out.'

'What?'

'It's coming tomorrow morning. Don't worry. They'll be fine. Oh Lord,' he says, craning his neck to see beyond me. 'What now?'

Uncle Al strides toward us in red waistcoat and top hat, his plaid-swaddled legs swallowing the ground. His grovelers follow, jogging in nervous spurts to keep up.

August sighs and holds the flap open for me. 'You might as well come in and have a seat. Looks like you're about to get your first business lesson.'

I duck inside. Marlena sits at her vanity, her arms folded and legs crossed. Her foot jiggles in anger.

'My dear,' says August. 'Collect yourself.'

'Marlena?' says Uncle Al from just behind the tent flap. 'Marlena? May I come in, dear? I need a word with August.'

Marlena smacks her lips and rolls her eyes. 'Yes, Uncle Al. Of course, Uncle Al. Won't you please come in, Uncle Al,' she intones.

The tent flap opens, and Uncle Al enters, perspiring visibly and beaming from ear to ear.

'The deal is done,' he says, coming to a stop in front of August.

'So you got him, then,' says August.

'Eh? What?' replies Uncle Al, blinking in surprise.

'The freak,' says August. 'Charles Whatsit.'

'No, no, no, never mind about him.'

'What do you mean, "never mind about him"?' says August. 'I thought he was the whole reason we came here. What happened?'

'What?' says Uncle Al vaguely. Heads pop out from behind him, shaking vehemently. One man makes the motion of slitting his throat.

August looks at them and sighs. 'Oh. Ringling got him.'

'Never mind that,' says Uncle Al. 'I have news – big news! You might even say jumbo-sized news!' He looks back at his followers, and is met with hearty guffaws. He swings around again. 'Guess.'

'I have no idea, Al,' says August.

He turns expectantly toward Marlena.

'I don't know,' she says crossly.

'We scored a bull!' Uncle Al shouts, spreading his arms wide in jubilation. His cane smacks a groveler, who leaps backward.

August's face freezes. 'What?'

'A bull! An elephant!'

'You have an elephant?'

'No, August – *you* have an elephant. Her name is Rosie, she's fifty-three, and she's perfectly brilliant. The best bull they had. I can't wait to see the act you come up with—' He closes his eyes, the better to summon up an image. His fingers wriggle in front of his face. He smiles in closed-eyed ecstasy. 'I'm thinking it involves Marlena. She can ride her during the parade and Grand Spec, and then you can follow with a feature act in the center ring. Oh, here!' He turns around and snaps his fingers. 'Where is it? Come on, come on, you idiots!'

A bottle of champagne appears. He presents it for Marlena's inspection with a deep bow. Then he unwinds the wire top and pops the cork.

Fluted glasses appear from somewhere behind him and are set up on Marlena's vanity.

Uncle Al pours a small amount into each and passes one to Marlena, August, and me.

He lifts the final one high. His eyes mist over. He sighs deeply and clasps a hand to his breast.

'It is my great pleasure to celebrate this momentous occasion with you – my dearest friends in the world.' He rocks forward on his spatted feet and squeezes out a real tear. It rolls over his fat cheek. 'Not only do we have a veterinarian – and a Cornell-educated one at that – we have a bull. A bull!' He sniffs with happiness and pauses, overcome. 'I have waited for this day for years. And this is just the beginning, my friends. We are in the big leagues now. A show to be reckoned with.'

There is scattered clapping from behind him. Marlena balances her glass on her knee. August holds his stiffly in front of him. Except for grasping the glass, he hasn't moved a muscle.

Uncle Al thrusts his champagne into the air. 'To the Benzini Brothers Most Spectacular Show on Earth!' he shouts.

'Benzini Brothers! Benzini Brothers!' cry voices from behind him. Marlena and August are silent.

Al drains his glass and tosses it to the nearest member of his entourage, who drops it into a jacket pocket and follows Al from the tent. The flap closes, and once again it's just the three of us.

There is a moment of utter stillness. Then August's head jerks, as though he's coming to.

'I guess we'd better go see this rubber mule,' he says, draining his glass in a single gulp. 'Jacob, you can see to those damned animals now. You happy?'

I look at him, wide-eyed. Then I also drain my glass. From the corner of my eye, I see Marlena do the same.

The Fox Brothers menagerie is now swarming with Benzini Brothers men. They run back and forth, filling troughs, tossing hay, and hauling away dung. Some sections of sidewall have been raised, creating a cross-breeze. I scan the tent as we enter, looking for animals in distress. Fortunately, they all look very much alive.

The elephant looms against the far sidewall, an enormous beast the color of storm clouds.

We push through the workmen and stop in front of her. She is gargantuan – at least ten feet tall at the shoulder. Her skin is mottled and cracked like a scorched riverbed from the tip of her trunk all the way down to her wide feet. Only her ears are smooth. She peers out at us with eerily human eyes. They're amber, set deep in her head, and fringed with outrageously long lashes.

'Good God,' says August.

Her trunk reaches out to us, moving like an independent creature. It waves in front of August, then Marlena, and finally, me. At the end of it, a fingerlike protrusion wiggles and grasps. The nostrils open and close, snuffing and blowing, and then the trunk retreats. It swings in front of her like a pendulum, an enormous and muscled worm. Its finger grasps stray pieces of hay from the ground and then drops them again. I watch the swaying trunk and wish it would come back. I hold my hand out in offering, but it doesn't return.

August stares in consternation, and Marlena simply stares. I don't know what to think. I've never encountered an animal this large. She rises almost four feet above my head.

'You the bull man?' says a man approaching from the right. His shirt is filthy and untucked, puffing out from behind his suspenders.

'I am the equestrian director and superintendent of animals,' replies August, drawing himself up to full height.

'Where's your bull man?' says the man, squirting a wad of tobacco juice from the corner of his mouth.

The elephant reaches out with her trunk and taps him on the shoulder. He whacks her and steps out of reach. The elephant opens her shovel-shaped mouth in what can only be described as a smile and starts to sway, keeping time with the movement of her trunk.

'Why do you want to know?' asks August.

'Just want a word with him, is all.'

'Why?'

'To let him know what he's in for,' says the man.

'How do you mean?'

'Show me your bull man, and I'll tell you.'

August grabs my arm and swings me forward. 'Him. This is my bull man. So what are we in for?'

The man looks at me, pushes his wad of tobacco deep in his cheek, and continues to address August.

'This here's the stupidest goddamned animal on the face of the earth.'

August looks stunned. 'I thought she was supposed to be the best bull. Al said she was the best bull.'

The man snorts and squirts a stream of brown saliva toward the great beast. 'If she was the best bull, why was she the only one left? You think you're the first show to turn up picking the bones? You didn't even get here for three days. Well, good luck on ya.' He turns to leave.

'Wait,' August says quickly. 'Tell me more. Is she a rogue?'

'Naw, just dumb as a bag of hammers.'

'Where did she come from?'

'An elephant tramp – some dirty Polack who dropped dead in Libertyville. City gave her up for a song. Wasn't no bargain though, 'cuz she ain't done a damned thing since but eat.'

August stares at him, pale. 'You mean she wasn't even with a circus?'

The man steps over the rope and disappears behind the elephant. He returns with a wooden rod about three feet long with a four-inch metal pick coming off the end.

'Here's your bull hook. You're gonna need it. Good luck on ya. As for me, if I never see another bull as long as I live it'll be too soon.' He spits again and walks away.

August and Marlena stare after him. I look back just in time to see the elephant pull her trunk from the trough. She lifts it, aims, and blasts the man with such force his hat sails off his head on a stream of water.

He stops, his hair and clothes dripping. He is still for a moment. Then he wipes his face, leans over to retrieve his hat, bows to the astonished audience of menagerie workers, and continues on his way.

TEN

August huffs and puffs and turns so red he's actually closer to purple. Then he marches off, presumably to have it out with Uncle Al.

Marlena and I glance at each other. By unspoken agreement, neither of us follows.

One by one the menagerie men leave. The animals, finally fed and watered, settle in for the night. At the end of a desperate day is peace.

Marlena and I are alone, holding various bits of foodstuff toward Rosie's inquisitive trunk. When its strange rubbery finger grabs a wisp of hay from my fingers, Marlena squeals with laughter. Rosie tosses her head and opens her mouth in a smile.

I turn to find Marlena staring at me. The only sounds from within the menagerie are shuffling, snorting, and quiet munching. Outside, in the distance, someone plays a harmonica – a haunting tune in triple time, although I can't place it.

I'm not sure how it happens – do I reach for her? does she reach for me? – but next thing I know she's in my arms and we're waltzing, dipping, and skipping in front of the low-slung rope. As we twirl, I catch sight of Rosie's raised trunk and smiling face.

Marlena pulls suddenly away.

I stand motionless, my arms still slightly raised, unsure what to do.

'Uh,' says Marlena, blushing furiously and looking at everything but me. 'Well. Yes. Let's go wait for August, shall we?'

I stare at her for a long moment. I want to kiss her. I want to kiss her more than I've ever wanted anything in my life.

'Yes,' I finally say. 'Yes. Let's.'

An hour later August returns to the stateroom. He storms in and slams the door. Marlena goes immediately to a cupboard.

'That useless son-of-a-bitch paid two thousand for that useless son-of-a-bitch bull,' he says, throwing his hat in the corner and ripping off his jacket. *Two thousand fucking clams!* He flops into the nearest chair and drops his head into his hands.

Marlena removes a bottle of blended whiskey, pauses, looks at August, and then puts it back. She reaches for the single malt instead.

'And that's not the worst of it – oh no,' says August,

ripping his tie loose and clawing at his shirt collar. 'You wanna know what else he did? *Hmmmm?* Go on, guess.'

He's looking at Marlena, who is utterly unperturbed. She pours a good four fingers' worth of whiskey into three tumblers.

'I said guess!' barks August.

'I don't know, I'm sure,' Marlena says calmly. She puts the cap back on the whiskey.

'He spent the rest of the money on a goddamned elephant car.'

Marlena turns, suddenly paying attention. 'He didn't pick up any performers?'

'Sure he did.'

'But—'

'Yes. Exactly,' says August, cutting her off.

Marlena hands him a glass, motions me over for mine, and then takes a seat.

I take a slug and wait as long as I can. 'Yes, well, both of you may know what the hell you're talking about, but I don't. Do you mind filling me in?'

August exhales through puffed cheeks and brushes away the shock of hair that has fallen across his forehead. He leans forward, his elbows on his knees. Then he lifts his face so his eyes are locked on mine. 'It means, *Jacob*, that we hired more people without having anywhere to put them. It means, *Jacob*, that Uncle Al has seized one of the working men's bunk cars and declared it a performers' sleeping car. And because he hired two women, he has to partition it. It means, *Jacob*, that in order to accommodate less than a dozen performers, we will now have sixty-four working men sleeping under wagons on the flats.'

'That's stupid,' I say. 'He should just fill the bunk car with whoever needs a bunk.'

'He can't do that,' says Marlena.

'Why not?'

'Because you can't mix working men and performers.'

'Isn't that exactly what Kinko and I are doing?'

'Ha!' August snorts and sits forward, a lopsided smirk etched on his face. 'Do tell us – please, I'm dying to know. How's that going?' He cocks his head and smiles.

Marlena takes a deep breath and crosses her legs. A moment later, that red leather shoe starts pumping up and down.

I throw my whiskey down my throat and leave.

It was a big whiskey, and it starts to take effect somewhere between the staterooms and the coaches. I'm clearly not the only one under the influence either – now that 'business' has been concluded, everyone connected with the Benzini Brothers Most Spectacular Show on Earth is letting off steam. The gatherings run the entire gamut, from celebratory soirées characterized by radio jazz and outbursts of laughter to the desultory gatherings of dirty men who huddle some distance from the train and pass around various types of intoxicant. I catch sight of Camel, who lifts a hand in greeting before passing along the Sterno fluid.

I hear thrashing in the long grass and pause to investigate. I see a woman's bare legs spread wide with a man between them. He grunts and ruts like a billy goat. His trousers are down around his knees, his hairy buttocks pumping up and down. She grasps his shirt in her fists, moaning with each thrust. It takes me a moment to realize what I'm looking at – when I do, I wrench my eyes away and wobble forward.

As I approach the ring stock car, I see people sitting on the open doorway and milling around outside.

There are even more inside. Kinko is lording over a party with a bottle in his hand and drunken hospitality on his face. When he catches sight of me, he trips and lurches forward. Hands reach out to catch him.

'Jacob! My man!' he shouts, his eyes fiercely bright. He shakes free of his friends and straightens up. 'Folks – friends!' he calls across the crowd of about thirty people who take up the space usually occupied by Marlena's horses. He walks over and places his arm around my waist. 'This is my dear, dear friend Jacob.' He pauses to take a swig from the bottle. 'Please make him welcome,' he says. 'As a favor to me.'

His guests whistle and laugh. Kinko laughs until he coughs. He lets go of my waist and waves his hand in front of his purple face until he stops sputtering. Then he throws his arm around the waist of the man next to us. They stagger off.

Since the goat room is jammed tight, I head for the other end of the car, where Silver Star used to reside, and slump down against the slatted wall.

The pile of straw next to me rustles. I reach out and poke it, hoping I won't find a rat. Queenie's white tail stump is visible for only a moment before she burrows further into the straw, like a crab in sand.

From here on in, I'm not entirely sure of the order. Bottles are passed to me, and I'm pretty sure I drink from most of them. Before long, things are swimming and I'm filled with the warmth of human kindness toward everyone and everything. People have their arms around my shoulders, and I have mine around theirs. We laugh uproariously – at what, I don't remember, but everything is a riot.

There is some game where you have to toss something, and if you miss the target you have to take a drink. I miss quite a lot. Eventually I begin to think I'm going to throw up and crawl away, to the great mirth of everyone.

I'm sitting in the corner. I can't quite remember getting here, but I'm leaning against the wall with my head resting on my knees. I do so wish the world would stop spinning, but it doesn't, so I try leaning my head back against the wall instead.

'Well now, what have we here?' says a sultry voice from somewhere very nearby.

My eyes pop open. A foot's length of tightly packed cleavage is directly under my nose. I run my eyes up it until I see a face. It's Barbara. I blink quickly, trying to see only one of her. Oh God – it's no use. But no – wait. It's okay. It's not multiple Barbaras. It's multiple women.

'Hi, honey,' says Barbara, reaching out and stroking my face. 'You doing okay?'

'*Mmm,*' I say, trying to nod.

Her fingertips linger under my chin as she turns to the blonde crouching beside her. 'So young. Oh, he's cute as a button, isn't he, Nell?'

Nell takes a drag from a cigarette and blows the smoke from the side of her mouth. 'Sure is. Don't think I've seen him before.'

'He was helping out at the cooch tent a few nights ago,'

says Barbara. She turns back to me. 'What's your name, honey?' she says softly, running the backs of her fingers up and down my cheek.

'Jacob,' I say, around the edges of a belch.

'Jacob,' she says. 'Oh, say, I know who you are. He's the one Walter was talking about,' she says to Nell. 'He's brand new, a First of May. Handled himself real well at the cooch tent.'

She grabs my chin and raises it, gazing deep into my eyes. I try to return the favor but am having some trouble focusing. 'Oh, you are a sweet thing. So, tell me, Jacob – you ever been with a woman?'

'I . . . uh . . . ,' I say. 'Uh . . .'

Nell giggles. Barbara leans back and puts her hands on her waist. 'Whadya think? Wanna give him a proper welcome?'

'We practically have to,' says Nell. 'A First of May *and* a virgin?' Her hand slips between my legs and slides over my crotch. My head, which had been wobbling on its stem, snaps upright. 'You think his hair is red down there, too?' she says, cupping me in her palm.

Barbara leans forward, unclasps my hands, and lifts one to her mouth. She turns it over, runs a long nail across the palm and then stares me in the eye while running her tongue along the same path. Then she takes my hand and places it on her left breast, right where the nipple must be.

Oh God. Oh God. I'm touching a breast. Through a dress, but still—

Barbara stands up for a moment, smoothes her skirt, looks furtively around, and then crouches. I'm pondering this change of position when she takes hold of my hand again. This time she pulls it under her skirt and presses my fingers against hot, moist silk.

I catch my breath. The whiskey, the moonshine, the gin, the God-knows-what – all of it dissipates instantly. She moves my hand up and down, over her strange and wonderful valleys.

Oh shit. I may come right now.

'*Hmmmm?*' she purrs, rearranging my hand so that my middle finger presses further into her. Warm silk bulges around both sides of my finger, pulsing under my touch. She removes my hand, places it back on my knee, and then gives my crotch an experimental squeeze.

'*Mmmmm,*' she says, her eyes half-closed. 'He's ready, Nell. Damn, I love them at this age.'

The rest of the night passes in epileptic flashes. I am aware of being propped up between two women, but I think I fall out the door of the stock car. At least, I am aware of finding myself cheek down in the dirt. Then I'm swept upward again and jostled along in the dark until I'm sitting on the edge of a bed.

There are definitely two Barbaras now. And two of the other one, as well. Nell, was it?

Barbara steps backward and raises her arms in the air. She throws her head back and runs her hands over her body, dancing and moving by candle-light. I'm interested – there is no question about that. But I simply can't sit upright anymore. So I fall back.

Someone's yanking on my pants. I mumble something, not sure what, but I don't think it's encouragement. I'm suddenly not feeling well.

Oh God. She's touching me – *it* – stroking experimentally. I prop myself up on my elbows and look down. It's limp, a tiny pink turtle hiding in its shell. It also seems to be stuck to my leg. She peels it free, delves both her hands between my thighs to spread them, and reaches down for my balls. She rests them on one hand, juggling them like eggs while she examines my penis. It flops hopelessly under her manipulations while I watch, mortified.

The other woman – now there's only one again, how the hell am I ever going to keep this straight – lies next to me on the bed. She fishes a skinny breast from her dress and lifts it to my mouth. She rubs it all over my face. Now her lipsticked mouth is coming at me, a gaping maw with tongue extended. I turn my head to the right, where there is no woman. Then I feel a mouth close around the head of my penis.

I gasp. The women giggle, but it's a purring sound, an encouraging sound, as they continue trying to get a response.

Oh God, oh God, she's sucking it. *Sucking* it, for God's sake.

I'm not going to be able to—

Oh my God, I need to—

I turn my head and hurl the unfortunately varied contents of my stomach onto Nell.

There's a hideous scraping noise. Then the blackness above me is broken by a sliver of light.

Kinko peers in at me. 'Wake up, sunshine. Your boss is looking for you.'

He's holding a lid open. All of which starts to make sense, because as my cramped body realizes my brain is open for business, it soon becomes clear I am stuffed into a trunk.

Kinko props the lid open and walks away. I work my bent neck free and struggle into a sitting position. The trunk is in a tent, surrounded by rack after rack of vibrant costumes, props, and vanities with mirrors.

'Where am I?' I croak. I cough and try to clear my parched throat.

'Clown Alley,' says Kinko, fingering some paint jars on a dresser.

I lift an arm to cover my eyes and notice it is clad in silk. A red silk dressing gown, to be exact. A red silk dressing gown that is wide open. I look down and discover that someone has shaved my genitals.

I snatch the edges of the gown together, wondering if Kinko saw.

Dear God, what did I do last night? I have no idea. Nothing but scraps of memory, and—

Oh God. I threw up on a woman.

I struggle to my feet, tying the dressing gown. I wipe my forehead, which feels unusually slick. My hand comes away white.

'What the—?' I say, staring at my hand.

Kinko turns and hands me a mirror. I take it with great trepidation. When I raise it to my face, a clown looks back at me.

I poke my head out of the tent, look left and right, and then streak across to the stock car. I am followed by guffaws and catcalls.

'*Whooeeee*, look at that hot mama!'

'Hey, Fred – check out the new cooch girl!'

'Say, honey – got plans tonight?'

I dive into the goat room and slam the door, leaning against it. I breathe heavily, listening until the laughter outside dies down. I grab a rag and wipe my face again. I rubbed it raw before I left Clown Alley, but somehow I still don't believe it's clean. I don't think any part of me will ever be clean again. And the worst part is that I don't even know what I did. I have only snippets, and as horri-fying as those are it's even more horrifying not knowing what happened in between.

It suddenly occurs to me that I have no idea whether I'm still a virgin.

I reach inside the dressing gown and scratch my stubbly balls.

Kinko comes in a few minutes later. I'm lying on my bedroll, my arms over my head.

'You'd better get your ass out there,' he says. 'He's still looking for you.'

Something snuffles in my ear. I lift my head and bang into a wet nose. Queenie leaps backward as though launched from a catapult. She surveys me from a distance of three feet, sniffing cautiously. Oh, I bet I'm just a medley of smells this morning. I drop my head again.

'You want to get fired, or what?' Kinko says.

'At this point, I really don't care,' I mumble.

'What?'

'I'm leaving anyway.'

'What the hell are you talking about?'

I can't answer. I can't tell him that not only have I

disgraced myself beyond belief or redemption, but I have also failed at my first opportunity to have sex – something I've thought about pretty much constantly for the last eight years. Not to mention throwing up on one of the women who was offering and then passing out and having somebody shave my balls and paint my face and stuff me into a trunk. Although he must know at least parts of it, since he knew where to find me this morning. Perhaps he was even involved in the festivities.

'Don't be a pussy,' he says. 'You want to end up walking the tracks like those poor bums out there? Now get on out there before you get yourself fired.'

I remain inert.

'I said get up!'

'What do you care?' I grumble. 'And stop shouting. My head hurts.'

'Just get the hell up or I'll hurt the rest of you, too!'

'All right! Just stop yelling!'

I drag myself upright and throw him a dirty look. My head pounds and it feels as though lead weights are tied to each of my joints. Since he continues watching me, I turn toward the wall, keeping the red gown on until I pull my pants up in an effort to hide my hairlessness. Nevertheless, my face burns.

'Oh, and a word to the wise?' says Kinko. 'Some flowers for Barbara wouldn't go amiss. The other one's just a whore, but Barbara's a friend.'

I am so flooded with shame my consciousness flickers. After the urge to faint passes, I stare at the ground, sure I'll never bring myself to look anyone in the eyes again.

* * *

The Fox Brothers train has been moved off the siding, and the hotly disputed elephant car is now hitched directly behind our engine, where the ride will be smoothest. It has vents instead of slats and is made of metal. The boys from the Flying Squadron are busy tearing down tents – they've already dropped most of the larger ones, revealing the buildings of Joliet in the background. A small crowd of towners has gathered to watch the activity.

I find August in the menagerie tent, standing in front of the elephant.

'Move!' he screams, waving the bull hook around her face.

She swings her trunk and blinks.

'I said *move!*' He steps behind her and thwacks her in the back of the leg. 'Move, goddammit!' Her eyes narrow and her enormous ears flatten against her head.

August catches sight of me and freezes. He drops the bull hook to his side. 'Rough night?' he sneers.

A blush prickles up the back of my neck and spreads over my entire head.

'Never mind. Get a stick and help me move this stupid beast.'

Pete comes up behind him, twisting his hat in his hands. 'August?'

August turns, furious. 'Oh, for Christ's sake. What is it, Pete? Can't you see I'm busy?'

'The cat meat is here.'

'Good. Take care of it. We don't have much time.'

'What exactly do you want me to do with it?'

'What the hell do you think I want you to do with it?'

'But, boss—' says Pete, clearly distressed.

'Goddammit!' says August. The vein on his temple bulges dangerously. 'Do I have to do every damned thing myself? Here,' he says, thrusting the bull hook at me. 'Teach the brute something. Anything will do. As far as I can tell, all she knows how to do is shit and eat.'

I take the bull hook and watch as he storms from the tent. I'm still staring after him when the elephant's trunk sweeps past my face, blowing warm air into my ear. I spin and find myself looking into an amber eye. It blinks at me. My gaze shifts from that eye to the bull hook in my hand.

I look back up at the eye and again it blinks. I lean over and lay the bull hook on the ground.

She swings her trunk across the ground in front of her, fanning her ears like enormous leaves. Her mouth opens in a smile.

'Hi,' I say. 'Hi, Rosie. I'm Jacob.'

After a moment's hesitation, I extend my hand, just a bit. The trunk whooshes past, blowing. Emboldened, I reach out and lay a hand on her shoulder. Her skin is rough and stubbly and surprisingly warm.

'Hi,' I say again, giving her an experimental pat.

Her windsail of an ear moves forward and then back, and the trunk returns. I touch it tentatively, and then stroke it. I am entirely enamored, and so engrossed that I don't see August until he comes to an abrupt stop in front of me.

'What the hell is wrong with you people this morning? I should fire every goddamned one of you, what with Pete not wanting to take care of business and you pulling a disappearing act and then playing kissy-face with the bull. Where's the damned bull hook?'

I lean over and retrieve it. August snatches it from my hand, and the elephant's ears settle back against her head.

'Here, princess,' says August, addressing me. 'I have a job you might be able to handle. Go find Marlena. Make sure she doesn't go behind the menagerie for a bit.'

'Why?'

August takes a deep breath and grips the bull hook so hard his knuckles whiten. 'Because I said so. All right?' he says through clenched teeth.

Naturally, I head behind the menagerie to find out what Marlena's not supposed to see. I round the corner just as Pete slits the throat of a decrepit gray horse. The horse screams as blood shoots six feet from the gaping hole in its neck.

'Jesus Christ!' I yelp, taking a step backward.

The horse's heart slows, and the spurts weaken. Eventually the horse drops to its knees and crashes forward. It scrapes the ground with its front hooves and then falls still. Its eyes are open wide. A lake of dark blood spreads from its neck.

Pete glances up at me, still leaning over the twitching animal.

An emaciated bay horse is tethered to a stake beside him, out of its head with terror. Its nostrils are flared, showing red, its muzzle straight in the air. The lead rope is so taut it looks like it's going to snap. Pete steps across the dead horse, grabs the rope near the bay's head, and slices its throat. More spurting blood, more death throes, another collapsing body.

Pete stands with his arms slack at his sides, his sleeves rolled up past his elbows, still holding the bloody knife.

He watches the horse until it dies and then raises his face to me.

He wipes his nose, spits, and gets back to the task at hand.

'Marlena? You in there?' I say, rapping on the door of their stateroom.

'Jacob?' calls a small voice from inside.

'Yes,' I say.

'Come in.'

She's standing by one of the open windows, looking toward the front of the train. As I enter, she turns her head. Her eyes are wide, her face drained of blood.

'Oh, Jacob . . .' Her voice is wavering. She's on the verge of tears.

'What is it? What's the matter?' I say, crossing the room.

She presses her hand to her mouth and turns back to the window.

August and Rosie are making their noisy way to the front of the train. Their progress is excruciating, and everyone on the lot has stopped to watch.

August smacks her from behind, and Rosie hurries a few steps forward. When August catches up, he whacks her again, this time hard enough that she raises her trunk, bellows, and scampers sideways. August lets loose a long string of curses and runs up beside her, swinging the bull hook and driving the pick end into her shoulder. Rosie whimpers and this time doesn't move an inch. Even from this distance, we can see that she's trembling.

Marlena chokes back a sob. On impulse I reach for

her hand. When I find it, she clutches my fingers so tightly they hurt.

After a few more thumps and whacks, Rosie catches sight of the elephant car at the front of the train. She lifts her trunk and trumpets, taking off at a thunderous run. August disappears in a cloud of dust behind her, and panicked roustabouts dive out of her way. She climbs aboard with obvious relief.

The dust subsides and August reappears, shouting and waving his arms. Diamond Joe and Otis trudge up to the elephant car, slowly, matter-of-factly, and set about shutting it.

ELEVEN

Kinko spends the first few hours of the jump to Chicago using bits of beef jerky to teach Queenie, who has apparently recovered from her diarrhea, to walk on her hind legs.

'Up! Up, Queenie, up! Atta girl. Good girl!'

I'm lying on my bedroll, curled up and facing the wall. My physical state is every bit as sorry as my mental one, and that's saying something. My head is crammed with visions, all jumbled up like a ball of string: My parents alive, depositing me at Cornell. My parents dead, and the green and white floor tiles beneath them. Marlena, waltzing with me in the menagerie. Marlena this morning, fighting tears at the window. Rosie and her snuffing, inquisitive trunk. Rosie, ten feet tall and solid as a mountain, whimpering under August's blows. August, tap-dancing across the roof of a moving train. August as a bull-hook-wielding madman. Barbara, swinging those melons onstage. Barbara and Nell, and their expert ministrations.

The memory of last night hits me like a wrecking ball. I squeeze my eyes shut, trying to force my mind to go blank, but it won't. The more distressing the memory, the more persistent its presence.

Eventually Queenie's excited yipping stops. After a few seconds, the springs on Kinko's cot squeak. Then there's silence. He's watching me. I can feel it. I roll over to face him.

He's on the edge of the cot, his bare feet crossed and his red hair mussed. Queenie creeps into his lap, leaving her hind legs sticking straight out, like a frog.

'So, what's your story, anyway?' says Kinko.

The sunlight flashes like knives through the slats behind him. I cover my eyes and grimace.

'No, I mean it. Where'd you come from?'

'Nowhere,' I say, rolling back to the wall. I pull my pillow over my head.

'What are you so sore about? Last night?'

The mere mention causes bile to rise in my throat.

'You embarrassed or something?'

'Oh, for Christ's sake, would you just leave me alone?' I snap.

He is quiet. After a few seconds I roll over again. He's still looking at me, fingering Queenie's ears. She licks his other hand, wagging her stump.

'Sorry,' I say. 'I've never done anything like that before.'

'Well, yeah – I think that was pretty obvious.'

I grasp my pounding head with both hands. What I wouldn't give for about a gallon of water—

'Look, it's no big deal,' he continues. 'You'll learn to hold your liquor. As for the other stuff – well, I had to get you back for the other day. The way I see it, this makes us even. In fact, I may even owe you one. That honey stopped Queenie up like a cork. So, you know how to read?'

I blink a few times. 'Huh?' I say.

'You wanna read maybe, instead of just lying there stewing?'

'I think I'll just lie here stewing.' I squeeze my eyes shut and cover them with my hand. My brain feels too big for my skull, my eyes hurt, and I may throw up. And my balls itch.

'Suit yourself,' he says.

'Maybe some other time,' I say.

'Sure. Whatever.'

A pause.

'Kinko?'

'Yeah?'

'I appreciate the offer.'

'Sure.'

A longer pause.

'Jacob?'

'Yeah?'

'You can call me Walter if you want.'

Under my hand, my eyes open wide.

His cot squeaks as he rearranges himself. I sneak a look through splayed fingers. He folds his pillow in half, lies back, and grabs a book from the crate. Queenie settles at his feet, watching me. Her eyebrows twitch with worry.

* * *

The train approaches Chicago in the late afternoon. Despite my pounding head and aching body, I stand in the open door of the stock car craning my neck to get a good look. After all, this is the city of the St Valentine's Day Massacre, of jazz, gangsters, and speakeasies.

I can see a handful of tall buildings in the distance, and just as I'm trying to make out which one of them is the fabled Allerton we reach the stockyards. There are miles of them, and we slow to a crawl as we pass. The buildings are flat and ugly, and the pens, crammed with panicked, lowing cattle and filthy, snuffing pigs, butt right up against the tracks. But that is nothing compared to the noises and smells coming from the buildings: within minutes the bloody stench and piercing shrieks send me flying back to the goat room to press my nose against the mildewed horse blanket – anything to replace the smell of death.

My stomach is fragile enough that even though the lot is well beyond the stockyards, I stay inside the stock car until everything's been set up. Afterward, seeking the company of animals, I enter the menagerie and tour the perimeter.

It's impossible to describe how tenderly I suddenly feel toward them – hyenas, camels, and all. Even the polar bear, who sits on his backside chewing his four-inch claws with his four-inch teeth. A love for these animals wells up in me suddenly, a flash flood, and there it is, solid as an obelisk and viscous as water.

My father felt it his duty to continue to treat animals long after he stopped getting paid. He couldn't stand by and watch a horse colic or a cow labor with a breech calf

even though it meant personal ruin. The parallel is un-
deniable. There is no question that I am the only thing
standing between these animals and the business prac-
tices of August and Uncle Al, and what my father would
do – what my father would want *me* to do – is look after
them, and I am filled with that absolute and unwavering
conviction. No matter what I did last night, I cannot leave
these animals. I am their shepherd, their protector. And
it's more than a duty. It's a covenant with my father.

One of the chimps needs a cuddle, so I let him ride
on my hip as I make my way around the tent. I reach a
wide empty spot, and realize it's for the elephant. August
must be having trouble getting her out of her car. If I
were feeling at all kindly toward him, I'd see if I could
help. But I'm not.

'Hey, Doc,' says Pete. 'Otis thinks one of the giraffes
has a cold. You wanna take a look?'

'Sure,' I say.

'Come on, Bobo,' says Pete, reaching for the chimp.

The chimp's hairy arms and legs tighten around me.

'Come on now,' I say, trying to pluck his arms free. 'I'll
come back.'

Bobo moves not a muscle.

'Come on now,' I say.

Nothing.

'All right. One last hug and that's it,' I say, pressing my
face against his dark fur.

The chimp flashes a toothy smile and kisses me on the
cheek. Then he climbs down, slips his hand inside Pete's,
and ambles off on bowed legs.

There's a small amount of pus flowing down the giraffe's

long nasal passage. It's not something I'd find alarming in a horse, but since I don't know giraffes I decide to play it safe and fit her with a neck poultice, an operation that requires a stepladder with Otis at the bottom, handing me supplies.

The giraffe is timid and beautiful and quite possibly the strangest creature I've ever seen. Her legs and neck are delicate, her body sloped and covered with markings like puzzle pieces. Strange furry knobs poke out from the top of her triangular head, above her large ears. Her eyes are huge and dark, and she has the velvet-soft lips of a horse. She's wearing a halter and I hold on to it, but mostly she stays still as I swab out her nostrils and swaddle her throat in flannel. When I'm finished, I climb down.

'Can you cover for me for a bit?' I ask Otis, wiping my hands on a rag.

'Sure. Why?'

'I've got somewhere to go,' I say.

Otis's eyes narrow. 'You ain't moping off, are you?'

'What? No. Of course not.'

'You better tell me now, 'cuz if you're moping off, I ain't covering for you while you do it.'

'I'm not moping off. Why would I mope off?'

'On account of . . . Well, you know. Certain events.'

'No! I'm not moping off. Just let it drop, would you?'

Is there no one who hasn't heard the details of my disgrace?

I head out on foot and after a couple of miles find myself in a residential area. The houses are in disrepair, and many have boards over their windows. I pass a breadline – a long row of shabby dispirited people leading to the door of a mission. A black boy offers to shine my shoes, and while I'd like to let him, I don't have a cent to my name.

Finally I see a Catholic church. I sit in a pew near the back for a long time, staring at the stained glass behind the altar. Although I want absolution dearly, I am unable to face confession. Eventually I leave the pew and go to light votive candles for my parents.

As I turn to leave, I catch sight of Marlena – she must have come in while I was in the alcove. I can only see her back, but it's definitely her. She's in the front pew, wearing a pale yellow dress and matching hat. Her throat is delicate, her shoulders square. A few curls of light brown hair peek from beneath the brim of her hat.

She kneels on a cushion to pray, and a vice grip tightens around my heart.

I retreat from the church before I can further damage my soul.

When I return to the lot, Rosie has been installed in the menagerie tent. I don't know how, and I don't ask.

She smiles when I approach and then rubs her eye, curling the tip of her trunk like a fist. I watch her for a couple of minutes and then step over the rope. Her ears flatten and her eyes narrow. My heart sinks, because I think she's responding to me. Then I hear his voice.

'Jacob?'

I watch Rosie for a few seconds longer and then turn to face him.

'Look here,' says August, scrubbing the toe of his boot in the dirt. 'I know I've been a bit rough on you the last couple of days.'

I'm supposed to say something here, something to make him feel better, but I don't. I'm not feeling particularly conciliatory.

'What I'm trying to say is that I went a bit far. Pressures of the job, you know. They can get to a man.' He holds out his hand. 'So, friends again?'

I pause a few seconds longer, and then take his hand. He is my boss, after all. Having made the decision to stay, it would be stupid to get myself fired.

'Good man,' he says, grasping it firmly and clapping me on the shoulder with his other hand. 'I'll take you and Marlena out tonight. Make it up to you both. I know a great little place.'

'What about the show?'

'There's no point in doing a show. No one knows we're here yet. That's what happens when you blow your route and wildcat all over the damned place.' He sighs. 'But Uncle Al knows best. Apparently.'

'I don't know,' I say. 'Last night was kind of . . . rough.'

'Hair of the dog, Jacob! Hair of the dog. Come by at nine.' He smiles brightly and marches off.

I watch him leave, struck by how very much I don't want to spend any time with him – and by how very much I'd like to spend time with Marlena.

The door to the stateroom swings open, revealing Marlena, gorgeous in red satin.

'What?' she says, looking down at herself. 'Is there

something on my dress?' She twists, inspecting her body and legs.

'No,' I say. 'You look swell.'

She raises her eyes to mine.

August comes out from behind the green curtain, wearing white tie. He takes one look at me and says, 'You can't go like that.'

'I don't have anything else.'

'Then you'll have to borrow. Go on. Hurry up, though. The taxi's waiting.'

We zip through a maze of parking lots and back alleys before coming to an abrupt stop at a corner in an industrial area. August climbs out and hands the driver a rolled bill.

'Come on,' he says, extracting Marlena from the back-seat. I follow.

We're in an alley surrounded by large redbrick warehouses. The streetlights illuminate the asphalt's rough texture. On one side of the alley trash is blown up against the wall. On the other are parked cars – roadsters, coupes, sedans, even limousines – all flashy, all new.

August stops in front of a recessed wooden door. He raps sharply and then stands, tapping his foot. A rectangular peephole slides open, revealing male eyes under a single bushy brow. The sounds of a party pulse from behind him.

'Yeah?'

'We're here for the show,' says August.

'What show?'

'Why, Frankie's, of course,' August says, smiling.

The peephole shuts. There's clicking and clanking

followed by the unmistakable sound of a deadbolt. The door swings open.

The man looks us over quickly. Then he beckons us inside and slams the door. We step through a tiled foyer, past a coat check with uniformed clerks, and descend a few steps into a marble-floored dance hall. Elaborate crystal chandeliers hang from the high ceiling. A band plays on a raised platform, and the dance floor is jammed with couples. Tables and U-shaped booths surround the dance floor. Up a few steps and along the back wall is a wood-paneled bar with tuxedoed bartenders and hundreds of bottles lined up on shelves in front of a smoky mirror.

Marlena and I wait in one of the leather-lined booths while August goes to get the drinks. Marlena watches the band. Her legs are crossed and that foot is bobbing again. She moves it in time with the music, rolling her ankle.

A glass is plunked in front of me. A second later August drops down beside Marlena. I investigate the glass and find it contains ice cubes and scotch.

'You okay?' says Marlena.

'Fine,' I say.

'You look a little green,' she continues.

'Our Jacob here is suffering from a teensy hangover,' says August. 'We're trying the hair of the dog.'

'Well, make sure you let me know if I need to get out of the way,' Marlena says dubiously, turning back to the band.

August lifts his glass. 'To friends!'

Marlena looks back just long enough to locate her

frothy drink and then holds it over the table while we clink. She sips daintily from her straw, fingering it with lacquered nails. August tosses his scotch back. The second mine hits my lips, my tongue instinctively blocks its progress. August is watching, so I pretend to swallow before setting the glass down.

'There you are, my boy. A few more of those and you'll be right as rain.'

I don't know about me, but after a second brandy alexander Marlena certainly comes to life. She drags August onto the dance floor. As he twirls her around, I lean over and tip the contents of my scotch into a potted palm.

Marlena and August return to the booth, flushed from dancing. Marlena sighs and fans herself with a menu. August lights a cigarette.

His eyes land on my empty glass. 'Oh – I see I've been neglectful,' he says. He stands up. 'Same again?'

'Oh, what the hell,' I say without enthusiasm. Marlena simply nods, once again absorbed by what's happening on the dance floor.

August is gone about thirty seconds when she leaps up and grabs my hand.

'What are you doing?' I say, laughing as she yanks my arm.

'Come on! Let's dance!'

'What?'

'I love this song!'

'No – I—'

But it's no use. I'm already on my feet. She drags me onto the dance floor, jiving and snapping her fingers.

When we're surrounded by other couples she turns to me. I take a deep breath and then take her in my arms. We wait a couple of beats and then we're off, floating around the dance floor in a swirling sea of people.

She's light as air – doesn't miss a step, and that's a feat considering how clumsy I am. And it's not as though I don't know how to dance, because I do. I don't know what the hell is wrong with me. I'm sure as hell not drunk.

She spins away from me and then returns, passing beneath my arm so her back is pressed against me. My forearm rests on her collarbone, skin to skin. Her chest rises and falls under my arm. Her head is under my chin, her hair fragrant, her body warm from exertion. And then she's gone again, unwinding herself like a ribbon.

When the music stops, the dancers whistle and clap with their hands above their heads, and none more enthusiastically than Marlena. I glance over at our booth. August is staring with his arms crossed, seething. Startled, I step away from Marlena.

'*Raid!*'

There is one frozen moment, and then the second cry goes up.

'*RAID! Everybody get out!*'

I'm swept forward in a crush of bodies. People scream, shoving past each other in a frenzied attempt to reach the exit. Marlena is a few people in front of me, looking back through bobbing heads and desperate faces.

'Jacob!' she cries. 'Jacob!'

I struggle toward her, launching myself through bodies. I clasp a hand in a sea of flesh and know it's Marlena's from the look on her face. I grip her tightly, scanning the crowd for August. All I see are strangers.

Marlena and I are ripped apart at the doorway. Seconds later I'm expelled into an alley. People are screaming, piling into cars. Engines start, horns bleat, and tires squeal.

'*Come on! Come on! Get the hell out of here!*'

'*Move it!*'

Marlena appears from nowhere and grabs my hand. We flee as sirens blare and whistles blow. When the crackle of gunfire rings out, I grab Marlena and duck into a smaller alley.

'Hang on,' she gasps, pausing and hopping on one foot as she removes a shoe. She grasps my arm as she pulls off the other. 'Okay,' she says, holding both shoes in one hand.

We run until the sirens and crowds and screeching tires are out of earshot, winding our way through back streets and alleys. Finally, we stop under an iron fire escape, gasping for air.

'Oh my Lord,' says Marlena. 'Oh my Lord, that was close. I wonder if August got out.'

'I sure hope so,' I say, also struggling for air. I lean over, resting my hands on my thighs.

After a moment, I look up at Marlena. She's staring straight at me, breathing through her mouth. She starts laughing hysterically.

'What?' I say.

'Oh, nothing,' she says. 'Nothing.' She continues to laugh, but looks perilously close to tears.

'What is it?' I say.

'Oh,' she says, sniffing and bringing a finger to the

corner of her eye. 'It's just a crazy damned life, that's all. Do you have a handkerchief?'

I pat my pockets, and retrieve one. She takes it and wipes her forehead, then dabs the rest of her face. 'Oh, but I'm a mess. And just look at my stockings!' she shrieks, pointing at her shoeless feet. Her toes poke through their ruined ends. 'Oh, and they're *silk*, too!' Her voice is high and unnatural.

'Marlena?' I say gently. 'Are you all right?'

She presses her fist to her mouth and moans. I reach for her arm but she turns away. I expect her to stay facing the wall, but instead she continues turning, spinning in some kind of dervish. On the third rotation, I take her by the shoulders and press my mouth to hers. She stiffens and gasps, sucking air from between my lips. A moment later she softens. Her fingertips rise to my face. Then she yanks away, taking several steps backward and staring at me with stricken eyes.

'Jacob,' she says, her voice cracking. 'Oh God – Jacob.'

'Marlena.' I step forward and then stop. 'I'm so sorry. I shouldn't have done that.'

She stares at me with a hand pressed to her mouth. Her eyes are dark hollows. Then she leans against the wall, pulling on her shoes and looking at the asphalt.

'Marlena, please.' I hold my hands out helplessly.

She adjusts her second shoe and rushes off. She stumbles and wobbles forward.

'Marlena!' I say, running a few steps.

Her speed increases and she brings a hand up alongside her face, shielding it from my view.

I stop.

She keeps walking, tap-tapping down the alley.

'Marlena! Please!'

I watch until she turns the corner. Her hand remains beside her face, presumably in case I'm still there.

It takes me several hours to find my way back to the lot.

I pass legs sticking out of doorways, and signs advertising breadlines. I pass signs in windows that say CLOSED, and it's clear they don't mean for the night. I pass signs that say NO MEN WANTED and signs in second-story windows that say TRAINING FOR THE CLASS STRUGGLE. I pass a sign in a grocery store that says

DON'T HAVE MONEY?

WHAT HAVE YOU GOT?

WE'LL TAKE ANYTHING!

I pass a newspaper box, and the headline reads PRETTY BOY FLOYD STRIKES AGAIN: MAKES OFF WITH $4,000 AS CROWDS CHEER.

Less than a mile from the lot, I pass a hobo jungle. There's a fire in the center and people stretched out around it. Some are awake, sitting forward and staring into the fire. Some are lying back on folded clothes. I'm close enough to see their faces and to register that most of them are young – younger than me. There are some girls there, too, and one couple is copulating. They're not even in the bushes, just a little farther from the fire than the others. One or two of the boys watch in a disinterested manner. The ones who are asleep have taken off their shoes but tied them to their ankles.

An older man sits by the fire, his jaw covered with

stubble, scabs, or both. He has the sunken face of a person with no teeth. We make eye contact and hold it for a long time. I wonder why he's looking at me with such hostility until I remember I'm wearing an evening suit. He has no way of knowing that it's about the only thing separating us. I fight an illogical urge to explain this and continue on my way.

When I finally reach the lot, I stop and gaze at the menagerie tent. It's huge, outlined against the night sky. A few minutes later I find myself standing in front of the elephant. I can only see her in silhouette and even then only after my eyes have adjusted to the light. She's sleeping, her great body still but for her slow, slumbered breathing. I want to touch her, to lay my hands on that rough, warm skin, but I can't bring myself to wake her up.

Bobo is lying in the corner of his den, with one arm stretched out over his head and the other resting on his chest. He sighs deeply, smacks his lips, and then rolls onto his side. So human.

Eventually I make my way back to the ring stock car and settle on the bedroll. Queenie and Walter both sleep through my arrival.

I lie awake until dawn, listening to Queenie snore and feeling utterly miserable. Less than a month ago, I was within days of an Ivy League degree and a career at my father's side. Now I'm one step away from being a bum – a circus worker who has disgraced himself not once, but twice, in as many days.

Yesterday, I wouldn't have thought it possible to top

throwing up on Nell, but I believe that last night I managed to do just that. What the hell was I thinking?

I wonder if she will tell August. I have brief visions of the bull hook flying at my head and then even briefer visions of getting up right now, this minute, and walking back to the hobo camp. But I don't, because I can't bear the thought of abandoning Rosie, Bobo, and the others.

I'll pull myself together. I'll stop drinking. I'll make sure I'm never alone with Marlena again. I'll go to confession.

I use the corner of my pillow to wipe tears from my eyes. Then I squeeze them shut and conjure up an image of my mother. I try to hang on to it, but before long Marlena has replaced her. Coolly distant, when she was watching the band and jiggling that foot. Glowing, while we were spinning around the dance floor. Hysterical – and then horrified – in the alley.

But my final thoughts are tactile: the underside of my forearm lying above the swell of her breasts. Her lips under mine, soft and full. And the one detail I can neither fathom nor shake, the one that haunts me into sleep: the feel of her fingertips tracing the outline of my face.

Kinko – Walter – wakes me a few hours later.

'Hey, Sleeping Beauty,' he says, shaking me. 'Flag's up.'

'Okay. Thanks,' I say without moving.

'You're not getting up.'

'You're a genius, you know that?'

Walter's voice rises by about an octave. 'Hey, Queenie – here girl! Here girl! Come on, Queenie. Give him a lick. Come on!'

Queenie launches herself onto my head.

'Hey, stop it!' I say, raising an arm protectively because Queenie's tongue is rooting in my ear and she's dancing on my face. 'Stop it! Come on now!'

But she is unstoppable, so I jerk upright. This sends Queenie flying to the floor. Walter looks at me and laughs. Queenie wriggles onto my lap and stands on her hind legs, licking my chin and neck.

'Good girl, Queenie. Good baby,' says Walter. 'So, Jacob – you look like you had another . . . er . . . interesting evening.'

'Not exactly,' I reply. Since Queenie is on my lap anyway, I stroke her. It's the first time she's let me touch her. Her body is warm, her hair wiry.

'You'll find your sea legs soon. Come get some breakfast. Food'll help settle your stomach.'

'I wasn't drinking.'

He looks at me for a moment. 'Ah,' he says, nodding sagely.

'What's that supposed to mean?' I say.

'Woman trouble,' he says.

'No.'

'Yes.'

'No, it isn't!'

'I'm surprised Barbara forgave you already. Or did she?' He watches my face for a few seconds and then resumes nodding. 'Uh-huh. I do believe I'm starting to get the picture. You didn't get her flowers, did you? You need to start taking my advice.'

'Why don't you mind your own business?' I snap. I set Queenie on the floor and stand up.

'Sheesh, you're a first-class grump. You know that? Come on. Let's get some grub.'

After we fill our plates, I try to follow Walter to his table.

'What the hell do you think you're doing?' he says, coming to a stop.

'I thought I'd sit with you.'

'You can't. Everyone has assigned spots. Besides, you'd be coming down in the world.'

I hesitate.

'What's wrong with you, anyway?' he says. He looks over at my usual table. August and Marlena eat in silence, staring at their plates. Walter's eyelids flicker.

'Oh man – don't tell me.'

'I didn't tell you a damned thing,' I say.

'You didn't need to. Listen, kid, that's somewhere you just don't want to go, you hear me? I mean in the figurative sense. In the literal sense, you get your ass over to that table and act normal.'

I glance again at August and Marlena. They're clearly ignoring each other.

'Jacob, you listen to me,' says Walter. 'He's the meanest son of a bitch I've ever met, so whatever the hell is going on—'

'There's nothing going on. Absolutely nothing—'

'—it better stop now or you're going to find yourself dead. Redlighted, if you're lucky, and probably off a trestle. I mean it. Now get on over there.'

I glare down at him.

'Shoo!' he says, flicking his hand toward the table.

August looks up as I approach.

'Jacob!' he cries. 'Good to see you. Wasn't sure if you'd found your way back last night. Wouldn't have looked very good if I'd had to bail you out of jail, you know. Might have caught some heat.'

'I was worried about you two as well,' I say, taking a seat.

'Were you?' he says with exaggerated surprise.

I look up at him. His eyes are glowing. His smile has a peculiar tilt.

'Oh, but we found our way back all right, didn't we, darling?' he says, shooting Marlena a look. 'But do tell me, Jacob – how on earth did you two manage to get separated anyway? You were so . . . *close* on the dance floor.'

Marlena looks up quickly, red spots burning on her cheeks. 'I told you last night,' she says. 'We got pushed apart by the crowd.'

'I was asking Jacob, darling. But thank you.' August lifts a piece of toast with flourish, smiling broadly with closed lips.

'There was quite a crush,' I say, picking up my fork and sliding it under my eggs. 'I tried to keep track of her but couldn't. I looked for both of you out back, but after a while I figured I'd better just get out of there.'

'Wise choice, my boy.'

'So, did you two manage to hook up?' I ask, lifting my fork to my mouth and trying to sound casual.

'No, we arrived in separate taxis. Twice the expense, but I'd pay it a hundred times over to make sure my darling wife was safe – wouldn't I, darling?'

Marlena stares at her plate.

'I said wouldn't I, darling?'

'Yes, of course you would,' she says flatly.

'Because if I thought she was in any danger at all, there's no knowing what I might do.'

I look up quickly. August is staring right at me.

TWELVE

As soon as I can do it without attracting attention, I flee to the menagerie.

I replace the giraffe's neck poultice, cold-soak a camel for a suspected hoof abscess, and survive my first cat procedure – treating Rex for an ingrown claw while Clive strokes his head. Then I swing by to pick up Bobo while I check the rest. The only animals I don't run my eyes or hands over are the baggage stock, and that's only because they're in constant use and I know someone would alert me at the first sign of trouble.

By late morning, I'm just another menagerie man: cleaning dens, chopping food, and hauling manure with the rest of them. My shirt is soaked, my throat parched. When the flag finally goes up, Diamond Joe, Otis, and I trudge out of the great tent and toward the cook-house.

Clive falls into stride beside us.

'Keep your distance from August if you can,' he says. 'He's in a right state.'

'Why? What now?' says Joe.

'He's steamed because Uncle Al wants the bull in the parade today, and he's taking it out on anyone who crosses his path. Like that poor sod over there,' he says, pointing at three men crossing the field.

Bill and Grady are dragging Camel across the lot to the Flying Squadron. He's suspended between them, his legs dragging behind.

I jerk around to Clive. 'August didn't hit him, did he?'

'Naw,' says Clive. 'Gave him a good tongue lashing, though. It's not even noon, and he's already skunked. But that guy who looked at Marlena – *whooeeee*, he won't make that mistake again soon.' Clive shakes his head.

'That damned bull ain't gonna walk in no parade,' says Otis. 'He can't get her to walk in a straight line from her car to the menagerie.'

'I know that, and you know that, but apparently Uncle Al does not,' says Clive.

'Why is Al so set on having her in the parade?' I ask.

'Because he's been waiting his whole life to say "Hold your horses! Here come the elephants!"' says Clive.

'The hell with that,' Joe says. 'There ain't no horses to hold anymore these days, and we don't have elephants, anyway. We have elephant.'

'Why does he want to say that so badly?' I ask.

They turn in unison to stare at me.

'Fair question,' says Otis finally, although it's clear he

thinks I'm brain-damaged. 'It's because that's what Ringling says. Course, he actually *has* elephants.'

I watch from a distance as August attempts to line Rosie up among the parade wagons. The horses leap sideways, dancing nervously in their hitches. The drivers hold tight to the reins, shouting warnings. The result is a kind of contagion of panic, and before long the men leading the zebras and llamas are struggling to maintain control.

After several minutes of this, Uncle Al approaches. He gesticulates wildly toward Rosie, ranting without pause. When his mouth finally closes, August's opens, and he also gesticulates toward Rosie, waving the bull hook and thumping her on the shoulder for good measure. Uncle Al turns to his entourage. Two of them turn tail and sprint across the lot.

Not long after, the hippopotamus wagon pulls up beside Rosie, drawn by six highly doubtful Percherons. August opens the door and whacks Rosie until she enters.

Not long after, someone starts up the calliope and the parade begins.

They return an hour later with a sizable crowd. The towners hang around the edges of the lot, growing in numbers as word spreads.

Rosie is driven right up to the back end of the big top, which is already connected to the menagerie. August takes her through and to her spot. It is only after she is behind her rope with one foot chained to a stake that the menagerie is opened to the public.

I watch in awe as she is rushed by children and adults

alike. She is easily the most popular animal. Her big ears flap back and forth as she accepts candy and popcorn and even chewing gum from delighted circus-goers. One man is brave enough to lean forward and dump a box of Cracker Jack into her open mouth. She rewards him by removing his hat, placing it on her head, and then posing with her trunk curled in the air. The crowd roars and she calmly hands the delighted patron his hat. August stands beside her with his bull hook, beaming like a proud father.

There's something wrong here. This animal isn't stupid.

As the last of the crowd goes through to the big top and performers line up for the Grand Spec, Uncle Al pulls August aside. I watch from across the menagerie as August's mouth opens in shock, then outrage, and then vociferous complaint. His face darkens and he waves his top hat and hook. Uncle Al gazes on, completely impervious. Eventually he lifts a hand, shakes his head, and walks away. August stares after him, stunned.

'What the heck do you suppose happened there?' I say to Pete.

'God only knows,' he says. 'But I have the feeling we're going to find out.'

It turns out that Uncle Al was so delighted by Rosie's popularity in the menagerie that not only is he insisting she take part in the Spec but also that she put on a full elephant act in the center ring immediately after the show begins. By the time I hear about it, the outcome of said events is already the source of furious wagering in the back end.

My only thoughts are of Marlena.

I sprint around back to where the performers and ring stock are lined up behind the big top in preparation for the Spec. Rosie heads up the line. Marlena straddles her head, clad in pink sequins and grasping Rosie's ugly leather head harness. August stands beside her left shoulder, grim-faced, his fingers alternately clutching and releasing the bull hook.

The band falls quiet. The performers make last-minute adjustments to their costumes, and the animal handlers give their charges one last check. And then the music for the Spec starts.

August leans forward and bellows into Rosie's ear. The elephant hesitates, in response to which August strikes her with the bull hook. This sends her flying through the back end of the big top. Marlena ducks flat against her head to avoid being scraped off by the pole that runs across the top.

I gasp and run forward, curling around the edge of the sidewall.

Rosie comes to a stop about twenty feet down the hippo-drome track and Marlena undergoes a change that defies belief. One moment she is askew on Rosie's head, lying flat. The next, she yanks herself upright, turns on a smile, and thrusts an arm into the air. Her back is arched, her toes pointed. The crowd goes crazy – standing on the bleachers, clapping, whistling, and tossing peanuts onto the track.

August catches up. He lifts the bull hook high and then freezes. He turns his head and scans the audience. His hair flops over his forehead. He grins as he lowers the bull hook, and removes his top hat. He bows deeply, three times, aiming at different segments of the audience. When he turns back to Rosie, his face hardens.

By poking the bull hook in and around her underarms and legs, he persuades her to make a tour of sorts around the hippodrome. They go in fits and starts, stopping so many times the rest of the Spec is forced to continue around them, parting like water around a stone.

The audience loves it. Each time Rosie trots ahead of August and stops, they roar with laughter. And each time August approaches, red-faced and waving his bull hook, they explode with glee. Finally, about three-quarters of the way around, Rosie curls her trunk in the air and takes off at a run, leaving a series of thunderous farts in her wake as she barrels toward the back end of the tent. I am pressed against the bleachers, right by the entrance. Marlena grasps the head halter with both hands, and as they approach I catch my breath. Unless she bails, she is going to be knocked off.

A couple of feet from the entrance, Marlena lets go of the halter and leans hard to the left. Rosie disappears from the tent, and Marlena is left clinging to the top pole. The crowd falls silent, no longer sure that this is part of the act.

Marlena hangs limply, not a dozen feet from me. She's breathing hard, with eyes closed and head down. I'm just about to step forward and lift her down when she opens her eyes, removes her left hand from the pole, and in one graceful movement swings around so she's facing the audience.

Her face lights up and she points those toes. The band

leader, watching from his post, signals furiously for a drum roll. Marlena begins swinging.

The drum roll mounts as she gains momentum. Before long she's swinging parallel to the ground. I wonder how long she's going to keep this up and just what the heck she's planning to do when she suddenly releases the pole. She sails through the air, tucking her body into a ball and rolling forward twice. She uncurls for one sideways rotation, and lands firmly in a burst of sawdust. She looks at her feet, straightens up, and thrusts both arms into the air. The band launches into victory music and the crowd goes wild. Moments later, coins rain down on the hippodrome track.

As soon as she turns, I can see that she's hurt. She limps from the big top and I rush out behind her.

'Marlena—' I say.

She turns and collapses against me. I grasp her around the waist, holding her upright.

August rushes out. 'Darling – my darling! You were brilliant. Brilliant! I've never seen anything more—'

He stops cold when he sees my arms around her.

Then she lifts her head and wails.

August and I lock eyes. Then we lock arms, beneath and behind her, forming a chair. Marlena whimpers, leaning against August's shoulder. She tucks her slippered feet under our arms, clenching her muscles in pain.

August presses his mouth into her hair. 'It's okay, darling. I've got you now. *Shhh* . . . It's okay. I've got you.'

'Where should we go? Her dressing tent?' I ask.

'There's nowhere to lie down.'

'The train?'

'Too far. Let's go to the cooch girl's tent.'

'Barbara's?'

August shoots me a look over Marlena's head.

We enter Barbara's tent without any warning. She's sitting in a chair in front of her vanity, dressed in a midnight blue negligee and smoking a cigarette. Her expression of bored disdain drops immediately.

'Oh my God. What's going on?' she says, stubbing out her cigarette and leaping up. 'Here. Put her on the bed. Here, right here,' she says, rushing in front of us.

When we lay Marlena down, she rolls onto her side, clutching her feet. Her face is contorted, her teeth clenched.

'My feet—'

'Hush, sweetie,' Barbara says. 'It's going to be okay. Everything's going to be okay.' She leans over and loosens the ribbons on Marlena's slippers.

'Oh God, oh God, they hurt . . .'

'Get the scissors from my top drawer,' says Barbara, glancing back at me.

When I return with them, Barbara cuts the toes off Marlena's tights and rolls them up her legs. Then she lifts her bare feet into her lap.

'Go to the cookhouse and get some ice,' she says.

After a second, both she and August turn to look at me.

'I'm already there,' I say.

I'm barreling toward the cookhouse when I hear Uncle Al shouting behind me. 'Jacob! Wait!'

I pause while he catches up.

'Where are they? Where did they go?' he says.

'They're in Barbara's tent,' I gasp.

'Eh?'

'The cooch girl.'

'Why?'

'Marlena's hurt. I've got to get ice.'

He turns and barks at a follower. 'You, go get ice. Take it to the cooch girl's tent. *Go!*' He turns back to me. 'And you, go retrieve our goddamned bull before we get run out of town.'

'Where is she?'

'Munching cabbages in someone's backyard, apparently. The lady of the house is not amused. West side of the lot. Get her out of there before the cops come.'

Rosie stands in a trampled vegetable patch, running her trunk lazily across the rows. When I approach she looks me straight in the eye and plucks a purple cabbage. She drops it in her shovel-scoop of a mouth and then reaches for a cucumber.

The lady of the house opens the door a crack and shrieks, 'Get that thing out of here! Get it out of here!'

'Sorry, ma'am,' I say. 'I'll surely do my best.'

I stand at Rosie's shoulder. 'Come on, Rosie. Please?'

Her ears wave forward, she pauses, and then she reaches for a tomato.

'No!' I say. 'Bad elephant!'

Rosie pops the red globe in her mouth and smiles as she chews it. Laughing at me, no doubt.

'Oh Jesus,' I say, at a complete loss.

Rosie wraps her trunk around some turnip greens and

rips them from the ground. Still looking at me, she pops them in her mouth and begins munching. I turn and smile desperately at the still-gawking housewife.

Two men approach from the lot. One is wearing a suit, a derby hat, and a smile. To my immense relief, I recognize him as one of the patches. The other man wears filthy overalls and carries a bucket.

'Good afternoon, ma'am,' says the patch, tipping his hat and picking his way carefully across the ruined garden. It looks as though a tank has plowed through it. He climbs the cement stairs to the back door. 'I see you've met Rosie, the largest and most magnificent elephant in the world. You're lucky – she doesn't normally make house calls.'

The woman's face is still in the crack of the door. 'What?' she says, dumbfounded.

The patch smiles brightly. 'Oh yes. It's an honor indeed. I'm willing to bet no one else in your neighborhood – heck, probably the whole city – can say they've had an elephant in their backyard. Our men here will remove her – naturally, we'll fix up your garden and compensate you for your produce, too. Would you like us to arrange for a photograph of you and Rosie? Something to show your family and friends?'

'I . . . I . . . What?' she stammers.

'If I may be so bold, ma'am,' the patch says with the slightest hint of a bow. 'Perhaps it would be easier if we discussed this inside.'

After a reluctant pause the door swings open. He disappears inside the house and I turn back to Rosie.

The other man stands directly in front of her, holding the bucket.

She is rapt. Her trunk hovers over its top, sniffing and trying to squirm its way around his arms into the clear liquid.

'*Przestań!*' he says, brushing her away. '*Nie!*'

My eyes widen.

'You got a fucking problem?' he says.

'No,' I say quickly. 'No. I'm Polish, too.'

'Oh. Sorry.' He waves the ever-present trunk away, wipes his right hand on his thigh, and offers it to me. 'Grzegorz Grabowski,' he says. 'Call me Greg.'

'Jacob Jankowski,' I say, shaking his hand. He pulls his away to protect the contents of the bucket.

'*Nie! Teraz nie!*' he says crossly, pushing at the insistent trunk. 'Jacob Jankowski, huh? Yeah, Camel told me about you.'

'What is that anyway?' I ask.

'Gin and ginger ale,' he says.

'You're kidding.'

'Elephants love alcohol. See? One whiff of this and she doesn't care about cabbages anymore. Ah!' he says, batting the trunk away. '*Powiedziałem przestań! Później!*'

'How the hell did you know that?'

'The last show I was on had a dozen bulls. One of them used to fake a bellyache every night trying to get a dose of whiskey. Say, go get the bull hook, will you? She'll probably follow us back to the lot just to get at this gin – isn't that right, *mój mąlutki paczuszek?* – but better get it just in case.'

'Sure,' I say. I remove my hat and scratch my head. 'Does August know this?'

'Know what?'

'That you know so much about elephants? I bet he'd hire you on as a—'

Greg's hand shoots up. 'Nuh-uh. No way. Jacob, no offense to you personally, but there's no way in hell I'll work for that man. None. Besides, I'm no bull man. I just like the big beasts. Now, you want to run and get that hook, please?'

When I return with the hook, Greg and Rosie are gone. I turn, scanning the lot.

In the distance, Greg walks toward the menagerie. Rosie plods along a few feet behind. Every once in a while he stops and lets her slip her trunk into the bucket. Then he yanks it away and keeps walking. She follows like an obedient puppy.

With Rosie safely restored to the menagerie, I return to Barbara's tent, still clutching the bull hook.

I pause outside the closed flap. 'Uh, Barbara?' I say. 'Can I come in?'

'Yup,' she says.

She's alone, sitting in her chair with her bare legs crossed.

'They've gone back to the train to wait for the doctor,' she says, taking a drag from her cigarette. 'If that's what you came for.'

I feel my face turn red. I look at the sidewall. I look at the ceiling. I look at my feet.

'Ah heck, ain't you cute,' she says, tapping the cigarette over the grass. She brings it to her mouth and takes a deep drag. 'You're blushing.'

She stares at me for a long time, clearly amused.

'Ah, go on,' she says finally, blowing smoke from the

side of her mouth. 'Go on. Get out of here before I decide to give you another go.'

I scramble out of Barbara's tent and run smack into August. His face is dark as thunder.

'How is she?' I ask.

'We're waiting for the doctor,' he says. 'Did you catch the bull?'

'She's back in the menagerie,' I say.

'Good,' he says. He rips the bull hook from my hand.

'August, wait! Where are you going?'

'I'm going to teach her a lesson,' he says without stopping.

'But August!' I shout after him. 'Wait! She was good! She came back of her own accord. Besides, you can't do anything now. The show is still going!'

He stops so abruptly a cloud of dust temporarily obscures his feet. He stands absolutely still, staring at the ground.

After a long while he speaks. 'Good. The band will drown out the noise.'

I stare after him, my mouth open in horror.

I return to the ring stock car and lie on my bedroll, sickened beyond belief by the thought of what's going on in the menagerie and even more sickened that I'm doing nothing to prevent it.

A few minutes later, Walter and Queenie come back. He's still in costume – a billowing white affair with multi-colored polka dots, a triangular hat, and Elizabethan ruff. He's wiping his face with a rag.

'What the hell was that?' he says, standing so that I'm looking at his oversized red shoes.

'What?' I say.

'In the Spec. Was that part of the act?'

'No,' I say.

'Holy cow,' he says. 'Holy cow. In that case, what a save. Marlena's really something. But you already knew that, didn't you?' He clicks his tongue and leans over to poke my shoulder.

'Would you knock if off?'

'What?' he says, spreading his hands in feigned innocence.

'It's not funny. She's hurt, okay?'

He drops the goofy grin. 'Oh. Hey, man, I'm sorry. I didn't know. She gonna be okay?'

'I don't know yet. They're waiting for the doctor.'

'Shit. I'm sorry, Jacob. I really am.' He turns toward the door and takes a deep breath. 'But not half as sorry as that poor bull's gonna be.'

I pause. 'She's already sorry, Walter. Trust me.'

He stares out the door. 'Ah jeez,' he says. He puts his hands on his hips and looks across the lot. 'Ah jeez. I'll just bet.'

I stay in the stock car through dinner, and then through the evening show as well. I'm afraid that if I see August I'll kill him.

I hate him. I hate him for being so brutal. I hate that I'm beholden to him. I hate that I'm in love with his wife and something damned close to that with the elephant. And most of all, I hate that I've let them both down.

I don't know if the elephant is smart enough to connect me to her punishment and wonder why I didn't do anything to stop it, but I am and I do.

'Bruised heels,' says Walter when he returns. 'Come on, Queenie, up! Up!'

'What?' I mumble. I haven't moved since he left.

'Marlena bruised her heels. She'll be out a couple of weeks. Thought you might want to know.'

'Oh. Thanks,' I say.

He sits on his cot and looks at me for a long time.

'So, what's the story with you and August, anyway?'

'What do you mean?'

'Are you guys tight, or what?'

I haul my body into a sitting position and lean against the wall. 'I hate the bastard,' I say finally.

'Ha!' Walter snorts. 'Okay, so you do have some sense. So why do you spend all your time with them?'

I don't answer.

'Oh, sorry. I forgot.'

'You've got it all wrong,' I say, hauling myself upright.

'Yeah?'

'He's my boss and I have no choice.'

'That's true. But it's also about the woman, and you know it.'

I raise my head and glare at him.

'Okay, okay,' he says, raising his hands in surrender. 'I'll shut up. You know the score.' He turns and rummages in his crate. 'Here,' he says, tossing me an eight-pager. It skids across the floor and stops beside me. 'It's not Marlena, but it's better than nothing.'

After he turns away, I pick it up and thumb through it.

But despite the explicit and exaggerated drawings, I can't muster any interest whatever in Mr Big Studio Director boning the skinny would-be starlet with the horse face.

THIRTEEN

I blink rapidly, trying to get my bearings – that skinny nurse with the horse face has dropped a tray of food at the end of the hall, and it's woken me up. I wasn't aware of dozing, but that's how it goes these days. I seem to slip in and out of time and space. Either I'm finally going senile, or else it's my mind's way of coping with being entirely unchallenged in the present.

The nurse crouches down, collecting the spilled food. I don't like her – she's the one who's always trying to keep me from walking. I think I'm just too wobbly for her nerves, because even Dr Rashid admits that walking is good for me as long as I don't overdo it or get stranded.

I'm parked in the hallway just outside my door, but it's still several hours before my family comes and I think I'd like to look out the window.

I could just call the nurse. But what fun would that be?

I shift my bottom to the edge of my wheelchair, and reach for my walker.

One, two, three—

Her pale face thrusts itself in front of mine. 'Can I help you, Mr Jankowski?'

Heh. That was almost too easy.

'Why, I'm just going to look out the window for a while,' I say, feigning surprise.

'Why don't you sit tight and let me take you?' she says, planting both hands firmly on the arms of my chair.

'Oh, well then. Yes, that's very kind of you,' I say. I lean back in my seat, lift my feet onto the footrests, and fold my hands in my lap.

The nurse looks puzzled. Dear Lord, that's an impressive overbite. She straightens up and waits, I guess to see if I'm going to make a run for it. I smile pleasantly and train my gaze on the window at the end of the hall. Finally, she goes behind me and takes the handles of my wheelchair.

'Well, I must say, Mr Jankowski, I'm a little surprised. You're normally . . . uh . . . rather *adamant* about walking.'

'Oh, I could have made it. I'm only letting you push me because there aren't any chairs by the window. Why is that, anyway?'

'Because there's nothing to see, Mr Jankowski.'

'There's a circus to see.'

'Well, this weekend, maybe. But normally there's just a parking lot.'

'What if I want to look at a parking lot?'

'Then you shall, Mr Jankowski,' she says, pushing me up to the window.

My brow furrows. She was supposed to argue with me. Why didn't she argue with me? Oh, but I know why. She thinks I'm just an addled old man. Don't upset the residents, oh no – especially not that old Jankowski fellow. He'll fling pockmarked Jell-O at you and then call it an accident.

She starts to walk away.

'Hey!' I call after her. 'I haven't got my walker!'

'Just call me when you're ready,' she says. 'I'll come get you.'

'No, I want my walker! I always have my walker. Get me my walker.'

'Mr Jankowski—' says the girl. She folds her arms and sighs deeply.

Rosemary appears from a side hall like an angel from heaven.

'Is there a problem?' she says, looking from me to the horse-faced girl and then back again.

'I want my walker and she won't get it,' I say.

'I didn't say I wouldn't. All I said was—'

Rosemary holds up a hand. 'Mr Jankowski likes to have his walker beside him. He always does. If he asked for it, please bring it.'

'But—'

'But nothing. Get his walker.'

Outrage flashes across the horse girl's face, replaced almost instantly by hostile resignation. She throws a murderous glance my direction and goes back for my walker. She holds it conspicuously in front of her, storming down the hall. When she reaches me, she slams it in front of me. Which would be more impressive if it didn't have rubber leg caps, making it land with a squeak rather than a bang.

I smirk. I can't help it.

She stands there, arms akimbo, staring at me. Waiting for a thank you, no doubt. I turn my head slowly, chin raised like an Egyptian pharaoh, training my gaze on the magenta and white striped big top.

I find the stripes jarring – in my day, only the concession stands were striped. The big top was plain white, or at least started out that way. By the end of the season it may have been streaked with mud and grass, but it was never striped. And that's not the only difference between this show and the shows from my past – this one doesn't even have a midway, just a big top with a ticket gate at the door and concession and souvenir stand beside it. It looks like they still sell the same old fare – popcorn, candy, and balloons – but the children also carry flashing swords, and other moving, blinking toys I can't make out at this distance. Bet their parents paid an arm and a leg for them, too. Some things never change. Rubes are still rubes, and you can still tell the performers from the workers.

'Mr Jankowski?'

Rosemary is leaning over me, seeking my eyes with hers.

'Eh?'

'Are you ready for lunch, Mr Jankowski?' she says.

'It can't be lunchtime. I only just got here.'

She looks at her watch – a real one, with arms. Those digital ones came and went, thank God. When will people learn that just because you can make something doesn't mean you should?

'It's three minutes to twelve,' she says.

'Oh. All right then. What day is it, anyway?'

'Why, it's Sunday, Mr Jankowski. The Lord's Day. The day your people come.'

'I know that. I meant what's for lunch?'

'Nothing you'll like, I'm sure,' she says.

I raise my head, prepared to be angry.

'Oh, come now, Mr Jankowski,' she says, laughing. 'I was only joking.'

'I know that,' I say. 'What, now I have no sense of humor?'

But I'm grumpy, because maybe I don't. I don't know anymore. I'm so used to being scolded and herded and managed and handled that I'm no longer sure how to react when someone treats me like a real person.

Rosemary tries to steer me toward my usual table, but I'm having none of that. Not with Old Fart McGuinty there. He's wearing his clown hat again – must have asked the nurses to put it on him again first thing this morning, the damned fool, or maybe he slept in it – and he's still got helium balloons tied to the back of his chair. They're not really floating anymore, though. They're starting to pucker, hovering above limp lengths of string.

When Rosemary turns my chair toward him I bark, 'Oh no you don't. There! Over there!' I point at an empty table in the corner. It's the one farthest from my usual table. I just hope it's out of earshot.

'Oh, come now, Mr Jankowski,' Rosemary says. She

stops my chair and comes around to face me. 'You can't keep this up forever.'

'I don't see why not. Forever might be next week for me.'

She puts her hands on her hips. 'Do you even remember why you're so angry?'

'Yes, I do. Because he's lying.'

'Are you talking about the elephants again?'

I purse my lips by way of an answer.

'He doesn't see it that way, you know.'

'That's cockamamie. When you're lying, you're lying.'

'He's an old man,' she says.

'He's ten years younger than me,' I say, straightening up indignantly.

'Oh, Mr Jankowski,' Rosemary says. She sighs and gazes toward heaven as though asking for help. Then she crouches in front of my chair and places her hand on mine. 'I thought you and I had an understanding.'

I frown. This is not part of the usual nurse/Jacob repertoire.

'He may be wrong in the details, but he's not lying,' she says. 'He really *believes* that he carried water for the elephants. He does.'

I don't answer.

'Sometimes when you get older – and I'm not talking about you, I'm talking generally, because everyone ages differently – things you think on and wish on start to seem real. And then you believe them, and before you know it they're a part of your history, and if someone challenges you on them and says they're not true – why, then you get offended. Because you don't remember the first part.

All you know is that you've been called a liar. So even if you're right about the technical details, can you understand why Mr McGuinty might be upset?'

I scowl into my lap.

'Mr Jankowski?' she continues softly. 'Let me take you to the table with your friends. Go on, now. As a favor to me.'

Well, isn't that just dandy. The first time in years a woman wants a favor from me, and I can't stomach the idea.

'Mr Jankowski?'

I look up at her. Her smooth face is two feet from mine. She looks me in the eye, waiting for an answer.

'Oh, all right. But don't expect me to talk to anyone,' I say, waving a hand in disgust.

And I don't. I sit and listen as Old Liar McGuinty talks about the wonders of the circus and his experiences as a boy and I watch as the blue-haired old ladies lean toward him and listen, their eyes growing misty with admiration. It drives me completely berserk.

Just as I open my mouth to say something, I catch sight of Rosemary. She's on the opposite end of the room, bending over an old woman and tucking a napkin into her collar. But her eyes are on me.

I close my mouth again. I just hope she appreciates how hard I'm trying.

She does. When she comes to retrieve me after the tan-colored pudding with edible-oil-product topping has made its appearance, sat for a while, and been removed, she leans down and whispers, 'I knew you could do it, Mr Jankowski. I just knew it.'

'Yes. Well. It wasn't easy.'

'But it's better than sitting alone at a table, isn't it?'

'Maybe.'

She rolls her eyes toward heaven again.

'All right. Yes,' I say grudgingly. 'I suppose it's better than sitting alone.'

FOURTEEN

It's been six days since Marlena's accident, and she has yet to reappear. August no longer comes to the cookhouse for meals, so I sit conspicuously alone at our table. When I run across him in the course of looking after the animals, he is polite but distant.

For her part, Rosie is carted out through each town in the hippopotamus wagon and then displayed in the menagerie. She has learned to follow August from the elephant car to the menagerie tent, and in return for this he has stopped beating the hell out of her. Instead, she trudges alongside him, and he walks with the bull hook snagged firmly in the flesh behind her front leg. Once in the menagerie, she stands behind her rope, happily charming the crowds and accepting candy. Uncle Al hasn't actually said so, but there don't appear to be any immediate plans to attempt another elephant act.

As the days pass I grow more anxious about Marlena. Each time I approach the cookhouse I hope that I'll find her there. And each time I don't, my heart sinks.

It's the end of another long day in some damned city or other – they all look about the same from a railroad siding – and the Flying Squadron is preparing to pull out. I'm lounging on my bedroll reading *Othello* and Walter is on his cot reading Wordsworth. Queenie is tucked up against him.

She lifts her head and growls. Both Walter and I jerk upright.

Earl's large bald head pokes around the edge of the doorframe. 'Doc!' he says, looking at me. 'Hey! Doc!'

'Hi, Earl. What's up?'

'I need your help.'

'Sure. What is it?' I say, putting my book down. I shoot a glance at Walter, who has pinned the squirming Queenie against his side. She's still grumbling.

'It's Camel,' Earl says in a hushed voice. 'He's got trouble.'

'What kind of trouble?'

'Foot trouble. They've gone all floppy. He kind of slaps them down. His hands aren't so great neither.'

'Is he drunk?'

'Not at this particular moment. But it don't make no difference no-how.'

'Well damn, Earl,' I say. 'He's got to see a doctor.'

Earl's forehead crinkles. 'Well, yeah. That's why I'm here.'

'Earl, I'm no doctor.'

'You're an animal doctor.'

'It's not the same.'

I glance at Walter, who is pretending to read.

Earl blinks expectantly at me.

'Look,' I say finally, 'if he's in bad shape, let me talk to August or Uncle Al and see if we can get a doctor out in Dubuque.'

'They won't get him a doctor.'

'Why not?'

Earl straightens in righteous indignation. 'Damn. You don't know nothin' at all, do you?'

'If there's something seriously wrong with him, surely they'll—'

'Throw him off the train, is what,' says Earl definitively. 'Now, if he was one of the animals . . .'

I ponder this for only a moment before realizing he's right. 'Okay. I'll arrange for a doctor myself.'

'How? You got money?'

'Uh, well, no,' I say, embarrassed. 'Does he?'

'If he had any money, do you think he'd be drinking jake and canned heat? Aw, come on, won't you at least have a look? The old feller went out of his way to help you.'

'I know that, Earl, I know that,' I say quickly. 'But I don't know what you expect me to do.'

'You're the doctor. Just have a look.'

In the distance, a whistle blows.

'Come on,' says Earl. 'That's the five-minute whistle. We gotta move.'

I follow him to the car that carries the big top. The wedge horses are already in place, and all over the Flying

Squadron men are lifting ramps, climbing aboard, and sliding doors shut.

'Hey, Camel,' Earl shouts into the open door. 'I brought the doc.'

'Jacob?' croaks a voice from inside.

I jump up. It takes me a moment to adjust to the darkness. When I do, I make out Camel's figure in the corner, huddled on a pile of feed sacks. I walk over and kneel down. 'What's up, Camel?'

'I don't rightly know, Jacob. I woke up a few days ago and my feet was all floppy. Jes' can't feel 'em right.'

'Can you walk?'

'A bit. But I have to lift my knees real high 'cuz my feet are so floppy.' His voice drops to a whisper. 'It ain't just that, though,' he says. 'It's other stuff, too.'

'What other stuff?'

His eyes grow wide and fearful. 'Man's stuff. I can't feel nothing . . . in front.'

The train jolts forward, slowly, lurching as the couplings tighten.

'We're pulling out. You gotta get off now,' says Earl, tapping me on the shoulder. He moves to the open door and waves me toward him.

'I'll ride this leg with you,' I say.

'You can't.'

'Why not?'

'Because someone'll hear you been fraternizing with roustabouts and chuck you – or more likely these guys – off this thing,' he says.

'Well damn, Earl, aren't you security? Tell them to get lost.'

'I'm on the main train. This here's Blackie's territory,' he says, waving with increasing urgency. 'Come on!'

I look into Camel's eyes. They're fearful, pleading. 'I've got to go,' I say. 'I'll catch up with you in Dubuque. You'll be okay. We'll get you to a doctor.'

'I ain't got no money.'

'It's okay. We'll find a way.'

'Come on!' shouts Earl.

I lay a hand on the old man's shoulder. 'We'll figure something out. Okay?'

Camel's rheumy eyes flicker.

'Okay?'

He nods. Just once.

I rise from my haunches and walk to the doorway. 'Damn,' I say, gazing out on the fast-moving scenery. 'The train picked up speed faster than I thought.'

'And it ain't gonna get any slower,' says Earl, placing a hand square in the middle of my back and shoving me out the door.

'What the hell!' I shout, flailing my arms like a windmill. I hit the gravel and roll onto my side. There's a thunk as another body hits behind me.

'See?' Earl says, getting up and wiping off his backside. 'I told you he was bad.'

I stare in amazement.

'What?' he says, looking baffled.

'Nothing,' I say. I get up and brush the dust and gravel from my clothes.

'Come on. You better get back before anyone sees you up here.'

'Just tell them I was checking out the baggage stock.'

'Oh. Good one. Yeah. Guess that's why you're the doc and I'm not, huh?'

My head swivels, but his expression is completely without guile. I give up and start walking toward the main train.

'What's the matter?' Earl calls after me. 'Why are you shaking your head, Doc?'

'What was all that about?' says Walter as I walk in the door.

'Nothing,' I say.

'Yeah, right. I was here for most of it. Spill the beans, "Doc."'

I hesitate. 'It's one of the guys from the Flying Squadron. He's in a bad way.'

'Well, that much was obvious. How did he seem to you?'

'Scared. And quite frankly, I don't blame him. I want to get him to a doctor, but I'm flat broke and so is he.'

'You won't be for long. Tomorrow's payday. But what are his symptoms?'

'Loss of feeling in his legs and arms, and . . . well, other stuff, too.'

'What other stuff?'

I glance downward. 'You know . . .'

'Aw, shit,' says Walter. He sits upright. 'That's what I thought. You don't need a doctor. He's got jake leg.'

'He's got *what?*'

'Jake leg. Jake walk. Limber leg. Whatever – it's all the same thing.'

'Never heard of it.'

'Someone made a big batch of bad jake – put plasticizers in it or something. It went out all over the country. One bad bottle, and you're done for.'

'What do mean, "done for"'

'Paralyzed. It can start anytime within two weeks of drinking the shit.'

I am horrified. 'How the hell do you know this?'

He shrugs. 'It's in the papers. They only just figured out what it was, but there's lots been affected. Maybe tens of thousands. Mostly in the South. We passed through there on our way up to Canada. Maybe that's where he picked up the jake.'

I pause before asking my next question. 'Can they fix it?'

'Nope.'

'They can't do anything at all?'

'I already told you. He's done for. But if you want to waste your money on a doctor to tell you that, be my guest.'

Black and white fireworks explode across my field of vision, a shifting, shimmering pattern that blanks out everything else. I drop onto my bedroll.

'Hey, you okay?' says Walter. 'Whoa, pal. You're looking a little green there. You're not going to throw up, are you?'

'No,' I say. My heart pounds. Blood whooshes through my ears. I have just remembered the small bottle of brackish liquid Camel offered me my first day on the show. 'I'm okay. Thank God.'

The next day, right after breakfast, Walter and I line up in front of the red ticket wagon along with everyone else.

At nine on the nose, the man in the wagon beckons forth the first person, a roustabout. Moments later he stalks off, cursing and spitting on the ground. The next one – another roustabout – also leaves in a fit of pique.

The people in the line turn to each other, muttering behind their hands.

'Uh-oh,' says Walter.

'What's going on?'

'It looks like he's holding back Uncle Al–style.'

'What do you mean?'

'Most shows hold back some pay till end of season. But when Uncle Al runs out of money he holds it all back.'

'Damn!' I say, as a third man storms off. Two other working men – grim-faced and with hand-rolled cigarettes between their lips – leave the lineup. 'Why are we bothering then?'

'It only applies to working men.' Walter says. 'Performers and bosses always get paid.'

'I'm neither of those.'

Walter regards me for a couple of seconds. 'No, you're not. I don't actually know what the heck you are, but anyone who sits at the same table as the equestrian director is not a working man. That much I know.'

'So, does this happen often?'

'Yup,' says Walter. He's bored, scuffing the ground with his foot.

'Does he ever make it up to them?'

'Don't think anyone's ever tested the theory. The general wisdom is that if he owes you more than four weeks pay, you better stop showing up on payday.'

'Why?' I say, watching as yet another filthy man stomps off in a maelstrom of curses. Three other working men leave the line from in front of us. They head back to the train with stooped shoulders.

'Basically you don't want Uncle Al to start thinking of you as a financial liability. 'Cuz if he does, you disappear one night.'

'What? You get redlighted?'

'Damn right.'

'That seems a bit extreme. I mean, why not just leave them behind?'

''Cuz he owes them money. How well do you think that would go over?'

I'm second in line now, behind Lottie. Her blonde hair gleams in the sun, arranged into neat finger curls. The man at the window of the red wagon waves her forward. They chat pleasantly as he peels a few bills off his stack. When he hands them to her, she licks her forefinger and counts them. Then she rolls them up and slips them inside the top of her dress.

'Next!'

I step forward.

'Name?' says the man without looking up. He's a small, bald fellow with a fringe of thin hair and wire-rimmed glasses. He stares at the ledger book in front of him.

'Jacob Jankowski,' I say, peering past him. The wagon's interior is lined with carved wood panels and a painted ceiling. There's a desk and a safe at the back and a sink along one wall. On the opposite wall is a map of the United States with colored pins stuck in it. Our route, presumably.

The man runs his finger down the ledger. It comes to a stop and then moves to the far right column. 'Sorry,' he says.

'What do you mean, "sorry"?'

He looks up at me, the picture of sincerity. 'Uncle Al doesn't like anyone to finish the season broke. He always holds back four weeks pay. You'll get it at the end of season. *Next!*'

'But I need it now.'

He fixes his eyes upon me, his face implacable. 'You'll get it at the end of season. *Next!*'

As Walter approaches the open window, I stalk off, pausing just long enough to spit in the dust.

The answer comes to me as I'm chopping fruit for the orangutan. It's a mental flash, a vision of a sign.

Don't have money?
What have you got?
We'll take anything!

I walk back and forth in front of car 48 at least five times before I finally climb inside and knock on the door of stateroom 3.

'Who is it?' says August.

'It's me. Jacob.'

There's a slight pause. 'Come in,' he says.

I open the door and step inside.

August stands by one of the windows. Marlena is in one of the plush chairs, her bare feet resting on an ottoman.

'Hi,' she says, blushing. She pulls her skirt over her knees and then smoothes it across her thighs.

'Hello, Marlena,' I say. 'How are you?'

'Doing better. I'm walking a bit now. Won't be long before I'm back in the saddle, as it were.'

'So what brings you here?' August interjects. 'Not that we're not delighted to see you. We've missed you. Haven't we, darling?'

'Uh . . . yes,' says Marlena. She raises her eyes to mine and I flush.

'Oh, where *are* my manners? Would you like a drink?' says August. His eyes are unnaturally hard, set above a stern mouth.

'No. Thank you.' I'm caught off-guard by his hostility. 'I can't stay. I just wanted to ask you something.'

'And what's that?'

'I need to arrange to get a doctor out here.'

'Why?'

I hesitate. 'I'd rather not say.'

'Ah,' he says, winking at me. 'I understand.'

'What?' I say, horrified. 'No. It's nothing like that.' I glance at Marlena, who turns quickly toward the window. 'It's for a friend of mine.'

'Yes, of course it is,' says August, smiling.

'No, it really is. And it's not . . . Look, I just wondered if you knew of anyone. Never mind. I'll walk into town and see what I can find.' I turn to leave.

'Jacob!' Marlena calls after me.

I stop in the doorway, staring out the window across the narrow hall. I take a couple of breaths before turning to face her.

'There's a doctor coming to see me in Davenport

tomorrow,' she says quietly. 'Shall I send for you when we're finished?'

'I'd be much obliged,' I say. I tip my hat and leave.

The next morning, the line in the cookhouse is buzzing.

'It's because of that damned bull,' says the man in front of me. 'She can't do nothing, anyway.'

'Poor buggers,' says his friend. 'It's a shame when a man's worth less than a beast.'

'Excuse me,' I say. 'What do you mean, it's because of the bull?'

The first man stares at me. He's large across the shoulders, wearing a dirty brown jacket. His face is deeply creased, weathered and brown as a raisin. ''Cuz she costs so much. Plus they bought that elephant car.'

'No, but what's because of her?'

'A bunch of men went missing overnight. Six at least, maybe more.'

'What, from the train?'

'Yup.'

I set my half-full plate down on the steam table and walk toward the Flying Squadron. After a few strides I break into a run.

'Hey, pal!' the man calls after me. 'You ain't even et yet!'

'Leave him alone, Jock,' says his friend. 'He probably needs to lay eyes on someone.'

'Camel! Camel, you in there?' I stand in front of the train car, trying to see into its musty interior. 'Camel! You in there?'

There's no answer.

'Camel!'

Nothing.

I spin around, facing the lot. 'Shit!' I kick the gravel, and then kick it again. 'Shit!'

Just then, I hear a mewling from inside the car.

'Camel, is that you?'

A muffled noise comes from one of the darkened corners. I hop inside. Camel is lying up against the far wall.

He's passed out cold, holding an empty bottle. I lean over and pluck it from his hand. Lemon extract.

'Who the hell are you and what the hell do you think you're doing?' says a voice from behind me. I turn. It's Grady. He's standing on the ground in front of the open door, smoking a ready-made. 'Oh – hey. Sorry, Jacob. Didn't recognize you from the back.'

'Hi, Grady,' I say. 'How's he been?'

'Kind of hard to tell,' he answers. 'He's been tight since last night.'

Camel snorts and tries to roll over. His left arm flops limply across his chest. He smacks his lips and starts snoring.

'I'm getting a doctor out today,' I say. 'Keep an eye on him in the meantime, will you?'

'Of course I will,' says Grady, affronted. 'What the hell do you think I am? Blackie? Who the hell do you think kept him safe last night?'

'Of course I don't think you're – aw, hell, just forget it. Look, if he sobers up, try to keep him that way, okay? I'll catch up with you later with the doctor.'

*   *   *

The doctor holds my father's pocket watch in his pudgy hand, turning it over and inspecting it through his pince-nez. He pops it open to examine the face.

'Yes. This will do. So, what is it then?' he says, slipping it into his vest pocket.

We're in the hallway just outside August and Marlena's stateroom. The door is still open.

'We need to go somewhere else,' I say, lowering my voice.

The doctor shrugs. 'Fine. Let's go.'

As soon as we're outside, the doctor turns to me. 'So where are we going to perform this examination?'

'It's not me. It's a friend of mine. He's having problems with his feet and hands. And other stuff. He'll tell you when we get there.'

'Ah,' says the doctor. 'Mr Rosenbluth led me to believe that you were having difficulties of a . . . personal nature.'

The doctor's expression changes as he follows me down the track. By the time we leave the shiny painted cars of the first section behind, he looks alarmed. By the time we reach the battered cars of the Flying Squadron, his face is pinched in disgust.

'He's in here,' I say, hopping into the car.

'And how, pray tell, am I supposed to get in?' he says.

Earl emerges from the shadows with a wooden crate. He jumps down, sets it in front of the doorway, and gives it a loud pat. The doctor gazes upon it for a moment and then climbs up, clutching his black bag primly in front of him.

'Where's the patient?' he says, squinting and scanning the interior.

'Over there,' says Earl. Camel is huddled against a corner. Grady and Bill hover over him.

The doctor walks over to them. 'Some privacy, please,' he says.

The other men scatter, murmuring in surprise. They move to the other end of the car and crane their necks, trying to see.

The doctor approaches Camel and crouches beside him. I can't help noticing that he keeps the knees of his suit off the floorboards.

A few minutes later, he straightens up and says, 'Jamaica ginger paralysis. No question about it.'

I suck my breath in through my teeth.

'What? What's that?' Camel croaks.

'You get it from drinking Jamaica ginger extract.' The doctor puts great emphasis on the final three words. 'Or jake, as it's commonly known.'

'But . . . How? Why?' says Camel, his eyes desperately seeking the doctor's face. 'I don't understand. I've been drinking it for years.'

'Yes. Yes. I would have guessed that,' says the doctor.

Anger rises like bile in my throat. I step up beside the doctor. 'I don't believe you answered the question,' I say as calmly as I can.

The doctor turns and surveys me through his pince-nez. After a pause of a few beats he says, 'It's caused by a cresol compound used by a manufacturer.'

'Dear God,' I say.

'Quite.'

'Why did they add it?'

'To get around the regulations that require that Jamaica

ginger extract be rendered unpalatable.' He turns back to Camel and raises his voice. *'So it won't be used as an alcoholic beverage.'*

'Will it go away?' Camel's voice is high, cracking with fear.

'No. I'm afraid not,' the doctor says.

Behind me, the others catch their breath. Grady comes forward until we're touching shoulders. 'Wait a minute – you mean there's nothing you can do?'

The doctor straightens up and hooks his thumbs in his pockets. 'Me? No. Absolutely not,' he says. His expression is compressed as a pug's, as though he's trying to close his nostrils through facial muscles alone. He picks up his bag and edges toward the door.

'Hold on just a cotton-pickin' moment,' says Grady. 'If you can't do anything, is there anyone else who can?'

The doctor turns to address me specifically, I suppose because I'm the one who paid him. 'Oh, there's plenty who will take your money and offer a cure – wading in oil slush pools, electrical shock therapy – but none of it does a lick of good. He may recover some function over time, but it will be minimal at best. Really, he shouldn't have been drinking in the first place. It is against federal law, you know.'

I am speechless. I think my mouth may actually be open.

'Is that everything?' he says.

'I beg your pardon?'

'Do . . . you . . . need . . . anything . . . else?' he says as though I'm an idiot.

'No,' I say.

'Then I'll bid you good day.' He tips his hat, steps gingerly onto the crate, and dismounts. He walks a dozen yards away, sets his bag on the ground, and pulls a handkerchief from his pocket. He wipes his hands carefully, getting in between each finger. Then he picks up his bag, puffs out his chest, and walks off, taking Camel's last scrap of hope and my father's pocket watch with him.

When I turn back, Earl, Grady, and Bill are kneeling around Camel. Tears stream down the old man's face.

'Walter, I need to talk to you,' I say, bursting into the goat room. Queenie raises her head, sees that it's me, and sets it back on her paws.

Walter sets his book down. 'Why? What's up?'

'I need to ask a favor.'

'Well, go on then, what is it?'

'A friend of mine is in a bad way.'

'That guy with jake leg?'

I pause. 'Yes.'

I walk over to my bedroll but am too anxious to sit down.

'Well, spit it out then,' Walter says impatiently.

'I want to bring him here.'

'What?'

'He's going to get redlighted otherwise. His friends had to hide him behind a roll of canvas last night.'

Walter looks at me in horror. 'You have got to be kidding.'

'Look, I know you were less than thrilled when I showed up, and I know he's a working man and all, but he's an old man and he's in bad shape and he needs help.'

'And what exactly are we supposed to do with him?'

'Just keep him away from Blackie.'

'For how long? Forever?'

I drop to the edge of my bedroll. He's right, of course. We can't keep Camel hidden forever. 'Shit,' I say. I bang my forehead with the heel of my palm. And then again. And then again.

'Hey, stop that,' says Walter. He sits forward, closing his book. 'Those were serious questions. What would we do with him?'

'I don't know.'

'Does he have any family?'

I look up at him suddenly. 'He mentioned a son once.'

'Okay, well now we're getting somewhere. Do you know where this son is?'

'No. I gather they aren't in touch.'

Walter stares at me, tapping his fingers against his leg. After half a minute of silence he says, 'All right. Bring him on over. Don't let anyone see you or we'll all catch hell.'

I look up in surprise.

'What?' he says, brushing a fly from his forehead.

'Nothing. No. Actually, I mean thank you. Very much.'

'Hey, I got a heart,' he says, lying back and picking up his book. 'Not like some people we all know and love.'

Walter and I are relaxing between the matinée and evening show when there's a soft rapping on our door.

He leaps to his feet, knocking over the wooden crate and cursing as he keeps the kerosene lamp from hitting the floor. I approach the door and glance nervously at the trunks laid end-to-end across the back wall.

Walter rights the lamp and gives me the briefest of nods.

I open the door.

'Marlena!' I say, swinging the door farther open than I intend to. 'What are you doing up? I mean, are you okay? Do you want to sit down?'

'No,' she says. Her face is inches from mine. 'I'm all right. But I'd like to speak to you for a moment. Are you alone?'

'Uh, no. Not exactly,' I say, glancing back at Walter, who's shaking his head and waving his hands furiously.

'Can you come to the stateroom?' Marlena says. 'It won't take but a moment.'

'Yes. Of course.'

She turns and walks gingerly to the doorway. She's wearing slippers, not shoes. She sits on the edge and eases herself down. I watch for a moment, relieved to see that while she moves carefully, she's not limping obviously.

I close the door.

'Man, oh man,' says Walter, shaking his head. 'I nearly had a heart attack. Shit, man. What the hell are we doing?'

'Hey, Camel,' I say. 'You okay back there?'

'Yup,' says a thin voice from behind the trunks. 'Reckon she saw anything?'

'No. You're in the clear. For now. But we're going to have to be very careful.'

Marlena is in the plush chair with her legs crossed. When I first come in, she's sitting forward, rubbing the arch of one foot. When she sees me, she stops and leans back.

'Jacob. Thank you for coming.'

'Certainly,' I say. I remove my hat, and hold it awkwardly to my chest.

'Please sit down.'

'Thank you,' I say, sitting on the edge of the nearest chair. I look around. 'Where's August?'

'He and Uncle Al are meeting with the railroad authority.'

'Oh,' I say. 'Anything serious?'

'Just rumors. Someone reported that we were redlighting men. They'll sort it out, I'm sure.'

'Rumors. Yes,' I say. I hold my hat in my lap, fingering its edge and waiting.

'So . . . um . . . I was worried about you,' she says.

'You were?'

'Are you all right?' she asks quietly.

'Yes. Of course,' I say. Then it dawns on me what she's asking. 'Oh God – no, it's not what you think. The doctor wasn't for me. I needed him to see a friend, and it wasn't . . . it wasn't for *that*.'

'Oh,' she says, with a nervous laugh. 'I'm so glad. I'm sorry, Jacob. I didn't mean to embarrass you. I was just worried.'

'I'm fine. Really.'

'And your friend?'

I hold my breath for a moment. 'Not so fine.'

'Will she be okay?'

'She?' I look up, caught off-guard.

Marlena looks down, twisting her fingers in her lap. 'I just assumed it was Barbara.'

I cough, and then I choke.

'Oh, Jacob – oh, goodness. I'm making an awful mess

of this. It's none of my business. Really. Please for-give me.'

'No. I hardly know Barbara.' I blush so hard my scalp prickles.

'It's all right. I know she's a . . .' Marlena twists her fingers awkwardly and lets the sentence go unfinished. 'Well, despite that, she's not a bad sort. Quite decent, really, although you want to—'

'Marlena,' I say with enough force to stop her from talking. I clear my throat and continue. 'I'm not involved with Barbara. I hardly know her. I don't think we've exchanged more than a dozen words in our lives.'

'Oh,' she says. 'It's just Auggie said . . .'

We sit in excruciating silence for nearly half a minute.

'So, your feet are better then?' I ask.

'Yes, thank you.' Her hands are clasped so tightly her knuckles are white. She swallows and looks at her lap. 'There was something else I wanted to talk to you about. What happened in the alley. In Chicago.'

'That was entirely my fault,' I say quickly. 'I can't imagine what came over me. Temporary insanity or some-thing. I'm so very sorry. I can assure you it will never happen again.'

'Oh,' she says quietly.

I look up, startled. Unless I'm very much mistaken, I think I've just managed to offend her. 'I'm not saying . . . It's not that you're not . . . I just . . .'

'Are you saying you didn't want to kiss me?'

I drop my hat and raise my hands. 'Marlena, please help me. I don't know what you want me to say.'

'Because it would be easier if you didn't.'

'If I didn't what?'

'If you didn't want to kiss me,' she says quietly.

My jaw moves, but it's several seconds before anything comes out. 'Marlena, what are you saying?'

'I . . . I'm not really sure,' she says. 'I hardly know what to think anymore. I haven't been able to stop thinking about you. I know what I'm feeling is wrong, but I just . . . Well, I guess I just wondered . . .'

When I look up, her face is cherry red. She's clasping and unclasping her hands, staring hard at her lap.

'Marlena,' I say, rising and taking a step forward.

'I think you should go now,' she says.

I stare at her for a few seconds.

'Please,' she says, without looking up.

And so I leave, although every bone in my body screams against it.

FIFTEEN

Camel spends his days hidden behind the trunks, lying on blankets that Walter and I arrange to cushion his ruined body from the floor. His paralysis is so bad I'm not sure he could crawl out even if he wanted to, but he's so terrified of being caught that he doesn't try. Each night, after the train is in motion, we pull the trunks out and lean him up in the corner or lay him on the cot, depending on whether he wants to sit up or continue lying down. It's Walter who insists he take the cot, and in turn I insist that Walter take the bedroll. And so I am back to sleeping on the horse blanket in the corner.

Barely two days into our cohabitation, Camel's tremors are so bad he can't even speak. Walter notices at noon when he returns to the train to bring Camel some food. Camel is in such bad shape Walter seeks me out in the menagerie to tell me about it, but August is watching, so I can't return to the train.

At nearly midnight, Walter and I are sitting side by side on the cot, waiting for the train to pull out. The second it moves, we get up and drag the trunks from the wall.

Walter kneels, puts his hands under Camel's armpits, and lifts him into a sitting position. Then he pulls a flask from his pocket.

When Camel's eyes light on it, they jerk up to Walter's face. Then they fill with tears.

'What's that?' I ask quickly.

'What the hell do you think it is?' Walter says. 'It's liquor. Real liquor. The good stuff.'

Camel reaches for the bottle with shaking hands. Walter, still holding him upright, removes the cap and holds it to the old man's lips.

Another week passes, and Marlena remains cloistered in her stateroom. I'm now so desperate to lay eyes on her that I find myself trying to figure out ways of peeking into the window without getting caught. Fortunately, good sense prevails.

Every night, I lie on my smelly horse blanket in the corner and replay our last conversation, word for precious word. I follow the same tortured trajectory over and over – from my rush of disbelieving joy to my crashing defla-tion. I know that dismissing me was the only thing she could do, but even so, I can barely stand it. Just thinking about it leaves me so agitated I toss and writhe until Walter tells me to knock it off because I'm keeping him up.

*　　*　　*

Onward and upward. Mostly we stay one day in each town, although we usually make a two-day stopover Sunday. During the jump between Burlington and Keokuk, Walter – with the help of generous amounts of whiskey – manages to extract the name and last known location of Camel's son. For the next few stops, Walter marches off to town immediately after breakfast and doesn't return until it's nearly show time. By Springfield, he has made contact.

At first, Camel's son denies the association. But Walter is persistent. Day after day he marches into town, negotiating by telegram, and by the following Friday the son has agreed to meet us in Providence and take custody of the old man. It means we will have to continue the current housing arrangements for several more weeks, but at least it's a solution. And that's a good deal more than we've had up to this point.

In Terre Haute, the Lovely Lucinda drops dead. After Uncle Al recovers from his violent but short-lived bereavement, he organizes a farewell befitting 'our beloved Lucinda.'

An hour after the death certificate is signed, Lucinda is laid out in the water well of the hippopotamus car and hitched to a team of twenty-four black Percherons with feathers on their headbands.

Uncle Al climbs onto the bench with the driver, practically collapsing with grief. After a moment he wiggles his fingers, signaling the start of Lucinda's procession. She is hauled slowly through town, followed on foot by every member of the Benzini Brothers Most Spectacular

Show on Earth deemed fit to be seen. Uncle Al is desolate, weeping and honking into his red handkerchief and allowing himself only the occasional upward glance to gauge whether the procession's speed allows for maximum crowd enlargement.

The women follow immediately behind the hippopotamus wagon, dressed all in black and pressing elegant lace hankies to the corners of their eyes. I am farther back, surrounded on all sides by wailing men, their faces shiny with tears. Uncle Al has promised three dollars and a bottle of Canadian whiskey to the man who puts on the best show. You've never seen such grief – even the dogs are howling.

Almost a thousand townspeople follow us back to the lot. When Uncle Al stands up on the carriage, they fall silent.

He removes his hat and presses it to his chest. He digs out a hankie and dabs his eyes. He delivers a heart-wrenching speech, so distraught he can barely contain himself. At the end of it, he says that if it were up to him, he'd cancel tonight's show out of respect for Lucinda. But he cannot. It's out of his control. He is a man of honor, and on her deathbed she grasped his hand and made him promise – no, *vow* – that he wouldn't let what was clearly her imminent end disrupt the show's routine and disappoint the thousands of people who were expecting it to be circus day.

'Because after all . . .' Uncle Al pauses, clasping his hand to his heart and sniffing piteously. He looks heavenward as tears stream down his face.

The women and children in the crowd cry openly.

A woman near the front throws an arm across her forehead and collapses as the men on either side scramble to catch her.

Uncle Al collects himself with obvious effort, although he cannot keep his lower lip from quivering. He nods slowly and continues. 'Because, after all, as our dearest Lucinda knew only too well . . . *the show must go on!*'

We have an enormous crowd that night – a 'straw house,' so named because after all the regular seats sell out, roustabouts spread straw on the hippodrome track for the overflow crowd to sit on.

Uncle Al begins the show with a moment of silence. He bows his head, summons real tears, and dedicates the performance to Lucinda, whose great and absolute selflessness is the only reason we are able to continue in the face of our loss. And we will do her proud – oh yes, such was our singular love for Lucinda that despite the grief that consumes us, tugging on our breaking hearts, we will summon the strength to honor her final wish and do her proud. Such wonders you have never seen, ladies and gentlemen, acts and performers gathered from the four corners of the earth to delight and entertain you, acrobats, and tumblers, and aerialists of the highest caliber . . .

The show is about a quarter of the way through when she walks into the menagerie. I sense her presence even before I hear the surprised murmurs around me.

I set Bobo on the floor of his den. I turn and, sure enough, there she is, gorgeous in pink sequins and feathered headdress, removing her horses' halters and letting them drop to the ground. Only Boaz – a black Arabian and presumably Silver Star's counterpart – remains tethered, and he's clearly unhappy about it.

I lean against Bobo's den, mesmerized.

Those horses, with whom I've spent every night riding from town to town to town and who normally look like regular horses, have transformed. They blow and snort, their necks arched and tails aloft. They gather into two dancing groups, one black, one white. Marlena faces them, carrying a long whip in each hand. She raises one and waves it over her head. Then she walks backward, leading them from the menagerie. The horses are completely free. They wear no halters, no side reins, no surcingles – nothing. They simply follow her, shaking their heads and flinging their legs forward like Saddlebreds.

I've never seen her act – those of us who work behind the scenes don't have time for that luxury – but this time nothing could stop me. I secure Bobo's door and slip into the connection, the roofless canvas tunnel that joins the menagerie to the big top. The reserved-seat ticket seller glances at me quickly, and when he realizes I'm not a cop goes back to his business. His pockets jingle, swollen with money. I stand beside him, looking across the three rings to the back end of the big top.

Uncle Al announces her, and she steps inside. She spins, holding both whips high in the air. She flicks one and takes a few steps backward. The two groups of horses hurry in behind her.

Marlena sashays to the center ring and they follow, high-kicking, prancing clouds of black and white.

Once she's in the center of the ring, she slaps the air

lightly. The horses start circling the ring at a trot, five white followed by five black. After two complete rotations, she wiggles the whip. The black horses speed up until each is trotting beside a white horse. Another wiggle, and they ease into line so that the horses are now alternating black and white.

She moves only minimally, her pink sequins shimmering under the bright lights. She walks a small circle in the center of the ring, flicking the whips in combinations of signals.

The horses continue circling, with the white horses passing the black horses and then the black horses passing the white horses, with the end result always being alternating colors.

She calls out and they stop. She says something else, and they turn and step up so their front hooves are on the ring curb. They walk sideways, their tails toward Marlena and their hooves up on the rim. They do an entire rotation before she stops them again. They climb down and swing around to face her. Then she calls forth Midnight.

He is a magnificent black, all Arabian fire with a perfect white diamond on his forehead. She speaks to him, taking both whips in one hand, and offering him her other palm. He presses his muzzle into it, his neck arched and nostrils flared.

Marlena steps backward and raises a whip. The other horses watch, dancing on the spot. She lifts the other whip and flicks its tip back and forth. Midnight rises up on his hind legs, his forelegs curled in front of him. She shouts something now – the first time she has raised her voice

– and strides backward. The horse follows, walking on his hind legs and pawing the air in front of him. She keeps him upright all the way around the ring. Then she motions him down. Another cryptic circling of the whip, and Midnight bows, going down on the knee of one foreleg with the other extended. Marlena drops into a low curtsy and the crowd goes wild. With Midnight still bowing, she lifts both whips and flicks them. The rest of the horses pirouette, turning circles on the spot.

More cheering, more adulation. Marlena spreads her arms in the air, turning to give each section of the audience a chance to adore her. Then she turns to Midnight and perches delicately on his lowered back. He rises, arches his neck, and carries Marlena from the big top. The rest of the horses follow, once again grouped by color, crowding each other to stay close to their mistress.

My heart pounds so hard that, despite the roaring of the crowd, I am aware of blood whooshing through my ears. I am filled to overflowing, bursting with love.

That night, after whiskey has rendered Camel dead to the world and Walter is snoring on the bedroll, I leave the little room and stand looking over the backs of the ring stock.

I care for these horses daily. I muck out their stalls, fill their water and feed buckets, and groom them for the show. I check their teeth and comb their manes and feel their legs for heat. I give them treats and pat their necks. They had become as familiar a part of my scenery as Queenie, but after seeing Marlena's act I'll never view them the same way again. These horses are an extension of Marlena – a part of her that is here, right now, with me.

I reach over the stall divider and place my hand on a sleek black rump. Midnight, who had been asleep, rumbles in surprise and turns his head.

When he sees that it's just me, he turns away. His ears droop, his eyes close, and he shifts his weight so he's resting one hind leg.

I go back to the goat room and check that Camel is still breathing. Then I lie down on the horse blanket and drift into a dream about Marlena that will probably cost me my soul.

In front of the steam tables the next morning:

'Check that out,' says Walter, lifting his arm to poke me in the ribs.

'What?'

He points.

August and Marlena are sitting at our table. It's the first time they've shown up for a meal since her accident.

Walter eyeballs me. 'You gonna be okay?'

'Yes, of course,' I say irritably.

'Okay. Just checking,' he says. We pass the ever-vigilant Ezra and head for our separate tables.

'Good morning, Jacob,' August says as I set my plate on the table and take a seat.

'August. Marlena,' I say, nodding at each.

Marlena looks up quickly and then back at her plate.

'And how are you this fine day?' says August. He digs into a pile of scrambled eggs.

'Fine. And you?'

'Wonderful,' he says.

'And how are you, Marlena?' I ask.

'Very much better, thank you,' she says.

'I saw your act last night,' I say.

'Did you?'

'Yes,' I say, shaking my napkin and spreading it across my lap. 'It's . . . I don't quite know what to say. It was amazing. I've never seen anything like it.'

'Oh?' says August, cocking one eyebrow. 'Never?'

'No. Never.'

'Really.'

He stares at me without blinking. 'I thought it was Marlena's act that inspired you to join this show in the first place, Jacob. Was I wrong?'

My heart flips in my chest. I pick up my cutlery: fork in my left hand, knife in my right – European-style, like my mother.

'I lied,' I say.

I stab the end of a sausage and begin sawing it, waiting for a response.

'I beg your pardon?' he says.

'I lied. *I lied!*' I slam my cutlery down, a nub of sausage impaled on the fork. 'Okay? Of course I'd never heard of the Benzini Brothers before I jumped your train. Who the hell has heard of the Benzini Brothers? The only circus I'd seen in my entire life was the Ringling Brothers, and they were great. *Great!* Do you hear me?'

There's an eerie silence. I look around, horrified. Everyone in the tent is staring at me. Walter's jaw is open. Queenie's ears are pressed against her head. In the distance, a camel bellows.

Finally I turn my eyes to August. He, too, is staring. One edge of his moustache quivers. I tuck my napkin under the edge of my plate, wondering if he's going to come across the table at me.

August's eyes widen farther. I tense my knuckles under the table. Then August explodes. He laughs so hard he turns red, clutching his midriff and fighting for breath. He laughs and howls until tears run down his face and his lips tremble from exertion.

'Oh, Jacob,' he says, wiping his cheeks. 'Oh, Jacob. I think I may have misjudged you. Yes. Indeed. I think I may have misjudged you.' He cackles and sniffs, swabbing his face with his napkin. 'Oh dear,' he sighs. 'Oh dear.' He clears his throat and picks up his utensils. He scoops some egg onto his fork and then sets it down again, once more overcome with mirth.

The other diners return to their food, but reluctantly, like the crowd that watched as I expelled the man from the lot that first day. And I can't help but notice that when they return to their meals, it's with a look of apprehension.

Lucinda's death leaves us with a serious deficiency in the freak lineup. And it must be filled – all the big shows have fat ladies, and therefore so must we.

Uncle Al and August scour *Billboard* and at each stop make telephone calls and send telegrams in an effort to recruit a new one, but all known fat ladies appear either to be happy in their current situation or else leery of Uncle Al's reputation. After two weeks and ten jumps, Uncle Al is so desperate he approaches a woman of generous proportions in the audience. Unfortunately, she turns out to be Mrs Police Superintendent, and Uncle Al ends up with a shiny purple eye instead of a fat lady, along with summary instructions to leave town.

We have two hours. The performers immediately sequester themselves in their train cars. The roustabouts, once roused, run around like headless chickens. Uncle Al is breathless and purple, waving his cane and whacking people if they're not moving fast enough for his liking. Tents drop so quickly that men get trapped inside, and then men who are dropping other tents must come and retrieve them before they suffocate in a vast expanse of canvas, or – worse, in Uncle Al's estimation – use their pocketknives to cut a breathing hole.

After all the stock is loaded I retire to the ring stock car. I don't like the look of the townsmen hovering around the edge of the lot. Many are armed, and a bad feeling ferments in the pit of my stomach.

I haven't seen Walter yet, and I pace back and forth in front of the open door, scanning the lot. The black men have long since hidden themselves aboard the Flying Squadron, and I'm not at all convinced that the mob won't content themselves with a redheaded dwarf instead.

One hour and fifty-five minutes after we get our marching orders, his face appears in the doorway.

'Where the hell have you been?' I shout.

'Is that him?' croaks Camel from behind the trunks.

'Yeah, that's him. Get on up here,' I say, waving Walter inside. 'The crowd's looking nasty.'

He doesn't move. He's flushed and out of breath. 'Where's Queenie? You seen Queenie?'

'No. Why?'

He disappears.

'Walter!' I jump up and follow him to the door. 'Walter! Where the hell are you going? They've already blown the five-minute whistle!'

He's running alongside the train, ducking to look between its wheels. 'Come on, Queenie! Here, girl!' He straightens up, pausing in front of each stock car, yelling through the slats and then waiting for a response. 'Queenie! Here, girl!' Each time he calls, his voice reaches a new level of desperation.

A whistle blows, a long sustained warning followed by the hissing and sputtering of the engine.

Walter's voice cracks, hoarse with yelling. 'Queenie! Where the hell are you? Queenie! *Come!*'

Up ahead, the last stragglers are leaping onto flat cars.

'Walter, come on!' I shout. 'Don't mess around. You've got to get on now.'

He ignores me. He's up at the flat cars now, peering between wagon wheels. 'Queenie, *come!*' he shouts. He stops and suddenly stands straight up. He looks lost. 'Queenie?' he says to no one in particular.

'Aw hell,' I say.

'Is he coming back or what?' asks Camel.

'Doesn't look like it,' I say.

'Well go git 'im!' he barks.

The train lurches forward, the cars jerking as the engine pulls the slack from their couplings.

I jump to the gravel and run ahead to the flat cars. Walter stands facing the engine.

I touch his shoulder. 'Walter, it's time to go.'

He turns to me, his eyes pleading. 'Where is she? Have you seen her?'

'No. Come on, Walter,' I say. 'We've got to get on the train now.'

'I can't,' he says. His face is blank. 'I can't leave her. I just can't.'

The train is chugging forward now, gathering steam.

I glance behind me. The townsmen, armed with rifles, baseball bats, and sticks are surging forward. I look back at the train long enough to get a sense of speed, and count, praying to God that I'm right: *one, two, three, four*.

I scoop Walter up like a sack of flour and toss him inside. There's a crash and a yelp as he hits the floor. I sprint beside the train and grasp the iron bar beside the door. I let the train pull me along for three long strides, and then use its velocity to vault up and inside.

My face skids across the bucking floorboards. When I realize I'm safe, I look for Walter, prepared for a fight.

He is huddled in the corner, crying.

Walter is inconsolable. He remains in the corner as I pull the trunks out and retrieve Camel. I manage the old man's shave – a task that usually involves all three of us – and then drag him out to the area in front of the horses.

'Aw, come on, Walter,' says Camel. I'm holding him by his armpits, dangling his naked posterior over what Walter calls the honey bucket. 'You did what you could.' He looks over his shoulder at me. 'Hey, lower me a bit, would ya? I'm swinging in the breeze here.'

I shift my feet so they're further apart, trying to lower

Camel while keeping my back straight. Usually Walter takes care of this part because he's the right height.

'Walter, I could use a hand here,' I say as a spasm shoots across my back.

'Shut up,' he says.

Camel looks back again, this time with a raised eyebrow.

'It's okay,' I say.

'No, it's not okay,' Walter yells from the corner. 'Nothing's okay! Queenie was all I had. You understand that?' His voice drops to whimper. 'She was all I had.'

Camel waves his hand at me to indicate he's finished. I shuffle over a couple of feet and lay him on his side.

'Now, that can't be true,' says Camel as I clean him up. 'A young fella like you's gotta have somebody somewhere.'

'You don't know nothing.'

'You ain't got a mother somewhere?' says Camel, persisting.

'None I got a use for.'

'Now don't you talk like that,' says Camel.

'Why the hell not? She sold me to this outfit when I was fourteen.' He glares at us. 'And don't you go looking at me like you feel sorry for me,' he snaps. 'She was an old crow, anyway. Who the hell needs her.'

'What do you mean *sold* you?' says Camel.

'Well, I'm not exactly cut out for farmwork, am I? Just leave me the hell alone, will you?' He shuffles around so his back is to us.

I fasten Camel's pants, grab him by the armpits, and haul him back into the room. His legs drag behind him, his heels scraping the floor.

'Man, oh man,' he says as I arrange him on the cot. 'Ain't that something?'

'You ready for some food?' I say, trying to change the subject.

'Naw, not yet. But a drop of whiskey would go down well.' He shakes his head sadly. 'I ain't never heard of a woman so coldhearted.'

'I can still hear you, you know,' barks Walter. 'And besides, you ain't got no talking room, old man. When was the last time you saw your son?'

Camel goes pale.

'Eh? Can't answer that, can you?' continues Walter from outside the room. 'Ain't such a big difference in what you did and what my mother did, is there?'

'Yes there is,' shouts Camel. 'There's a world of difference. And how the hell do you know what I did, anyway?'

'You mentioned your son one night when you were tight,' I say quietly.

Camel stares at me for a moment. Then his face contorts. He raises a limp hand to his forehead and turns away from me. 'Aw shit,' he says. 'Aw shit. I never knew you knew,' he says. 'You shoulda' told me.'

'I thought you remembered,' I say. 'Anyway, he didn't say much. He just said you wandered off.'

'"He just said"?' Camel's head shoots around. '"*He just said*"? What the hell does that mean? You been in touch with him?'

I sink to the floor and rest my head on my knees. It's shaping up to be a long night.

'What do you mean, "*he just said*"?' shrieks Camel. 'I asked you a question!'

I sigh. 'Yes, we got in touch with him.'

'When?'

'A while ago.'

He stares at me, stunned. 'But why?'

'He's meeting us in Providence. He's taking you home.'

'Oh no,' says Camel, shaking his head vehemently. 'Oh no he's not.'

'Camel—'

'What the hell'd you go and do that for? You ain't got no right!'

'We had no choice!' I shout. I stop, close my eyes, and collect myself. 'We had no choice,' I repeat. 'We had to do something.'

'I can't go back! You don't know what happened. They don't want me no more.'

His lip quivers, and his mouth shuts. He turns his face away. A moment later, his shoulders start heaving.

'Aw hell,' I say. I raise my voice, shouting through the open door. 'Hey, thanks Walter! You've been a big help tonight! Sure appreciate it!'

'Fuck off!' he answers.

I shut off the kerosene lamp and crawl over to my horse blanket. I lie down on its scratchy surface and then sit up again.

'Walter!' I shout. 'Hey, Walter! If you're not coming back in, I'm using the bedroll.'

There's no answer.

'Did you hear me? I said I'm using the bedroll.'

I wait for a minute or two and then crawl across the floor.

Walter and Camel spend the night making the noises

men make when they're trying not to cry, and I spend the night punching my pillow up around my ears trying not to hear them.

I awake to Marlena's voice.

'Knock knock. May I come in?'

My eyes snap open. The train has stopped, and somehow I slept through it. I'm also startled because I was dreaming about Marlena, and for a moment I wonder if I'm still asleep.

'Hello? Anyone in there?'

I jerk up onto my elbows and look at Camel. He's help-less on the cot, his eyes wide with fear. The interior door has stayed open all night. I leap up.

'Uh, hang on a second!' I rush out to meet her, pulling the door shut behind me.

She's already climbing into the car. 'Oh, hello,' she says, looking at Walter. He's still huddled in the corner. 'I was actually looking for you. Isn't this your dog?'

Walter's head snaps around. *'Queenie!'*

Marlena leans over to release her, but before she can, Queenie squirms free, hitting the floor with a thunk. She scrabbles across the floor and leaps onto Walter, licking his face and wagging so hard she topples backward.

'Oh, Queenie! Where were you, you *bad, bad* girl? You had me so worried, you *bad, bad* girl!' Walter offers his face and head for licking, and Queenie wiggles and squirms in delight.

'Where was she?' I ask, turning to Marlena.

'She was running alongside the train when we pulled out yesterday,' she says, keeping her eyes trained on Walter and Queenie. 'I saw her from the window and sent Auggie out. He got down on his belly on the platform and scooped her up.'

'August did?' I say. 'Really?'

'Yes. And then she bit him for his trouble.'

Walter wraps both arms around his dog and buries his face in her coat.

Marlena watches for a moment longer and then turns toward the door. 'Well, I guess I'll be on my way,' she says.

'Marlena,' I say, reaching for her arm.

She stops.

'Thank you,' I say, dropping my hand. 'You have no idea what this means to him. To us, really.'

She throws me the quickest of glances – with just the merest hint of a smile – and then looks over the backs of her horses. 'Yes. Yes. I think I do.'

My eyes are moist as she climbs down from the car.

'Well, whadya know,' says Camel. 'Maybe he's human after all.'

'Who? August?' says Walter. He leans, grabs the handle of a trunk, and drags it across the floor. We're arranging the room into its daytime configuration, although Walter does everything at half speed because he insists on holding Queenie under one arm. 'Never.'

'You can let her go, you know,' I say. 'The door's closed.'

'He saved your dog,' Camel points out.

'He wouldn't have if he'd known she was mine. Queenie knows that. That's why she bit him. Yes, you knew, didn't you, baby?' he says, pulling her snout up to his face and reverting to baby talk. 'Yes, Queenie is a clever girl.'

'What makes you think he didn't know?' I say. 'Marlena knew.'

'Because I just know. There's not a human bone in that kike's body.'

'Watch your damned mouth!' I shout.

Walter stops to look at me. 'What? Oh, hey, you're not Jewish, are you? Look, I'm sorry. I didn't mean that. It was just a cheap shot,' he says.

'Yes, it was a cheap shot,' I say, still shouting. 'They're all cheap shots and I'm getting mighty damned sick of them. If you're a performer, you take shots at the working men. If you're a working man, you take shots at Poles. If you're a Pole, you take shots at Jews. And if you're a dwarf – well, you tell me, Walter? Is it just Jews and working men you hate, or do you also hate Poles?'

Walter reddens and looks down. 'I don't hate 'em. I don't hate anybody.' After a moment he adds, 'Well, okay, I really do hate August. But I hate him because he's a crazy son of a bitch.'

'Can't argue with that,' croaks Camel.

I look from Camel to Walter, and then back again. 'No,' I say with a sigh. 'No, I suppose you can't.'

In Hamilton, the temperature creeps up into the nineties, the sun beats relentlessly on the lot, and the lemonade goes missing.

The man from the juice joint, who left the great mixing vat for no more than a few minutes, storms off to Uncle Al, convinced that roustabouts are responsible.

Uncle Al has them rounded up. They emerge from behind the stable tent and menagerie, sleepy, with straw in their hair. I observe from some distance, but it's hard not to think they have an air of innocence about them.

Apparently Uncle Al doesn't agree. He storms back and forth, bellowing like Genghis Khan at a troop inspection. He screams in their faces, details the cost – both in supplies and lost sales – of the stolen lemonade and tells them that every one of them will have his pay docked the next time it happens. He whacks a few upside the head and dismisses them. They creep back to their resting spots, rubbing their heads and eyeing each other with suspicion.

With only ten minutes before the gate opens, the men at the juice joint mix up another batch using water from the animal troughs. They filter out the stray oats, hay, and whiskers through a pair of hose donated by a clown, and by the time they toss in the 'floaters' – wax lemon slices designed to give the impression that the concoction actually met fruit somewhere along the line – a swell of rubes is already approaching the midway. I don't know if the hose were clean, but I do notice that everyone on the show abstains from drinking lemonade that day.

The lemonade goes missing again in Dayton. Once again, a new batch is mixed up with trough water and set out moments before the rubes descend.

This time, when Uncle Al rounds up all the usual suspects, rather than docking their pay – a meaningless threat anyway since not one of them has been paid in more than eight weeks – he forces them to fish out the chamois grouch bags that hang around their necks and hand over two quarters each. The holders of the grouch bags become grouchy indeed.

The lemonade thief has hit the roustabouts where it hurts, and they're prepared to take action. When we get to Columbus, a few of them hide near the mixing vat and wait.

Shortly before showtime, August summons me to Marlena's dressing tent to look at an advertisement for a white liberty horse. Marlena needs another because twelve horses are more spectacular then ten, and spectacular is what it's all about. Besides, Marlena thinks Boaz is getting depressed at being left by himself in the menagerie while the others perform. This is what August says, but I think I'm being restored to favor after my blowup in the cookhouse. That, or August has decided to keep his friends close and his enemies even closer.

I'm sitting in a folding chair with *Billboard* on my lap and a bottle of sarsaparilla in my hand. Marlena is at the mirror adjusting her costume, and I'm trying not to stare. The one time our eyes meet in the mirror, I catch my breath, she reddens, and we both look elsewhere.

August is oblivious, buttoning his waistcoat and chatting amiably when Uncle Al bursts through the flap.

Marlena turns, outraged. 'Hey – ever heard of asking before you barge into a lady's dressing tent?'

Uncle Al pays no attention to her at all. He marches straight to August and jabs his finger in his chest.

'It's your *goddamned bull!*' he screams.

August looks down at the finger sticking into his chest, pauses a few beats, and then takes it daintily between thumb and forefinger. He moves Uncle Al's hand aside, and then flicks a handkerchief from his pocket to wipe the spit from his face.

'I beg your pardon?' he asks at the end of this operation.

'It's your *goddamned thieving bull!*' screams Uncle Al, once again showering August with spit. 'She pulls out her stake, takes it with her, drinks the goddamned lemonade, then goes back and sticks her stake in the ground!'

Marlena claps a hand over her mouth, but not in time.

Uncle Al spins, furious. 'You think it's funny? *You think it's funny?*'

The blood drains from her face.

I rise from my chair and step forward. 'Well, you have to admit there's a certain—'

Uncle Al turns, plants both hands squarely on my chest and shoves me so hard I fall backward onto a trunk.

He twists around to August. 'That fucking bull cost me a *fortune!* She's the reason I couldn't pay the men and had to take care of business and caught heat from the goddamned railroad authority! And for what? The goddamned thing won't perform and she steals the fucking lemonade!'

'Al!' August says sharply. 'Watch your mouth. I'll have you remember you're in the presence of a lady.'

Uncle Al's head swivels. He regards Marlena without remorse and turns back to August.

'Woody's going to tally up the losses,' he says. 'I'm taking it from your pay.'

'You've already taken it from the roustabouts,' Marlena says quietly. 'Are you planning to return their money?'

Uncle Al gazes upon her and I like his expression so

little I step forward until I'm between them. He turns his gaze to me, his jaw grinding in anger. Then he turns and marches out.

'What a jerk,' says Marlena, going back to her dressing table. 'I could have been getting dressed.'

August stands utterly still. Then he reaches for his top hat and bull hook.

Marlena sees this in the mirror. 'Where are you going?' she says quickly. 'August, what are you doing?'

He heads for the doorway.

She grabs his arm. 'Auggie! Where are you going?'

'I'm not the only one who's going to pay for the lemonade,' he says, shaking her off.

'August, no!' She grabs his elbow again. This time she throws her weight into it, trying to prevent him from leaving. 'August, wait! For God's sake. She didn't know. We'll secure her better next time—'

August wrenches free and Marlena crashes to the ground. He looks at her in utter disgust. Then he plants his hat on his head and turns away.

'August!' she shrieks. 'Stop!'

He pushes the flap open and is gone. Marlena sits, stunned, exactly where she fell. I look from her to the flap and then back again.

'I'm going after him,' I say, heading for the doorway.

'No! Wait!'

I freeze.

'There's no use,' she says, her voice hollow and small. 'You can't stop him.'

'I can sure as hell try. I did nothing last time and I'll never forgive myself.'

'You don't understand! You'll only make it worse! Jacob, please! You don't understand!'

I spin to face her. 'No! I don't! I don't understand anything anymore. Not a damned thing. Would you care to enlighten me?'

Her eyes open wide. Her mouth forms an *O*. Then she buries her face in her hands and bursts into tears.

I stare, horrified. Then I fall to my knees and gather her in my arms.

'Oh, Marlena, Marlena—'

'Jacob,' she whispers into my shirt. She clings to me as tightly as if I were keeping her from being sucked into a vortex.

SIXTEEN

My name isn't Rosie. It's Rose*mary*. You know that, Mr Jankowski.'

I am startled into awareness, blinking up into the unmistakable glare of fluorescent lighting.

'Eh? What?' My voice is thin, reedy. A black woman leans over me, tucking something around my legs. Her hair is fragrant and smooth.

'You called me Rosie just a minute ago. My name is Rose*mary*,' she says, straightening up. 'There, now isn't that better?'

I stare at her. Oh God. That's right. I'm old. And I'm in bed. Wait a minute – I called her Rosie?

'I was talking? *Out loud?*'

She laughs. 'Oh dear, yes. Oh yes, Mr Jankowski. You've been talking a blue streak since we left the lunchroom. Just talking my ear off.'

My face flushes. I stare at the clawed hands in my lap. God only knows what I've been saying. I only know what I've been thinking, and even that's in retrospect – until I suddenly found myself here, now, I thought I was *there*.

'Why, what's the matter?' Rosemary says.

'Did I . . . Did I say anything . . . you know, *embarrassing?*'

'Heavens, no! I don't understand why you haven't told the others, what with everyone going to the circus and all. I'll bet you've never even mentioned it though, have you?'

Rosemary watches me expectantly. Then her brow furrows. She pulls a chair over and sits next to me. 'You don't remember talking to me, do you?' she says gently.

I shake my head.

She takes both my hands in hers. They are warm and firmly fleshed. 'You said nothing to be embarrassed of, Mr Jankowski. You're a fine gentleman and I'm honored to know you.'

My eyes fill, and I drop my head so she won't see.

'Mr Jankowski—'

'I don't want to talk about it.'

'About the circus?'

'No. About . . . Oh hell, don't you understand? *I didn't even realize I was talking.* It's the beginning of the end. It's all downhill from here, and I didn't have very far to go. But I was really hoping to hang on to my brains. I really was.'

'You still have your brains, Mr Jankowski. You're sharp as a tack.'

We sit in silence for a minute.

'I'm scared, Rosemary.'

'Do you want me to talk to Dr Rashid?' she asks.

I nod. A tear slips from my eye and into my lap. I hold my eyes wide, hoping to contain the rest.

'It's another hour before you have to be ready to go. Would you like to rest a spell?'

I nod again. She gives my hand a final pat, lowers the head of my bed, and leaves. I lie back, listening to the buzzing lights and staring at the square tiles of the dropped ceiling. An expanse of pressed popcorn, of tasteless rice cakes.

If I'm completely honest with myself, there have been hints I was slipping.

Last week, when my people came, I didn't know them. I faked it, though – when they made their way toward me and I realized it was me they had come to see, I smiled and made all the usual placating noises, the 'oh yesses' and 'goodness graciouses' that make up my end of most conversations these days. I thought it was going just fine until a peculiar look crossed the mother's face. A horrified look, with her forehead scrumpled and her jaw slightly open. I raced back over the last few minutes of the conversation and realized I'd said the wrong thing, the polar opposite of what I should have said, and then I was mortified, because I don't dislike Isabelle. I just don't know her, and so I was having trouble paying attention to the details of her disastrous dance recital.

But then this Isabelle turned and laughed and in that instant I saw my wife. This made me weepy and these people whom I didn't recognize exchanged furtive glances and shortly thereafter announced that it was time to leave because Grandpa needed his rest. They patted my hand and they tucked my blanket in around my knees, and they left. They went out into the world, and they left me here. And to this day I have no idea who they were.

I know my children, don't get me wrong – but these are not my children. These are the children of my children, and their children, too, and maybe even theirs. Did I coo into their baby faces? Did I dandle them on my knee? I had three sons and two daughters, a houseful indeed, and none of them exactly held back. You multiply five by four and then by five again, and it's no wonder I forget how some of them fit in. It doesn't help that they take turns coming to see me, because even if I manage to commit one group to memory, they may not come around again for another eight or nine months, by which time I've forgotten whatever it was I may have known.

But what happened today was entirely different, and much, much scarier.

What in God's name did I say?

I close my eyes and reach for the far corners of my mind. They're no longer clearly defined. My brain is like a universe whose gases get thinner and thinner at the edges. But it doesn't dissolve into nothingness. I can sense something out there, just beyond my grasp, hovering, waiting – and God help me if I'm not skidding toward it again, mouth open wide.

SEVENTEEN

While August is off doing God knows what to Rosie, Marlena and I crouch on the grass in her dressing tent, clinging to each other like spider monkeys. I say almost nothing, just hold her head to my chest as her history spills out in a rushed whisper.

She tells me about meeting August – she was seventeen, and it had just dawned on her that the recent spate of bachelors joining her family for dinner were actually being presented as potential husbands. When one middle-aged banker with a receding chin, thinning hair, and reedy fingers showed up for dinner one time too many, she heard the doors of her future slamming all around her.

But even as the banker sniveled something that made Marlena blanch and stare in horror at her bowl of clam chowder, posters were being slapped up on every surface in town. The wheels of fate were in motion. The Benzini Brothers Most Spectacular Show on Earth was chugging toward them at that very moment, bringing with it a very real fantasy and, for Marlena, an escape that would prove as romantic as it was terrifying.

Two days later, on a brilliantly sunny day, the L'Arche family went to the circus. Marlena was standing in the menagerie tent in front of a string of stunning black and white Arabians when August first approached her. Her parents had wandered off to look at the cats, oblivious to the force that was about to enter their lives.

And August *was* a force. Charming, gregarious, and handsome as the devil. Dressed immaculately in blinding white jodhpurs, top hat and tails, he radiated both authority and irresistible charisma. Within minutes, he had secured the promise of a surreptitious meeting and disappeared before the L'Arche seniors rejoined their daughter.

When she met him later, at an art gallery, he began wooing her in earnest. He was twelve years her senior and glamorous in the way only an equestrian director can be. Before the end of the date, he had proposed.

He was charming and relentless. He refused to budge until she married him. He regaled her with stories of Uncle Al's desperation, and Uncle Al himself made pleas on August's behalf. They had already missed two jumps. A circus could not survive if it blew its route. This was an important decision, yes, but surely she understood how this was affecting *them?* That the lives of countless others depended on her making the right choice?

The seventeen-year-old Marlena gazed upon her future

in Boston for three more evenings and on the fourth packed a suitcase.

At this point in her story, she dissolves into tears. I'm still holding her, still rocking back and forth. Eventually she pulls away, wiping her eyes with her hands.

'You should go,' she says.

'I don't want to.'

She whimpers, reaching across the divide to stroke my cheek with the back of her hand.

'I want to see you again,' I say.

'You see me every day.'

'You know what I mean.'

There's a long pause. She drops her gaze to the ground. Her mouth moves a few times before she finally speaks. 'I can't.'

'Marlena, for God's sake—'

'I just can't. I'm married. I made my bed, and now I have to lie in it.'

I kneel in front of her, searching her face for a signal to stay. After an agonizing wait, I realize I'm not going to find one.

I kiss her on the forehead and leave.

Before I've gone forty yards, I've heard more than I ever wanted to about how Rosie paid for the lemonade.

Apparently August stormed into the menagerie and banished everyone. The puzzled menagerie men and a handful of others stood outside, their ears pressed to the seams of the great canvas tent as a torrent of angry screaming began. This sent the rest of the animals into a panic – the chimps screeched, the cats roared, and the zebras yelped. Despite this, the distraught listeners could still make out the hollow thud of bull hook hitting flesh, again and again and again.

At first Rosie bellowed and whimpered. When she progressed to squealing and shrieking, many of the men turned away, unable to take any more. One of them ran for Earl, who entered the menagerie and hauled August out by his armpits. He kicked and struggled like a madman even as Earl dragged him across the lot and up the stairs into the privilege car.

The remaining men found Rosie lying on her side, quivering, her foot still chained to a stake.

'I hate that man,' says Walter as I climb into the stock car. He's sitting on the cot, stroking Queenie's ears. 'I really, really hate that man.'

'Someone wanna tell me what's going on?' Camel calls from behind the row of trunks. ''Cuz I know something is. Jacob? Help me out here. Walter ain't talking.'

I say nothing.

'There was no call to be that brutal. No call at all,' Walter continues. 'He damn near started a stampede, too. Could have killed the lot of us. Were you there? Did you hear any of it?'

Our eyes meet.

'No,' I say.

'Well, I wouldn't mind knowing what in blazes you're talking about,' says Camel. 'But it seems I don't count for squat here. Hey, ain't it dinnertime?'

'I'm not hungry,' I say.

'Me either,' says Walter.

'Well, I am,' says Camel, disgruntled. 'But I bet neither one of you thought of that. And I bet neither one of you picked up so much as a piece of bread for an old man.'

Walter and I look at each other. 'Well, I was there,' he says, his eyes full of accusation. 'You wanna know what I heard?' he says.

'No,' I say, staring at Queenie. She meets my gaze and whacks the blanket a few times with her stump.

'You sure?'

'Yes I'm sure.'

'Thought you might be interested, you being the vet and all.'

'I am interested,' I say loudly. 'But I'm also afraid of what it might make me do.'

Walter looks at me for a long time. 'So who's going to get that old git some grub? You or me?'

'Hey! Mind your manners!' cries the old git.

'I'll go,' I say. I turn and leave the stock car.

Halfway to the cookhouse, I realize I'm grinding my teeth.

When I come back with Camel's food, Walter is gone. A few minutes later he returns, carrying a large bottle of whiskey in each hand.

'Well, God bless your soul,' cackles Camel, who is now propped up in the corner. He points at Walter with a limp hand. 'Where in tarnation did you come up with that?'

'A friend on the pie car owed me a favor. I figured we could all use a little forgetting tonight.'

'Well, go on then,' says Camel. 'Stop yapping and hand it over.'

Walter and I turn in unison to glare.

The lines on Camel's grizzled face furrow deeper. 'Well, jeez, you two sure are a couple of sourpusses, ain't you? What's the matter? Someone spit in your soup?'

'Here. Pay him no mind,' says Walter, shoving a bottle of whiskey against my chest.

'What do you mean, "pay him no mind"? In my day, a boy was taught to respect his elders.'

Instead of answering, Walter carries the other bottle over and crouches down beside him. When Camel reaches for it, Walter bats his hand away.

'Hell no, old man. You spill that and we'll all three be sourpusses.'

He raises the bottle up to Camel's lips and holds it as he swallows a half-dozen times. He looks like a baby taking a bottle. Walter turns on his heels and leans against the wall. Then he takes a long swig himself.

'What's the matter – don't like the whiskey?' he says, wiping his mouth and gesturing at the unopened bottle in my hand.

'I like it just fine. Listen, I don't have any money so I don't know when or if I can ever make it up to you, but can I have this?'

'I already gave it to you.'

'No, I mean . . . can I take it for someone else?'

Walter looks at me for a moment, his eyes crinkled at the edges. 'It's a woman, isn't it?'

'Nope.'

'You're lying.'

'No I'm not.'

'I'll bet you five bucks it's a woman,' he says, taking

another drink. His Adam's apple bobs up and down and the brown liquid lowers by almost an inch. It's astounding how quickly he and Camel manage to get hard liquor down their gullets.

'She *is* female,' I say.

'Ha!' snorts Walter. 'You better not let her hear you say that. Although whoever or whatever she is, she's more suitable than where your mind's been lately.'

'I've got some making up to do,' I say. 'I let her down today.'

Walter looks up in sudden understanding.

'How 'bout a little more of that?' Camel says irritably. 'Maybe he don't want none, but I do. Not that I blame the boy for wanting a little action. You're only young once. You gotta get it while you can, I says. Yessir, get it while you can. Even if it costs you a bottle of sauce.'

Walter smiles. He holds the bottle up to Camel's lips again and lets him have several long swallows. Then he caps it, leans across, still on his haunches, and hands it to me.

'Take her this one, too. You tell her I'm also sorry. Real sorry, in fact.'

'Hey!' shouts Camel. 'There ain't no woman in the world worth two bottles of whiskey! Come on now!'

I rise to my feet and slip a bottle in each pocket of my jacket.

'Aw, come on now!' Camel pleads. 'Aw, that just ain't no fair.'

His wheedling and complaining follow me until I'm out of earshot.

* * *

It's dusk, and several parties have already started at the performers' end of the train, including – I can't help but notice – one in Marlena and August's car. I wouldn't have gone, but it's significant that I wasn't invited. I guess August and I are on the outs again; or rather, since I already hate him more than I've ever hated anyone or anything in my life, I guess I'm on the outs with him.

Rosie is at the far end of the menagerie, and as my eyes adjust to the twilight I see someone standing beside her. It's Greg, the man from the cabbage patch.

'Hey,' I say as I approach.

He turns his head. He's holding a tube of zinc ointment in one hand and is dabbing Rosie's punctured skin. There are a couple of dozen white spots on this side alone.

'Jesus,' I say, surveying her. Droplets of blood and histamine ooze up under the zinc.

Her amber eyes seek mine. She blinks those outrageously long lashes and sighs, a great whooshing exhalation that rattles all through her trunk.

I'm flooded with guilt.

'What do you want?' grunts Greg, continuing with his task.

'I just wanted to see how she was.'

'Well, you can see that, can't you? Now, if you'll excuse me,' he says, dismissing me. He turns back to her. '*Nogę*,' he says. '*No, daj nogę!*'

After a moment, the elephant lifts her foot and holds it in front of her. Greg kneels down and rubs some ointment in her armpit, right in front of her strange gray breast, which hangs from her chest, like a woman's.

'*Jesteś dobrą dziewczynką,*' he says, standing up and screwing the cap back on the ointment. '*Połóż nogę.*'

Rosie sets her foot back on the ground. '*Masz, moja piękna,*' he says, digging in his pocket. Her trunk swings around, investigating. He pulls out a mint, brushes off the lint, and hands it to her. She plucks it nimbly from his fingers and pops it in her mouth.

I stare in shock – I think my mouth may even be open. In the space of two seconds, my mind has zigzagged from her unwillingness to perform, to her history with the elephant tramp, to her lemonade thievery, and back to the cabbage patch.

'Jesus Christ,' I say.

'What?' says Greg, fondling her trunk.

'She understands you.'

'Yes, so what?'

'What do you mean, "*so what*"? My God, do you have any idea what this means?'

'Now wait just a cotton-pickin' minute,' Greg says as I come up to Rosie. He forces his shoulder between us, his face hard.

'Humor me,' I say. 'Please. About the last thing in the world I'd do is hurt this bull.'

He continues to stare at me. I'm still not entirely sure he won't clobber me from behind, but I turn to Rosie, anyway. She blinks at me.

'Rosie, *nogę!*' I say.

She blinks again and opens her mouth in a smile.

'*Nogę,* Rosie!'

She fans her ears and sighs.

'*Proszę?*' I say.

She sighs again. Then she shifts her weight and lifts her foot.

'Dear Mother of God.' I hear my voice as though from outside of my body. My heart is pounding, my head spinning. 'Rosie,' I say, laying a hand on her shoulder. 'Just one more thing.' I look her straight in the eye, pleading with her. Surely she knows how important this is. Please God please God please God—

'Do tyłu, Rosie! Do tyłu!'

Another deep sigh, another subtle shifting of weight, and then she takes a couple of steps backward.

I yelp with delight and turn to an astonished Greg. I leap forward, grab him by the shoulders, and kiss him full on the mouth.

'What the hell!'

I sprint for the exit. About fifteen feet away I stop and turn around. Greg is still spitting, wiping his mouth in disgust.

I dig the bottles out of my pockets. His expression changes to one of interest, the back of his hand still raised to his mouth.

'Here, catch!' I say, sending a bottle flying at him. He snags it from the air, looks at its label, and then glances up hopefully at the other. I toss it to him.

'Give those to our new star, will you?'

Greg cocks his head thoughtfully and turns to Rosie, who is already smiling and reaching for the bottles.

For the next ten days, I serve as August's personal Polish coach. In each city he has a practice ring set up in the back end, and day after day, the four of us – August,

Marlena, Rosie, and I – spend the hours between our arrival in town and the start of the matinée working on Rosie's act. Although she already takes part in the daily parade and Spec, she has yet to perform in the show. Although the wait is killing Uncle Al, August doesn't want to unveil her act until it's perfect.

I spend my days sitting on a chair just outside the ring curb with a knife in one hand and a bucket between my legs, cutting fruit and vegetables into chunks for the primates and shouting Polish phrases as required. August's accent is appalling, but Rosie – perhaps because August is usually repeating something I've just yelled – obeys without fail. He hasn't touched her with the bull hook since we discovered the language barrier. He just walks beside her, waving it under her belly and behind her legs, but never – not once – does it make contact.

It's hard to reconcile this August with the other one, and to be honest I don't try very hard. I've seen flashes of this August before – this brightness, this conviviality, this generosity of spirit – but I know what he's capable of, and I won't forget it. The others can believe what they like, but I don't believe for a second that this is the real August and the other an aberration. And yet I can see how they might be fooled—

He is delightful. He is charming. He shines like the sun. He lavishes attention on the great storm-colored beast and her tiny rider from the moment we meet in the morning until the moment they disappear for the parade. He is attentive and tender toward Marlena, and kindly and paternal toward Rosie.

He seems unaware that there ever was any bad blood

between us, despite my reserve. He smiles broadly; he pats me on the back. He notices that my clothes are shabby and that very afternoon the Monday Man arrives with more. He declares that the show's vet should not have to bathe with buckets of cold water and invites me to shower in the stateroom. And when he finds out that Rosie likes gin and ginger ale better than anything in the world except perhaps watermelon, he ensures that she gets both, every single day. He cozies up to her. He whispers in her ear, and she basks in the attention, trumpeting happily at the sight of him.

Doesn't she remember?

I scrutinize him, watching for chinks, but the new August persists. Before long, his optimism permeates the entire lot. Even Uncle Al is affected – he stops each day to observe our progress and within a couple of days orders up new posters that feature Rosie with Marlena sitting astride her head. He stops whacking people, and shortly thereafter people stop ducking. He becomes positively jolly. Rumors circulate that there may actually be money on payday, and even the working men begin to crack smiles.

It's only when I catch Rosie actually *purring* under August's loving ministrations that my conviction starts to crumble. And what I'm left looking at in its place is a terrible thing.

Maybe it was me. Maybe I wanted to hate him because I'm in love with his wife, and if that's the case, what kind of a man does that make me?

In Pittsburgh, I finally go to confession. I break down in the confessional and sob like a baby, telling the priest about my parents, my night of debauchery, and my adulterous thoughts. The somewhat startled priest mutters a few *there-theres* and then tells me to pray the rosary and forget about Marlena. I am too ashamed to admit that I haven't got a rosary, so when I return to the stock car I ask Walter and Camel if either of them has one. Walter looks at me strangely, and Camel offers me a green elk-tooth necklace.

I'm well aware of Walter's opinion. He still hates August beyond all expression, and although he doesn't say anything I know exactly what he thinks of my shifting opinion. We still share the care and feeding of Camel, but the three of us no longer exchange stories during the long nights spent on the rails. Instead, Walter reads Shakespeare and Camel gets drunk and cranky and increasingly demanding.

In Meadville, August decides that tonight is the night.

When he delivers the good news, Uncle Al is rendered speechless. He clasps his hand to his breast and looks starward with tear-filled eyes. Then, as his grovelers duck for cover, he reaches out and claps August on the shoulder. He gives him a manly shake and then, because he's clearly too overwhelmed to actually say anything, gives him another.

I'm examining a cracked hoof in the blacksmith tent when August sends for me.

'August?' I say, placing my face near the opening of Marlena's dressing tent. It billows slightly, snapping in the wind. 'You wanted to see me?'

'Jacob!' he calls out in a booming voice. 'So glad you could come! Please, come in! Come in, my boy!'

Marlena is in costume. She sits in front of her vanity with one foot up on its edge, wrapping the long pink ribbon from one of her slippers around her ankle. August sits nearby, in top hat and tails. He twirls a silver-tipped cane. Its handle is bent, like a bull hook.

'Please take a seat,' he says, rising from his chair and patting its seat.

I hesitate for a fraction of a second and then cross the tent. Once I am seated, August stands in front of us. I glance over at Marlena.

'Marlena, Jacob – my dearest dear, and my dearest friend,' says August, removing his hat and gazing upon us with moist eyes. 'This last week has been amazing in so many ways. I think it would not be an exaggeration to call it a journey of the soul. Just two weeks ago, this show was on the brink of collapse. The livelihood – and indeed, in this financial climate, I think I can safely say the lives, yes the very lives! – of everyone on this show were in danger. And do you want to know why?'

His bright eyes move from me to Marlena, from Marlena to me.

'Why?' Marlena asks obligingly, lifting her other leg and wrapping the broad satin ribbon around her ankle.

'Because we went into the hole acquiring an animal that was supposed to be the salvation of our show. And because we also had to buy a train car to house her. And because we then discovered that this animal apparently knew nothing, yet ate everything. And because keeping her fed meant that we couldn't afford to feed our employees and we had to let some of them go.'

My head snaps up at this oblique reference to

redlighting, but August stares beyond me, at a sidewall. He is silent uncomfortably long, almost as though he's forgotten we're here. Then he remembers himself with a start.

'But we have been saved,' he says, gazing down at me with love in his eyes, 'and the reason we have been saved is that we have been doubly blessed. Fate was smiling on us that day in June when she led Jacob to our train. She handed us not only a veterinarian with an Ivy League degree – a veterinarian befitting a big show like ours – but also a veterinarian so devoted to his charges that he made a most amazing discovery. A discovery that ended up saving the show.'

'No, really, all I—'

'Not a word, Jacob. I won't let you deny it. I had a feeling about you the very first time I laid eyes on you. Didn't I, dear?' August turns to Marlena and waggles his finger at her.

She nods. With her second slipper secured, she removes her foot from the edge of the vanity and crosses her legs. Her toes start bobbing immediately.

August gazes at her. 'But Jacob didn't work alone,' he continues. 'You, my beautiful and talented darling, have been brilliant. And Rosie – because she, of all of us, is not to be forgotten in this equation. So patient, so willing, so—' He stops, and inhales so deeply his nostrils flare. When he continues, his voice cracks. 'Because she is a beautiful, magnificent animal with a heart full of forgiveness and the capacity to appreciate misunderstanding. Because thanks to the three of you, the Benzini Brothers Most Spectacular Show on Earth is about to rise to a new level of greatness. We are truly joining the ranks of the big shows, and none of it could have happened without you.'

He beams at us, his cheeks so flushed I'm afraid he might burst into tears.

'Oh! I almost forgot,' he cries, clapping his hands in front of him. He rushes to a trunk and fishes around inside. He pulls two small boxes out. One is square, one is rectangular and flat. Both are gift-wrapped.

'For you, my dear,' he says, handing the flat one to Marlena.

'Oh, Auggie! You shouldn't have!'

'How do you know?' he says, smiling. 'Perhaps it's a pen set.'

Marlena tears off the gift wrap, revealing a blue velvet box. She glances up at him, unsure, and then opens its hinged lid. A diamond choker sparkles on the red satin lining.

'Oh, Auggie,' she says. She looks from the necklace to August, her brow creased with worry. 'Auggie, it's gorgeous. But surely we can't afford—'

'Hush,' he says, leaning over to grab her hand. He plants a kiss on its palm. 'Tonight heralds a new era. There is nothing too good for tonight.'

She picks the necklace up, letting it dangle from her fingers. She is clearly stunned.

August turns and hands me the square box.

I slide the ribbon off and carefully open the paper. The box inside is also of blue velvet. A lump rises in my throat.

'Come on now,' August says impatiently. 'Open it! Don't be shy!'

The lid opens with a pop. It's a gold pocket watch.

'August—' I say.

'Do you like it?'

'It's beautiful. But I can't accept it.'

'Yes, of course you can. And you will!' he says, grabbing Marlena's hand and pulling her to her feet. He plucks the necklace from her hand.

'No, I can't,' I say. 'It's a wonderful gesture. But it's too much.'

'You can and you will,' he says firmly. 'I am your boss and that is a direct order. Anyway, why shouldn't you accept that from me? I seem to remember you gave one up for a friend not too long ago.'

I squeeze my eyes shut. When I open them again, Marlena is standing with her back to August, holding her hair up as he fastens the necklace around her throat.

'There,' he says.

She twirls around and leans toward her vanity mirror. Her fingers reach tentatively for the diamonds on her throat.

'I gather you like it?' he says.

'I don't even know what to say. It's the most beautiful thing – Oh!' she squeals. 'I nearly forgot! I've got a surprise, too.'

She pulls the third drawer of her vanity open and digs through it, tossing aside gauzy bits of costume. Then she pulls out a great expanse of shimmering pink something. She holds it by its edges, giving it a little shake so that it sparkles, throwing a thousand points of light.

'So, what do you think? What do you think?' she says, beaming.

'It's . . . It's . . . What is it?' says August.

'It's a headpiece for Rosie,' she says, pinning it to her chest with her chin and spreading the rest of it across her front. 'Look, see? This part attaches to the back of her halter, and these parts go on the side, and this part comes down over her forehead. I made it. I've been working on it for two weeks. It matches mine.' She looks up. There's a small spot of red on each of her cheeks.

August stares at her. His lower jaw moves a bit, but no sound comes out. Then he reaches forward and clasps her in his arms.

I have to look away.

Thanks to Uncle Al's superior marketing techniques, the big top is packed solid. So many tickets sell that after Uncle Al entreats the crowd to shift closer together for the fourth time, it becomes clear that this won't be enough.

Roustabouts are sent to toss straw down on the hippodrome track. To keep the crowd occupied while this happens, the band plays a concert and the clowns, including Walter, tour the stands, handing out candy and chucking tots' chins.

The performers and animals are lined up out back, ready to start the Spec. They've been waiting for twenty minutes and are fidgety.

Uncle Al bursts out the back of the big top. 'Okay, folks, listen up,' he barks. 'We've got a straw house tonight, so keep to the inside track and make sure there's a good five feet between your animals and the rubes. If so much as one child gets run over, I'll personally flay the person whose animal did it. Got it?'

Nods, murmurs, more adjusting of outfits.

Uncle Al pops his head back inside the big top, raising his hand for the band leader. 'All right. Let's go! Knock 'em dead! But don't, if you know what I mean.'

Not a single child is run over. In fact, everyone is brilliant, and none more so than Rosie. She carries Marlena on her pink sequined head during the Spec, curling her trunk in a salute. There's a clown in front of her, a lanky man who alternately does back flips and cartwheels. At one point, Rosie reaches forward and grabs hold of his pants. She yanks so hard his feet leave the ground. He turns, outraged, to face a smiling elephant. The crowd whistles and applauds, but after that the clown keeps his distance.

When it's nearly time for Rosie's act, I sneak into the big top and stand flattened against a section of seats. While the acrobats are receiving their applause, roustabouts run into the center ring, rolling two balls ahead of them: one small, the other large, and both decorated with red stars and blue stripes. Uncle Al raises his arms and glances at the back end. He looks right past me, making eye contact with August. He gives a slight nod and flicks one hand at the band leader, who slides into a Gounod waltz.

Rosie enters the big top, promenading beside August. She carries Marlena on her head, her trunk curled in a salute and her mouth open in a smile. When they enter the center ring, Rosie lifts Marlena from her head and places her on the ground.

Marlena skips theatrically around the border, a whirl of shimmering pink. She smiles, spinning, throwing her arms out and blowing kisses to the crowd. Rosie follows at a fast clip, her trunk curled high in the air. August moves beside her, hovering with the silver-tipped cane rather than the bull hook. I watch his mouth, lip-reading the Polish phrases he's learned by rote.

Marlena dances around the ring's perimeter one more time and comes to a stop beside the smaller ball. August brings Rosie to the center of the ring. Marlena watches and then turns to the audience. She puffs up her cheeks and wipes a hand across her forehead in an exaggerated gesture of exhaustion. Then she sits on the ball. She crosses her legs and sets her elbows upon them, resting her chin in her hands. She taps her foot, rolling her eyes toward the heavens. Rosie observes, smiling, her trunk held high. After a moment, she turns slowly and lowers her enormous gray rear onto the larger ball. Laughter ripples through the crowd.

Marlena does a double take and stands, her jaw dropped in mock outrage. She turns her back on Rosie. The elephant also stands and then shambles around to present Marlena with her tail. The crowd roars with delight.

Marlena looks back and scowls. With dramatic flair, she lifts one foot and plants it on her ball. Then she crosses her arms in front of her and nods once, deeply, as if to say, *Take that, elephant.*

Rosie curls her trunk, lifts her right front foot, and sets it gently on her ball. Marlena glares, furious. Then she thrusts both arms out to the side and lifts her other foot from the ground. She straightens her knee slowly, her other leg pointing to the side, toes extended like a ballerina's. Once her leg is straight she lowers her second foot so that she's standing on the ball. She smiles broadly, sure that she has finally outsmarted the elephant. The audience claps and whistles, also sure. Marlena shuffles around so her back is to Rosie and lifts her arms in victory.

Rosie waits a moment, and then sets her other front foot on the ball. The crowd explodes. Marlena does a double take over her shoulder. She shuffles back around so that she's facing Rosie and once again places her hands on her hips. She frowns deeply, shaking her head in frustration. She lifts a finger and starts wagging it at Rosie, but after just a moment she freezes. Her face lights up. An idea! She raises her finger high in the air, turning so that the whole audience can absorb that she is about to outdo the elephant once and for all.

She concentrates for a moment, staring down at her satin slippers. And then, to a rising drum roll, she starts shuffling her feet, rolling the ball forward. She goes faster and faster, her feet a blur of motion, rolling the ball around the ring as the audience claps and whistles. Then there is a wild explosion of delighted cries—

Marlena stops and looks up. She has been so busy concentrating on her ball that she hasn't noticed the ridiculous sight behind her. The pachyderm is perched on the larger ball, with all four feet crowded together and her back arched. The drum roll begins again. At first, nothing. Then, slowly, slowly, the ball begins to roll under Rosie's feet.

The bandmaster signals the band into a fast number, and Rosie moves the ball a dozen feet. Marlena smiles in delight, clapping, extending her hands toward Rosie and inviting the crowd to adore her. Then she hops down from her ball and skips over to Rosie, who climbs rather more carefully down from hers. She drops her trunk and Marlena sits in its curve, hooks an arm around it, and points her toes daintily. Rosie raises her trunk, holding Marlena aloft. Then she deposits Marlena on her head and departs the big top to the cheers of an adoring crowd.

And then the shower of money starts – the sweet, sweet shower of money. Uncle Al is delirious, standing in the center of the hippodrome track with his arms and face raised, basking in the coins that rain down on him. He keeps his face raised even as coins bounce off his cheeks, nose, and forehead. I think he may actually be crying.

EIGHTEEN

I catch up with them as Marlena slides down from Rosie's head.

'You were brilliant! Brilliant!' says August, kissing her on the cheek. 'Did you see that, Jacob? Did you see how brilliant they were?'

'Sure did.'

'Do me a favor and take Rosie around, would you? I've got to go back inside.' He hands me the silver-tipped cane. He looks at Marlena, sighs deeply, and claps a hand to his breast. 'Brilliant. Simply brilliant. Don't forget,' he says, turning and walking a few strides backward, 'you're on with the horses right after Lottie.'

'I'll get them right now,' she says.

August heads back to the big top.

'You were spectacular,' I say.

'Yes, she was good, wasn't she?' Marlena leans over

and plants a loud kiss on Rosie's shoulder, leaving a perfect lip print on the gray hide. She reaches out and rubs it with her thumb.

'I meant you,' I say.

She blushes, her thumb still on Rosie's shoulder.

I regret saying it instantly. Not that she wasn't spectacular – she was, but that wasn't all I meant and she knew it and now I've made her uncomfortable. I decide to beat a hasty retreat.

'*Chodź*, Rosie,' I say, motioning her forward. '*Chodź, mój malutki pączuszek.*'

'Jacob, wait.' Marlena lays her fingers on the inside of my elbow.

In the distance, right at the entrance to the big top, August stops and stiffens. It's as though he sensed the physical contact. He turns around slowly, his face somber. Our eyes lock.

'Can you do me a favor?' Marlena asks.

'Sure. Of course,' I say, glancing nervously at August. Marlena hasn't noticed that he's watching us. I place my hand on my hip, causing her fingers to fall from my elbow.

'Can you bring Rosie to my dressing tent? I have a surprise planned.'

'Uh, sure. I guess so,' I say. 'When do you want her there?'

'Take her there now. I'll be along in a bit. Oh, and wear something nice. I want it to be a proper party.'

'Me?'

'Of course you. I've got to do my act now, but I won't be long. And if you see August ahead of time, not a word, okay?'

I nod. When I look back at the big top, August has disappeared inside.

Rosie is perfectly agreeable to the unusual arrangement. She plods along by my side to the edge of Marlena's dressing tent and then waits patiently as Grady and Bill untie the bottom of the sidewall from the stakes.

'So, how's Camel doing, anyway?' asks Grady, crouching down and working on a rope. Rosie reaches out to investigate.

'About the same,' I say. 'He thinks he's getting better, but I don't see it. I think he doesn't notice as much because he doesn't have to do anything. Well, that and he's usually drunk.'

'That sure sounds like Camel,' says Bill. 'Where's he getting liquor? It is liquor, ain't it? He ain't drinking that jake shit no more, is he?'

'No, it's liquor. My bunkmate's taken a shine to him.'

'Who? That Kinko guy?' says Grady.

'Yup.'

'I thought he hated working men.'

Rosie reaches out and takes Grady's hat. He turns around and swipes at it, but she holds it high. 'Hey, would you keep your bull under control?'

I look into her eye, which twinkles back at me. '*Połóż!*' I say sternly, although I'm finding it hard not to laugh. Her great ear waves forward and she drops the hat. I stoop to retrieve it.

'Walter – Kinko – could use some softening around the edges,' I say, handing the hat back to Grady, 'but he's been real decent to Camel. Gave up his bed for him.

Found his son, even. Talked him into meeting us in Providence to take Camel off our hands.'

'No kidding,' says Grady, stopping and looking at me in surprise. 'Does Camel know this?'

'Uh . . . Yeah.'

'And how did he take it?'

I grimace and suck the air in through my teeth.

'That well, huh?'

'It's not like we had a lot of alternatives.'

'No, that you didn't.' Grady pauses. 'What happened wasn't really his fault. His family probably even knows that by now. The war made a lot of men go funny. You knew he was a gunner, didn't you?'

'No. He doesn't talk about it.'

'Say, you don't think Camel could manage standing in line, do you?'

'I doubt it,' I say. 'Why?'

'We been hearing rumors that maybe there's money finally, maybe even for the working men. Hadn't given the story much credence up till now, but after what just happened in the big top, I'm beginning to think there might be half a chance.'

The bottom of the sidewall is now flapping free. Bill and Grady lift it, exposing the rearranged interior of Marlena's dressing tent. There's a table at one end, with a heavy linen tablecloth and three place settings. The other end of the tent has been completely cleared.

'Where do you want the stake? Over there?' says Grady, gesturing toward the open space.

'Guess so,' I say.

'Back in a sec,' he says, disappearing. A few minutes

later he's back, carrying two sixteen-pound sledges, one in each hand. He slings one through the air to Bill, who looks not even remotely alarmed. He catches its handle and follows Grady into the tent. They pound the iron stake into the ground in a battery of perfectly timed strokes.

I lead Rosie in and crouch on my hams while I secure her leg chain. She leaves that leg planted firmly on the ground, but is leaning hard on the others. When I rise again, I see she is inclining toward a large pile of watermelons in the corner.

'You want us to tie it back down?' says Grady, pointing at the flapping sidewall.

'Yes, if you don't mind. I don't think Marlena wants August to know Rosie's in here till he steps inside.'

Grady shrugs. 'No skin off my nose.'

'Say, Grady? Do you think you could keep an eye on Rosie for just a minute? I need to change my clothes.'

'I don't know,' he says, looking at Rosie with narrowed eyes. 'She's not going to pull her stake out or anything, is she?'

'I doubt it. But here,' I say, walking to the pile of watermelons. Rosie curls her trunk and opens her mouth in a wide smile. I carry one over and smash it to the ground in front of her. It explodes, and her trunk dives instantly into its red flesh. She scoops chunks into her mouth, rind and all. 'There's some insurance,' I say.

I duck under the sidewall and go get changed.

When I return, Marlena is there, wearing the beaded silk dress August gave her that night we had dinner in their stateroom. The diamond necklace sparkles on her throat.

Rosie is munching happily on another watermelon – it's at least her second, but there are still half a dozen in the corner. Marlena has removed Rosie's headpiece, which hangs over the chair in front of her vanity. There is now a serving table laden with silver-domed platters and wine bottles. I smell seared beef, and my stomach twists from hunger.

Marlena is flushed, digging through one of the drawers of her vanity. 'Oh, Jacob!' she says, looking over her shoulder. 'Good. I was getting worried. He'll be here any second. Oh heavens. Now I can't find it.' She straightens up suddenly, leaving the drawer open. Silk scarves spill over its edge. 'Can you do me a favor?'

'Of course,' I say.

She extracts a bottle of champagne from a three-legged silver cooler. The ice inside shifts and jingles. Water drips from the bottle's bottom as she hands it to me. 'Can you pop it just as he comes in? Also, yell "surprise!"'

'Sure,' I say, taking the bottle. I remove the wire contraption and wait with my thumb on the cork. Rosie reaches over with her trunk, trying to pry her way between my fingers and the bottle. Marlena continues to dig through the drawer.

'What is this?'

I look up. August stands in front of us.

'Oh!' cries Marlena, spinning around. 'Surprise!'

'Surprise!' I shout, twisting away from Rosie and popping the cork. It bounces off the canvas and lands in the grass. Champagne bubbles over my fingers, and I laugh. Marlena is there instantly with two champagne flutes, trying to catch the overflow. By the time we get coordinated, we've spilled a third of the bottle, which Rosie is still trying to take from me.

I look down. Marlena's rose silk shoes are dark with champagne. 'Oh, I'm so sorry!' I laugh.

'No, no! Don't be silly,' she says. 'We have another bottle.'

'I said *what is this?*'

Marlena and I freeze, our hands still tangled. She looks up, her eyes suddenly worried. She holds a mostly empty champagne flute in each hand. 'It's a surprise. A celebration.'

August stares. His tie is loose, his jacket open. His face is an utter blank.

'A surprise, yes,' he says. He removes his hat and turns it over in his hands, examining it. His hair rises in a wave from his forehead. He looks up suddenly, with one eyebrow cocked. 'Or so you think.'

'I beg your pardon?' Marlena asks in a hollow voice.

He flicks his wrist and sends his hat sailing into a corner. Then he removes his jacket, slowly, methodically. He walks to the vanity and swings his jacket as though he's going to place it over the back of the chair. When he sees Rosie's headpiece, he stops. Instead, he folds the jacket and places it neatly on the chair's seat. His eyes move down to the open drawer and silk scarves spilling over its sides.

'Did I catch you at a bad moment?' he says, looking up at us. He sounds as though he's just asked someone to pass the salt.

'Darling, I don't know what you're talking about,' Marlena says softly.

August reaches down and pulls a long, nearly transparent orange scarf free from the drawer. Then he weaves it through and around his fingers. 'Having a little fun with scarves, were you?' He pulls the end of the scarf, and it slips through his fingers again. 'Oh, you're a naughty one. But I guess I knew that.'

Marlena stares, speechless.

'So,' he says. 'Is this a postcoital celebration? Did I give you long enough? Or perhaps I should go away for a while and come back? I must say, the elephant is a new twist. I dread to think.'

'What in God's name are you talking about?' Marlena says.

'Two flutes,' he observes, nodding at her hands.

'What?' She lifts the flutes so quickly their contents slosh onto the grass. 'Are you talking about these? The third one is right—'

'Do you think I'm an idiot?'

'August—' I say.

'Shut up! Just shut the fuck up!'

His face is purple. His eyes bulge. He trembles with rage.

Marlena and I stand perfectly still, stunned into silence. Then August's face undergoes another transformation, melding into something close to complacency. He continues to play with the scarf, even smiles at it. Then he folds it carefully and places it back in the drawer. When he straightens up, he shakes his head slowly.

'You . . . You . . . You . . .' He raises a hand, stirring the air with his fingers. But then he trails off, his attention caught by the silver-tipped cane. It's leaning against the sidewall near the table, where I left it. He saunters over and picks it up.

I hear liquid hitting the ground behind me and turn quickly. Rosie is peeing into the grass, her ears flat against her head, her trunk curled under her face.

August holds the cane and slaps its silver handle repeatedly against his palm. 'How long did you think you could keep it from me?' He pauses for a second, and then looks me straight in the eye. 'Eh?'

'August,' I say. 'I have no idea what—'

'I said *shut up!*' He spins and swipes the cane across the serving table, knocking platters, cutlery, and bottles to the ground. Then he raises a foot and kicks the whole thing over. It crashes onto its side, sending china, glass, and food flying.

August stares down at the mess for a moment, and then looks up. 'You think I don't see what's going on?' His eyes drill into Marlena, his temple pulses. 'Oh, you're good, my dear,' he wiggles his finger at her and smiles, 'I'll give you that. You're very good.'

He walks back to the vanity and rests the cane against it. Then he leans over and peers into the mirror. He pushes the hair that's fallen over his forehead back into place and then smoothes it with his palm. Then he freezes, his hand still at his forehead. 'Peek-a-boo,' he says, looking at our reflections. 'I see you.'

Marlena's horrified face looks back at me from the mirror.

August turns and picks up Rosie's pink sequined headpiece. 'And that's the trouble, isn't it? I see you. You think I don't, but I do. This was a nice touch, I must admit,' he says, turning the shimmering headpiece over in his hands. 'The devoted wife, hiding away in a closet, sewing up a storm. Or was it a closet? Maybe it was right here. Or maybe you went to that whore's tent. Whores look after each other, don't they?' He looks at me. 'So, where did you do it, eh, Jacob? Where, exactly, have you fucked my wife?'

I take Marlena's elbow. 'Come on. Let's go,' I say.

'*Aha!* So you don't even deny it!' he screams. He clutches the headpiece in white-knuckled fists and pulls, screaming through gritted teeth, until a split zigzags across it.

Marlena shrieks. She drops the flutes and claps a hand to her mouth.

'You *whore!*' August screams. 'You *slut*. You *mangy bitch!*' With each epithet, he rips the headpiece further.

'August!' Marlena screams, stepping forward. 'Stop it! *Stop it!*'

The noise seems to shock him, because he stops. He looks at her and blinks. He looks at the headpiece. Then he looks back at her, confused.

After a pause of several seconds, Marlena steps forward. 'Auggie?' she says tentatively. She looks up at him, her eyes beseeching. 'Are you all right now?'

August stares at her, baffled, as though he's simply awakened and found himself here. Marlena approaches slowly. 'Darling?' she says.

His lower jaw moves. His forehead crumples, and the headpiece falls to the ground.

I think I've stopped breathing.

Marlena steps right up to him. 'Auggie?'

He looks down at her. His nose twitches. Then he shoves

her so violently she crashes back onto the overturned platters and food. He takes one long step forward, leans down,
and tries to rip the necklace from her throat. The clasp
holds, so he ends up dragging her by the neck as she
screams.

I launch across the open space and tackle him. Rosie
roars behind me as August and I fall backward onto
broken plates and spilled gravy. First I'm on top of him,
pounding his face. Then he's on top of me, cuffing me
in the eye. I buck him off and yank him to his feet.

'Auggie! Jacob!' shrieks Marlena. 'Stop!'

I shove him backward, but he grabs my lapels and so
we crash into the vanity together. I am vaguely aware of
tinkling as the mirror disintegrates around us. August
thrusts me away, and we grapple in the center of the tent.

We roll around, grunting, so close I can feel his breath
on my face. Now I'm on top of him, landing punches.
Now he's on top of me, banging my head against the
ground. Marlena is hovering, screaming at us to stop, but
we can't. Or at least I can't – all the rage and pain and
frustration of the past few months is channeled into my
fists.

Now I'm facing the overturned table. Now I'm facing
Rosie, who is pulling her leg chain and bellowing. Now
we're standing up again, grasping at each other's collars
and lapels, both blocking and landing blows. Eventually
we fall against the entrance flap and land in the middle
of the crowd that has gathered outside.

Within seconds, I'm hauled off, pinioned by Grady and
Bill. For a moment, August looks as though he's going to
come after me, but then the expression on his mashed

face shifts. He climbs to his feet and calmly dusts himself off.

'You're crazy. *Crazy!*' I scream.

He observes me coolly, straightens his sleeves, and goes back into the tent.

'Let me go,' I plead, jerking my head around first to Grady and then to Bill. 'For Christ's sake, let me go! He's nuts! He'll kill her!' I struggle hard enough that I manage to pull them forward a few feet. From inside the tent I hear the crash of broken dishes and then Marlena screams.

Grady and Bill are both grunting, bracing their legs to keep me from getting loose. 'No he won't,' says Grady. 'Don't you worry about that.'

Earl blasts from the crowd and ducks into the tent. The crashing stops. There are two soft thuds, then a louder one, and then conspicuous silence.

I freeze, staring at the blank expanse of canvas.

'There. See?' says Grady, still gripping my arm tightly. 'You okay? Can we let you go now?'

I nod, continuing to stare.

Grady and Bill release me, but in stages. First they loosen their grips. Then they let go, but stay close, keeping an eye on me.

A hand appears on my waist. Walter is standing beside me.

'Come on, Jacob,' he says. 'Walk away.'

'I can't,' I say.

'Yes. You can. Come on. Walk away.'

I stare at the silent tent. After another few seconds, I tear my eyes from the billowing flap and walk away.

* * *

Walter and I climb into the stock car. Queenie emerges from behind the trunks, where Camel is snoring. She wags her stump and then stops, sniffing the air.

'Sit,' Walter orders, pointing at the cot.

Queenie sits in the center of the floor. I sit on the edge of the cot. Now that my adrenaline is fading, I'm beginning to realize how badly I'm hurt. My hands are lacerated, I sound like I'm breathing through a gas mask, and I'm looking through a slit formed by the puffed lids of my right eye. When I touch my face, my hand comes away bloody.

Walter leans over an open trunk. When he turns around, he's got a jug of moonshine and a handkerchief. He stands in front of me and pulls the cork.

'Eh? Is that you? Walter?' Camel calls from behind the trunks. Trust him to wake up at the sound of a cork being pulled.

'You're a bloody mess,' Walter says, completely ignoring Camel. He holds the hankie against the neck of the jug and tips the whole thing upside down. He brings the wet cloth toward my face. 'Hold still. This is going to sting.'

That was the understatement of the century – when the alcohol encounters my face, I jerk back with a yelp.

Walter waits, hankie poised. 'You need something to bite on?' He bends down to retrieve the cork. 'Here.'

'No,' I say, clenching my teeth. 'Just give me a second.' I hug my chest, rocking back and forth.

'I've got a better idea,' says Walter. He hands me the jug. 'Go on. It burns like hell going down, but after a few swallows you don't notice so much. What the hell happened, anyway?'

I take the jug and use both my battered hands to raise it to my face. I feel clumsy, like I'm wearing boxing gloves. Walter steadies it. The alcohol burns my bruised lips, rips a path down my throat, and explodes in my stomach. I gasp and push the jug away so quickly liquid sloshes from its neck.

'Yeah. It's not the smoothest,' says Walter.

'You guys gonna get me outta here and share, or what?' cries Camel.

'Shut it, Camel,' says Walter.

'Hey now! That ain't no way to talk to a sick old—'

'I said shut it, Camel! I'm dealing with a situation here. Go on,' he says, pushing the jug back at me. 'Have some more.'

'What kind of a situation?' says Camel.

'Jacob's messed up.'

'What? How? Was there a Hey Rube?'

'No,' Walter says grimly. 'Worse.'

'What's a Hey Rube?' I mumble through fat lips.

'Drink,' he says, pushing the jug at me again. 'A fight between us and them. Show folk and rubes. You ready?'

I take another sip of the moonshine, which, despite Walter's assurances, still goes down like mustard gas. I set the jug on the floor and close my eyes. 'Yeah. I think so.'

Walter holds my chin in one hand and turns my head left and right, assessing the damage. 'Holy hell, Jacob. What on earth happened?' he says, picking through the hair at the back of my head. Apparently he has found some new atrocity.

'He pushed Marlena.'

'You mean physically?'

'Yeah.'

'Why?'

'He just went nuts. I don't know how else to describe it.'

'There's glass all through your hair. Hold still.' His fingers investigate my scalp, lifting and separating the hair. 'So, why did he go nuts?' he says, depositing glass shards on top of the nearest book.

'Damned if I know.'

'Like hell you don't. Did you mess with her?'

'No. Absolutely not,' I say, although I'm pretty sure I'd be blushing if my face weren't already ground beef.

'I hope not,' says Walter. 'For your sake, I sure hope not.'

There's shuffling and banging to my right. I try to look, but Walter holds my chin tight. 'Camel, what the hell are you up to?' he barks, his breath hot on my face.

'I wanna see if Jacob's all right.'

'For Christ's sake,' says Walter. 'Just stay put, will ya? I wouldn't be surprised if we had company in a bit. It may be Jacob they're after, but don't think they won't take you, too.'

When Walter has finished cleaning my cuts and removing glass from my hair, I creep over to the bedroll and try to find a comfortable place for my head, which is battered both front and back. My right eye is swollen completely shut. Queenie comes over to investigate, sniffing tentatively. She backs up a few feet and lies down, keeping an eye on me.

Walter puts the jug back in the trunk and then stays bent over, riffling through the bottom. When he straightens up again, he's holding a large knife.

He closes the interior door, and wedges it shut with a chunk of wood. Then he sits with his back to the wall and the knife at his side.

Some time later, we hear the clip-clopping of horses' hooves on the ramp. Pete, Otis, and Diamond Joe speak in hushed voices in the other part of the car, but no one knocks and no one tries the door. After a while, we hear them dismantle the ramp and slide the outside door shut.

When the train finally chugs forward, Walter sighs audibly. I look over at him. He drops his head between his knees and remains there for a moment. Then he climbs to his feet and slides the big knife behind the trunk.

'You're a lucky bastard,' he says, working the chunk of wood free. He swings the door open and walks to the row of trunks that obscures Camel.

'Me?' I say, through a haze of moonshine.

'Yeah, you. So far.'

Walter hauls the trunks away from the wall and retrieves Camel. Then he drags the old man out to the other part of the car to take care of the evening's ablutions.

I doze, flattened by a combination of trauma and moonshine.

I'm vaguely aware of Walter helping Camel with his dinner. I remember propping myself up to accept a drink of water and then collapsing back on the bedroll. The next time I surface, Camel is lying flat on the cot, snoring, and Walter sits on the horse blanket in the corner with the lamp beside him and a book in his lap.

I hear footsteps on the roof, and a moment later there's

a soft thud outside our door. My whole body snaps into awareness.

Walter scrambles across the floor, crablike, and grabs the knife from behind the trunk. Then he moves to beside the door, gripping the knife's handle tightly. He gestures to me, waving me toward the lamp. I dive across the room, but with one eye swelled shut I have no depth perception and come up short.

The door creaks inward. Walter's fingers clench and unclench around the knife's handle.

'Jacob?'

'Marlena!' I cry.

'Jesus Christ, woman!' Walter shouts, dropping the knife to his side. 'I nearly killed you.' He grabs the edge of the door. His head bobs as he tries to see around her. 'You alone?'

'Yes,' she says. 'I'm sorry. I need to talk to Jacob.'

Walter opens the door a bit more. Then his face falls. 'Aw jeez,' he says. 'You'd better come in.'

When she steps inside I lift the kerosene lamp. Her left eye is purple and swollen.

'Jesus Christ!' I say. 'Did he do that to you?'

'Oh God, look at you,' she says, reaching out. Her fingertips hover near my face. 'You need to see a doctor.'

'I'm fine,' I say.

'Who in blazes is that?' says Camel. 'Is that a dame? I can't see a thing. Someone turn me around.'

'Oh, I beg your pardon,' says Marlena, startled by the sight of the crippled body on the cot. 'I thought there were only the two of you . . . Oh, I'm so sorry. I'll go back now.'

'No you won't,' I say.

'I didn't mean . . . to him.'

'I don't want you walking around on the top of moving train cars, never mind leaping between them.'

'I agree with Jacob,' says Walter. 'We'll move out there with the horses and give you some privacy.'

'No, I couldn't possibly,' says Marlena.

'Then let me take the bedroll out there for you,' I say.

'No. I didn't mean to . . .' She shakes her head. 'Oh God. I shouldn't have come.' She cups her hands over her face. A moment later she starts to cry.

I hand the lamp to Walter and pull her against me. She sinks into me, sobbing, her face pressed to my shirt.

'Aw jeez,' Walter says again. 'This probably makes me an accomplice.'

'Let's go talk,' I say to Marlena.

She sniffs and pulls away. She walks out to the horses and I follow, pulling the door shut behind us.

There's a soft nicker of recognition. Marlena wanders over and strokes Midnight's flank. I sink down against the wall, waiting for her. After a while she joins me. As we round a curve, the floorboards jerk beneath us, throwing us together so our shoulders touch.

I speak first. 'Has he ever hit you before?'

'No.'

'If he does it again, I swear to God I'll kill him.'

'If he does it again, you won't have to,' she says quietly.

I look over at her. The moonlight comes through the slats behind her, and her profile is black, featureless.

'I'm leaving him,' she says, dropping her chin.

Instinctively, I reach for her hand. Her ring is gone.

'Have you told him?' I ask.

'In no uncertain terms.'

'How did he take it?'

'You saw his answer,' she says.

We sit listening to the clacking of the ties beneath us. I stare over the backs of the sleeping horses and at the snatches of night visible through the slats.

'What are you going to do?' I ask.

'I guess I'll talk to Uncle Al when we get to Erie and see if he can set me up with a bunk in the girls' sleeper.'

'And in the meantime?'

'In the meantime, I'll stay at a hotel.'

'You don't want to go back to your family?'

A pause. 'No. I don't think they'd have me, anyway.'

We lean against the wall in silence, still holding hands. After about an hour she falls asleep, sliding down until her head rests on my shoulder. I remain awake, every fiber of my body aware of her proximity.

NINETEEN

'Mr Jankowski? It's time to get ready.'

My eyes snap open at the voice's proximity. Rosemary hovers over me, framed by ceiling tiles.

'Eh? Oh, right,' I say, struggling up onto my elbows. Joy surges through me when I realize that not only do I remember where I am and who she is but also that it's circus day. Perhaps what happened earlier was just a brain belch?

'Stay put. I'll raise the head of your bed,' she says. 'Do you need to use the washroom?'

'No, but I want my good shirt. And my bow tie.'

'Your bow tie!' she hoots, throwing her head back and laughing.

'Yes, my bow tie.'

'Oh dear, oh dear. You are a funny one,' she says, going to my closet.

By the time she returns, I have managed to undo three buttons on my other shirt. Not bad for gnarled fingers. I'm rather pleased with myself. Brain and body, both in working order.

As Rosemary helps me out of my shirt, I look down at my skinny frame. My ribs show, and the a few hairs left on my chest are white. I remind myself of a greyhound, all sinews and skinny rib cage. Rosemary guides my arms into my good shirt, and a few minutes later leans over me, tugging the edges of my bow tie. She stands back, cocks her head, and makes a final adjustment.

'Well, I do declare the bow tie was a fine decision,' she says, nodding in approval. Her voice is deep and honeyed, lyrical. I could listen to her all day long. 'Would you like to have a look?'

'Did you get it straight?' I say.

'Of course I did!'

'Then no. I don't like the mirror much these days,' I grumble.

'Well, I think you look very handsome,' she says, placing her hands on her hips and surveying me.

'Oh, *psshhh.*' I wave a bony hand at her.

She laughs again, and the noise is like wine, warm in my veins. 'So, do you want to wait for your family here, or shall I take you out to the lobby?'

'What time does the show start?'

'It starts at three,' she says. 'It's two now.'

'I'll wait in the lobby. I want to leave straightaway when they get here.'

Rosemary waits patiently while I lower my creaking

body into the wheelchair. As she wheels me out to the lobby, I clasp my hands in my lap, fiddling nervously.

The lobby is full of other old folks in wheelchairs, lined up in front of the bucket seats meant for visitors. Rosemary parks me at the end, beside Ipphy Bailey.

She is hunched over, her dowager's hump forcing her to face her lap. Her hair is wispy and white, and someone – obviously not Ipphy – has combed it carefully to obscure the bald spots. She turns suddenly toward me. Her face lights up.

'Morty!' she cries, reaching out a skeletal hand and clapping it around my wrist. 'Oh, Morty, you came back!'

I yank my arm away, but the hand comes with it. She pulls me toward her as I recoil.

'Nurse!' I yell, trying to wrench free. 'Nurse!'

A few seconds later, someone pries me loose from Ipphy, who is convinced I am her dead husband. Furthermore, she is convinced I don't love her anymore. She leans over the arm of her chair, weeping, waving her arms in a desperate attempt to reach me. The horse-faced nurse backs me up, moves me some distance away, and then places my walker between us.

'Oh, Morty, Morty! Don't be like that!' Ipphy wails. 'You know it didn't mean anything. It was nothing – a terrible mistake. Oh, Morty! Don't you love me anymore?'

I sit rubbing my wrist, incensed. Why can't they have a separate wing for people like that? That old bird is clearly out of her head. She could have hurt me. Of course, if they did have a separate wing, I'd probably end up in it after what happened this morning. I sit up straight as an idea occurs to me. Maybe it was the new drug that caused the brain belch – oh, I must ask Rosemary about that. Or maybe not. The thought has cheered me, and I'd like to hang on to that. Must protect my little pockets of happiness.

Minutes pass and old people disappear until the row of wheelchairs resembles a jack-o-lantern's gap-toothed smile. Family after family arrives, each claiming a decrepit ancestor amid high-decibel greetings. Strong bodies lean over weak; kisses are planted on cheeks. Brakes are kicked free, and one by one old people exit the sliding doors surrounded by relatives.

When Ipphy's family arrives, they make a great show of being happy to see her. She gazes into their faces, eyes and mouth wide open, baffled but delighted.

There are only six of us left now, and we eye each other suspiciously. Each time the glass doors slide open our faces turn in unison and one of them brightens. And so it goes until I'm the only one left.

I glance at the wall clock. Two forty-five. Dammit! If they don't show up soon I'll miss the Spec. I shift in my seat, feeling querulous and old. Hell, I *am* querulous and old, but I must try not to lose my temper when they arrive. I'll just rush them out the door, make clear that there's no time for pleasantries. They can tell me about whoever's promotion or whatever vacation after the show.

Rosemary's head appears in the doorway. She looks both directions, taking in the fact that I'm alone in the lobby. She goes behind the nurses' station and sets her chart down on the counter. Then she comes and sits next to me.

'Still no sign of your family, Mr Jankowski?'

'No!' I shout. 'And if they don't show up soon there won't be much point. I'm sure the good seats are already taken and I'm already going to miss the Spec.' I turn back to the clock, miserable, whiney. 'Whatever is keeping them? They're always here by now.'

Rosemary looks at her watch. It's gold with stretchy links that look like they're pinching her flesh. I always wore my watch loose, back when I had one.

'Do you know who's coming today?' she asks.

'No. I never do. And it doesn't really matter, just so long as they get here in time.'

'Well, let me see what I can find out.'

She rises and goes behind the desk at the nurses' station.

I scan each person who passes on the sidewalk behind the sliding glass doors, seeking a familiar face. But they pass as a blur, one unto another. I look at Rosemary, who is standing behind the desk and speaking into the phone. She glances at me, hangs up, and makes another call.

The clock now says two fifty-three – just seven minutes to showtime. My blood pressure is so high my entire body buzzes like the fluorescent lights above me.

I've entirely given up on the idea of not losing my temper. Whoever shows up is going to get a piece of my mind, and that's for sure. Every other old bird or coot in the place will have seen the whole show, including the Spec, and where's the fairness in that? If there's anyone in this place who should be there, it's me. Oh, just wait until I lay eyes on whoever comes. If it's one of my children, I'll lay right into them. If it's one of the others, well, then I'll wait until—

'I'm so sorry, Mr Jankowski.'

'Eh?' I look up quickly. Rosemary's back, sitting in the chair next to me. In my panic, I hadn't noticed.

'They plum lost track of whose turn it was.'

'Well, who did they decide? How long is it going to take them to get here?'

Rosemary pauses. She presses her lips together and takes my hand between hers. It's the expression people wear when they're about to deliver bad news, and my adrenaline rises in anticipation. 'They can't make it,' she says. 'It was supposed to be your son, Simon. When I called, he remembered, but he'd already made other plans. There was no answer at the other numbers.'

'Other plans?' I croak.

'Yes, sir.'

'Did you tell him about the circus?'

'Yes, sir. And he was really very sorry. But it was something he just couldn't get out of.'

My face twists, and before I know it I'm sniveling like a child.

'I'm so sorry, Mr Jankowski. I know how important this was to you. I'd take you myself, but I'm working a twelve-hour shift.'

I bring my hands to my face, trying to hide my old man tears. A few seconds later, a tissue dangles in front of me.

'You're a good girl, Rosemary,' I say, taking the tissue and staunching my leaky nose. 'You know that, don't you? I don't know what I'd do without you.'

She looks at me for a long time. Too long. Finally she says, 'Mr Jankowski, you do know I'm leaving tomorrow, don't you?'

My head snaps up. 'Eh? For how long?' Oh, damn. That's just what I need. If she goes on vacation, I'll probably forget her name by the time she comes back.

'We're moving to Richmond. To be closer to my mother-in-law. She's not been well.'

I am stunned. My jaw flaps uselessly for a moment before I find words. 'You're married?'

'For twenty-six happy years, Mr Jankowski.'

'Twenty-six years? No. I don't believe it. You're just a girl.'

She laughs. 'I'm a grandmother, Mr Jankowski. Forty-seven years old.'

We sit in silence for a moment. She digs into her pale pink pocket and replaces my saturated tissue with a new one. I dab the deep sockets that house my eyes.

'He's a lucky man, your husband,' I sniff.

'We're both lucky. Very blessed indeed.'

'And so's your mother-in-law. Did you know there's not a single one of my children who could take me in?'

'Well . . . It's not always easy, you know.'

'I never said it was.'

She takes my hand. 'I know that, Mr Jankowski. I know that.'

I am overcome by the unfairness of it all. I close my eyes and picture drooling old Ipphy Bailey in the big top. She won't even notice she's there, never mind remember any of it.

After a couple of minutes, Rosemary says, 'Is there anything I can do for you?'

'No,' I say, and there isn't – not unless she can deliver me to the circus or the circus to me. Or take me with her to Richmond. 'I think I'd like to be alone now,' I add.

'I understand,' she says gently. 'Shall I take you back to your room?'

'No. I think I'll sit right here.'

She stands up, leans over long enough to plant a kiss on my forehead, and disappears into the hallway, her rubber soles squeaking on the tiled floor.

TWENTY

When I wake up, Marlena has disappeared. I immediately go in search of her and find her exiting Uncle Al's car with Earl. He accompanies her to car 48 and makes August vacate while she goes inside.

I am pleased to see that August looks much as I do, which is to say like a battered rotten tomato. When Marlena climbs into the car he calls her name and tries to follow, but Earl blocks his way. August is agitated and desperate, moving from window to window, hauling himself up by his fingertips, weeping, oozing contrition.

It will never happen again. He loves her more than life itself – surely she knows that. He doesn't know what came over him. He'll do anything – anything! – to make it up to her. She is a goddess, a queen, and he is a just a miserable puddle of remorse. Can't she see how sorry he is? Is she trying to torture him? Has she no heart?

When Marlena emerges with a suitcase, she passes him without so much as a glance. She wears a straw hat with a floppy brim pulled down over her black eye.

'Marlena,' he cries, reaching forward and grabbing her arm.

'Let her go,' says Earl.

'Please. I'm begging you,' says August. He drops to his knees in the dirt. His hands slide down her arm until he's holding her left hand. He brings it to his face, showering it with tears and kisses as she stares stonily ahead.

'Marlena. Darling. Look at me. I'm on my knees. I'm begging you. What more can I do? My darling – my sweet – please come inside with me. We'll talk about it. We'll work it out.' He digs through his pocket, and comes up with a ring, which he tries to slip onto her third finger. She jerks her hand free and starts walking.

'Marlena! Marlena!' He is screaming now, and even the unbruised parts of his face are discolored. His hair flops over his forehead. 'You can't do this! This is not the end! Do you hear me? You're my wife, Marlena! Till death do us part, remember?' He climbs to his feet and stands with fists clenched. 'Till death do us part!' he screams.

Marlena thrusts her suitcase at me without stopping. I turn and follow, staring at her narrow waist as she marches across the brown grass. Only at the edge of the lot does she slow down enough that I can walk beside her.

'May I help you?' says the hotel clerk, looking up as the bell above the door announces our arrival. His initial expression of solicitous pleasantry is replaced first by alarm and then by disdain. It's the same combination we've seen on the faces of everyone we passed on the way here. A middle-aged couple sitting on a bench by the front door gawks unabashedly.

And we do make quite a pair. The skin around Marlena's eye has turned an impressive blue, but at least her face has kept its shape – mine is pulpy and mashed, the bruises overlaid with oozing wounds.

'I need a room,' says Marlena.

The clerk peers at her with disgust. 'We haven't got any,' he replies, pushing his spectacles up with one finger. He returns to his ledger.

I set her suitcase down and stand beside her. 'Your sign says you've got vacancies.'

He presses his lips into an imperious line. 'Then it's wrong.'

Marlena touches my elbow. 'Come on, Jacob.'

'No, I won't "come on,"' I say, turning back to the clerk. 'The lady needs a room, and you've got vacancies.'

He glances conspicuously at her left hand and raises an eyebrow. 'We don't rent to unmarried couples.'

'It's not for us. Just her.'

'Uh-huh,' he says.

'You better watch it, pal,' I say. 'I don't like what you're implying.'

'Come on, Jacob,' Marlena says again. She is even paler than before, looking at the floor.

'I'm not *implying* anything,' the clerk says.

'Jacob, please,' says Marlena. 'Let's just go somewhere else.'

I give the clerk a final, searing stare that lets him know exactly what I'd do to him if Marlena weren't here and then pick up her suitcase. She marches to the door.

'Oh, say, I know who you are!' says the woman half of the couple on the bench. 'You're the girl from the poster! Yes! I'm sure of it.' She turns to the man sitting next to her. 'Norbert, that's the girl from the poster! Isn't it? Miss, you're the circus star, aren't you?'

Marlena swings the door open, adjusts the brim of her hat, and steps outside. I follow.

'Wait,' calls the clerk. 'I think we may have a—'

I slam the door behind me.

The hotel three doors down has no such qualms, although I dislike this clerk almost as much as the other. He's just dying to know what happened. His eyes sweep over us, shining, curious, lewd. I know what he'd assume if Marlena's black eye were the only injury between us, but because I am far worse off, the story is not so clear.

'Room 2B,' he says, dangling a key in front of him and still drinking in the sight of us. 'Up the stairs and to the right. End of the hall.'

I follow Marlena, watching her sculpted calves as she climbs the stairs.

She fusses with the key for a minute and then stands aside, leaving it in the lock. 'I can't get it. Can you try?'

I jiggle it in the cavity. After a few seconds, the dead-bolt slides. I push the door open and stand aside to let Marlena enter. She tosses her hat on the bed and walks to the window, which is open. A gust of wind inflates the curtain, first blowing it into the room and then sucking it back against the screen.

The room is plain but adequate. There are flowers on the wallpaper and curtains, and the bed is covered with chenille. The bathroom door is open. The bathroom itself is large, and the tub has clawed feet.

I set the suitcase down and stand awkwardly. Marlena has her back to me. There's a cut on her neck, from where the necklace clasp dug into it.

'Do you need anything else?' I ask, turning my hat over in my hands.

'No, thank you,' she says.

I watch her for a while longer. I want to cross the room and wrap her in my arms, but instead I leave, shutting the door quietly behind me.

Because I can't think of anything else to do, I head for the menagerie and do the usual. I cut up, stir, and measure food. I check a yak's abscessed tooth and hold hands with Bobo, leading him around as I check the rest of the animals.

I have progressed to mucking out when Diamond Joe comes up behind me. 'Uncle Al wants to see you.'

I stare at him for a moment, then lay my shovel in the straw.

Uncle Al is in the pie car, sitting behind a plate of steak and fries. He's holding a cigar and blowing smoke rings. His entourage stands behind him, sober-faced.

I remove my hat. 'You wanted to see me?'

'Ah, Jacob,' he says, leaning forward. 'Glad to see you. Did you get Marlena sorted out?'

'She's in a room, if that's what you mean.'

'That's part of it, yes.'

'Then I'm not sure what you mean.'

He is silent for a moment. Then he sets his cigar down and brings his hands together, forming a steeple with his fingers. 'It's quite simple. I can't afford to lose either one of them.'

'As far as I know, she has no intention of leaving the show.'

'And neither does he. Imagine, if you will, what it will be like if they both remain but don't get back together. August is simply beside himself with grief.'

'Surely you're not suggesting she go back to him.'

He smiles and cocks his head.

'He *hit* her, Al. He *hit* her.'

Uncle Al rubs his chin and ponders. 'Yes, well. I didn't care much for that, I must say.' He waves at the seat opposite him. 'Sit.'

I approach and perch on the edge.

Uncle Al leans his head to the side, surveying me. 'So was there any truth to it?'

'To what?'

He drums his fingers against the table and purses his lips. 'Are you and Marlena – *hmmm*, how shall I put this . . .'

'No.'

'*Mmmm*,' he says, continuing to ponder. 'Good. Didn't think so. But good. In that case, you can help me.'

'What?' I say.

'I'll work on him, you work on her.'

'The hell with that.'

'You're in a bad spot, yes. A friend to both.'

'I'm no friend of his.'

331

He sighs, and assumes an expression of great patience. 'You have to understand August. He does this occasionally. It's not his fault.' He leans forward, peering into my face. 'Good God. I think I'd better have a doctor out to look at you.'

'I don't need a doctor. And of course it's his fault.'

He stares at me, and then leans back in his chair. 'He's ill, Jacob.'

I say nothing.

'He's paragon schnitzophonic.'

'He's what?!'

'Paragon schnitzophonic,' repeats Uncle Al.

'You mean paranoid schizophrenic?'

'Sure. Whatever. But the bottom line is he's mad as a hatter. Of course, he's also brilliant, so we work around it. It's harder for Marlena than the rest of us, of course. Which is why we must support her.'

I shake my head, stunned. 'Do you even hear what you're saying?'

'I cannot lose either one of them. And if they don't get back together, August will be impossible to handle.'

'He *hit* her,' I repeat.

'Yes, I know, very upsetting, that. But he's her husband, isn't he?'

I place my hat on my head and rise.

'Where do you think you're going?'

'Back to work,' I say. 'I'm not going to sit here and listen to you tell me that it's okay for August to hit her because she's his wife. Or that it's not his fault because he's insane. If he's insane, that's all the more reason she should stay away.'

'If you want a job to go back to, you will sit back down.'

'You know what? I don't give a damn about your job,' I say, moving to the door. 'See you. Wish I could say it's been a pleasure.'

'What about your little friend?'

I freeze. My hand is on the doorknob.

'That little shit with the dog,' he says, musing. 'And that other one, too – oh, what's his name?' He snaps his fingers as he tries to come up with it.

I turn around slowly. I know what's coming.

'You know who I mean. That useless cripple who's been scarfing my food and taking up space on my train for weeks without doing a lick of work. How about him?'

I stare, my face burning with hatred.

'Did you really think you could keep a stowaway without me finding out about it? Without *him* finding out about it?' His face is hard, his eyes glinting.

His expression suddenly softens. He smiles warmly. He spreads his hands in supplication. 'You've got me all wrong, you know. The people on this show are my family. I care deeply about each and every one of them. But what I understand and you apparently do not as yet is that sometimes an individual has to make a sacrifice for the good of the rest of us. And what this family needs is for August and Marlena to work things out. Do we understand each other?'

I stare into his glowing eyes, thinking how very much I'd like to sink a hatchet between them.

'Yes, sir,' I say eventually. 'I believe we do.'

* * *

Rosie stands with one foot on a tub while I file her toenails. She has five on each foot, like a human. I'm working on one of her front feet when I'm suddenly aware that all human activity in the menagerie has ceased. The workers are frozen, staring at the entrance with widened eyes.

I look up. August approaches and comes to a stop in front of me. His hair flops forward, and he brushes it back with a swollen hand. His upper lip is bluish purple, split like a grilled sausage. His nose is flattened and off to the side, encrusted with blood. He holds a lit cigarette.

'Dear Lord,' he says. He tries to smile, but his split lip prevents him. He takes a drag from the cigarette. 'Hard to say who got the worst of it, eh, my boy?'

'What do you want?' I say, leaning over and rasping the edge off a huge toenail.

'You're not still sore, are you?'

I don't answer.

He watches me work for a moment. 'Look, I know I was out of line. Sometimes my imagination gets the better of me.'

'Oh, is that what happened?'

'Look here,' he says, blowing smoke. 'I was hoping we could let bygones be bygones. So what do you say, my boy – friends again?' He extends his hand.

I stand up straight, both arms at my sides. 'You *hit* her, August.'

The other men watch wordlessly. August looks stunned. His mouth moves. He pulls his hand back and transfers the lit cigarette to it. His hands are bruised, the nails cracked. 'Yes. I know.'

I stand back and appraise Rosie's toenails. '*Połóż nogę. Połóż nogę,* Rosie!'

She lifts her enormous foot and puts it back on the ground. I kick the overturned tub toward her other front foot. '*Nogę! Nogę!*' Rosie shifts her weight and places her foot in the center of the tub. '*Teraz do przodu,*' I say, poking the back of her leg with my fingers until her toenails hang over the front edge of the tub. 'Good girl,' I say, patting her shoulder. She lifts her trunk and opens her mouth in a smile. I reach in and stroke her tongue.

'Do you know where she is?' says August.

I lean over and evaluate Rosie's toenails, running my hands along the underside of her foot.

'I need to see her,' he continues.

I start filing. A fine spray of toenail powder shoots into the air.

'Fine. Be that way,' he says, his voice shrill. 'But she is my wife, and I will find her. Even if I have to go from hotel to hotel, I *will* find her.'

I look up just as he flicks the cigarette. It arcs through the air and lands in Rosie's open mouth, sizzling as it hits her tongue. She roars, panicked, throwing her head and fishing inside her mouth with her trunk.

August marches off. I turn back to Rosie. She stares at me, a look of unspeakable sadness on her face. Her amber eyes are filled with tears.

I should have known he'd go from hotel to hotel. But I wasn't thinking, and so she's in the second hotel we came across. Couldn't be easier to find.

I know I'm being watched, so I bide my time. At the

first opportunity, I slip from the lot and rush to the hotel. I wait around the corner for a minute, watching, making sure I wasn't followed. After I've caught my breath, I remove my hat, wipe my forehead, and enter the building.

The clerk looks up. It's a new one. His eyes glaze over.

'What do *you* want?' he says, as though he's seen me before, as though battered rotten tomatoes walk through his door every day.

'I'm here to see Miss L'Arche,' I say, remembering that Marlena has checked in using her maiden name. 'Marlena L'Arche.'

'There is no one here by that name,' he says.

'Yes, of course there is,' I say. 'I was with her when she checked in this morning.'

'I'm sorry, but you're incorrect.'

I stare at him for a moment and then sprint for the stairs.

'Hey, pal! You get back here!'

I mount the steps, two at a time.

'If you go up those stairs, I'm calling the police!' he shouts.

'Go ahead!'

'I'm doing it! I'm calling right now!'

'Good!'

I rap on her door with my least-bruised knuckles. 'Marlena?'

A second later, the clerk grabs me and spins me around, shoving me against the wall. He has me by the lapels, his face right in mine. 'I told you before, she's not here.'

'It's all right, Albert. This is a friend.' Marlena has come out into the hallway behind us.

He freezes, panting hot breath on me. His eyes widen in confusion. 'What?' he says.

'Albert?' I say, equally confused. 'Albert?'

'But what about earlier?' sputters Albert.

'This isn't the same man. This is another one.'

'August was here?' I say, finally clueing in. 'Are you okay?'

Albert jerks around from me to her and back again.

'This is a friend. This is the man who fought him,' Marlena explains.

Albert lets me down. He makes an awkward attempt to smooth my jacket and then extends his hand. 'Sorry, pal. You look an awful lot like that other guy.'

'Uh, that's all right,' I say, taking his hand. He squeezes and I wince.

'He's coming after you,' I say to Marlena. 'We've got to move you.'

'Don't be silly,' Marlena says.

'He's already been,' says Albert. 'I told him she wasn't here and he seemed to buy it. That's why I was surprised when you – he – er, showed up again.'

Downstairs, the bell over the front door tinkles. Albert and I lock eyes. I hustle Marlena into the room, and he hurries down.

'May I help you?' he says as I close the door. I can tell from his voice that it's not August.

I lean against the door, breathing hard with relief. 'I'd really feel better if you let me find you a room farther from the lot.'

'No. I want to stay here.'

'But why?'

'He's already been here and he thinks I'm somewhere else. Besides, it's not like I can avoid him forever. I have to go back to the train tomorrow.'

I hadn't even thought of that.

She crosses the room, dragging a hand across the top of the small table as she passes. Then she drops into a chair and rests her head against its back.

'He tried to apologize to me,' I say.

'And did you accept it?'

'Of course not,' I say, offended.

She shrugs. 'It would be easier for you if you did. If you don't, you'll probably get fired.'

'He *hit* you, Marlena!'

She closes her eyes.

'My God – has he always been like this?'

'Yes. Well, he's never hit me before. But these mood swings? Yes. I never know what I'm going to wake up to.'

'Uncle Al said he's a paranoid schizophrenic.'

She drops her head.

'How have you stood it?'

'I didn't have much choice, did I? I married him before I realized. You've seen it. When he's happy, he's the most charming creature on earth. But when something sets him off . . .' She sighs, and then waits so long I wonder if she's going to continue. When she does, her voice is tremulous. 'The first time it happened we'd only been married three weeks, and it scared me to death. He beat one of the menagerie workers so badly he lost an eye. I saw him do it. I called my parents and asked if I could come home, but they wouldn't even speak to me. It was bad enough that I'd married a Jew, but now I wanted a divorce as well? My father made Mother tell me that in his eyes I had died the day I eloped.'

I cross the room and kneel beside her. I raise my hand to stroke her hair, but after a few seconds place it on the arm of the chair instead.

'Three weeks later, another menagerie man lost his arm while helping August feed the cats. He died of blood loss before anyone could find out the details. Later in the season I found out that the only reason August had a string of liberty horses to give me was that the previous trainer – another woman – jumped from the moving train after joining August for an evening in his stateroom. There have been other incidents, too, although this is the first time he's turned on me.' She slumps forward. A moment later her shoulders shake.

'Oh, hey,' I say, helplessly. 'Hey now. Hey now. Marlena – look at me. Please.'

She sits up and wipes her face. She stares into my eyes. 'Will you stay with me, Jacob?' she says.

'Marlena—'

'*Shh.*' She scootches to the edge of her seat and touches a finger to my lips. Then she slides to the ground. She kneels in front of me, just inches away, her finger trembling against my lips.

'Please,' she says. 'I need you.' After the slightest pause, she traces my features – tentatively, softly, barely grazing my skin. I catch my breath and close my eyes.

'Marlena—'

'Don't say anything,' she says softly. Her fingers flutter their way around my ear and down the back of my neck. I shudder. Every hair on my body is standing on end.

When her hands move to my shirt, I open my eyes. She undoes the buttons slowly, methodically. I watch her, knowing I should stop her. But I can't. I am helpless.

When my shirt is open she pulls it free of my trousers and looks me in the eye. She leans forward and brushes her lips past mine – so softly it's not even a kiss, merely contact. She pauses for just a second, keeping her lips so close I can feel her breath on my face. Then she leans in and kisses me, a gentle kiss, tentative but lingering. The next kiss is stronger still, the next one even more so, and before I know it I'm kissing back, clutching her face in both my hands as she runs her fingers over my chest and down my body. When she reaches for my trousers, I gasp. She pauses, tracing the outline of my erection.

She stops. I am reeling, teetering on my knees. Still staring into my eyes, she takes my hands and brings them to her lips. She presses a kiss into each palm and then places my hands on her breasts.

'Touch me, Jacob.'

I am doomed, finished.

Her breasts are small and round, like lemons. I cup them, running my thumbs over them and feeling her nipples contract under the cotton of her dress. I crush my bruised mouth to hers, running my hands over her rib cage, her waist, her hips, her thighs—

When she undoes my trousers and takes me in her hand, I pull away.

'Please,' I gasp, my voice cracking. 'Please. Let me be inside you.'

Somehow, we make it to the bed. When I finally sink into her, I cry out.

Afterward, I curl around her like a spoon. We lie in silence until darkness falls, and then, haltingly, she begins to talk. She slides her feet between my ankles, plays with my fingertips, and before long the words are pouring out. She speaks without need or even room for response, so I simply hold her and stroke her hair. She talks of the pain, grief, and horror of the past four years; of learning to cope with being the wife of a man so violent and unpredictable his touch made her skin crawl and of thinking, until quite recently, that she'd finally managed to do that. And then, finally, of how my appearance had forced her to realize she hadn't learned to cope at all.

When she finally falls silent, I continue to stroke her, running my hands gently over her hair, her shoulders, her arms, her hips. Then I start to talk. I tell her about my childhood and my mother's apricot rugelach. I tell her about starting to go on rounds with my father during my teen years and of how proud he was when I was accepted into Cornell. I tell her about Cornell, and Catherine, and how I thought that was love. I tell her about Old Mr McPherson running my parents off the side of the bridge, and the bank taking our home, and how I broke down and ran out of the exam hall when all the heads lost their faces.

In the morning, we make love again. This time she takes my hand and guides my fingers, moving them against her flesh. At first I don't understand, but when she trembles and rises to my touch I realize what she's showing me and want to cry with joy at the knowledge of it.

Afterward, she lies nestled against me, her hair tickling my face. I stroke her lightly, memorizing her body. I want her to melt into me, like butter on toast. I want to absorb her and walk around for the rest of my days with her encased in my skin.

I want.

I lie motionless, savoring the feeling of her body against mine. I'm afraid to breathe in case I break the spell.

TWENTY-ONE

Marlena stirs suddenly. Then she jerks upright and grabs my watch from the bedside table.

'Oh Jesus,' she says, dropping it and swinging her legs around.

'What? What is it?' I ask.

'It's already noon. I've got to get back,' she says.

She darts to the bathroom and shuts the door. A moment later the toilet flushes and water runs. Then she bursts out the door, rushing around scooping clothing from the floor.

'Marlena, wait,' I say, getting up.

'I can't. I have to perform,' she says, struggling with her stockings.

I come up behind her and take her shoulders in my hands. 'Marlena, please.'

She stops and turns slowly to face me. She looks first at my chest and then at the floor.

I stare down at her, suddenly tongue-tied. 'Last night you said, "I need you." You never said the word "love," so I only know how I feel.' I swallow hard, blinking at the part in her hair. 'I love you, Marlena. I love you with my heart and soul, and I want to be with you.'

She continues to face the floor.

'Marlena?'

She lifts her head. There are tears in her eyes. 'I love you, too,' she whispers. 'I think I've loved you from the moment I laid eyes on you. But don't you see? I'm married to August.'

'We can fix that.'

'But—'

'But nothing. I want to be with you. If that's what you also want, we'll find a way.'

There's a long silence. 'I've never wanted anything more in all my life,' she says finally.

I take her face in my hands and kiss her.

'We'll have to leave the show,' I say, wiping her tears with my thumbs.

She nods, sniffling.

'But not until Providence.'

'Why there?'

'Because that's where Camel's son is meeting us. He's taking him home.'

'Can't Walter look after him until then?'

I close my eyes and lean my forehead against hers. 'It's a little more complicated than that.'

'How so?'

'Uncle Al called me in yesterday. He wants me to persuade you to go back to August. He made threats.'

'Well, of course he did. He's Uncle Al.'

'No, I mean he was threatening to redlight Walter and Camel.'

'Oh, that's just talk,' she says. 'Don't pay any attention. He'd never have anyone redlighted.'

'Says who? August? Uncle Al?'

She looks up, startled.

'Do you remember when the railroad authority came out in Davenport?' I say. 'Six men went missing from the Flying Squadron the night before.'

She frowns. 'I thought the railroad authority came out because someone was trying to cause trouble for Uncle Al.'

'No, they came out because half a dozen men got redlighted. Camel was supposed to be among them.'

She stares at me for a moment, and then puts her hands over her face. 'Dear God. Dear God. I've been so stupid.'

'Not stupid. Not stupid at all. It's hard to conceive of such evil,' I say, wrapping my arms around her.

She presses her face to my chest. 'Oh, Jacob – what are we going to do?'

'I don't know,' I say, stroking her hair. 'We'll figure something out, but we're going to have to be very, very careful.'

We return to the lot separately, surreptitiously. I carry her suitcase until a block away, and then watch as she crosses the lot and disappears into her dressing tent. I hang around for a few minutes in case August turns out to be inside. When there aren't any obvious signs of trouble, I return to the ring stock car.

'So, the tomcat returns,' says Walter. He's pushing trunks against the wall, obscuring Camel. The old man lies with his eyes closed and mouth open, snoring. Walter must have just given him booze.

'You don't need to do that anymore,' I say.

Walter straightens up. 'What?'

'You don't need to hide Camel anymore.'

He stares at me. 'What the hell are you talking about?'

I sit on the bedroll. Queenie comes over, wagging her tail. I scratch her head. She sniffs me all over.

'Jacob, what's going on?'

When I tell him, his expression changes from shock to horror to disbelief.

'You bastard,' he says at the end.

'Walter, please—'

'So, you're going to take off after Providence. That's very big of you to wait that long.'

'It's because of Cam—'

'I know it's because of Camel,' he shouts. Then he pounds his chest with his fist. 'What about me?'

My mouth opens, but nothing comes out.

'Yeah. That's what I thought,' he says. His voice drips with sarcasm.

'Come with us,' I blurt.

'Oh yeah, that'll be cozy. Just the three of us. And where the hell are we supposed to go, anyway?'

'We'll check *Billboard* and see what's available.'

'There's nothing available. Shows are collapsing all over

346

the damned country. There's people starving. Starving! In the United States of America!'

'We'll find something, somewhere.'

'The hell we will,' he says, shaking his head. 'Damn, Jacob. I hope she's worth it, that's all I can say.'

I head for the menagerie, watching all the while for August. He's not there, but the tension among the menagerie men is palpable.

In the middle of the afternoon, I am summoned to the privilege car.

'Sit,' says Uncle Al, when I enter. He waves at the opposite chair.

I sit.

He leans back in his chair, twiddling his moustache. His eyes are narrowed. 'Any progress to report?' he asks.

'Not yet,' I say. 'But I think she'll come around.'

His eyes widen. His fingers stop twiddling. 'You do?'

'Not right away, of course. She's still angry.'

'Yes, yes, of course,' he says, leaning forward eagerly. 'But you *do* think . . . ?' He lets the question trail off. His eyes gleam with hope.

I sigh deeply and lean back, crossing my legs. 'When two people are meant to be together, they will be together. It's fate.'

He stares into my eyes as a smile seeps across his face. He lifts his hand and snaps his fingers. 'A brandy for Jacob,' he orders. 'And one for me as well.'

A minute later, we are each holding large snifters.

'So, tell me then, how long do you think . . . ?' he says, stirring the air beside his head.

347

'I think she wants to make a point.'

'Yes, yes, of course,' he says. He shifts forward, eyes shining. 'Yes. I quite understand.'

'Also, it's important that she feel we are supporting her, not him. You know how women are. If she thinks that we're in any way unsympathetic, it will only set things back.'

'Of course,' he says, nodding and shaking his head all at once so it bobs in a circle. 'Absolutely. And what do you recommend we do in that regard?'

'Well, naturally August should keep his distance. That would give her a chance to miss him. It might even be beneficial for him to pretend *he's* no longer interested. Women are funny that way. Also, she *mustn't* think that we're pushing them back together. It's critical that she think it's her idea.'

'Mmmm, yes,' he says, nodding thoughtfully. 'Good point. And how long do you think . . . ?'

'I shouldn't think more than a few weeks.'

He stops nodding. His eyes pop open. 'That long?'

'I can try to speed things up, but there's a risk it will backfire. You know women.' I shrug. 'It might take two weeks, and it might be tomorrow. But if she feels any pressure, she'll hold off just to prove a point.'

'Yes, quite,' says Uncle Al, bringing a finger to his lips. He scrutinizes me for what feels like a very long time. 'So, tell me,' he says, 'what changed your mind since yesterday?'

I lift my glass and swirl the brandy, staring at the point where the stem meets the glass. 'Let's just say that the way things are suddenly became very clear to me.'

His eyes narrow.

'To August and Marlena,' I say, thrusting my glass upward. The brandy sloshes up the sides.

He lifts his glass slowly.

I toss back the rest of my brandy and smile.

He lowers his glass without drinking. I cock my head and keep smiling. Let him examine me. Just let him. Today I am invincible.

He starts to nod, satisfied. He takes a drink. 'Yes. Good. I have to admit I wasn't so sure about you after yesterday. I'm glad you've come around. You won't be sorry, Jacob. It's the best thing for everyone. And especially you,' he says, pointing at me with his snifter. He tips it back and drains it. 'I look after those who look after me.' He smacks his lips, stares at me, and adds, 'I also look after those who don't.'

That evening, Marlena conceals her black eye with pancake makeup and does her liberty act. But August's face is not so easily fixed, so there will be no elephant act until he looks like a human being again. The towns-folk – who have been staring at poster after poster of Rosie balancing on a ball for the last two weeks – are unhappy in the extreme when the show ends and they realize that the pachyderm who cheerfully accepted candy, popcorn, and peanuts in the menagerie tent never made an appearance in the big top at all. A handful of men wanting their money back are hustled away to be molli-fied by the patches before their train of thought has an opportunity to spread.

A few days later, the sequined headpiece reappears – mended carefully with pink thread – and so Rosie looks glamorous as she charms the crowd in the menagerie. But she still doesn't perform, and after every show there are complaints.

Life goes on with fragile normalcy. I perform my usual duties in the morning and retire to the back end when the crowd comes in. Uncle Al does not consider battered rotten tomatoes to be good ambassadors for the show, and I can't say I blame him. My wounds look significantly worse before they start to look better, and when the swelling subsides it's clear that my nose will be off-kilter for life.

Except for mealtimes, we don't see August at all. Uncle Al reassigns him to Earl's table, but after it becomes clear that all he will do is sit and sulk and stare at Marlena, he is ordered to take his meals in the dining car with Uncle Al. And so it happens that three times a day, Marlena and I sit across from each other, strangely alone in the most public of places.

Uncle Al tries to keep up his end of the deal, I'll give him that. But August is too far gone to be controlled. The day after his extraction from the cookhouse, Marlena turns and sees him ducking behind a tent flap. An hour later, he accosts her in the midway, drops to his knees, and wraps his arms around her legs. When she wrestles to get free, he knocks her onto the grass and pins her there, trying to force her ring back on her finger, alternately murmuring entreaties and spitting threats.

Walter sprints to the menagerie to get me, but by the time I get there Earl has already hauled August away. Fuming, I head for the privilege car.

When I tell Uncle Al that August's outburst has just returned us to square one, he vents his frustration by smashing a decanter against the wall.

August disappears entirely for three days, and Uncle Al begins whacking heads again.

August is not the only one consumed by thoughts of Marlena. I lie on my horse blanket at night wanting her so badly I ache. A part of me wishes she would come to me – but not really, because it's too dangerous. I also can't go to her, because she's sharing a bunk in the virgin car with one of the bally broads.

We manage to make love twice in the space of six days – ducking behind sidewalls and grappling frantically, re-arranging our clothing because there is no time to remove it. These encounters leave me both exhausted and recharged, desperate and fulfilled. The rest of the time we interact with focused formality in the cookhouse. We are so careful to maintain the facade that even though no one could possibly hear our conversations, we conduct them as though others were sitting at our table. Even so, I wonder whether our affair isn't obvious. It seems to me that the bonds between us must be visible.

The night after our third unexpected and frenzied encounter, while the taste of her is still on my lips, I have a vivid dream. The train is stopped in the forest, for no reason I can make out because it's the middle of the night and nobody stirs. There's yelping outside, insistent and distressed. I leave the stock car, following the noise to the edge of a steep bank. Queenie struggles at the bottom of a ravine, a badger hanging from her leg. I call to her, frantically scanning the bank for a way to get down. I grab a ropy branch and clutch it while I try to descend, but the mud slips under my feet and I end up hauling myself back up.

In the meantime, Queenie breaks free and scrabbles up the hill. I scoop her up and check her for injuries. Incredibly, she is fine. I tuck her under my arm and turn toward the stock car. An eight-foot alligator blocks its entrance. I head for the next car over, but the alligator turns as well, shambling beside the train, its blunt, toothy snout open, grinning. I turn in panic. Another huge alligator approaches from the other direction.

There are noises behind us, leaves crackling and twigs snapping. I spin around to find that the badger has come up the bank and multiplied.

Behind us, a wall of badgers. In front of us, a dozen alligators.

I wake up in a cold sweat.

The situation is entirely untenable, and I know it.

In Poughkeepsie, we are raided, and for once the social strata are bridged: working men, performers, and bosses alike weep and snizzle as all that scotch, all that wine, all that fine Canadian whiskey, all that beer, all that gin, and even moonshine is poured onto the gravel by straight-armed, sour-faced men. It winnows through the stones as we watch, bubbling into the undeserving earth.

And then we are run out of town.

In Hartford, a handful of patrons take serious exception to Rosie's nonperformance, as well as the continued presence of the Lovely Lucinda sideshow banner despite the unfortunate absence of the Lovely Lucinda. The patches aren't fast enough, and before we know it disgruntled men swarm the ticket wagon demanding refunds. With the police closing in on one side and townsfolk on the other, Uncle Al is forced to refund the whole day's proceeds.

And then we are run out of town.

The following morning is payday, and the employees of the Benzini Brothers Most Spectacular Show on Earth line up in front of the red ticket wagon. The working men are in a foul humor – they know which way the wind is blowing. The first person to approach the red wagon is a roustabout, and when he leaves empty-handed the line buzzes with angry curses. The rest of the working men stalk off, spitting and swearing, leaving only performers and bosses in line. A few minutes later, another angry buzz runs down the line, this one tinged with surprise. For the first time in the show's history, there is no money for performers. Only the bosses are getting paid.

Walter is outraged.

'What the *fuck* is this?' he shouts as he enters the stock car. He throws his hat into the corner and then drops onto the bedroll.

Camel whimpers from the cot. Ever since the raid, he spends his time either staring at the wall or crying. The only time he speaks is when we're trying to feed or clean him, and even then it's only to beg us not to deliver him to his son. Walter and I take turns muttering placating things about family and forgiveness, but we both have misgivings. Whatever he was when he wandered away from his family, he is incalculably worse now, damaged beyond repair and probably even recognition. And if they're not in a forgiving frame of mind, what will it be like for him to be so helpless in their hands?

'Calm down, Walter,' I say. I'm sitting on my horse blanket in the corner, brushing away the flies that have been tormenting me all morning, flitting from scab to scab.

'No, I will not *fucking calm down*. I'm a performer! A performer! Performers get paid!' Walter shouts, thumping his chest. He pulls off a shoe and heaves it against the wall. He stares at it for a moment, then pulls off the other and slams it into the corner. It lands on his hat. Walter brings his fist down on the blanket beneath him and Queenie scurries behind the row of trunks that used to hide Camel.

'We don't have much longer,' I say. 'Just hang on for a few more days.'

'Yeah? Why's that?'

'Because that's when Camel gets picked up?' – there's a keening wail from the cot – 'and we get the hell out of here.'

'Yeah?' says Walter. 'And just what the hell are we going to do? Have you figured that out yet?'

I meet his gaze and hold it for a few seconds. Then I turn my head.

'Yeah. That's what I thought. That's why I needed to get paid. We're going to end up as fucking *hoboes*,' he says.

'No we won't,' I say unconvincingly.

'You better think of something, Jacob. You're the one who got us into this mess, not me. You and your girl-friend might be able to take to the road, but I can't. This may be all fun and games for you—'

'It is *not* fun and games!'

'—but my life is at stake here. You've at least got the option of hopping trains and moving around. I don't.'

He is quiet. I stare at his short, compact limbs.

He nods curtly, bitterly. 'Yeah. That's right. And like I said before, I'm not exactly cut out for farmwork, either.'

My mind churns as I go through the line in the cook-house. Walter is absolutely right – I got us into this mess, and I've got to get us out. Damned if I know how, though. Not one of us has a home to go to. Never mind that Walter can't hop trains – hell will freeze over before I let Marlena spend a single night in a hobo jungle. I'm so preoccupied that I'm almost at the table before I look up. Marlena is already there.

'Hi,' I say, taking my seat.

'Hi,' she says after a slight pause, and I know imme-diately that something is wrong.

'What is it? What happened?'

'Nothing.'

'Are you okay? Did he hurt you?'

'No. I'm fine,' she whispers, staring at her plate.

'No you're not. What is it? What did he do?' I say. Other diners start to look.

'Nothing,' she hisses. 'Keep your voice down.'

I straighten up and, with a great show of restraint, spread my napkin across my lap. I pick up my cutlery and carefully slice my pork chop. 'Marlena, please talk to me,' I say quietly. I concentrate on making my face look as though we're discussing the weather. Slowly, the people around us return to their meals.

'I'm late,' she says.

'I beg your pardon?'

'I'm late.'

'For what?'

She raises her head and turns beet red. 'I think I'm going to have a baby.'

When Earl comes to fetch me, I'm not even surprised. It's just the way the day is going.

Uncle Al is sitting in his chair, his face pinched and sour. There is no brandy today. He gnaws on the end of a cigar and stabs his cane repeatedly into the carpet.

'It's been almost three weeks, Jacob.'

'I know,' I say. My voice is shaky. I'm still absorbing Marlena's news.

'I'm disappointed in you. I thought we had an understanding.'

'We did. We do.' I shift restlessly. 'Look, I'm doing my best, but August isn't helping. She'd have gone back to him a long time ago if he'd just leave her the hell alone for a while.'

'I've done what I could,' says Uncle Al. He takes the cigar from his lips, looks at it, and then picks a piece of tobacco from his tongue. He flicks it against the wall, where it sticks.

'Well, it's not enough,' I say. 'He follows her around. He yells at her. He cries outside her window. She's *scared* of him. Having Earl follow him around and haul him off whenever he gets out of hand is not enough. Would you go back to him if you were her?'

Uncle Al stares at me. I suddenly realize I've been yelling.

'I'm sorry,' I say. 'I'll work on her. I swear, if you can just get him to leave her alone for a few more days—'

'No,' he says quietly. 'We're going to do it my way now.'

'What?'

'I said we're going to do it my way. You can leave now.' He flicks the ends of his fingers toward the door. 'Go.'

I stare at him, blinking stupidly. 'What do you mean, your way?'

Next thing I know, Earl's arms encircle me like a steel band. He lifts me from the chair and carries me to the door. 'What do you mean, Al?' I shout over Earl's shoulder. 'I want to know what you mean! What are you going to do?'

Earl handles me significantly more gently once he's closed the door. When he finally sets me on the gravel, he brushes off my jacket.

'Sorry, pal,' he says. 'I really did try.'

'Earl!'

He stops and turns back to me, his face grim.

'What's he got in mind?'

He looks at me but says nothing.

'Earl, please. I'm begging you. What's he going to do?'

'I'm sorry, Jacob,' he says. He climbs back inside the train.

* * *

Quarter to seven, fifteen minutes to showtime. The crowd mills around the menagerie, viewing the animals on their way to the big top. I'm standing by Rosie, supervising as she accepts donations of candy, gum, and even lemonade from the crowd. From the corner of my eye I see a tall man stride toward me. It's Diamond Joe.

'You gotta get out of here,' he says, stepping over the rope.

'Why? What's going on?'

'August's on his way. The bull's performing tonight.'

'What? You mean with Marlena?'

'Yeah. And he don't want to see you. He's in one of those moods. Go on, get out.'

I scan the tent for Marlena. She's standing in front of her horses, chatting with a family of five. Her eyes flit over to me and then, when she sees my expression, dart back at regular intervals.

I hand Diamond Joe the silver-tipped cane that passes for a bull hook these days and step over the rope. I see August's top hat approaching on my left and move instead to my right, past the line of zebras. I stop beside Marlena.

'Did you know you're supposed to perform with Rosie tonight?' I say.

'Excuse me,' she says, smiling at the family in front of her. She turns around and leans in close. 'Yes. Uncle Al called me in. He says the show is on the verge of collapse.'

'But can you? I mean, in your . . . um . . .'

'I'm fine. I don't have to do anything strenuous.'

'What if you fall off?'

'I won't. Besides, I don't have a choice. Uncle Al also

said – oh hell, here's August. You'd better get out of here.'

'I don't want to.'

'I'll be fine. He won't do anything with rubes around. You've got to go. *Please.*'

I look over my shoulder. August is approaching, looking up from a downturned face like a charging bull.

'*Please,*' Marlena says desperately.

I head through the big top, following the hippodrome track to the back entrance. I pause, and then slip beneath the seats.

I watch the Spec from between a man's work boots. About half-way through, I realize I'm not alone. An ancient roustabout is also looking through the stands but facing the other direction. He's looking up a woman's skirt.

'Hey!' I shout. 'Hey, knock it off!'

The crowd roars in delight as a great gray mass passes the edge of the risers. It's Rosie. I turn back to the roustabout. He stands on tiptoe, holding the edge of a floorboard with his fingertips and peering upward. He licks his lips.

I can't stand it. I'm guilty of terrible, terrible things – things that will damn my soul to hell – but the idea of some random woman being violated in this manner is more than I can bear, and so even as Marlena and Rosie are stepping into the center ring, I grab the roustabout by the jacket and drag him from beneath the seats.

'Lemme go!' he squeals. 'What's the matter with you?'

I keep him in my grasp, but my attention is on the center ring.

Marlena balances gamely on her ball, but Rosie stands utterly still, all four feet planted squarely on the ground. August's arms wave up and down. He swings the cane. He shakes his fist. His mouth opens and closes. Rosie's ears flatten against her head, and I lean forward, looking more closely. Her expression is unmistakably belligerent.

Oh God, Rosie. Not now. Don't do this now.

'Aw, come on!' screeches the filthy gnome in my hands. 'This ain't no Sunday School show. It's just a harmless bit of fun. Come on! Lemme go!'

I look down at him. He is panting, his breath rank, his lower jaw punctuated by long brown teeth. Disgusted, I shove him away from me.

He looks quickly from side to side, and when he realizes that no one in the crowd has noticed anything, he straightens his lapels in righteous indignation and swaggers toward the back entrance. Just before he steps outside, he throws me a dirty look. But his narrowed eyes bounce off me, glomming on to something beyond. He dives through the air, his face frozen in a mask of terror.

I spin and find Rosie hurtling toward me, her trunk raised and mouth open. I throw myself against the risers and she passes, trumpeting and pounding the sawdust with such force that a three-foot cloud of particles trails her. August follows, waving his cane.

The crowd explodes, laughing and cheering – they think it's part of the act. Uncle Al stands in the center of the hippodrome, stupefied. He watches the back entrance of the tent for a moment with his mouth open. Then he snaps into action and cues Lottie.

I climb to my feet and look for Marlena. She passes me, a pink blur.

'Marlena!'

In the distance, August is already hammering Rosie. She bellows and screams, throwing her head and backing away, but he's like a machine. He raises that damned cane and brings it down hook first, again and again and again. When Marlena reaches them, he turns to face her. The cane falls to the ground. He stares at her with burning intensity, completely oblivious to Rosie.

I know that look.

I charge forward. Before I've gone a dozen strides, my feet are swept out from under me and I'm facedown on the ground with a knee on my cheek and one of my arms twisted behind my back.

'Get the hell off me!' I scream, twisting to get free. 'What the hell's the matter with you? Let me go!'

'Just shut up,' says Blackie's voice from above me. 'You ain't goin' nowhere.'

August leans over and straightens up with Marlena over his shoulder. She pounds his back with her fists, kicking her legs and screaming. She almost manages to slide off his shoulder, but he just hitches her back up and marches off.

'Marlena! *Marlena!*' I bellow, renewing my struggle.

I twist out from under Blackie's knee and am halfway to my feet before something crashes into the back of my head. My brain and eyes jolt in their cavities. My vision fills with black and white sparkles and I think I might also be deaf. After a moment my vision starts to return, from the outside in. Faces appear and mouths move, but all I hear is an earsplitting buzz. I weave on my knees trying to figure out who and what and where but now the ground comes screaming toward me. I'm powerless to stop it so I brace myself, but in the end it isn't necessary because the blackness swallows me before it hits.

TWENTY-TWO

hh, don't move.'

I'm not, although my head jiggles and jerks with the motion of the train. The engine's whistle blows mournfully, a distant sound that somehow cuts through the insistent buzzing in my ears. My whole body feels like lead.

Something cold and wet hits my forehead. I open my eyes and see a panoply of shifting color and forms. Four blurred arms cross my face and then merge into a single foreshortened limb. I gag, my lips involuntarily forming a tunnel. I turn my head, but nothing comes out.

'Keep your eyes closed,' says Walter. 'Just lie still.'

'*Hrrmph*,' I mumble. I let my head fall to the side, and the cloth falls from it. A moment later it's replaced.

'You took a good hit. Glad to see you back.'

'Is he coming around?' says Camel. 'Hey, Jacob, you still with us?'

I feel like I'm rising from a deep mine, am having trouble placing myself. I appear to be on the bedroll. The train is already moving. But how did I get here and why was I asleep?

Marlena!

My eyes snap open. I struggle to rise.

'Didn't I tell you to lie still?' Walter scolds.

'Marlena! Where's Marlena?' I gasp, falling back on the pillow. My brain rolls in my head. I think it's been shaken loose. It's worse when my eyes are open and so I close them again. With all visual stimulus removed, the blackness feels larger than my head, as though my cranial cavity has turned inside out.

Walter is kneeling beside me. He removes the rag from my forehead, dips it in water, and then squeezes out the excess. The water trickles back into the bowl, a clean, clear sound, a familiar tinkling. The buzzing starts to subside, replaced by a pounding ache that sweeps from ear to ear around the back of my skull.

Walter brings the rag back to my face. He wipes my forehead, cheeks, and chin, leaving my skin damp. The cooling tingle is grounding, helps me concentrate on the outside of my head.

'Where is she? Did he hurt her?'

'I don't know.'

I open my eyes again, and the world tilts violently. I struggle up on my elbows and this time Walter doesn't push me down. Instead, he leans over and peers into my eyes. 'Shit. Your pupils are different sizes. You feel up to drinking something?' he says.

'Uh . . . yeah,' I gasp. Finding words is hard. I know what I want to express, but the pathway between my mouth and brain might as well be stuffed with cotton.

Walter crosses the room, and a bottle cap clinks to the floor. He comes back and holds a bottle to my lips. It's sarsaparilla. 'It's the best I've got, I'm afraid,' he says ruefully.

'Damned cops,' Camel grumbles. 'You okay, Jacob?'

I'd like to answer, but staying upright is taking all my concentration.

'Walter, is he okay?' Camel sounds significantly more worried this time.

'I think so,' says Walter. He puts the bottle on the floor. 'You want to try sitting up? Or you want to wait a few minutes?'

'I've got to get Marlena.'

'Forget it, Jacob. There's nothing you can do right now.'

'I've got to. What if he . . . ?' My voice cracks. I can't even finish the sentence. Walter helps me into a sitting position.

'There's nothing you can do right now.'

'I don't accept that.'

Walter turns in fury. 'For Christ's sake, would you just listen to me for once?'

His anger startles me into silence. I rearrange my knees and lean forward so my head is resting on my arms. It feels heavy, huge – at least as large as my body.

'Never mind that we're on a moving train and you've got a concussion. We're in a mess. A big mess. And the only thing you can do right now is make it worse. Hell, if you hadn't been knocked flat and if we didn't still have

Camel here, I'd have never gotten back on this train tonight.'

I stare between my knees at the bedroll, trying to concentrate on the largest fold of material. Things are steadier now, not shifting so much. With each passing minute, additional parts of my brain are kicking in.

'Look,' Walter continues, his voice softer, 'we've got three days left before we off-load Camel. And we're just going to have to cope the best we can in the meantime. That means watching our backs and not doing anything stupid.'

'Off-load Camel?' says Camel. 'Is that how you think of me?'

'At the moment, yes!' barks Walter. 'And you should be grateful we do, because what the hell do you think would happen to you if we took off right now? *Hmmm?*'

There is no answer from the cot.

Walter pauses and sighs. 'Look, what's happening with Marlena is terrible, but for God's sake! If we leave before Providence, Camel's done for. She's going to have to look after herself for the next three days. Hell, she's done it for four years. I think she can last another three days.'

'She's pregnant, Walter.'

'What?'

There is a long silence. I look up.

Walter's forehead is creased. 'Are you sure?'

'So she says.'

He stares into my eyes for a long time. I try to meet his gaze, but my eyes jerk rhythmically to the side.

'All the more reason to play this carefully. Jacob, look at me!'

'I'm trying!' I say.

'We're going to get out of here. But if we're all going to make it, we've got to play it right. We can't do anything – anything! – until Camel's gone. The sooner you get used to that, the better.'

There's a sob from the cot. Walter turns his head. 'Shut it, Camel! They wouldn't be taking you back if they hadn't forgiven you. Or would you rather be redlighted?'

'I don't rightly know,' he cries.

Walter turns back to me. 'Look at me, Jacob. Look at me.' When I do, he continues. 'She'll handle him. I tell you, she'll handle him. She's the only one who can. She knows what's at stake. It's only for three days.'

'And then what? Like you've said all along, we have nowhere to go.'

He turns his face away in anger. Then he spins back. 'Do you truly comprehend the situation here, Jacob? Because sometimes I wonder.'

'Of course I do! It's just I'm not liking any of the options.'

'Me neither. But like I said, we'll have to sort that out later. Right now let's just concentrate on getting out of here alive.'

Camel sobs and sniffs his way to sleep, despite Walter's repeated assurances that his family will welcome him with open arms.

Eventually he drifts off. Walter checks him one more time and then turns off the lamp. He and Queenie retire to the horse blanket in the corner. A few minutes later he begins to snore.

I rise carefully, testing my balance at every point. When I've got myself successfully upright, I step tentatively forward. I'm dizzy but seem able to compensate. I take a few steps in a row, and when that works out all right I cross the floor to the trunk.

Six minutes later, I'm creeping across the top of the stock car on my hands and knees with Walter's knife in my teeth.

What sounds like gentle clacking from inside the train is a violent banging up here. The cars shift and jerk as we round a corner, and I stop, clinging to the top rail until we're once again on a straightaway.

At the end of the car I pause to consider my options. In theory, I could climb down the ladder, leap over to the platform, and walk through the various cars until I reach the one in question. But I can't risk being seen.

So. And so.

I stand, still holding the knife in my teeth. My legs are spread, my knees bent, my arms moving jerkily to the side, like the tightrope walker's.

The divide between this car and the next seems immense, a great span over eternity. I gather myself, pressing my tongue against the bitter metal of the knife. Then I leap, throwing every ounce of muscle into propelling myself through the air. I swing my arms and legs wildly, preparing to catch hold of anything – anything at all – if I miss.

I hit roof. I cling to the top rail, panting like a dog around the sides of the blade. Something warm trickles from the corner of my mouth. Still kneeling on the rail, I remove the knife from my mouth and lick blood from my lips. Then I put it back, taking care to keep my lips retracted.

In this manner I traverse five sleepers. Each time I leap, I land a little more cleanly, a little more cavalierly. By the sixth, I have to remind myself to be careful.

When I reach the privilege car, I sit on the roof and take stock. My muscles are aching, my head is spinning, and I'm gasping for breath.

The train jags around another curve and I grasp the rails, looking toward the engine. We're hugging the side of a forested hill, headed for a trestle. From what I can see in the darkness, the trestle drops down to a rocky river bank twenty yards below. The train jerks again, and I make my decision. The rest of my journey to car 48 will be on the interior.

Still clenching the knife in my teeth, I ease myself off the edge of the platform. The cars that house the performers and bosses are connected by metal plates, so all I have to do is make sure I land on it. I'm hanging by my fingertips when the train lurches once again, swinging my legs off to the side. I clutch desperately, my sweaty fingers sliding on the cross-hatched metal.

When the train straightens out again, I drop onto the plate. The platform has a railing and I lean against it for a moment, collecting myself. With aching, trembling fingers I pull the watch from my pocket. It's nearly three in the morning. The chances of running into someone are slim. But still.

The knife is a problem. It is too long to go in a pocket, too sharp to stick in my waistband. In the end, I wrap my jacket around it and tuck it under my arm. Then I run my fingers through my hair, wipe the blood off my lips, and slide the door open.

The corridor is empty, illuminated by moonlight coming through the windows. I pause long enough to look out. We're on the trestle now. I had underestimated its height – we're a good forty yards above the boulders of the river-bank and facing a wide area of nothingness. As the train sways, I'm grateful I'm no longer on the roof.

Soon I'm staring at the doorknob of stateroom 3. I unwrap the knife and lay it on the floor while I put my jacket back on. Then I pick it up and stare at the door-knob a moment longer.

There's a loud click as I turn the knob, and I freeze, keeping it turned, waiting to see if there's a reaction. After several seconds, I continue twisting and push the door inward.

I leave the door open, afraid that if I close it I'll wake him up.

If he's on his back, a single quick slash across the wind-pipe will do it. If he's on his stomach or side, I'll plunge it straight through, making sure the blade crosses his wind-pipe. Either way, I'll hit him in the neck. I just can't falter, because it must be deep enough that he bleeds out quickly, without crying out.

I creep toward the bedroom, clutching the knife. The velvet curtain is closed. I pull the edge of it toward me and peek in. When I see that he's alone, I exhale in relief. She's safe, probably in the virgin car. In fact, I must have crawled right over her on my way here.

I slip in and stand by the bed. He's sleeping on the near side, leaving space for the absent Marlena. The curtains on the windows are tied back, and moonlight flashes through the trees, alternately illuminating and hiding his face.

I stare down at him. He's in striped pajamas and looks peaceful, boyish even. His dark hair is mussed, and the edge of his mouth moves in and out of a smile. He's dreaming. He moves suddenly, smacking his lips and rolling from his back onto his side. He reaches over to Marlena's side of the bed and pats the empty space a few times. Then he pats his way up to her pillow. He takes hold of it and pulls it to his chest, hugging it, burrowing his face into it.

I raise the knife, holding it in both hands, its tip poised two feet above his throat. I need to do this right. I adjust the blade's angle to maximize side-to-side damage. The train passes out of the trees, and a thin streak of moonlight catches the blade. It glints, throwing tiny shards of light as I make adjustments to the angle. August moves again, snorting and rolling violently onto his back. His left arm flops off the bed and comes to a stop inches from my thigh. The knife is still gleaming, still catching and throwing light. But the movement is no longer a result of my making adjustments. My hands are shaking. August's lower jaw opens, and he inhales with a terrible rumbling and smacking of lips. The hand beside my thigh is slack. The fingers of his other hand twitch.

I lean over him and lay the knife carefully on Marlena's pillow. I stare for a few seconds longer and then leave.

* * *

No longer riding a wave of adrenaline, my head once again feels larger than my body, and I stagger through the corridors until I reach the end of the staterooms.

I have a choice to make. I must either go up top again or else continue through the privilege car – where there's every possibility someone is still up gambling – and then also pass through all the sleepers, at which point I'll still have to go back up top to get to the stock car. And so I decide to make the ascent earlier rather than later.

It's almost more than I can manage. My head is pounding, and my balance seriously compromised. I climb onto the railing of a connecting platform and somehow scrape my way up to the top. Once there, I lie on the top rail, queasy and limp. I spend ten minutes recovering and then crawl forth. I rest again at the end of the car, prostrate between the top rails. I am utterly drained. I can't imagine how I'll keep going, but I must, because if I fall asleep here I'll fall off the first time we hit a curve.

The buzzing returns, and my eyes are jerking. I dive across the great divide four times, each time sure I won't make it. On the fifth, I nearly don't. My hands hit the thin iron rails, but the edge of the car hits me in the gut. I hang there, stunned, so tired that it crosses my mind how much easier it would be to simply let go. It's how drowning people must feel in the last few seconds, when they finally stop fighting and sink into the water's embrace. Only what's waiting for me is not a watery embrace. It's a violent dismemberment.

I snap to, scrabbling with my legs until I get purchase

on the top edge of the car. From there, it's easy enough to haul myself up and a second later I'm once again lying on the top rail, gasping for breath.

The train whistle blows, and I lift my huge head. I'm on top of the stock car. I only have to make it to the vent and drop down. I crawl to the vent in fits and starts. It's open, which is odd because I thought I closed it. I lower myself inside and crash to the floor. One of the horses whinnies and continues to snort and stamp, riled up about something.

I turn my head. The exterior door is now open.

I jerk up and scooch around so I'm facing the interior door. It is also open.

'Walter! Camel!' I shout.

Nothing but the sound of the door gently hitting the wall behind it, keeping time with the ties clacking beneath us.

I scramble to my feet and lunge for the door. Doubled over and supporting myself with one hand against the doorframe and the other on my thigh, I scan the interior of the room with sightless eyes. All the blood has left my head, and my vision once again fills with black and white explosions.

'Walter! Camel!'

My eyesight starts to return, from the outside in so that I find myself turning my head to try to catch things in the periphery. The only light is what comes through the slats, and it reveals an empty cot. The bedroll is also empty, as is the horse blanket in the corner.

I stagger to the row of trunks against the back wall and lean over them.

'Walter?'

All I find is Queenie, shivering and curled into a ball. She looks up at me in terror, and I am left with no doubt.

I sink to the floor, overcome with grief and guilt. I throw a book at the wall. I pound the floorboards. I shake my fists at heaven and God, and when I finally subside into uncontrolled sobbing Queenie creeps out from behind the trunks and slides into my lap. I hold her warm body until finally we are rocking in silence.

I want to believe that taking Walter's knife didn't make a difference. But still, I left him without a knife, without even a chance.

I want to believe they survived. I try to picture it – the two of them rolling out onto the mossy forest floor amid indignant curses. Why, at this very moment, Walter is probably going for help. He has made Camel comfortable in some sheltered spot and is going for help.

Okay. Okay. It's not as bad as I thought. I'll go back for them. In the morning, I'll grab Marlena and we'll go back to the nearest town and ask at the hospital. Maybe even the jail, in case the town decided they were vagrants. It should be easy enough to figure out which town is closest. I can locate it by proximity to the—

They didn't. They couldn't have. Nobody could have redlighted a crippled old man and a dwarf over a *trestle*. Not even August. Not even Uncle Al.

I spend the rest of the night planning all the ways I can kill them, rolling the ideas around in my head and savoring them, as though I were fingering smooth stones.

* * *

The screech of the air brakes snaps me out of my trance. Before the train has even stopped, I drop to the gravel and stride toward the sleepers. I climb the iron stairs to the first one shabby enough to house working men and slide the door open so violently it bounces closed again. I reopen it and march through.

'Earl! Earl! Where are you?' My voice is guttural with hate and rage. 'Earl!'

I stalk down the aisle, peering into bunks. None of the surprised faces I encounter is Earl's.

Onto the next car.

'Earl! You in here?'

I pause and turn to a bewildered man in a bunk. 'Where the hell is he? Is he in here?'

'You mean Earl from security?'

'Yeah. That's who I mean, all right.'

He jerks his thumb over his shoulder. 'Two cars that-away.'

I pass through another car, trying to avoid the limbs that stick out from under bunks, the arms that spill over their edges.

I slide the door open with a crash. 'Earl! Where the hell are you? I know you're in here!'

There's an astonished pause, with men on both sides of the car shifting in their bunks to get a look at this loud intruder. Three-quarters of the way down I see Earl. I charge him.

'You son of a bitch!' I say, reaching down to grab him by the neck. 'How could you do it? How could you?'

Earl leaps from his bunk, holding my arms out to the side. 'Whoa – hang on, Jacob. Calm down. What's going on?'

375

'You know *fucking well* what I'm talking about!' I shriek, twisting my forearms around and out, breaking his grasp. I hurl myself at him, but before I make contact he once again has me at arm's length.

'How could you do it?' Tears are running down my face. 'How could you? You were supposed to be Camel's friend! And what the hell did Walter ever do to you?'

Earl goes pale. He freezes with his hands still closed around my wrists. The shock on his face is so genuine I stop struggling.

We blink at each other in horror. Seconds pass. A panicked buzz ripples through the rest of the car.

Earl releases me and says, 'Follow me.'

We step down from the train, and once we are a good dozen yards away, he turns to me. 'They're gone?'

I stare at him, seeking answers in his face. There aren't any. 'Yeah.'

Earl sucks in his breath. His eyes close. For a moment I think he might cry.

'Are you telling me you didn't know anything?' I say.

'Hell no! What do you think I am? I'd never do something like that. Aw shit. Aw hell. The poor old fella. Wait a minute—' he says, training his eyes on me suddenly. 'Where were you?'

'Somewhere else,' I say.

Earl stares for a moment and then drops his gaze to the ground. He puts his hands on his waist and sighs, bobbing his head and thinking. 'Okay,' he says. 'I'm going to find out how many other poor bastards got tossed, but let me tell you something – kinkers don't get tossed, even lowly ones. If Walter got it, they were after you. And if

I were you, I'd start walking right now and never look back.'

'And if I can't do that?'

He looks up sharply. His jaw moves from side to side. He regards me for a very long time. 'You'll be safe on the lot, in daylight,' he says finally. 'If you get back on the train tonight, don't go anywhere near that stock car. Move around the flats and rest under wagons. Don't get caught, and don't let your guard down. And blow the show as soon as you can.'

'I will. Believe me. But I've got a couple of loose ends to wrap up first.'

Earl gives me a long last look. 'I'll try to catch up with you later,' he says. Then he strides off toward the cook-house where the men from the Flying Squadron are congregating in small groups, their eyes darting, their faces fearful.

In addition to Camel and Walter, eight other men are missing, three from the main train and the rest from the Flying Squadron, which means that Blackie and his group broke up into squads, riding different sections of the train. With the show on the brink of collapse, the working men probably would have been red-lighted anyway, but not over a trestle. That was meant for me.

It occurs to me that my conscience stopped me from killing August at the very moment someone was attempting to carry out his orders to kill me.

I wonder how he felt waking up beside that knife. I hope he understands that while it started out as a threat,

SARA GRUEN

it's since transformed into a promise. I owe it to each and every one of the men who got tossed.

I skulk around all morning, searching desperately for Marlena. She is nowhere to be seen.

Uncle Al strides around in his black and white checked pants and scarlet waistcoat, slapping the head of anyone who isn't quick enough to jump out of his way. At one point he catches sight of me and stops cold. We face each other, eighty yards apart. I stare and stare, trying to focus all my hatred through my eyes. After a few seconds, his lips form a cold smile. Then he makes a sharp right turn and continues on his way, his grovelers straggling behind.

I watch from a distance when the flag goes up over the cookhouse at lunchtime. Marlena is there, dressed in street clothes and lined up for food. Her eyes scan the crowd; I know she's looking for me, and I hope she knows I'm okay. Almost as soon as she sits down, August comes out of nowhere and sits opposite. He has no food. He says something and then reaches across and grabs her wrist. She pulls backward, spilling her coffee. The people around them turn to watch. He lets go and rises so quickly the bench falls backward onto the grass. Then he storms out. As soon as he's gone, I sprint to the cookhouse.

Marlena looks up, sees me, and goes pale.

'Jacob!' she gasps.

I set the bench upright and sit on its edge.

'Did he hurt you? Are you okay?' I say.

'I'm fine. But what about you? I heard—' Her words

378

catch in her throat, and she covers her mouth with her hand.

'We're getting out today. I'll watch you. Just leave the lot when you can and I'll follow.'

She stares at me, pale. 'What about Walter and Camel?'

'We'll go back and see what we can find out.'

'I need a couple of hours.'

'What for?'

Uncle Al stands at the perimeter of the cookhouse, snapping his fingers in the air. From across the tent, Earl approaches.

'There's some money in our room. I'll go in when he's not there,' she says.

'No. It's not worth the risk,' I say.

'I'll be careful.'

'No!'

'Come on, Jacob,' says Earl, taking hold of my upper arm. 'The boss wants you to move along.'

'Give me just a second, Earl,' I say.

He sighs deeply. 'Fine. Struggle a bit. But only for a couple of seconds, and then I gotta take you out of here.'

'Marlena,' I say desperately, 'promise me you won't go in there.'

'I have to. The money's half mine, and if I don't get it we won't have a cent to our names.'

I break free of Earl's grasp and stand facing him. Or his chest, anyway.

'Tell me where it is and I'll get it,' I growl, poking my finger into Earl's chest.

'Under the window seat,' Marlena whispers urgently. She rises and comes around the table so that she's beside me.

'The bench opens. It's in a coffee can. But it's probably easier for me—'

'Okay, I gotta take you out now,' says Earl. He turns me around and bends my arm behind my back. He pushes me forward so I'm bent in the middle.

I turn my head to Marlena. 'I'll get it. You stay away from that train car. Promise me!'

I wriggle a bit, and Earl lets me.

'I said promise me!' I hiss.

'I promise,' Marlena says. 'Be careful!'

'Let me go, you son of a bitch!' I shout at Earl. For effect, of course.

He and I make a great spectacle of leaving the tent. I wonder if anyone can tell that he's not bending my arm far enough for it to hurt. But he makes up for that detail by chucking me a good ten feet across the grass.

I spend the entire afternoon peering around corners, slipping behind tent flaps, and ducking under wagons. But not once can I get near car 48 without being seen – and besides, I haven't laid eyes on August since lunchtime, so it's entirely possible that he's in there. So I bide my time.

There is no matinée. At about three in the afternoon, Uncle Al stands on a box in the middle of the lot and informs everyone that the evening show better be the best of their lives. He doesn't say what will happen if it isn't, and no one asks.

And so an impromptu parade is thrown together, after which the animals are led to the menagerie and the candy butchers and other concessionaires set up their wares.

The crowd that followed the parade back from town gathers in the midway, and before long Cecil is working the suckers in front of the sideshow.

I'm pressed up against the outside of the menagerie tent, pulling the laced seam open so I can peek through.

I see August inside, bringing in Rosie. He swings the silver-tipped cane under her belly and behind her front legs, essentially threatening her with it. She follows obediently, but her eyes are glazed with hostility. He leads her to her usual spot and chains her foot to a stake. She gazes upon his bent back with flattened ears and then seems to adjust her attitude, swinging her trunk and investigating the ground in front of her. She finds some tidbit on the ground and picks it up. She curls her trunk inward and rubs the object on it, testing it for texture. Then she pops it in her mouth.

Marlena's horses are already lined up, but she's not there yet. Most of the rubes have already filed through on their way to the big top. She ought to be here by now. *Come on, come on, where are you—*

It occurs to me that despite her promise, she's probably gone to their stateroom. *Damn it, damn it, damn it.* August is still fussing with Rosie's chain, but it won't be long before he notices Marlena's absence and investigates.

There's a tug on my sleeve. I spin around with fists clenched.

Grady raises both hands in a gesture of surrender. 'Whoa there, fella. Take it easy.'

I drop my fists. 'I'm a bit jittery. That's all.'

'Yeah, well. You got reason,' he says, glancing around.

'Say, you eaten yet? I saw you get tossed from the cook-house.'

'No,' I say.

'Come on. We'll go around to the grease joint.'

'No. I can't. I'm flat broke,' I say, desperate for him to leave. I turn back to the seam and pry its edges apart. Marlena's still not there.

'I'll spot you,' says Grady.

'I'm okay, really.' I keep my back to him, hoping he'll take the hint and leave.

'Listen, we gotta talk,' he says quietly. 'It's safer on the midway.'

I turn my head and lock eyes with him.

I follow him through to the midway. From inside the big top, the band launches into the music for the Spec.

We join the lineup in front of the grease joint. The man behind the counter flips and assembles burgers at lightning speed, catering to the few but anxious stragglers.

Grady and I work our way to the front of the line. He holds up two fingers. 'A couple of burgers, Sammy. No rush.'

Within seconds, the man behind the counter holds out two tin plates. I take one, and Grady takes the other. He also extends a rolled bill.

'Get outta here,' says the cook, waving his hand. 'Your money's no good here.'

'Thanks, Sammy,' says Grady, pocketing the bill. 'Sure do appreciate it.'

He goes to a battered wooden table and swings his leg over the bench. I go around to the other side.

'So, what's up?' I say, fingering a burl in the wood.

Grady looks around furtively. 'A few of the guys that got done last night caught up again,' he says. He lifts his burger and waits as three drops of grease fall onto his plate.

'What, they're here now?' I say, straightening up and scanning the midway. With the exception of a handful of men in front of the sideshow – probably waiting to be led to Barbara – all the rubes are in the big top.

'Keep it down,' says Grady. 'Yeah, five of 'em.'

'Is Walter . . . ?' My heart is beating fast. No sooner do I get his name out than Grady's eyes flicker and I have my answer.

'Oh Jesus,' I say, turning my head. I blink back tears and swallow. It takes me a moment to compose myself. 'What happened?'

Grady sets his burger on his plate. There are a full five seconds of silence before he answers, and when he does, it's quietly, without inflection. 'They got tossed over the trestle, all of them. Camel's head hit the rocks. He died right away. Walter's legs were smashed up bad. They had to leave him.' He swallows and adds, 'They don't reckon he lasted the night.'

I stare into the distance. A fly lands on my hand. I flick it away. 'What about the others?'

'They survived. A couple moped off, and the rest caught up.' His eyes sweep from side to side. 'Bill's one of them.'

'What are they going to do?' I ask.

'He didn't say,' says Grady. 'But one way or another, they're taking Uncle Al down. I aim to help if I can.'

'Why are you telling me?'

'To give you a chance to steer clear. You were a pal to

Camel, and we won't forget that.' He leans forward so his chest is pressed against the table. 'Besides,' he continues quietly, 'it seems to me you've got a lot to lose right now.'

I look up sharply. He's staring right into my eyes, one eyebrow cocked.

Oh God. He knows. And if he knows, everyone knows. We've got to leave now, this very minute.

Thunderous applause explodes from the big top, and the band slides seamlessly into the Gounod waltz. I turn toward the menagerie. It's a reflex, because Marlena is either preparing to mount or else is already astride Rosie's head.

'I've got to go,' I say.

'Sit,' says Grady. 'Eat. If you're thinking of clearing out, it may be a while before you see food again.'

He plants his elbows on the rough gray wood of the table and picks up his burger.

I stare at mine, wondering if I can choke it down.

I reach for it, but before I can pick it up the music crashes to a halt. There's an ungodly collision of brass that finishes with a cymbal's hollow clang. It wavers out of the big top and across the lot, leaving nothing in its wake.

Grady freezes, crouched over his burger.

I look from left to right. No one moves a muscle – all eyes point at the big top. A few wisps of hay swirl lazily across the hard dirt.

'What is it? What's going on?' I ask.

'*Shh*,' Grady says sharply.

The band starts up again, this time playing 'Stars and Stripes Forever.'

'Oh Christ. Oh shit,' Grady jumps up and backward, knocking over the bench.

'What? What is it?'

'The Disaster March!' he shouts, turning and bolting.

Everyone associated with the show is barreling toward the big top. I dismount the bench and stand behind it, stunned, not understanding. I jerk around to the fry cook, who struggles with his apron. 'What the hell's he talking about?' I shout.

'The Disaster March,' he says, wrestling the apron over his head. 'It means something's gone bad – real bad.'

Someone thumps my shoulder as he passes. It's Diamond Joe. 'Jacob – it's the menagerie,' he screams over his shoulder. 'The animals are loose. Go, go, *go!*'

He doesn't need to tell me twice. As I approach the menagerie, the ground rumbles beneath my feet and it scares the hell out of me because it's not noise. It's motion, the vibration of hooves and paws on hard dirt.

I throw myself through the flap and then immediately up against the sidewall as the yak thunders past, his crooked horn just inches from my chest. A hyena clings to his back, its eyes spinning in terror.

I'm facing a full-fledged stampede. The animal dens are all open, and the center of the menagerie is a blur; staring into it, I see bits of chimp, orangutan, llama, zebra, lion, giraffe, camel, hyena, and horse – in fact, I see dozens of horses, including Marlena's, and every one of them is mad with terror. Creatures of every sort zigzag, bolt, scream, swing, gallop, grunt, and whinny; they are every-where, swinging on ropes and slithering up poles, hiding under wagons, pressed against sidewalls, and skidding across the center.

I scan the tent for Marlena and instead see a panther slide through the connection into the big top. As its lithe, black body disappears, I brace myself. It takes several seconds to come, but come it does – one prolonged scream, followed by another, and then another, and then the whole place explodes with the thunderous sound of bodies shoving past other bodies and off the stands.

Please God let them leave by the back end. Please God don't let them try to come through here.

Beyond the roiling sea of animals, I catch sight of two men. They're swinging ropes, stirring the animals into an ever-higher frenzy. One of them is Bill. He catches my gaze and holds it for a moment. Then he slips into the big top with the other man. The band screeches to a halt again and this time stays silent.

My eyes sweep the tent, desperate to the point of panic. *Where are you? Where are you? Where the hell are you?*

I catch sight of pink sequins and my head jerks around. When I see Marlena standing beside Rosie, I cry out in relief.

August is in front of them – of course he is, where else would he be? Marlena's hands cover her mouth. She hasn't seen me yet, but Rosie has. She stares at me long and hard, and something about her expression stops me cold. August is oblivious – red-faced and bellowing, flapping his arms and swinging his cane. His top hat lies in the straw beside him, punctured, as though he'd put a foot through it.

Rosie stretches out her trunk, reaching for something.

A giraffe passes between us, its long neck bobbing gracefully even in panic, and when it's gone I see that Rosie has pulled her stake from the ground. She holds it loosely, resting its end on the hard dirt. The chain is still attached to her foot. She looks at me with bemused eyes. Then her gaze shifts to the back of August's bare head.

'Oh Jesus,' I say, suddenly understanding. I stumble forward and bounce off a horse's passing haunch. 'Don't do it! *Don't do it!*'

She lifts the stake as though it weighs nothing and splits his head in a single clean movement – *ponk* – like cracking a hardboiled egg. She continues to hold the stake until he topples forward, and then she slides it almost lazily back into the earth. She takes a step backward, revealing Marlena, who may or may not have seen what just happened.

Almost immediately a herd of zebras passes in front of them. Flailing human limbs flash between pounding black and white legs. Up and down, a hand, a foot, twisting and bouncing bonelessly. When the herd passes, the thing that was August is a tangled mass of flesh, innards, and straw.

Marlena stares at it, wide-eyed. Then she crumples to the ground. Rosie fans her ears, opens her mouth, and steps sideways so she's standing directly over top of Marlena.

Although the stampede continues unabated, at least I know Marlena won't be trampled before I can navigate the perimeter of the tent.

Inevitably, people try to exit the big top the way they entered it – through the menagerie. I'm kneeling beside

Marlena, cradling her head in my hands when people spew forth from the connection. They are a few feet in before they realize what's going on.

The ones at the front come to a dead stop and are flung to the ground by the people behind them. They would be trampled except that the people behind them have now also seen the stampede.

The mass of animals suddenly changes direction, an interspecies flock – lions, llamas, and zebras running side by side with orangutans and chimps; a hyena shoulder to shoulder with a tiger. Twelve horses and a giraffe with a spider monkey hanging from its neck. The polar bear, lumbering on all fours. And all of them headed for the knot of people.

The crowd turns, shrieking, and trying to recede into the big top. The people at the very back, shoved so recently to the ground, dance in desperation, pounding the backs and shoulders of the people in front of them. The clog bursts free, and people and animals flee together in a great squealing mass. It's hard to say who is more terrified – certainly the only thing any of the animals have in mind is saving their own hides. A Bengal tiger forces itself between a woman's legs, sweeping her from the ground. She looks down and faints. Her husband grabs her by the armpits, lifting her off the tiger and dragging her into the big top.

In a matter of seconds, there are only three living creatures in the menagerie besides me: Rosie, Marlena, and Rex. The mangy old lion has crept back into his den and is huddled in the corner, quivering.

Marlena moans. She lifts a hand and drops it. I glance

quickly at the thing that was August and decide I cannot let her see it again. I scoop her up and carry her out through the ticket gate.

The lot is nearly empty, the outer perimeter defined by people and animals, all running as far and as fast as they can, expanding and dispersing like a ring on the surface of a pond.

TWENTY-THREE

Post-stampede, day one.

We're still finding and retrieving animals. We've caught a great many, but the ones that lend themselves to catching are not the ones the townsfolk are concerned about. Most of the cats are still missing, as is the bear.

Immediately after lunch we are summoned to a local restaurant. When we arrive, we find Leo hiding under the kitchen sink, shivering in terror. Wedged in beside him is an equally terrified dishwasher. Man and lion, cheek by jowl.

Uncle Al is also missing, but no one is surprised. The lot is crawling with police. August's body was found and removed last night, and they're performing an investigation. It will be perfunctory, since it's clear he was trampled. The word is that Uncle Al is keeping away until he's sure he won't be charged with anything.

Post-stampede, day two.

Animal by animal, the menagerie fills. The sheriff returns to the lot with railroad officials and makes noises about vagrancy laws. He wants us off the siding. He wants to know who's in charge here.

In the evening, the cookhouse runs out of food.

Post-stampede, day three.

In late morning, the Nesci Brothers Circus train pulls up on a siding next to ours. The sheriff and the railroad officials return and greet the general manager as though he were visiting royalty. They stroll the lot together and finish up with hearty handshakes and booming laughter.

When Nesci Brothers men start moving Benzini Brothers animals and equipment into their tents and onto their train, even the most fervently optimistic among us can no longer deny the obvious.

Uncle Al has done a runner. Each and every one of us is out of work.

Think, Jacob. *Think.*

We have enough money to get ourselves out of here, but what good is that with nowhere to go? We have a baby coming. We need a plan. I need a job.

I walk into town to the post office and call Dean Wilkins. I had been afraid that he wouldn't remember me, but he sounds relieved to hear from me. He says he's often wondered where I went and whether I was okay, and by the way, what *had* I been up to for the last three and a half months?

I take a deep breath and even as I'm thinking about how hard it will be to explain everything, the words start spilling out of me. They tumble forth, competing for precedence and sometimes coming out so tangled I have to back up and pick up a different thread. When I finally fall quiet, Dean Wilkins is silent for so long I wonder if the line has gone dead.

'Dean Wilkins? Are you there?' I say. I take the earpiece from my ear and look at it. I consider tapping it against the wall but don't, because the postmistress is watching. Staring at me agog, in fact, because she's been listening to every word. I turn toward the wall and bring the phone back to my ear.

Dean Wilkins clears his throat, stammers for a second, and then says that yes, by all means, I am welcome to return and sit my exams.

When I get back to the lot, Rosie is standing some distance from the menagerie with the general manager of the Nesci Brothers, the sheriff, and a railroad official. I break into a jog.

'What the hell is going on?' I say, coming to a stop by Rosie's shoulder.

The sheriff turns to me. 'Are you in charge of this show?'

'No,' I say.

'Then it's none of your business,' he says.

'This is my bull. That makes it my business.'

'This animal is part of the chattel of the Benzini Brothers circus, and as sheriff I am authorized on behalf of—'

'The hell she is. She's mine.'

A crowd is gathering, mostly made up of displaced Benzini Brothers roustabouts. The sheriff and railroad official exchange nervous glances.

Greg steps forward. We lock eyes. Then he addresses the sheriff. 'It's true. She's his. He's an elephant tramp. He's been traveling with us, but the bull's his.'

'I assume you can prove this.'

My face burns. Greg stares at the sheriff with blunt hostility. After a couple of seconds, he starts grinding his teeth.

'In that case,' the sheriff says with a tight smile, 'please leave us to conduct our business.'

I spin around to the Nesci Brothers general manager. His eyes widen in surprise.

'You don't want her,' I say. 'She's dumb as a bag of hammers. I can make her do a few things, but you won't get anything out of her.'

His eyebrows raise. 'Eh?'

'Go on, make her do something,' I urge.

He stares at me as though I've sprouted horns.

'I mean it,' I say. 'You got a bull man here? Try to make her do something. She's useless, stupid.'

He continues staring for a moment. Then he turns his head. 'Dick,' he barks. 'Make her do something.'

A man with a bull hook steps forward.

I stare Rosie in the eye. Please, Rosie. Understand what's going on here. *Please.*

'What's her name?' says Dick, looking over his shoulder at me.

'Gertrude.'

He turns to Rosie. 'Gertrude, step up to me. Step up to me now.' His voice is raised, sharp.

Rosie blows, and starts swinging her trunk.

'Gertrude, step up to me *now*,' he repeats.

Rosie blinks. She sweeps her trunk along the ground and then pauses. She curls its tip and pushes dirt onto it with her foot. Then she swings it around, throwing the collected dirt across her back and over the people around her. Several in the crowd laugh.

'Gertrude, lift your foot,' says Dick, stepping forward so that he's right at her shoulder. He taps the back of her leg with the bull hook. 'Lift it!'

Rosie swings her ears and sniffs him with her trunk.

'Lift it!' he says, tapping her leg harder.

Rosie smiles and checks his pockets. Her four feet remain firmly on the ground.

The bull man pushes her trunk away and turns to his boss. 'He's right. She doesn't know a damned thing. How'd you even get her out here?'

'This fella brought her,' says the manager, pointing at Greg. He turns back to me. 'So what does she do?'

'She stands in the menagerie and takes candy.'

'*That's it?*' he asks incredulously.

'Yup,' I answer.

'No wonder the damned show collapsed,' he says, shaking his head. He turns back to the sheriff. 'So, what else you got?'

I don't hear anything after that because my ears are buzzing.

What the hell have I done?

*   *   *

394

I stare forlornly at the windows of car 48, wondering how to break the news to Marlena that we now own an elephant, when she suddenly comes flying out the door, leaping from the platform like a gazelle. She hits the ground running, her arms and legs pumping.

I turn to follow her trajectory and immediately see why. The sheriff and the general manager of the Nesci Brothers are standing beside the menagerie tent, shaking hands and smiling. Her horses are lined up behind them, held by Nesci Brothers men.

The manager and sheriff whip around when she reaches them. I'm too far away to make out much, but snatches of her diatribe – the bits in the uppermost register – cut through. Things like 'how dare you,' 'appalling nerve,' and 'unspeakable gall.' She gesticulates wildly, arms flailing. 'Grand theft' and 'prosecution' make their way across the lot. Or was that 'prison'?

The men stare, astonished.

Finally she stops. She crosses her arms, scowls, and taps her foot. The men look at each other, wide-eyed. The sheriff turns and opens his mouth, but before he has time to utter a word Marlena explodes again, shrieking like a banshee, poking a finger in his face. He takes a step backward but she moves with him. He stops and braces, his chest puffed and eyes closed. When she stops wagging her finger, she crosses her arms again. The foot taps, the head bobs.

The sheriff's eyes open, and he turns to look at the general manager. After a pregnant pause, he shrugs feebly. The general manager frowns and turns to Marlena.

He lasts approximately five seconds before stepping

backward with hands raised in surrender. His face has 'Uncle' written all over it. Marlena puts her hands on her waist and waits, glaring. Eventually he turns, red-faced, and barks something to the men holding her horses.

Marlena watches until all eleven have been returned to the menagerie. Then she marches back to car 48.

Dear God. Not only am I unemployed and homeless, but I also have a pregnant woman, bereaved dog, elephant, and eleven horses to take care of.

I return to the post office and call Dean Wilkins. He is silent for even longer this time. He finally stammers out an apology: he's really very sorry – he wishes he could help – I'm still welcome to sit my final exams, of course, but he hasn't the faintest idea what I should do with the elephant.

I return to the lot rigid with panic. I can't leave Marlena and the animals here while I return to Ithaca to write my exams. What if the sheriff sells the menagerie in the meantime? The horses we can board, and we can afford for Marlena and Queenie to stay in a hotel for a while, but Rosie?

I cross the lot, making a wide arc around scattered piles of canvas. Workmen from the Nesci Brothers show are unrolling various pieces of the big top under the watchful eye of the boss canvasman. It looks like they're checking for tears before making an offer.

As I mount the stairs to car 48, my heart is pounding, my breath coming fast. I need to calm down – my mind is spinning in ever smaller circles. This is no good, no good at all.

I push open the door. Queenie comes to my feet and stares up at me with a pathetic combination of bewilderment and gratitude. She wags her stump uncertainly. I lean down and scratch her head.

'Marlena?' I say, straightening up.

She comes out from behind the green curtain. She looks apprehensive, twisting her fingers and avoiding making eye contact. 'Jacob – oh, Jacob, I've done something really stupid.'

'What?' I ask. 'Do you mean the horses? It's okay. I already know.'

She looks up quickly. 'You do?'

'I was watching. It was pretty obvious what was going on.'

She blushes. 'I'm sorry. I just . . . reacted. I wasn't thinking about what we'd do with them afterward. It's just that I love them so much and I couldn't stand to let him take them. He's no better than Uncle Al.'

'It's okay. I understand.' I pause. 'Marlena, I have something to tell you, too.'

'You do?'

My jaw opens and closes, but no words come out.

She looks worried. 'What is it? What's going on? Is it something bad?'

'I called the Dean at Cornell, and he's willing to let me sit my exams.'

Her face lights up. 'That's wonderful!'

'And we've also got Rosie.'

'*We've what?*'

'It was the same as with you and the horses,' I say quickly, rushing to explain myself. 'I don't like the look of their bull man and I couldn't let him take her – God only knows where she'd end up. I love that bull. I couldn't let her go. So I pretended she belonged to me. And now I guess she does.'

Marlena stares at me for a long time. Then – to my enormous relief – she nods, saying, 'You did right. I love her, too. She deserves better than what she's had. But it does mean we're in a pickle.' She looks out the window, her eyes narrowed in thought. 'We've got to get on another show,' she says finally. 'That's all there is to it.'

'How? Nobody's hiring.'

'Ringling is always hiring, if you're good enough.'

'Do you think we actually have a shot?'

'Sure we do. We've got one hell of an elephant act, and you're a Cornell-educated veterinarian. We have a definite shot. We'll have to be married, though. They're a real Sunday School outfit.'

'Honey, I plan to marry you the moment the ink is dry on that death certificate.'

The blood drains from her face.

'Oh, Marlena. I'm so sorry,' I say. 'That came out all wrong. I just meant that there's never been an instant of doubt that I'm going to marry you.'

After a moment's pause, she reaches up and lays her hand on my cheek. Then she grabs her purse and hat.

'Where are you going?' I say.

She rolls forward onto her toes and kisses me. 'To make that phone call. Wish me luck.'

'Good luck,' I say.

I follow her outside and sit on the metal platform watching as she recedes into the distance. She walks with such certainty, placing each foot directly in front of the other and holding her shoulders square. As she passes, all the men on the lot turn to look. I watch until she disappears around the corner of a building.

As I rise to return to the stateroom, there's a shout of surprise from the men unrolling the canvas. One man takes a long step backward, clutching his stomach. Then he doubles over, vomiting onto the grass. The rest continue to stare at the thing they've uncovered. The boss canvasman removes his hat and clutches it to his chest. One by one, the others do the same.

I walk over, staring at the darkened bundle. It's large, and as I get closer I make out bits of scarlet, gold brocade, and black and white checks.

It's Uncle Al. A makeshift garrote is tightened around his blackened neck.

Later that night, Marlena and I sneak into the menagerie and bring Bobo back to our stateroom.

In for a penny, in for a pound.

TWENTY-FOUR

S o this is what it boils down to, is it? Sitting alone in a lobby waiting for family that's not going to come?

I can't believe Simon forgot. Especially today. Especially Simon – that boy spent the first seven years of his life on the Ringling show.

To be fair, I suppose the boy is seventy-one. Or is that sixty-nine? Dammit, I'm tired of not knowing. When Rosemary comes back I'll ask her what year it is and settle the matter once and for all. She's very kind to me, that Rosemary. She won't make me feel foolish even if I am. A man ought to know how old he is.

I remember so many things as clear as a bell. Like the day of Simon's birth. God, such joy. Such relief! The vertigo as I approached the bed, the trepidation. And there was my angel, my Marlena, smiling up at me, tired, radiant, with a blanketed bundle nestled in the crook of her arm. His face was so dark and scrunched he hardly looked like a person at all. But then when Marlena pulled the blanket back from his hair and I saw that it was red, I thought I might actually faint from joy. I never really doubted – not really, and I would have loved and raised him, anyway – but still. I damn near dropped over when I saw that red hair.

I glance at the clock, antsy with despair. The Spec is over for sure. Oh, it's just not fair! All those decrepit old people who won't even know what they're looking at, and here's me! Trapped in this lobby!

Or am I?

I furrow my brow and blink. What, exactly, makes me think I'm trapped?

I glance from side to side. No one. I turn and look toward the hall. A nurse whizzes past, clutching a chart and looking at her shoes.

I scooch to the edge of my seat and reach for my walker. By my estimation, I'm only eighteen feet from freedom. Well, there's an entire city block to traverse after that, but if I hoof it I bet I can catch the last few acts. And the finale – it won't make up for missing the Spec, but it's something. A warm glow tingles through me and I snort back a giggle. I may be in my nineties, but who says I'm helpless?

The glass door slides open as I approach. Thank God for that – I don't think I could manage the walker and a regular door. No, I'm wobbly, all right. But that's okay. I can work with wobbly.

I reach the sidewalk and stop, blinded by the sun.

I've been away from the real world for so long that the combination of engines running, dogs barking, and horns honking brings a lump to my throat. The people on the sidewalk part and pass me like I'm a stone in a stream. Nobody seems to think it odd that an old man is standing in his slippers on the sidewalk right outside an old folks' home. But it occurs to me that I'm still in plain sight if one of the nurses comes into the lobby.

I lift my walker, twist it a couple of inches to the left, and plunk it down again. Its plastic wheels scrape the concrete, and the sound makes me giddy. It's a real noise, a gritty noise, not the squeak or patter of rubber. I shuffle around behind it, savoring the way my slippers scuffle. Two more manipulations like that, and I'm facing the right way. A perfect three-point turn. I grab hold and shuffle off, concentrating on my feet.

I mustn't go too fast. Falling would be disastrous in so many ways. There are no floor tiles, so I measure my progress in feet – my feet. Each time I take a step, I bring the heel of one foot parallel to the toes of the other. And so it goes, ten inches at a time. I stop occasionally to gauge my progress. It's slow but steady. The magenta and white tent is a little bigger each time I look up.

It takes me half an hour and I have to stop twice, but I'm practically there and already feeling the thrill of victory. I'm huffing a little, but my legs are still steady. There was that one woman I thought might make trouble, but I managed to get rid of her. I'm not proud of it – I don't normally speak to people in that manner, and especially women – but damned if I was going to let some busybody do-gooder foil my outing. I'm not setting foot in that facility again until I've seen what's left of the show, and woe to the person who tries to make me. Even if the nurses catch up with me right now, I'll make a scene. I'll make noise. I'll embarrass them in public and make them fetch Rosemary. When she realizes how determined I am, she'll take me to the show. Even if she misses the rest of her shift, she'll take me – it is her last shift, after all.

Oh Lord. How am I going to survive that place when she's gone? The remembrance of her imminent departure wracks my old body with grief, but it's quickly displaced by joy – I am now close enough to hear the music thumping from the big top. Oh, the sweet, sweet sound of circus music. I lodge my tongue in the corner of my mouth and hurry. I'm almost there now. Just a few yards farther—

'Yo, Gramps. Where do you think you're going?'

I stop, startled. I look up. A kid sits behind the ticket wicket, his face framed by bags of pink and blue cotton candy. Flashing toys blink from the glass counter under his arms. There's a ring through his eyebrow, a stud through his bottom lip, a large tattoo on each shoulder. His hands are tipped with black nails.

'Where does it look like I'm going?' I say querulously. I don't have time for this. I've missed enough of the show as it is.

'Tickets are twelve bucks.'

'I don't have any money.'

403

'Then you can't go in.'

I am flabbergasted, still struggling for words when a man comes up beside me. He's older, clean-shaven, well dressed. The manager, I'm willing to bet.

'What's going on here, Russ?'

The kid jerks his thumb at me. 'I caught this old guy trying to sneak in.'

'Sneak!' I exclaim in righteous indignation.

The man takes one look at me and turns back to the kid. 'What the hell is the matter with you?'

Russ scowls and looks down.

The manager stands in front of me, smiling graciously. 'Sir, I'd be happy to show you in. Would it be easier if you had a wheelchair? Then we wouldn't have to worry about finding you a good seat.'

'That would be nice. Thank you,' I say, ready to weep with relief. My altercation with Russ left me shaking – the idea that I could make it this far only to be turned away by a teenager with a pierced lip was horrifying. But all is okay. Not only have I made it, but I think maybe I'm going to get a ringside seat.

The manager goes around the side of the big top and returns with a standard hospital-issue wheelchair. I let him help me into it and then relax my aching muscles as he pushes me toward the entrance.

'Don't mind Russ,' he says. 'He's a good kid under-neath all those holes, although it's a wonder he doesn't spring a leak when he drinks.'

'In my day they put the old fellows in the ticket booth. Kind of the end of the road.'

'You were on a show?' the man asks. 'Which one?'

'I was on two. The first was the Benzini Brothers Most Spectacular Show on Earth,' I say proudly, rolling each syllable off my tongue. 'The second was Ringling.'

The chair stops. The man's face suddenly appears in front of mine. 'You were with the Benzini Brothers? What years?'

'The summer of 1931.'

'You were there for the stampede?'

'Sure was!' I exclaim. 'Hell, I was in the thick of it. In the menagerie itself. I was the show's vet.'

He stares at me, incredulous. 'I don't believe this! After the Hartford fire and Hagenbeck-Wallace wreck, that's probably the most famous circus disaster of all time.'

'It was something, all right. I remember it like yesterday. Hell, I remember it *better* than yesterday.'

The man blinks and sticks his hand out. 'Charlie O'Brien the third.'

'Jacob Jankowski,' I say, taking his hand. 'The first.'

Charlie O'Brien stares at me for a very long time, his hand spread on his chest as though he were pledging an oath. 'Mr Jankowski, I'm going to get you into the show now before there's nothing left to see, but it would be an honor and a privilege if you would join me for a drink in my trailer after the show. You're a living piece of history, and I'd surely love to hear about that collapse firsthand. I'd be happy to see you home afterward.'

'I'd be delighted,' I say.

He snaps to, and moves around to the back of the chair. 'All righty then. I hope you enjoy our show.'

An honor and a privilege.

I smile serenely as he wheels me right up to the ring curb.

TWENTY-FIVE

I t's after the show – a damn good show, too, although not of the magnitude of either the Benzini Brothers or Ringling, but how could it be? For that you need a train.

I'm sitting at a Formica table in the back of an impressively appointed RV sipping an equally impressive single malt – Laphroaig, if I'm not mistaken – and singing like a canary. I tell Charlie everything: about my parents, my affair with Marlena, and the deaths of Camel and Walter. I tell him about crawling across the train in the night with a knife in my teeth and murder on my mind. I tell him about the redlighted men, and the stampede, and about Uncle Al being strangled. And finally I tell him what Rosie did. I don't even think about it. I just open my mouth and the words tumble out.

The relief is instant and palpable. All these years it's

been pent up inside me. I thought I'd feel guilty, like I betrayed her, but what I feel – particularly in light of Charlie's sympathetic nodding – is more like absolution. Redemption, even.

I was never entirely sure whether Marlena knew – there was so much going on in the menagerie at that moment that I have no idea what she saw, and I never brought it up. I couldn't, because I couldn't risk changing how she felt about Rosie – or, if it comes right down to it, how she felt about me. Rosie may have been the one who killed August, but I also wanted him dead.

At first, I stayed silent to protect Rosie – and there was no question she needed protecting, in those days elephant executions were not uncommon – but there was never any excuse for keeping it from Marlena. Even if it caused her to harden toward Rosie, she'd never have caused her harm. In the entire history of our marriage, it was the only secret I kept from her, and eventually it became impossible to fix. With a secret like that, at some point the secret itself becomes irrelevant. The fact that you kept it does not.

Having heard my story, Charlie looks not in the least bit shocked or judgmental, and my relief is so great that when I finish telling him about the stampede, I keep going. I tell him about our years with Ringling and how we left after the birth of our third child. Marlena had simply had enough of being on the road – kind of a nesting thing, I figure – and besides, Rosie was getting on in years. Fortunately, the staff veterinarian at Brookfield Zoo in Chicago chose that spring to drop dead, and I was a shoo-in – not only did I have seven years of experience with exotics and a damned good degree, but I also came with an elephant.

We bought a rural property far enough from the zoo that we could keep the horses but close enough that the drive to work wasn't that bad. The horses more or less retired, although Marlena and the kids still rode them occasionally. They grew fat and happy – the horses, not the children, or Marlena for that matter. Bobo came with us, of course. He got into more trouble over the years than all the kids put together, but we loved him just the same.

Those were the salad days, the halcyon years! The sleepless nights, the wailing babies; the days the interior of the house looked like it had been hit by a hurricane; the times I had five kids, a chimpanzee, and a wife in bed with fever. Even when the fourth glass of milk got spilled in a single night, or the shrill screeching threatened to split my skull, or when I was bailing out some son or other – or, in one memorable instance, Bobo – from a minor predicament at the police station, they were good years, grand years.

But it all zipped by. One minute Marlena and I were in it up to our eyeballs, and next thing we knew the kids were borrowing the car and fleeing the coop for college. And now, here I am. In my nineties and alone.

Charlie, bless his heart, is actually interested in my story. He picks up the bottle and leans forward. As I push my glass toward him, there's a knock on the door. I yank my hand back as though it's been singed.

Charlie slides off the bench and leans toward a window, pulling the plaid curtain back with two fingers.

'Shit,' he says. 'It's the heat. I wonder what's up?'

'They're here for me.'

He glances at me, hard and precise. 'What?'

'They're here for me,' I say, trying to keep my eyes level with his. It's hard – I have nystagmus, the result of a long-ago concussion. The harder I try to look steadily at someone, the more my eyes jerk back and forth.

Charlie lets the curtain fall and goes to the door.

'Good evening,' says a deep voice from the doorway. 'I'm looking for a Charlie O'Brien. Someone said I could find him here.'

'You can and did. What can I do for you, officer?'

'I was hoping you could help us out. An elderly man went missing from a nursing home just down the street. The staff seems to think he probably came here.'

'Wouldn't be surprised. Folks of all ages enjoy the circus.'

'Sure. Of course. Thing is, this guy is ninety-three and pretty frail. They were hoping he'd come back on his own after the show, but it's been a couple of hours and he still hasn't showed up. They're mighty worried about him.'

Charlie blinks pleasantly at the cop. 'Even if he did come here, I doubt he's still around. We're fixing to leave real soon.'

'Do you remember seeing anyone fitting that description tonight?'

'Sure. Lots. All sorts of families brought their old folks.'

'How about an old man on his own?'

'I didn't notice, but then again we get so many people coming through I kind of tune out after a while.'

The cop pokes his head inside the trailer. His eyes light on me with obvious interest. 'Who's that?'

'Who – him?' says Charlie, waving in my direction.

'Yes.'

'That's my dad.'

'Do you mind if I come in for a moment?'

After just the slightest pause, Charlie steps aside. 'Sure, be my guest.'

The cop climbs inside the trailer. He's so tall he has to stoop. He has a jutting chin and fiercely hooked nose. His eyes are set too close together, like an orangutan's. 'How are you doing, sir?' he asks, coming closer. He squints, examining me closely.

Charlie shoots me a look. 'Dad can't talk. He had a major stroke a few years ago.'

'Wouldn't he better off staying at home?' says the officer.

'This is home.'

I drop my jaw and let it quaver. I reach for my glass with a trembling hand and nearly knock it over. Nearly, because it would be a shame to waste such good scotch.

'Here, Pops, let me help you,' says Charlie, rushing over. He slides onto the bench beside me and reaches for my glass. He lifts it to my lips.

I point my tongue like a parrot's, letting it touch the ice cubes that tumble toward my mouth.

The cop watches. I'm not looking directly at him, but I can see him in my peripheral vision.

Charlie sets my glass down and gazes placidly at him.

The cop watches us for a while, then scans the room with narrowed eyes. Charlie's face is blank as a wall, and I do my best to drool.

Finally the cop tips his cap. 'Thank you, gentlemen. If you see or hear anything, please let us know right away. This old guy is in no shape to be out on his own.'

'I surely will,' says Charlie. 'Feel free to have a look around the lot. I'll have my guys keep an eye out for him. It would be a terrible shame if something happened to him.'

'Here's my number,' says the cop, handing Charlie a card. 'Give me a call if you hear anything.'

'You bet.'

The cop takes one final look around and then steps toward the door. 'Well, good night then,' he says.

'Good night,' says Charlie, following him to the door. After he shuts it, he comes back to the table. He sits and pours us each another whiskey. We each take a sip and then sit in silence.

'Are you sure about this?' he finally asks.

'Yup.'

'What about your health? You need any medicine?'

'Nope. There's nothing wrong with me but old age. And I reckon that will take care of itself eventually.'

'What about your family?'

I take another sip of whiskey, swirl the remaining liquid around the bottom, and then drain the glass. 'I'll send them postcards.'

I look at his face and realize that didn't come out right.

'I didn't mean it like that. I love them and I know they love me, but I'm no longer really a part of their lives. I'm more like a duty. That's why I had to find my own way over here tonight. They plum forgot about me.'

Charlie's brow is furrowed. He looks dubious.

I barrel on, desperate. 'I'm ninety-three. What have I got to lose? I can still mostly take care of myself. I'll need some help for some things, but nothing like what you're thinking.' I feel my eyes grow moist and try to rearrange my ruined face into some semblance of toughness. I'm no wimp, by God. 'Let me come along. I can sell tickets. Russ can do anything – he's young. Give me his job. I can still count, and I don't short-change. I know you don't run a grift show.'

Charlie's eyes mist over. I swear to God they do.

I continue, on a roll. 'If they catch up with me, they catch up with me. If they don't, well, then at end of season I'll call and go back. And if something goes wrong in the meantime, just call and they'll come get me. What's the harm in that?'

Charlie stares at me. I've never seen a man look more serious.

One, two, three, four, five, six – he's not going to answer – *seven, eight, nine* – he's going to send me back there, and why shouldn't he, he doesn't know me from Adam – *ten, eleven, twelve* –

'All right,' he says.

'All right?'

'All right. Let's give you something to tell your grandkids about. Or great-grandkids. Or great-great-grandkids.'

I snort with glee, delirious with excitement. Charlie winks and pours me another finger's worth of whiskey. Then, on second thought, he tips the bottle again.

I reach out and grab its neck. 'Better not,' I say. 'Don't want to get tipsy and break a hip.'

And then I laugh, because it's so ridiculous and so

gorgeous and it's all I can do to not melt into a fit of giggles. So what if I'm ninety-three? So what if I'm ancient and cranky and my body's a wreck? If they're willing to accept me and my guilty conscience, why the hell shouldn't I run away with the circus?

It's like Charlie told the cop. For this old man, this *is* home.

AUTHOR'S NOTE

The idea for this book came unexpectedly: In early 2003 I was gearing up to write an entirely different book when the *Chicago Tribune* ran an article on Edward J. Kelty, a photographer who followed traveling circuses around America in the 1920s and '30s. The photograph that accompanied the article so fascinated me that I bought two books of old-time circus photographs: *Step Right This Way: The Photographs of Edward J. Kelty* and *Wild, Weird, and Wonderful: The American Circus as Seen by F. W. Glasier*. By the time I'd thumbed through them, I was hooked. I abandoned the book I'd planned to write and dove instead into the world of the train circus.

I started by getting a bibliography of suggested reading from the archivist at Circus World, in Baraboo, Wisconsin, which is the original winter quarters of the Ringling

Brothers. Many of the books were out of print, but I managed to get them through rare booksellers. Within weeks I was off to Sarasota, Florida, to visit the Ringling Circus Museum, which happened to be selling off duplicates of books in its rare book collection. I came home poorer by several hundred dollars and richer by more books than I could carry.

I spent the next four and a half months acquiring the knowledge necessary to do justice to this subject, including taking three additional research trips (a return to Sarasota, a visit to Circus World in Baraboo, and a weekend trip to the Kansas City Zoo with one of its former elephant handlers to learn about elephant body language and behavior).

The history of the American circus is so rich that I plucked many of this story's most outrageous details from fact or anecdote (in circus history, the line between the two is famously blurred). These include the display of a hippo pickled in formaldehyde, a deceased four-hundred-pound 'strong lady' being paraded around town in an elephant cage, an elephant who repeatedly pulled her stake and stole the lemonade, another elephant who ran off and was retrieved from a backyard vegetable patch, a lion and a dishwasher wedged together under a sink, a general manager who was murdered and his body rolled up in the big top, and so on. I also incorporated the horrific and very real tragedy of Jamaica ginger paralysis, which devastated the lives of approximately one hundred thousand Americans between 1930 and 1931.

And finally, I'd like to draw attention to two old-time circus elephants, not just because they inspired major plot points, but also because these old girls deserve to be remembered.

In 1903 an elephant named Topsy killed her trainer after he fed her a lit cigarette. Most circus elephants at the time were forgiven a killing or two – as long as they didn't kill a rube – but this was Topsy's third strike. Topsy's owners at Coney Island's Luna Park decided to turn her execution into a public spectacle, but the announcement that they were going to hang her met with uproar – after all, wasn't hanging a cruel and unusual punishment? Ever resourceful, Topsy's owners contacted Thomas Edison. For years, Edison had been 'proving' the dangers of rival George Westinghouse's alternating current by publicly electrocuting stray dogs and cats, along with the occasional horse or cow – but nothing as ambitious as an elephant. He accepted the challenge. Because the electric chair had replaced the gallows as New York's official method of execution, the protests stopped.

Accounts differ as to whether Topsy was fed cyanide-laced carrots in an early, failed, execution attempt or whether she ate them immediately before she was electrocuted, but what is not disputed is that Edison brought a movie camera, had Topsy strapped into copper-lined sandals, and shot sixty-six hundred volts through her in front of fifteen hundred spectators, killing her in about ten seconds. Edison, convinced that this feat discredited alternating current, went on to show the film to audiences across the country.

On to a less sobering note. Also in 1903, an outfit in Dallas acquired an elephant named Old Mom from Carl Hagenbeck, a circus legend who declared her to be the smartest elephant he'd ever had. Their hopes thus raised, Old Mom's new trainers were dismayed to find they could persuade her to do nothing more than shuffle around. Indeed, she was so useless she 'had to be pushed and pulled from one circus lot to another.' When Hagenbeck later visited Old Mom at her new home, he was aggrieved to hear her described as stupid and said so – in German. It suddenly dawned on everyone that Old Mom only understood German. After this watershed, Old Mom was retrained in English and went on to an illustrious career. She died in 1933 at the ripe old age of eighty, surrounded by her friends and fellow troupers.

Here's to Topsy and Old Mom—

What to read next...

Catch-22

Joseph Heller

It's not always easy trying to decide what to read when you've finished a book you've loved.

So we asked Sara Gruen to recommend a book she loves and that you might enjoy next. She chose *Catch-22* by Joseph Heller.

Turn the page for more information about the book and to read an exclusive extract...

About
Catch-22

Explosive, subversive, wild and funny, 50 years
on the novel's strength is undiminished. Reading
Joseph Heller's classic satire is nothing less than a
rite of passage.

Set in the closing months of World War II, this is the
story of a bombardier named Yossarian who is frantic
and furious because thousands of people he has never
met are trying to kill him. His real problem is not the
enemy – it is his own army which keeps increasing the
number of missions the men must fly to complete their
service. If Yossarian makes any attempts to excuse
himself from the perilous missions then he is caught in
Catch-22: if he flies he is crazy, and doesn't have to;
but if he doesn't want to he must be sane and has to.
That's some catch...

I

THE TEXAN

IT WAS LOVE at first sight.

The first time Yossarian saw the chaplain he fell madly in love with him.

Yossarian was in the hospital with a pain in his liver that fell just short of being jaundice. The doctors were puzzled by the fact that it wasn't quite jaundice. If it became jaundice they could treat it. If it didn't become jaundice and went away they could discharge him. But this just being short of jaundice all the time confused them.

Each morning they came around, three brisk and serious men with efficient mouths and inefficient eyes, accompanied by brisk and serious Nurse Duckett, one of the ward nurses who didn't like Yossarian. They read the chart at the foot of the bed and asked impatiently about the pain. They seemed irritated when he told them it was exactly the same.

'Still no movement?' the full colonel demanded.

The doctors exchanged a look when he shook his head.

'Give him another pill.'

Nurse Duckett made a note to give Yossarian another pill, and the four of them moved along to the next bed. None of the nurses liked Yossarian. Actually, the pain in his liver had gone away, but Yossarian didn't say anything and the doctors never suspected. They just suspected that he had been moving his bowels and not telling anyone.

Yossarian had everything he wanted in the hospital. The food wasn't too bad, and his meals were brought to him in bed. There were extra rations of fresh meat, and during the hot part of the afternoon he and the others were served chilled fruit juice or chilled chocolate milk. Apart from the doctors and the nurses, no one ever disturbed him. For a little while in the morning he had to censor letters, but he was free after that to spend the rest of each day lying around idly with a clear conscience. He was comfortable in the hospital, and it was easy to stay on because he always ran a temperature of 101. He was even more comfortable than Dunbar, who had to keep falling down on his face in order to get *his* meals brought to him in bed.

After he had made up his mind to spend the rest of the war in the hospital, Yossarian wrote letters to everyone he knew saying that he was in the hospital but never mentioning why. One day he had a better idea. To everyone he knew he wrote that he was going on a very dangerous mission. 'They asked for volunteers. It's very dangerous, but someone has to do it. I'll write you the instant I get back.' And he had not written anyone since.

All the officer patients in the ward were forced to censor letters written by all the enlisted-men patients, who were kept in residence in wards of their own. It was a monotonous job, and Yossarian was disappointed to learn that the lives of enlisted men were only slightly more interesting than the lives of officers. After the first day he had no curiosity at all. To break the monotony he invented games. Death to all modifiers, he declared one day, and out of every letter that passed through his hands went every adverb and every adjective. The next day he made war on articles. He reached a much higher plane of creativity the following day when he blacked out everything in the letters but *a*, *an* and *the*. That erected more dynamic intralinear tensions, he felt, and in just about every case left a message far more universal. Soon he was proscribing parts of salutations and signatures and leaving the text untouched. One time he blacked out all but the salutation 'Dear Mary' from a letter, and at the bottom he wrote, 'I yearn for you tragically. R. O. Shipman, Chaplain, U.S. Army.' R. O. Shipman was the group chaplain's name.

When he had exhausted all possibilities in the letters, he began attacking the names and addresses on the envelopes, obliterating whole homes and streets, annihilating entire metropolises with careless flicks of his wrist as though he were God. Catch-22 required that each censored letter bear the censoring officer's name. Most letters he didn't read at all. On those he didn't read at all he wrote his own name. On those he did read he wrote, 'Washington Irving.' When that grew monotonous he wrote, 'Irving Washington.' Censoring the envelopes had serious repercussions, produced a ripple of anxiety on some ethereal military echelon that floated a C.I.D. man back into the ward posing as a patient. They all knew he was a C.I.D. man because he kept inquiring about an officer named Irving or Washington and because after his first day there he wouldn't censor letters. He found them too monotonous.

It was a good ward this time, one of the best he and Dunbar had ever enjoyed. With them this time was the twenty-four-year-old fighter-pilot captain with the sparse golden mustache who had been shot into the Adriatic Sea in midwinter and not even caught cold. Now the summer was upon them, the captain had not been shot down, and he said he had the grippe. In the bed on Yossarian's right, still lying amorously on his belly, was the startled captain with malaria in his blood and a mosquito bite on his ass. Across the aisle from Yossarian was Dunbar, and next to Dunbar was the artillery captain with whom Yossarian had stopped playing chess. The captain was a good chess player, and the games were always interesting. Yossarian had stopped playing chess with him because the games were so interesting they were foolish. Then there was the educated Texan from Texas who looked like someone in Technicolor and felt, patriotically, that people of means – decent folk – should be given more votes than drifters, whores, criminals, degenerates, atheists and indecent folk – people without means.

Yossarian was unspringing rhythms in the letters the day they brought the Texan in. It was another quiet, hot, untroubled day. The heat pressed heavily on the roof, stifling sound. Dunbar was lying motionless on his back again with his eyes staring up at the ceiling like a doll's. He was working hard at increasing his life span. He did it by cultivating boredom. Dunbar was working so hard at increasing his life span that Yossarian thought he was dead. They put the Texan in a bed in the middle of the ward, and it wasn't long before he donated his views.

Dunbar sat up like a shot. 'That's it,' he cried excitedly. 'There was something missing – all the time I knew there was something missing – and now I know what it is.' He banged his fist down into his palm. 'No patriotism,' he declared.

'You're right,' Yossarian shouted back. 'You're right, you're right, you're right. The hot dog, the Brooklyn Dodgers. Mom's apple pie. That's what everyone's fighting for. But who's fighting for the decent folk? Who's fighting for more votes for the decent folk? There's no patriotism, that's what it is. And no matriotism, either.'

The warrant officer on Yossarian's left was unimpressed. 'Who gives a shit?' he asked tiredly, and turned over on his side to go to sleep.

The Texan turned out to be good-natured, generous and likable. In three days no one could stand him.

He sent shudders of annoyance scampering up ticklish spines, and everybody fled from him – everybody but the soldier in white, who had no choice. The soldier in white was encased from head to toe in plaster and gauze. He had two useless legs and two useless arms. He had been smuggled into the ward during the night, and the men had no idea he was among them until they awoke in the morning and saw the two strange legs hoisted from the hips, the two strange arms anchored up perpendicularly, all four limbs pinioned strangely in air by lead weights suspended darkly above him that never moved. Sewn into the bandages over the insides of both elbows were zippered lips through which he was fed clear fluid from a clear jar. A silent zinc pipe rose from the cement on his groin and was coupled to a slim rubber hose that carried waste from his kidneys and dripped it efficiently into a clear, stoppered jar on the floor. When the jar on the floor was full, the jar feeding his elbow was empty, and the two were simply switched quickly so that the stuff could drip back into him. All they ever really saw of the soldier in white was a frayed black hole over his mouth.

The soldier in white had been filed next to the Texan, and the Texan sat sideways on his own bed and talked to him throughout the morning, afternoon and evening in a pleasant, sympathetic drawl. The Texan never minded that he got no reply.

Temperatures were taken twice a day in the ward. Early each morning and late each afternoon Nurse Cramer entered with a jar full of thermometers and worked her way up one side of the ward and down the other, distributing a thermometer to each patient. She managed the soldier in white by inserting a thermometer into the hole over his mouth and leaving it balanced there on the lower rim. When she returned to the man in the first bed, she took his thermometer and recorded his temperature, and then moved on to the next bed and continued around the ward again. One afternoon when she had completed her first circuit of the ward and came a second time to the soldier in white, she read his thermometer and discovered that he was dead.

'Murderer,' Dunbar said quietly.

The Texan looked up at him with an uncertain grin.

'Killer,' Yossarian said.

'What are you fellas talkin' about?' the Texan asked nervously.

'You murdered him,' said Dunbar.

'You killed him,' said Yossarian.

The Texan shrank back. 'You fellas are crazy. I didn't even touch him.'

'You murdered him,' said Dunbar.

'I heard you kill him,' said Yossarian.

'You killed him because he was a nigger,' Dunbar said.

'You fellas are crazy,' the Texan cried. 'They don't allow niggers in here. They got a special place for niggers.'

'The sergeant smuggled him in,' Dunbar said.

'The Communist sergeant,' said Yossarian.

'And you knew it.'

The warrant officer on Yossarian's left was unimpressed by the entire incident of the soldier in white. The warrant officer was unimpressed by everything and never spoke at all unless it was to show irritation.

The day before Yossarian met the chaplain, a stove exploded in the mess hall and set fire to one side of the kitchen.

An intense heat flashed through the area. Even in Yossarian's ward, almost three hundred feet away, they could hear the roar of the blaze and the sharp cracks of flaming timber. Smoke sped past the orange-tinted windows. In about fifteen minutes the crash trucks from the airfield arrived to fight the fire. For a frantic half hour it was touch and go. Then the firemen began to get the upper hand. Suddenly there was the monotonous old drone of bombers returning from a mission, and the firemen had to roll up their hoses and speed back to the field in case one of the planes crashed and caught fire. The planes landed safely. As soon as the last one was down, the firemen wheeled their trucks around and raced back up the hill to resume their fight with the fire at the hospital. When they got there, the blaze was out. It had died of its own accord, expired completely without even an ember to be watered down, and there was nothing for the disappointed firemen to do but drink tepid coffee and hang around trying to screw the nurses.

The chaplain arrived the day after the fire. Yossarian was busy expurgating all but romance words from the letters when the chaplain sat down in a chair between the beds and asked him how he was feeling. He had placed himself a bit to one side, and the captain's bars on the tab of his shirt collar were all the insignia Yossarian could see. Yossarian had no idea who he was and just took it for granted that he was either another doctor or another madman.

'Oh, pretty good,' he answered. 'I've got a slight pain in my liver and I haven't been the most regular of fellows, I guess, but all in all I must admit that I feel pretty good.'

'That's good,' said the chaplain.

'Yes,' Yossarian said. 'Yes, that is good.'

'I meant to come around sooner,' the chaplain said, 'but I really haven't been well.'

'That's too bad,' Yossarian said.

'Just a head cold,' the chaplain added quickly.

'I've got a fever of a hundred and one,' Yossarian added just as quickly.

'That's too bad,' said the chaplain.

'Yes,' Yossarian agreed. 'Yes, that is too bad.'

The chaplain fidgeted. 'Is there anything I can do for you?' he asked after a while.

'No, no.' Yossarian sighed. 'The doctors are doing all that's humanly possible, I suppose.'

'No, no.' The chaplain colored faintly. 'I didn't mean anything like that. I meant cigarettes . . . or books . . . or . . . toys.'

'No, no,' Yossarian said. 'Thank you. I have everything I need, I suppose – everything but good health.'

'That's too bad.'

'Yes,' Yossarian said. 'Yes, that is too bad.'

The chaplain stirred again. He looked from side to side a few times, then gazed up at the ceiling, then down at the floor. He drew a deep breath.

'Lieutenant Nately sends his regards,' he said.

Yossarian was sorry to hear they had a mutual friend. It seemed there was a basis to their conversation after all. 'You know Lieutenant Nately?' he asked regretfully.

'Yes, I know Lieutenant Nately quite well.'

'He's a bit loony, isn't he?'

The chaplain's smile was embarrassed. 'I'm afraid I couldn't say. I don't think I know him that well.'

'You can take my word for it,' Yossarian said. 'He's as goofy as they come.'

The chaplain weighed the next silence heavily and then shattered it with an abrupt question. 'You are Captain Yossarian, aren't you?'

'Nately had a bad start. He came from a good family.'

'Please excuse me,' the chaplain persisted timorously. 'I may be committing a very grave error. Are you Captain Yossarian?'

'Yes,' Captain Yossarian confessed. 'I am Captain Yossarian.'

'Of the 256th Squadron?'

'Of the fighting 256th Squadron,' Yossarian replied. 'I didn't know there were any other Captain Yossarians. As far as I know, I'm the only Captain Yossarian I know, but that's only as far as I know.'

'I see,' the chaplain said unhappily.

'That's two to the fighting eighth power,' Yossarian

pointed out, 'if you're thinking of writing a symbolic poem about our squadron.'

'No,' mumbled the chaplain. 'I'm not thinking of writing a symbolic poem about your squadron.'

Yossarian straightened sharply when he spied the tiny silver cross on the other side of the chaplain's collar. He was thoroughly astonished, for he had never really talked with a chaplain before.

'You're a chaplain,' he exclaimed ecstatically. 'I didn't know you were a chaplain.'

'Why, yes,' the chaplain answered. 'Didn't you know I was a chaplain?'

'Why, no. I didn't know you were a chaplain.' Yossarian stared at him with a big, fascinated grin. 'I've never really seen a chaplain before.'

The chaplain flushed again and gazed down at this hands. He was a slight man of about thirty-two with tan hair and brown diffident eyes. His face was narrow and rather pale. An innocent nest of ancient pimple pricks lay in the basin of each cheek. Yossarian wanted to help him.

'Can I do anything at all to help you?' the chaplain asked.

Yossarian shook his head, still grinning. 'No, I'm sorry. I have everything I need and I'm quite comfortable. In fact, I'm not even sick.'

Sara Gruen Photograph © Lynne Harty

Sara Gruen is the internationally bestselling author of *Water for Elephants* and *Ape House*. Her works have been translated into forty-three languages and have sold more than ten million copies worldwide. *Water for Elephants* was adapted into a major motion picture starring Reese Witherspoon, Rob Pattinson, and Christoph Waltz.

Her new novel, *At The Water's Edge*, will be published by Two Roads in May 2015.

She lives in Western North Carolina with her husband and three children.

saragruen.com
facebook.com/SaraGruenBooks
twitter.com/saragruen

TWO
ROADS

We hope you enjoyed *Water for Elephants*.
If you'd like to know more about this book
or any other title on our list, please go to
www.tworoadsbooks.com

For news on forthcoming Two Roads titles,
please sign up for our newsletter.

enquiries@tworoadsbooks.com

TwoRoadsBooks

Continuing your reading journey

As well as World Book Night, The Reading Agency runs lots of programmes to help keep you reading.

The **Six Book Challenge** invites you to pick six reads and record your reading in a diary in order to get a certificate. If you're thinking about improving your reading or would like to read more, then this is for you. Find out more at **readingagency.org.uk/sixbookchallenge**

Reading Groups for Everyone helps you discover and share new books. Find a reading group near you, or register a group you already belong to and get free books and offers from publishers at **readinggroups.org**

Reading together with a child will help them to develop a lifelong love of reading. Our **Chatterbooks** children's reading groups and **Summer Reading Challenge** inspire children to read more and share the books they love. **summerreadingchallenge.org.uk**

THE
READING
AGENCY

Partners and Supporters

World Book Night is run by The Reading Agency, and would not be possible without the support of many generous partners.

 Supported using public funding by
**ARTS COUNCIL
ENGLAND**

Our primary partners are:

BBC

The Publishers Association

The Booksellers Association of UK and Ireland

Quick Reads

We are supported by the generosity of:

Jerwood Charitable Foundation, who funded the printing of the
World Book Night 2015 edition of *Essential Poems from the Staying Alive Trilogy*,
ed. Neil Astley

Booker Prize Foundation, who funded the printing of the World Book Night 2015
edition of *Dead Man Talking* by 1993 Booker Prize winner Roddy Doyle

The Paul Hamlyn Foundation

John Laing Charitable Trust

A range of private donors who believe in the value of our work

The publishers who fund the printing and production of the books

The authors who waive their royalties on these copies of the books

The libraries and booksellers across the country who promote reading
every day and participate as collection points

The volunteers who give their time, energy and passion to promote reading
in their communities.

**You can join them and help get more books to more people –
just text* READ15 £3 to 70070**

Book design
Pentagram (2011)
Richard Bravery (2014)
Fiona Carpenter (artwork)

Book printing
Clays
CPI Group (UK)

World Book Night is run by the charity The Reading Agency
(registered charity number 1085443, registered number 3904882, England & Wales)
Registered Office: Free Word Centre, 60 Farringdon Road, London, EC1R 3GA.
*Text costs £3 plus network charge. The Reading Agency receives 100% of your donation.
Obtain bill payer's permission. Customer care 0345 078 2063.

9112 0000498539

'It's a broad canvas Kane is painting on, but he does it with **vivid** colours and, like the Romans themselves, he can show great admiration for a Greek enemy and still kick them in the balls'
Robert Low, author of the Oathsworn series

'Ben Kane manages to marry broad narrative invention with detailed historical research . . . in taut, authoritative prose . . . **his passion for the past, and for the craft of story-telling, shines from every page**'
Toby Clements, author of the Kingmaker series

'This **thrilling** series opener delivers every cough, spit, curse and gush of blood to set up the mighty clash of the title. Can't really fault this one'
Jon Wise, *Weekend Sport*

'Ben Kane's new series **explores the bloody final clash between ancient Greece and upstart Rome**, focusing on soldiers and leaders from both worlds and **telling the story of a bloody war with style**'
Charlotte Heathcote, *Sunday Express S Magazine*

'**A thumping good read.** You can feel the earth tremble from the great battle scenes and feel the desperation of those caught up in the conflict. Kane's brilliant research weaves its way lightly throughout'
David Gilman, author of the Master of War series

BEN KANE is one of the most hard-working and successful historical writers in the industry. His third book, *The Road to Rome*, was a *Sunday Times* number four bestseller, and almost every title since has been a top ten bestseller. Born in Kenya, Kane moved to Ireland at the age of seven. After qualifying as a veterinarian, he worked in small animal practice and during the terrible Foot and Mouth Disease outbreak in 2001. Despite his veterinary career, he retained a deep love of history; this led him to begin writing.

His first novel, *The Forgotten Legion*, was published in 2008; since then he has written five series of Roman novels. Kane lives in Somerset with his two children.